High Praise for Elizabeth Stuart's
HEARTSTORM

An opulent epic of passion, loyalty, and betrayal as wild and wondrous as all of Scotland...

"A vibrant tapestry of highland castles and lochs, of passionate love and conflicting loyalties."
—**Elizabeth Kary, author of *Love, Honor and Betray***

"Beautifully evokes the atmosphere of the highlands... lyrically written... readers will be reminded of the brand of sexual tension that Johanna Lindsey creates... memorable... [A] KEEPER!"
—*Romantic Times*

"A sweeping book of pageantry, intrigue and suspense, with a strong plotline that keeps moving. ... HIGHLY RECOMMENDED!"
—*Rendezvous*

"Well-crafted... in the tradition of Rebecca Brandewyne, Jude Deveraux and Karen Robards ... breathtaking romance.... The author has captured the flavor of the times."
—*Inside Books*

"WHEN IT COMES TO ROMANCE... [STUART] OBVIOUSLY HAS WHAT IT TAKES!"
—*...nal*

St. Martin's Paperbacks by
Elizabeth Stuart

HEARTSTORM

WHERE LOVE DWELLS

WHERE LOVE DWELLS

ELIZABETH STUART

ST. MARTIN'S PAPERBACKS

WHERE LOVE DWELLS

Copyright © 1990 by Elizabeth Stuart.

ISBN: 0-312-92358-9

Printed in the United States of America

St. Martin's Paperbacks edition/September 1990

10 9 8 7 6 5 4 3 2 1

Life is more than taking the easy road. For my husband, John, who shares the laughter and tears, and who makes each step an adventure not to be missed.

And for my own Welsh ancestors whose lives were the inspiration for this book.

CHAPTER ONE
Middle Wales, December 1282

Against the oppressive gray of a leaden sky, the swirling snowflakes settled softly to earth, carpeting the frozen ground. In the deepening twilight, the sharp, angry bark of a fox sounded from the growth of birch wood and spruce lining the narrow pathway.

At the sound, a slender female figure slipped from the trees, hugging her arms tightly against the boy's wool tunic she wore. The girl ignored the cry of the fox. Animals had never frightened her, at least not the four-legged kind. But it would be dark soon and the men of Teifi should be coming home . . . if they'd been successful.

The girl strained to see in the failing light, studying the trail ahead with rising anxiety. But there was nothing—no movement, no sound, nothing save the hushed fall of snow and the chill brush of wind against her cheek, a chill that penetrated her rough clothing, adding to the tight knot of fear gathering in the pit of her stomach.

She began to pray as she had never prayed before. "Holy Mary, Mother of God, bring them home safe," she whispered earnestly. "Please, *please*, bring them home safe."

The small group of bedraggled men, scattered through the forest, followed in the wake of a single horseman. The rider's head was bent, his broad shoulders sagging with defeat. It was over. All was lost. The only reality was that of keeping his mount headed in the right direction, of keeping the wounded going until they reached Teifi.

Home, but then what? That refuge was good for a few hours at best.

The grizzled old soldier half turned in his saddle, glancing back at the men following on foot. Scarce two dozen men, he thought bitterly. Naught but a handful left from the eight score that had followed Lord Aldwyn so eagerly into battle. And how was he to take care of them?

Acid bile rose in his throat as the searing memory of the last few hours surged over him. Llywelyn ap Gruffydd, Prince of Wales, was dead, run through by an English broadsword in an unexpectedly early skirmish that took them by surprise. In the blink of an eye Llywelyn was dead, and the hope of every loyal Welshman would be buried with that brave prince.

Turning back to the trail, the horseman stared straight ahead, scarcely noticing the snowflakes melting against the blood-soaked rags that wrapped his arm. His horse picked up its pace, reassured by the firm hand still gripping the reins.

Yea, Llywelyn was dead, Owain told himself dazedly, and with him the only other man with the wisdom and power to unite the jealous, squabbling Welsh lords against the English devils invading their heartland. In that same evil hour that had taken Llywelyn, his own dear lord, Aldwyn of Teifi, had been struck down in the fierce skirmishing about the fallen prince.

And not Aldwyn alone. Aldwyn's only son, Lord Rhodri, had been lost too, and Lord Enion, the Lady Elen's betrothed. The young lords had been fighting shoulder to shoulder, struggling to reach their prince when they fell, hacked down before Owain's eyes by the swarming Englishmen.

A low groan sounded, and Owain realized dimly it had come from his own throat. The memory of that nightmare hour was a crushing burden his warrior's heart could scarcely bear—Rhodri and Enion, inseparable since early childhood when Enion had fostered at Teifi. Young lords yes, but dear to him as if sprung from his own body.

And Elen. Christ, have mercy! How would he tell Elen?

Suddenly, his chest heaved with greater anguish than any he had known in his near two score years as a fighting man. Tears of pain and hopelessness gathered in his gray eyes, trickling slowly down his proud, furrowed cheeks to drip unnoticed onto his gloved hand. Better to have ended his life on that field with the pride of Wales. He'd have taken a good half-dozen of those haughty devils with him, he thought with a bitter smile. Maybe even more.

But Aldwyn would have none of it. "Elen..." the old lord had murmured as Owain knelt, cradling Aldwyn's dying form in his arms. "Take my men... as many as can break free...." His words had trailed off as he had struggled to maintain consciousness. "Elen... get Elen and Gweneth to safety," he had rasped. "Owain... there's no one else. Elen... you must... you must...." Slowly his blood-soaked body had gone limp in Owain's arms.

Lord Aldwyn was right. There was no one else. And God alone knew how he would manage to fulfill his pledge to see his lord's wife and daughter to safety. In less than an hour, these woods would be crawling with ravening English soldiers drunk with a blood lust nothing but time and more Welsh blood would appease. At the thought, he prodded his weary mount into a trot.

The dull thud of horses' hooves beat a rhythmic accompaniment to the ideas churning in his brain. Llywelyn was dead and his brother, Dafydd, was a treacherous hothead who would never succeed in uniting this wild country. Owain smiled grimly. At least Dafydd would be repaid for his plots to betray his royal brother. The English would never rest until the last male of Llywelyn's blood was dead.

But with their prince dead, the people would need a rallying point, something to keep their hope of freedom alive else they would be crushed beneath King Edward's oppressive heel. Owain's eyes narrowed thoughtfully, his cold-numbed fingers gripping the reins in sudden excitement. Elen! Was that what Aldwyn had meant? She might be naught but a girl of sixteen, but she was the descendant of a proud line of warrior lords, a line of fighting Celtic princes claiming lineage to King Arthur himself. And she was a distant kinswoman to Llywelyn.

As if conjured by his thoughts, a slim, boyish figure stepped unexpectedly from a screen of trees lining the frozen creek. Despite the concealing knee-boots and archer's cap, the drab tunic of brown wool and the light sword resting in its sheath at the youth's elbow, Owain recognized his young mistress at once.

"Lady Elen!" he exclaimed, jerking his mount to a halt as the girl stepped into his path. "What in God's name are you doing here alone?"

Great blue eyes, heavily lashed and anxious, stared up at him from a face pale with cold. "Waiting for Father," she said calmly. Her eyes left his, moving over the men, quickly assessing the injuries. "I see you've brought the wounded home. Mother's taken to her bed with worry, but I have everything prepared in the hall. Tangwen and I will see to them."

Her eyes returned to his. Her full lips trembled slightly, but her voice, when she spoke, was steady. "I suppose Father and Enion and my brother stayed behind to secure the field?"

Owain motioned the men behind him to move up the path toward the keep. This was the moment he had dreaded most and he wasn't prepared. He stared into Elen's lovely, heart-shaped face. He had known Aldwyn's beautiful daughter almost from the moment of her first lusty cry in the midwife's arms. He wasn't deceived by her calm mien. "You're going to have to be strong, little one," he whispered, using a nickname her willowy frame had outgrown years ago.

Swinging down from his mount, he took one step toward her, wishing there was something he might say to ease the blow. "The field was secured some time ago—by Edward's knights." He halted before her. "Our men won't be coming home, child. Lord Llywelyn is dead and most of the rest slaughtered about him. What you see is all that's left of us—these and a few bowmen who fled to the forest afoot."

Her eyes widened in disbelief. "It's not true! The prophecy . . . Merlin's prophecy! Llywelyn will wear the crown of all Britain. It's been promised for hundreds of years!"

She lifted a beseeching hand, her eyes searching his desperately. "It's not true," she repeated. "It can't be! You must have left before the battle was done. Father must be looking for you now. How *dare* you leave him!"

Owain caught her slender shoulders and gave her a rough shake. "Listen to me, Elen, and listen well for there's little time. Merlin's prophecy obviously wasn't meant for our Llywelyn. The battle is done and all are lost save a few miserable bands that managed to fight their way into the forest. Your menfolk are dead. All dead," he repeated with characteristic bluntness.

With a strangled sob, Elen tore herself from his arms and stumbled away a few feet. "I . . . I don't believe you. I *won't* believe you!"

"I saw your brother go down with two English lances through his chest," Owain said harshly. "Enion fell at the hand of that hellspawn, Richard of Kent. And Lord Aldwyn died in my arms," he added, his rough voice hoarse with emotion. "Never tell me it's not true, Elen, for I'll see that sight so long as I live!"

The girl turned back toward him, her great eyes luminous with unshed tears. "Enion . . ." The cry trembled with anguish and she broke off abruptly. "You're sure?" she whispered at last. "All are dead?"

"Aye."

Bowing her head, she clenched her gloved fists before her face, battling hard for self-control. Owain watched her painful struggle, his own heart near to breaking. He longed to reach out a comforting hand, but nothing could ease this pain for either of them.

The girl's shoulders convulsed with several shaking sobs before she mastered herself. "How far . . . how far are the English behind us?" she choked at last, lifting grief-stricken eyes to his.

"An hour at most. They'll come through these woods slowly, though, fearing an ambush."

She moved toward him, nodding in agreement. The snow was falling faster now, the woodland sounds silenced by the eerie stillness of the storm and the approaching night. They stood together, shoulder to shoulder, listening intently for any sound of pursuit.

Suddenly the wind picked up, tugging a long strand of dark chestnut hair from beneath Elen's cap. It whipped across her face and she dashed it back, wiping impatiently at her tears. "Let's give this Richard of Kent an ambush he'll not forget!" she cried out. "For my father and Rhodri . . . for Enion! By God, we'll make him pay!"

Resting a hand on her sword hilt, she turned toward him, her unusual height placing her glittering, angry gaze on a level with his own. "I'll need five of your best men to see my lady mother to safety. Once they're away, we'll secure the keep. We'll teach these English dogs we Welsh sell our lives dearly!"

Overhead, the wind moaned through the shivering pine boughs with the tormented whisper of restless spirits. Owain stared at Elen in surprise, half convinced it was Lord Aldwyn's furious glare he faced. Shaking his head, he resisted the ridiculous impulse to cross himself. "Nay, Elen, 'twould be foolish to end our lives for a futile gesture."

His eyes narrowed and he gazed at her intently. "Listen to me now, girl. We must be wise, you and I. Wise enough to forgo this thirst for revenge for a time. I have a better plan, a plan to make the English hurt, and hurt badly. But I'll need your help."

CHAPTER TWO

Gwynedd, North Wales, April 1283

*A*ieyaa!

The low groan of agony trembled on the chill evening air. Elen glanced nervously at the mud-and-wattle hut a few yards away. Something had gone wrong with Enid's birthing. Something had gone terribly wrong.

Rising from her seat on a log, Elen resumed her anxious pacing. Tangwen's low, encouraging voice drifted from the hut, but Elen couldn't make out what the midwife was saying. She frowned. Until a few hours ago, she had been helping at her friend's birthing, but just after midday Tangwen had unexpectedly ordered her out. And the midwife's sharp voice brooked no argument, not even from Elen.

All at once Elen could stand the uncertainty no longer. She moved to the hut entrance. "Tangwen. Tangwen!" she called softly.

The midwife appeared in the doorway. In the last few hours her weary, wrinkled face seemed to have aged another year. "Tangwen, Enid's been at this since dawn," Elen whispered. "Surely you know some potion or spell to make the babe come."

Tangwen shook her graying head from side to side. "Enid's too weak for the birthing. I've suspected it these two months past. The winter in these mountains was too harsh, the dearth of food too much for such as her." The old woman's dark eyes rested on Elen, assessing her. "This child will be her death," she added softly. "She's lost more blood now than she can stand."

Elen stared at her old nurse in amazement. This was only the third time she had helped the older women of the camp with a birthing. The first two had gone as smooth as nature would allow, and she wasn't prepared for Tangwen's words.

A sudden, helpless fear came near to choking her. Not Enid. She couldn't lose Enid too! Except for Owain, the lively young woman and her man Dylan had become the closest thing to family Elen had left. "She won't die. She can't!" Elen burst out. "Do something. Surely there's something!"

Tangwen gazed at Elen pityingly. She had stood by her impetuous young mistress through all the joys and sorrows of her sixteen summers. The girl was full young yet to know such hurt, but many a woman died in childbirth under the best of conditions. Running and hiding from the English in these northern mountains certainly wasn't the best of conditions.

"She's near gone now," Tangwen responded. "There's naught to do but try to save the child."

"But . . ."

Another muffled groan sounded from inside the hut, and Tangwen disappeared into the smoky interior. Elen closed her eyes against the pain of Tangwen's words, clenching her fists so tightly her nails bit into her palms. Dear God in heaven, she was tired of the pain! So tired of the stench of blood and death, of the festering wounds of the men and the bleak, hollow-eyed women and hungry children who followed them in this hole-and-corner war they couldn't win. Perhaps her mother had been right after all. Perhaps they should have given up, sailed for France. . . .

Her mind shied away from the guilt that thought evoked. It was she who had insisted on remaining in Wales after the crushing defeat at Irfon Bridge near Builth. But her mother's frail health and broken spirit hadn't been equal to the harsh conditions they had met. She had died of a wasting fever soon after the harrowing flight from Teifi.

A weak, mewling cry jerked Elen back to the present. Shoving the door aside, she entered the torchlit hut. Two camp women were efficiently wiping down a squalling, struggling infant. "A girl child," Tangwen said matter-of-factly. Her eyes rested on Elen. "But I doubt she'll last without her mother."

Elen didn't speak. For a moment, she stared at Enid's lifeless form, keeping the tears at bay by sheer force of will. How often had her father told her? A Welsh princess didn't cry.

Her thoughts began to spin in a jumble of recent memories. Dylan riding out on a raid with Owain yesterday, so excited about the coming child he had forgotten his knife and had had to return for it. Enid laughing with her over a sparse dinner last night. Now, just a few hours later, Enid was dead. And there wasn't a priest to bless her grave. There hadn't even been one for her mother.

Whirling through the doorway, Elen stumbled from the hut without a backward glance. She moved blindly between the thick trees and scattered huts, instinctively heading toward the camp stream. She was tired of acting brave and too bitter to keep up the pretense any longer. She would return to pray for Enid's immortal soul. But not now. Now she was overwhelmed by the unfairness of it all. And what good would it do, anyway? God obviously didn't hear his Welsh children.

Reaching the rocky embankment, Elen flung herself down on a soft mattress of moss. The stream cut a dancing path from high in the gaunt, dark mountains of Eryri. Its water was clear and cold, earth-dark, as wild and unfettered in its tumble down the mountainside as the eagles that soared above the cliffs.

Turning onto her belly, Elen plunged both hands deep into the stream, welcoming the sting of cold water that had so recently been ice. She held her breath against the ache, and submerged both arms to the elbows, wishing she dared fling herself bodily into the stream for a thorough purging.

Slowly, the sharp ache dulled to a tingling numbness. Her arms felt curiously weightless—unattached. They wavered helplessly in the swift-rushing current, tugging at her as if to pull her downward into the stream.

With an effort, she drew them from the water. Was that how death crept upon one? First the pain of an unexpected sword thrust, a burning fever, a childbirth gone awry, then the welcoming numbness that drained the fight from its victims.

Enid had looked peaceful in death, so too had her own mother. Elen stared hopelessly into the dark water. Her reflection, wavering unsteadily across the shivering surface of the pool, revealed a hard-faced young woman she scarcely recognized gazing back at her. Perhaps it was the living who were most to be pitied, she mused. After all, it was they who bore the cold and hunger, the deaths of the others . . . the living who had still to face another day.

Rolling onto her back, she stared thoughtfully at the darkening sky through the bare, twisted branches above her. This bitterness and despair were new to her and not to be indulged in. They weakened the arm and destroyed the spirit, Owain had told her often enough.

But why did she thrive and grow strong on their pitiful rations? The pangs of cold and hunger only strengthened her hatred for the English; hardened her resolve to fight on.

The image of her older brother Rhodri flashed before her eyes. If Rhodri were alive, he would laugh and say it was the devil of perversity in her soul, evidenced, as he'd oft pointed out, by the cursed red in her gleaming chestnut hair. That devil-red crowning the face of an angel, was the way Enion had described it, long before he had asked Lord Aldwyn for her hand.

Oh, Enion . . . Enion . . .

An uncontrollable wave of pain and homesickness washed over her for a place and time that would never come again. She and Rhodri and Enion, laughing, carefree children racing their surefooted ponies along the river Teifi or dueling furiously with wooden swords, mimicking Lord Aldwyn and his men.

And Lord Aldwyn, her magnificent father, the most powerful lord in Mid Wales and a distant kinsman to Llewelyn himself. Holy Mary, how she missed him! How she longed for his comforting strength. At the surge of memories, she fought back tears, tears she had thought conquered months ago. Her father had never slighted her for a girl child but had proudly encouraged her to play at war games with Enion and Rhodri—the war games so essential to the survival of their race.

The three Teifi youngsters had been inseparable, even after Elen's disapproving mother had forced her to give up the freedom of her short tunic and boots for the long confining skirts of a maiden's cotte, even after she had turned her hand to stitchery instead of the light sword her over-indulgent father had had specially made . . . even after Enion had wanted her for his woman.

Elen choked back a sob, squeezing her eyes tight shut as if to block out the memories. *Why, God? Why?*

A light footstep sounded in the nearby rotting leaves, instantly banishing the vision of the three men Elen had loved more than life. She jumped to her feet, reaching instinctively for her sword even as she realized it lay sheathed in its leather scabbard on the floor back at the hut.

"Easy, child. 'Tis I, Owain."

A breath of relief hissed between her clenched teeth. "Owain. Thank God!" She glanced to her empty belt where both knife and sword usually rode. "I've been careless," she admitted contritely. "I fear I left Tangwen's hut without thinking. Enid's dead."

"I know. I followed you after Tangwen told me. I knew you'd come here."

The simple words were full of a warm comfort that somehow steadied her. She stared at Owain, struggling to read his gray eyes in the deepening twilight. He knew what she was thinking—he always did. From the day she was three years old and he had sat her astride her first pony, Owain had been her special friend and protector. Despite her royal blood and his position as a leader of her father's men, there was no gulf between them. Bound together by a mutual worship of Lord Aldwyn, the impetuous child and the stern-faced warrior had become fast friends.

Staring at him, Elen found something infinitely reassuring about Owain's solid bulk. Thank God, he had returned safely from the raid. For now, at least, heaven was merciful.

She took a step toward him, her mind settling back to its accustomed practicality. "What news, Owain?"

She saw the white flash of his teeth in the dim light as he smiled. "News to your liking, I'll wager. Richard of Kent rides west for Gwenlyn Keep." He chuckled softly. "But he rides three knights the less. Your plan worked perfectly, Elen."

Elen grinned, barely suppressing the surge of exhilaration flooding through her. For she had hatched the plot to kill the armored knights by hamstringing the great destriers as they rode them. And no matter how badly her impoverished people needed horses, she allowed herself no remorse for the loss of the valuable animals—killing English knights was far more important to their cause. "So the Wolf of Kent loses some of his pack," she remarked easily. "Too bad Sir Richard Basset came not under your sword."

Owain shook his head. "God was not so generous today. But perhaps soon." Moving to her side, he placed his hand on her shoulder in a comradely gesture. "What's this?" he snapped. "You're wet through and shivering fit to scramble your wits! What do you mean, staying out in this cold without a cloak?"

She shrugged off his hand. "I was damp with sweat from running and now the air has grown chill. 'Tis nothing."

"And I suppose you'll think it nothing when you lie on your deathbed of a fever," he scolded. Quickly untying his heavy fox cloak, he settled it snugly around her shoulders. "Have a care, Elen. You are the last of your line. Your life is precious enough to me, but more valuable still for the hope it gives our countrymen."

Elen tucked her chin into the welcome warmth of the silky red fur. The costly cloak had once belonged to Lord Aldwyn and had been her gift to Owain during those first nightmare days after their escape from Teifi. In the bleak months that followed, the cloak had given rise to a foolish legend among the English.

Wherever the red fox cloak was seen, the lightning raids of the Welsh were sure to be successful. Foraging parties sent out by the English failed to return and supply trains were attacked and carried off into the mountains. Even well-garrisoned camps were struck.

But the success had been brief. As English soldiers poured north, the raiding Welsh were forced to fall back ever deeper into the Eryri mountains of Gwynedd. As King Edward's men cut great swathes through the dense forest for roadways, successful ambush became difficult. As his knights garrisoned Welsh fortresses, they easily controlled the lands around them. And as Richard Basset, nicknamed the Wolf of Kent, drew the king's forces inward in an ever-tightening circle about Gwynedd, he began nipping dangerously close to the heels of the Red Fox of Wales.

Elen glanced at Owain, mischievous lights twinkling in her blue eyes. "Would you make me the Welsh Fox? I doubt I'd sleep as sound nights knowing the price in English silver on my head."

Owain cocked a graying eyebrow at her and smiled. "'Tis your devious mind more than my own battle plans that have given us success thus far, child. I can almost believe Lord Aldwyn whispers in your ear from time to time."

Elen stroked the fox fur lovingly, the laughter in her eyes dying out. "He does, Owain. I hear his voice in my memories oft enough. Our Holy Lord be praised, Father didn't think it amiss to teach his daughter the same as his son." She smiled wryly. "To my own shame and that of my lady mother, I fear I remember his lessons of battle and ambush far better than hers of housewifery."

Owain's muscular arm encircled her shoulders. Again he had read the thoughts she dared not voice. "It's no matter, little one," he said softly. "The Lady Gweneth is at peace now with Lord Aldwyn. The fears and troubles of this world were not for one such as her."

Elen nodded, and together they started up the shadowy path toward the camp. The damp night air had grown increasingly cold, and she shivered despite the warmth of the cloak.

"What must we do next?" she asked, as they reached the open doorway of a hut set well back in the trees away from the others. "You know Richard Basset won't rest till he avenges your raid. He'll turn every rock in these mountains upside down to find our winter camp."

"First I'll build you a fire and we'll cook the hare I killed this evening," Owain said lightly, entering the hut behind her. "Fresh meat goes a long way to strengthening the spirit."

He sent her a frowning glance. "Then I must ride for Lywarch's camp. We must plan a concerted attack. We can't allow Richard to garrison Gwenlyn Keep. If he succeeds, it'll be the final step in overrunning these mountains. We've our backs to the sea, Elen, and Edward controls the coast. We've nowhere else to run. 'Tis here we make our stand."

Elen felt another chill shiver through her. They would fight and more of her people would die. And Owain would be in the thick of it. A sudden fear for him took her breath. "Must you ride tonight?" she asked unsteadily. "Can't it wait till morning?"

"It must be tonight if I'm to be of any use." He tugged at the heavy chestnut braid that hung over one shoulder halfway to her waist. "Don't fear for me, Elen. There's a moon tonight and the ride is one I could make in my sleep. If we can catch Richard in an ambush tomorrow, we will, but I fear he'll be too cautious after yesterday. The real test of wits between us will probably have to wait."

She nodded. There was nothing else to say. They had to fight on. Catching up the dead hare by its silky hind legs, she said, "I'll skin this blessed morsel while you start the fire. But I must borrow your knife. Tangwen still has mine."

Owain slipped his knife from his belt in a practiced movement, offering it to her, blade down. "I'll fetch your steel. But don't be so careless as to leave it again," he warned. "I'd like to think this camp safe, but I'm not such a fool. With the snows gone, 'tis only a matter of time till the foraging English stumble closer. I pray the Holy Virgin every night our sentries give us good warning. We must move higher into the mountains where that Satan's brood dare not climb."

The roasted hare was delicious and the first fresh meat Elen had tasted in more than a week. Food had been scarce over the winter, and she had insisted Owain see the fighting men and pregnant women and children have first choice. But now with the warm breath of spring touching the hidden mountain valleys, game was beginning to stir.

She sucked greedily at the last bit of marrow in the leg bone. Owain was right—fresh meat did strengthen the spirit. She allowed herself to hope. Perhaps the worst was over. Perhaps they could send Edward's forces on their way.

The simple meal over, Owain began making preparations for his trip. Elen watched in silence, finally rising to her feet to walk him to the doorway. Gripping her shoulders with both hands, he brushed a fatherly kiss across her forehead. "Now remember, Elen, if aught should go awry, young Gruffydd will see you to Conwy and book you safe passage for France. The lad knows your true identity, but he's trustworthy. He'd never betray you to the English no matter the prize offered."

Owain's dark, troubled eyes frowned down at her as though he struggled with a problem that had no answer. "Promise me you'll obey him and go this time. That you'll not insist on staying. If Edward succeeds in taking you hostage..." His words trailed off as if it were a fear he dared not voice.

Elen nodded. Only the handful of people from Teifi knew she was Lord Aldwyn's daughter. In her rough wool tunic and calfskin boots, she had easily passed herself off as Owain's niece. And the rest of the camp had believed his tale that the noblewomen of Teifi had escaped to France. "Gruffydd's a friend, I trust him as I do Tangwen and the others who know I'm Lord Aldwyn's daughter," she said slowly. "I'll go if he says I must."

Her eyes narrowed in concentration, her perfectly arched dark brows almost meeting above the bridge of her nose. "My concern is for you, Owain. With the English pressing so close and promising outrageous sums for information about your movements, I fear you may be taken."

Owain shrugged. "What will be will be, and God alone plans our course. Heaven knows, I'm naught but a simple soldier and this dark plotting is beyond me. I can see only so far as the next fight." He smiled grimly. "But I'm not so foolish I'll tempt my fate. Though my own cloak be not so warm as Lord Aldwyn's, I'll not ride out as the Welsh Fox this night. With Richard nearby, there's too much likelihood of prying eyes about."

With a sinking heart, Elen stood in the doorway to watch Owain mount his nervously shifting horse. "God go with you," she called as the animal pranced out of the trees into the moonlit clearing several paces before the hut. Owain lifted his hand in a gesture of farewell, and the shadows of night immediately swallowed him up.

CHAPTER THREE

$\mathcal{D}$usk crept slowly over the forested lower slopes of the brooding Welsh mountains. Despite the three score armor-clad men at his back and the southern Welsh allies acting as willing guides for his band, Richard of Kent rode uneasily, his keen eyes constantly searching the wood for shadowy figures slipping through the trees.

The men behind him bunched as closely as their high-spirited horses would allow. English stragglers met a harsh and speedy fate in this mountain fastness of North Wales. None wished to repeat the mistake of yesterday when three knights bringing up the rear had lost their lives. A screaming hoard of the mad Welsh had sprung from the trees to hack down the great war-horses and finish off the knights, clumsy in impeding armor, as they struggled to rise from the ground.

Richard's fists clenched in angry remembrance. It was all over in the blink of an eye. The Welsh had melted back into the gloomy, mist-shrouded forest in a dozen different directions, and he and his badly shaken men had quickly lost their trails. Even his own Welsh scouts had been loath to continue the search.

A scowl of frustration marred his lean, high-cheekboned face, a scowl mirrored by the unaccustomed bitterness in his eyes. Damn these stiff-necked northern Welsh! They had been beaten fairly enough. King Edward had invested their fortresses and set plans in motion for a string of stone castles to ring this mountain stronghold of Gwynedd. The king had wrung submission from every captured noble, and those who hadn't lost their heads had already sworn on bended knee to accept Edward as overlord.

Trouble was, this stubborn race refused to accept defeat. They didn't even *know* they'd been beaten! Small bands continued to strike from their lair deep in these mountains, roughly led by a canny warrior known as the Welsh Fox. Edward himself had entrusted Richard with the task of stamping out the last coals of rebellion. Nothing was left but to hunt the irregular armies down one by one, to starve them into submission and make an example of their leaders.

It was a task Richard had no stomach for. Give him a pitched fight in an open field and he was any man's equal, as ferocious in battle as the cold-eyed king he followed. But the ambush tactics of the Welsh and his own mission to destroy a people fighting for their homeland sat ill in his gut.

"A moment, Richard," a voice called out from down the line.

Richard swung about in the saddle, drawing rein as his friend Sir Giles Eversly cantered up the path toward him. Drawing off his uncomfortable steel helmet, Richard hooked it over his saddle and ran his hand through his thick golden hair.

Giles grinned at him as he drew alongside. "Better cover that head, my friend. No sense telling our enemies we've the Wolf of Kent leading this small band. That distinctive mane might as well be a beacon guiding the arrows of your Welsh admirers straight to your throat."

Richard frowned at the use of his nickname. Wolves traveled in packs, bringing down the old and sick, the young and helpless. It was a comparison he didn't appreciate. "So you think we're being watched, do you, Giles?" he asked, obliging his friend by slipping his helmet back in place. "I've had the feeling all afternoon."

Giles shrugged his shoulders. "Even the trees have eyes in these forests. We're on unfriendly ground and the men are wondering where we'll pass the night. We'll never make Beaufort Keep."

"I know. I've wondered if that was the real purpose behind that raid yesterday. If that handful of rebels hoped to drag us from the trail long enough for more men to arrive." Richard's mouth twisted in the cynical smile that was rapidly becoming his habitual expression. "If that's the case, we certainly fell into the trap."

"As any soldier would have done under like circumstances," Giles said quietly. "We don't leave comrades unavenged." His dark eyes searched Richard's face. "What is your plan, if you don't mind my asking?"

Richard jerked his head in the direction of the road. "There's a village just a mile or two ahead—if you can call anything in this godforsaken land a village. It's naught but a few huts squatting along the roadside, but from what I've been told, there's a burned-out keep nearby with the foundation wall still standing. We'll not have a comfortable night there, but mayhap it'll be a safe one."

His mailed fist slid to his sword hilt, and he glanced once more at the darkening wood. "At least the walls will offer protection if we're forced into a fight. At dawn we'll ride for Beaufort for supplies and what men Sir Thomas de Waurin can muster, then back to search these valleys. I'll not ride on to Gwenlyn till we find the Welsh camp." His eyes narrowed with determination. "This miserable skirmishing must be ended and the raiders punished, else all our forces will lose heart."

Giles nodded. "I'll pass the word among the men. They've seen bogarts under every bush this hour past. Just knowing there's cover ahead'll settle 'em."

Some fifteen minutes later the weary band trotted into the village. Though a half-dozen cooking fires spiraled lazily into the darkening sky, the tiny settlement appeared deserted. No ragged children played about the doorways of the huts; no dogs barked in questionable greeting. An unusual silence reigned over all.

Richard felt the hair rise in warning on the back of his neck. Instinctively, his hand tightened on the reins making Saladin, his big bay war-horse, quiver with anticipation. He unsheathed his sword, holding it in readiness across his muscular thigh as his horse sidestepped slowly past the row of scattered huts. His men followed his example, moving forward cautiously, swords in hand.

Reaching the edge of the village, Richard drew rein. A dense forest of mingled oak and beech began a few dozen yards away. Nothing moved along that dark line of trees.

A warning sounded loudly in his brain. *The Welsh were there; he could feel them watching.*

Squinting into the misty blackness beneath the trees, he caught a telltale flash of movement. "Form up!" he ordered softly.

His men moved into fighting position, knights at the fore, men-at-arms just behind, their shields held well forward. Richard continued to stare fixedly into the gloom. Were trained warriors waiting in readiness beneath those trees? If so how many? Enough to wipe them out? His own band of men was small, but it would be better to meet the foe head-on than be ambushed in the dark hours of the night when the Welsh preferred to strike.

"Giles," he hissed.

"Here, Richard." The voice came from close behind his right shoulder.

"Order them to come out. Tell them we mean no harm if they're innocent villagers, but that we take no chances. Tell them if they don't come out at once, we'll charge in and slaughter all we find, then destroy the village."

Giles nodded his dark head and immediately began translating loudly in the sing-song Welsh tongue.

For several long, heart-straining moments there was silence. Then, with a whir of wings, a startled flock of sparrows broke from the brush along Richard's left side. His men jerked nervously toward the sound, raising gleaming swords as if to fend off a blow.

Richard smiled in grim satisfaction as a figure emerged from the thicket. A bent old woman hobbled slowly toward him across the winter-cured grass. Was it a trick? The Welsh were shrewd. He had learned long ago not to underestimate them.

The woman paused a half-dozen yards from his horse. "What do you want of us?" she asked haltingly in Norman French.

Richard stared at her in surprise. These people never did what he expected. "Nothing, save to know yon forest harbors no ambush," he replied in the same cultured tongue. "Bring the rest of your villagers out. I give you my word we mean you no harm."

"Your *word*?"

Richard recognized the cold contempt in her tone. "I am Richard of Kent, knight of your sovereign lord, Edward of England," he snapped impatiently. "I tell you we mean no harm. I've coins here to buy food if you've aught to spare."

The woman moved closer, gazing up at him with clear brown eyes devoid of fear. "We know who you are. But Edward of England is none of ours. With Llywelyn dead, we wait for another to lead us." She chuckled mirthlessly. "You'd best beware the whelp of Aldwyn of Teifi. Another Llywelyn may yet rise to claim the crown."

Richard held his temper on a thin rein. Even the women of this accursed land flung their defiance in his teeth. Edward had been furious when he learned that the noblewomen of Lord Aldwyn's family escaped after Builth. It was said the women had made sanctuary in France. "Have a

care, old woman. You speak treason and your years may
not save you!" he growled.

With a shrug of one stooped shoulder, she met his angry
gaze with a bitter grin. "I am an old woman, true enough,
and what value my life and loyalty? You and your kind will
never make me claim an Englishman my king!"

She glanced over her shoulder toward the woods. "We've
women and children there and a few men too old to draw
a bowstring. None such as you need fear." She turned back
to him and spat disgustedly. "But unless you relish a handful
of moldy grain and a bit of leek soup, we've no food for
you. We lost seven to hunger this winter past."

Richard nodded. Her gaunt frame and pasty skin gave
the truth to her words. Truly she was naught but a bag of
bones. He frowned. He had seen more hungry women and
children in the last few months than he could wish in a
lifetime. "Tell your people to come out," he said gently,
wishing he had more than a half ration of salt pork and
two small bags of tough beans for his own men.

The woman turned her back on him and bit out several
terse words in Welsh. Slowly a stream of villagers began
filtering through the trees. Richard relaxed, when all
seemed to be as the woman had said. Most of the people
looked scarce strong enough to lift a bow, much less fit an
arrow and let it fly.

Suddenly a shrill scream rang out, and the war cry of the
dead Llywelyn quivered on the evening air. Richard swung
his mount toward the sound, raising his heavy shield to
fend off what he was sure must be an ambush. To his surprise
no hoard of fierce Welsh warriors swarmed from the trees.
A single ragged woman lay crumpled at the feet of one of
his men.

Gripping his sword, Richard spurred toward the scene,
his young squire, Simon, following hastily at his left shoulder. The woman lay in a widening pool of her own blood,
her head nearly cleft from her shoulders. The soldier had

dismounted, his bloody sword held in one shaking hand.

"Christ's mercy! What's this?" Richard snarled.

The soldier dropped to one knee. "My . . . my lord, I didn't see . . . in the shadows, I didn't see! She came at me out of the bush with a staff and that accursed cry. I swear I thought we were ambushed! I swear it, my lord."

Sheathing his sword, Richard swung down from his horse. He couldn't blame John Picard, for he had thought the same. Thrusting his reins into Simon's ready hand, he knelt beside the body, but there was really little use. The woman's life had ended the moment the blade touched her throat.

A small boy of some six or seven years pushed through the gathering crowd. He stared down at the woman, his anguished expression leaving little doubt of his identity.

Gazing at the boy in the twilight shadows, Richard experienced a sharp pain that went far deeper than regret. Something about the lad's expression reminded him of himself at just that age, watching in grieving disbelief as his lovely young mother had been lowered into her grave. No hurt on earth had ever equaled that pain.

With a low snarl, the boy launched himself across the woman's body, beating his small, impotent fists furiously against Richard's leather-clad thighs. Richard caught his arms, holding the lad away from him. "Giles!" he shouted, glancing around helplessly. "Giles . . ."

His friend stepped forward immediately.

"Tell him it was an accident. A mistake. Tell him we didn't mean this," Richard ordered furiously.

Giles sent him a long, thoughtful look. Squatting down beside the painfully thin child, he began a soft-voiced explanation.

The boy had stopped struggling. Richard released him and stepped back, chilled by the hatred that gleamed up at him from the lad's brown eyes. He had seen that look in the eyes of plenty of grown men, but in the face of an innocent child, the look was unsettling.

"Do you think soft words mean aught to the boy now?"

Richard swung around, flushing angrily as he met the scornful gaze of the stooped old woman who spoke.

"There's naught else to be done," he said shortly. "The woman was a fool to launch herself at a mailed soldier."

The old woman's eyes shifted to the boy who was now struggling manfully not to cry. "Perhaps. She lost her man at the battle of Builth, her daughter last month for lack of food. Ride on, my lord. We can see you mean us no harm!"

Richard met her contemptuous gaze, silently cursing this woman, the accident, and even his absent king. "Is there anyone to take charge of the boy?" he asked at last.

She shook her head. "I will care for him such as I may."

Richard reached into a pouch that hung at his belt. Grasping two silver pennies, he thrust them into her bony hand. "See he's cared for," he snapped. "I'll send food if it can be found."

The woman stared down at the coins then back to Richard's set face in amazement. It was more money than anyone in her village would see in a lifetime.

With a last glance at the forlorn child huddling beside the body of his mother, Richard seized his reins from his waiting squire. It was nearly nightfall, and they must yet make a safe camp. He had lingered here overlong as it was, and for what? One motherless boy who would wield a bow against England in a few short years? "Mount up," he ordered, stepping stiffly into the saddle. "We must be away."

As the cavalcade of knights and men-at-arms trotted across the field, the sound of a high-pitched childish voice followed them, screaming something in the unintelligible Welsh tongue. Richard sent Giles an inquiring look. "What's the little devil calling me?" he asked, forcing a light tone.

Giles cocked his head slightly to one side and frowned. "My friend, it's best you don't know."

Richard tightened his jaw and closed his heart, spurring Saladin forward viciously. God, *how he hated Wales!*

A half-dozen campfires flickered and danced amid the ruins of the old keep, throwing ghostly shadows over the soot-blackened stone foundations. Richard sat well back from the revealing glow of firelight, musing on the twisted fate that had brought him to this place.

His father, Sir John Basset, was naught but a minor vassal of Sir Gifford de Erley, a knight holding lands from the powerful Earl of Kent. Richard's Saxon ancestors had been dispossessed of vast lands by the conquering Norman knights of William's time. Slowly the men of his family had won back their honor and a small holding of land through service to Norman kings, but the Bassets were poor and unimportant compared with the great Norman families of the land.

They had been a happy family, though, until Richard's mother died of a winter fever the castle leech couldn't break. Her death was a shattering blow to the bewildered young boy, and when Sir John had remarried even before the proper year of mourning was over—to "bring a woman's touch about the place again," as he'd put it—Richard's life had been turned upside down.

Though of good family, Jeanne of Lewes was a penniless bride and as spiteful and selfish as she was beautiful. She had both disliked and feared Richard on sight, seeing him as a constant reminder of her husband's first wife and as a rival of the son she herself quickly bore. As a result, Richard was packed off to become a page in the household of Gifford de Erley.

Richard scowled at a memory that even now sent his insides churning. He had hated Jeanne for driving him from his home and for making his few holidays there times of misery. And yet indirectly it had all worked to his good.

Bereft of the love of both mother and father, he had turned to pleasing de Erley with a fierce passion that quickly made him a favorite in the household. And at a time when roistering Norman knights still strung men up for the "crime" of being English, it was Richard whom de Erley had taken as squire when he joined Prince Edward on crusade.

There in the sweltering camps of Acre, Richard conceived what almost amounted to a worship of Edward Plantagenet. The tall, dashing prince was a man to love and die for, the impressionable young Richard had decided, and he would do all in his power to become worthy of serving his prince.

Fortunately the crusade hadn't lasted long, and as Edward crossed into Sicily, news came that King Henry was dead and Edward himself proclaimed king. Later, at the infamous tournament of Burgundy against the Count of Chalons, Richard first came to his sovereign's notice.

As the friendly joust turned into a bloody melee, more akin to a battle than a honorable game among allies, it was Richard who unexpectedly came to his king's defense. He had stood at the edge of the field, anxiously straining his eyes amidst the dusty combatants, vainly striving to keep both master and king in sight. As he watched, three fresh Burgundian knights converged on Edward just as the king's lance splintered against an opponent's shield.

Without thought to his own danger, Richard grabbed up a fresh lance and dashed onto the field, ducking and diving amid the deadly, plunging hooves of the destriers to reach his king. For the fraction of a second, Edward's flashing blue gaze had held Richard's in grateful surprise. Then he had caught up the lance and gone on to unhorse all three opponents with a skill the passionate boy had burned to emulate.

Richard leaned back against the wall at his back, a rueful smile touching his face as he recalled what had happened the following day. Far from forgetting the incident, Edward had searched throughout camp until he came across the ardent young squire who had rushed to his defense. "You have done me great service, Richard of Kent," Edward had stated in a suitably grave tone. "What do you ask of me?"

Richard could still remember dropping to his knees and staring up at Edward in starry-eyed admiration. The King of England was actually speaking to him! "Only that I may be worthy to serve you, Your Grace," he had managed to choke out.

Edward had laughed and tousled his hair like an indulgent uncle. "And so you shall, young Richard of Kent, for your response pleases me well. Gifford, I envy you this lad," he said, turning to de Erley. "See you train him well, for I will be watching his progress."

And strangely enough, Edward had continued to take notice of Richard, personally knighting him and attaching him to the royal service when his years as a squire were ended. And Richard's strength and skill in battle were rewarded as he rose higher and higher in Edward's regard, though he had not yet won the riches he knew his family hoped to gain from the arrangement.

Richard shook his head and chewed the last piece of stringy salt pork that had made up his meal. He served Edward because the man was one he could follow for love and loyalty, not because he hoped for gain. Unlike England's preceding sovereigns, Henry and John, Edward was a king who treated men fairly be they English or Norman, who gave his word and kept it, who swore to hold the peace of a strife-torn England at the point of his sword if necessary.

Richard grinned wryly. And this cursed action in Wales wasn't one to gain any man riches and glory. It was more likely to get him kicked out of the royal favor if he didn't quickly succeed in bringing the Welsh Fox to earth for his impatient sovereign. There were plenty of ready tongues at court whispering against him, plenty of men jealous of his standing with Edward. Though Richard had no wealth and little power, it was rapidly becoming known he had something even more valuable—the ear of the king.

"My lord."

Richard glanced up. Henry Bloet, the master of his men-at-arms, was standing respectfully a few paces away. "What is it, man?"

"I hate ta disturb ye, m'lord," Henry said with a grin, "but there be a woman at the gate askin' for ye."

"A woman?" Richard repeated, scowling.

Henry nodded. "She says she's got news ye'll be eager for." Henry grinned again. "I suggest ye come quick, m'lord. She's young and clean, and the men be, ah . . . interested."

Richard rose to his feet, frowning with concern. He had removed his heavy steel hauberk, but now he lifted it over his head, drawing it down to fit over his chest in two practiced movements. "Tell the men to hold themselves in readiness," he commanded. "This may be a trick."

Henry nodded. "I've doubled the guard a'ready."

Richard followed his man to the western doorway of the old keep. Sure enough, a dark-cloaked woman stood stiff and anxious beside Giles, glancing nervously over her shoulder in the direction of the village. He glanced at his friend. "Tell her I am Richard."

The woman threw back her hood, revealing thick blond hair and wide-set eyes of fathomless brown. "I speak English, my lord," she said clearly. "I am Margaret of Chester. As you may guess, I am of mixed blood."

Richard gave Giles a nod of dismissal. Courteously holding out his hand, he gestured for the woman to enter the gate. "You told my man you have news. What is it you wish to say to me?"

She moved toward him until she was so close he could feel the warmth of her body. "I have news of the camp you seek," she murmured, "but it will mean my death if any learn I have spoken to you."

Richard schooled his features to hide his surge of eagerness. This was more likely a trap than not, but perhaps, just perhaps, his luck was about to change. "And what camp is that?"

"I'm no fool, m'lord," she said sharply. "You seek the camp of the Red Fox of Wales, and I tell you this night you lie within a few hours of the prize."

He studied her pleasing features. Her steady gaze didn't shift beneath his lengthy perusal. Either the woman was in earnest or so practiced in deceit that she was a master of the art. "How came you by this knowledge?"

"My man rides with the Fox from time to time. I've had enough bits of information from him to piece together the place."

The woman was foolish to think he would take the bait so readily. "And why do you bring this information to me?"

She lifted her head proudly to meet his keen gaze. "Because my man has shamed me before the village. He took his mistress into my house, casting me out because of my English blood." She smiled bitterly. "What is shaming to one people may bring victory to another, might it not, m'lord?"

Richard studied the arrogant lines of the woman's face. "Your man was a fool," he said softly, "but perhaps we may all profit by it. If your information is true, there'll be a bag of coins for you. If false, you'll rue the day you lied to me."

She studied his face as shrewdly as he had just studied hers. "Oh, it's true, my lord. I've nothing to fear from that. But how do I know you speak truth? That you'll not cast me out or give me to your men when the raid is done?"

"I give you my word as a knight of Edward of England. That is all the assurance I can offer you now."

She stared at him cynically. "And if that isn't enough?"

Richard's gaze hardened. Many miserable months and countless lives might be saved if they could take the main Welsh camp by surprise. And if he could only take the Fox, his exile in this savage land would be ended. "You've told me you have information. I'll have that information from you now . . . willingly or not. The choice is yours."

"Then my decision is easy, is it not, m'lord? The camp lies a few hours' ride to the northeast at the foot of a little-known mountain pass. Here, I'll draw the way on the ground."

Though he strained his eyes to look into the darkness, Richard could see nothing in the shadow of the tall cliff sheltering the trail to the Welsh camp.

Ahead in the open glen, moonlight turned every frost-spangled bush and blade of grass to shimmering silver, but the glen's inviting beauty was treacherous. He and his men must cross that open ground to reach the safety of the wood beyond where his enemy supposedly lay. And if this were a trick, they would be exposed to the efficient fire of the deadly Welsh longbows for sufficient time to be destroyed.

Easing quietly from the saddle, Richard slipped his sword from the scabbard and whispered the order for his men to do the same. They wore no armor for fear of the noise, only the thick leather of protective jerkins. And every piece of metal on saddle and bridle had been carefully wrapped with cloth to prevent the possibility of jangling steel. If they planned to lay an ambush for the canny Welsh, it must be laid carefully indeed.

Richard sniffed the air, recognizing the smell of wood smoke on the chill night breeze. At least one part of the woman's tale was true. The camp was definitely close by.

He longed to send one of his Welsh scouts forward to study the wood ahead, but his man might be seen by the sentries he knew stood between himself and the camp. Luckily, with nightfall, the guards would be few and posted in close. No one would dream the English would come upon them in the dark—that is, if this weren't a trap.

"Ready, m'lord." The whispered words came back to him from down the line. His squire stepped forward, taking the reins of his restive stallion. When the fighting began, four of the lads would bring the mounts of the knights nearby in case their masters had need of them, but Richard ordered Simon to remain there to oversee the rest of the squires and horses.

Holding his sword before him, Richard stepped boldly forward into the moonlight. His men followed readily enough. They were well-trained soldiers and eager to come at the Welsh in a real fight. It was the unexpected ambush from woodland and mountain pass that so preyed on their spirits.

Keeping low to the ground, Richard sprinted into the brightly lit meadow. His heart thudded painfully in his chest as he raced for the sheltering trees. Now he would learn if his gamble had paid off or was naught but a foolish mistake costing the lives of himself and his men. Now he expected the hiss of feathered death. *Now, if he'd been wrong...*

They reached the woods without mishap. A wild exhilaration sang through his veins; the enemy was just ahead! A few scattered fires glimmered in the darkness of the trees like winking fireflies. From somewhere close by, the laughing whisper of rushing water came to him, but all else in the wood was deathly silence.

A sudden furious cry of alarm rang out from just to his right, and a dark shape lunged from behind the thick trunk of a tree. The sword of Henry Bloet flashed briefly before it was buried in the heart of the Welsh sentry.

The alarm was raised. Ahead lay the Welsh Fox and the end of this miserable war. Lifting his sword above his head, Richard dashed forward into the camp.

"Edward and England!" he bellowed at the top of his lungs.

The men behind him took up the savage roar. "*Edward and England! Edward and England!*"

CHAPTER FOUR

*E*len shifted her head drowsily on her sweet-scented pallet of pine boughs, but the roaring in her ears wouldn't go away. Opening her eyes, she glanced sleepily toward the feebly glowing coals of the dying fire. A nightmare, she must be having a nightmare.

The surging roar formed itself into words. *England... England!*

Throwing back Owain's warm fox fur, she sat bolt upright, recognizing the clash of steel, the screams of pain and confusion signifying a battle. Leaping to her feet, she stumbled to the doorway and peered out.

In the flickering light of several pine torches held aloft, shadowy figures raced back and forth among the scattered huts. Before her disbelieving eyes, women and children were dragged from their shelters while men struggled against their attackers with swords, firewood, anything they could lay to hand.

A nightmare, her worst nightmare. But she was living it!

For a moment, she couldn't think. Sheer terror washed over her, leaving her helpless, unable to move. Owain... sweet, blessed Virgin! What would Owain do?

As she glanced about the hut in a panic, her gaze came to rest on his fur cloak. Owain would do something to save his people, and he would expect her to do the same.

The thought steadied her. Grabbing up her sword, she buckled it on, and reached for the fur cloak. At the door, she gazed out once again, but this time with a determination so strong it smothered her fear.

The hut she shared as Owain's avowed niece was away from the others, located in a dense stand of trees for both warmth and safety. It might be several minutes yet till her enemies discovered it.

Slipping through the doorway, she raced around back where her horse was kept tethered for just such an emergency. Owain had been wise. She could never have caught a mount in the maddening scene near the camp's center.

The big gray stallion sidled away at her approach, backing his ears and shaking his head in nervous excitement at the nearby sounds of battle. "Easy, boy. Easy, Moroedd," she whispered, groping for his bridle in the darkness and getting it over his nervously bobbing head with difficulty.

The animal was no mount for a lady, but it had been her father's boast that his slender daughter could bestride any horse in his stable—a boast she'd nearly killed herself to make truth. In the panicked flight after his death at Builth, it had seemed wise to take the strongest and fleetest of his horses. And the great beast had never yet failed her, carrying her miles over rough terrain without seeming to feel the pace. The English would never catch her on this devil.

The fox cloak thrown over her shoulders, she wrapped the reins securely around one hand and led the impatient stallion away a few paces to a log that served as her mounting block. There was no time to waste in saddling the beast. The unmistakable sound of soldiers charging into her hut confirmed her instincts; she hadn't a second to lose!

Moroedd sidled away from the log and she brought him back into position. The men would be on her in a moment. "Stand, Moroedd. Please stand!" she whispered desperately.

Flinging up his great head, the stallion hesitated, staring back through the trees at the flickering torches near the camp's center. It was now or never. Grasping a fistful of heavy black mane, Elen launched herself from the log, scarcely getting a leg across the stallion's back before he lunged forward, almost unseating her.

Using all the strength of her wiry body, she checked his headlong dash into the forest. But to her dismay, controlling the beast without the aid of a saddle was a feat scarcely within her skill. Determinedly, she worked him back toward the scene of noise and confusion. Her people were putting up a valiant fight. If she could create a diversion, perhaps some could escape.

At the edge of the trees, she drew rein and pulled the cloak's concealing hood up about her face. Edward of England wanted the Welsh Fox. If the Englishmen thought her the man, they would leave all to pursue her.

Elen held her sword before her, struggling to manage her fidgeting mount. Then, with a low growl of hatred, she dug her heels into Moroedd's sides. The animal leaped forward from the sheltering wood directly into a small cluster of English soldiers, scattering them in all directions. The men glanced up in confusion at the flash of red fur atop a huge gray beast of a horse. They set up a shout at once. "The Fox! The Fox!"

Elen bent low over Moroedd's neck, clinging to his slippery sides as he dashed through the ranks of struggling men. She felt the thud of impact as his flashing hooves connected with a body. She didn't dare look back. God grant it was an Englishman.

At the sound of hoofbeats, Richard glanced up. "Christ's blood! Our quarry flies!" With a shout at Giles, he swung out of the bloody melee in which he was involved, and leaped on a horse a squire held. With another shouted order, four of his knights followed suit.

Elen broke from the trees on the far side of the camp,

sawing back on the reins in an attempt to slow Moroedd's flight across the moonlit meadow. She wanted her enemies close by when she entered the mountain pass. Mayhap a few would break their necks in a tumble.

Daring a glance over her shoulder, she saw the riders gallop into the meadow behind her. Now! She swung Moroedd toward the pass, kicking him to full speed while her enemies streamed out several lengths to the rear.

She almost made it. A few more paces and the shielding darkness of the trees hugging the pass would make freedom a certainty. Suddenly, out of the blackness ahead, a blazing torch swung up, dazzling her with its unexpected brilliance. Moroedd lurched to a halt, rearing in fear as the flare twirled about him.

The stallion's abrupt stop flung Elen onto his neck. She grabbed for a handhold in his thick mane but found herself grasping at air. Landing on the ground with an impact that pushed the breath from her lungs, Elen rolled instinctively away from beneath the stallion's flailing hooves. She was on her feet in an instant, but to no avail. With a nervous snorting of flared nostrils, Moroedd galloped away. And in that moment, the English were upon her.

Elen scrambled desperately for her sword, her quick mind grasping for any possibility of escape. She knew these woods like the back of her hand. If she could fight her way into their concealing shadows, perhaps she could win free.

The unexpected sound of English voices came from behind her. There were more men there in the trees; bobbing torches told of their movements. She swung back to the knights rushing to encircle her. God have mercy, she was trapped!

Grasping her sword tightly in one sweating hand, Elen straightened herself proudly to face her attackers. One tall knight advanced slowly from the ring of enemies, his gleaming broadsword held high. Moonlight shimmered over a head of straight blond hair, making it glow like spun silver.

A realization washed over her, strengthening her—it was Richard of Kent she faced across her sword, Richard of Kent, the man who had slain Enion! A sudden rage burned through her, a rage so powerful, so elemental it left no room for fear. Her prayers were answered, her most fervent desire granted, if she had but the strength and wit to see it through. She might kill the Wolf of Kent . . . *with her own hand!*

"Lay down your sword," Richard ordered tersely, coming to a halt three blade lengths away. "You are taken."

Elen understood French clearly enough. Her father had fought bravely to keep his homeland free but had wisely planned for the possibility of defeat by a more powerful enemy. She had learned French as well as the hated English along with all the members of her family.

"He doesn't understand our speech, Richard," one of the knights called out gleefully. "Bark at him like a dog. Mayhap he'll recognize his own cowardly tongue!"

Richard didn't move a muscle as the men about him continued their laughter and vicious jibes at their enemy. He despised this reviling of a brave man, but he couldn't blame his men for their hatred. All had lost comrades in this accursed war. "You are taken, sir," he tried again in English. "I order you in King Edward's name to throw down your arms."

In those few seconds, Elen made her plan. She knew the strength of her arm would be as nothing to the battle-hardened knight standing before her, but she was light and quick, quicker than most men.

Though Owain had insisted on keeping her far from his raids, he had continued to engage her in the sword practice that had once been merely a pleasant pastime, teaching her many a trick to enhance what strength she possessed. And the hours of practice had paid off. Once, when a band of English men-at-arms stumbled upon her party, she had engaged and slain an attacking soldier.

Yes, she could kill a man, she reminded herself now.

And it would be a pleasure to kill this one. Her lips thinned to a tight, determined line. God in heaven strengthen and direct her aim!

Catching up the trailing hem of her cloak, she swung it over her left arm and edged forward a step, lightly saluting Richard's blade with the tip of her own steel. Then she backed away a few paces into the shadowy tree line. She must keep out of the betraying moonlight. The great Wolf of Kent would scorn to fight a woman.

"So you would fight me, would you," Richard said softly, "I think not, friend Fox. My king wishes for your hide undamaged by my steel."

"Coward! Base coward!" She hurled the insult in a guttural snarl of Norman French, shrewdly guessing the knights encircling them would hear and understand.

The men's laughter died abruptly. Richard stiffened. "Is that what you think, friend Fox? Then perhaps I should instruct you."

"Richard, don't be a fool!" Giles snapped, swinging down from his horse. "You don't even wear armor, for God's sake. Don't risk it!"

"He doesn't wear armor either," Richard pointed out. He followed Elen's backing figure slowly into the trees. "I'd say we're matched evenly enough."

Elen smiled in triumph. It was easy to goad these arrogant fools into a fight. But the next part of her plan would be more difficult, and she must keep all her wits about her if she was to be successful.

"Boy! Bring torches," Giles shouted to a hovering squire. Immediately the glow of torchlight ringed the space beneath the trees.

Abruptly, Elen halted, her raised blade forcing Richard to do likewise. As he shifted forward to test the strength of her arm, she ducked beneath his blade, circling to one side in a maneuver that almost won under his guard.

He followed swiftly, his heavy broadsword a flash of

deadly silver in the uncertain light. But Elen's guard was quicker yet, and his blade met hers with a resounding clash.

She danced sideways, shaken from the force of his blow. She must end the fight quickly. She was no match for this man, even for a moment. No wonder Enion had fallen before him.

She backed away, the thought of Enion giving deadly purpose to her movements. Again Richard followed as she circled warily. Unlike so many big men, her enemy was quick and easy on his feet. But she would be quicker.

Panting slightly from excitement and exertion, Elen engaged his blade several times in quick succession, always shifting away before Richard could bring his full weight behind the staggering blow of his sword.

He followed with an oath. "Stand and fight," he snarled. "You've not the strength of a woman!"

She repeated the maneuver, this time allowing him to press down against her steel. Stumbling back in feigned retreat, she darted close in as Richard followed, thrusting upward with a lightning stroke just as Richard recognized the ploy and jerked sideways.

Her blade missed his heart by a wide margin, sliding harmlessly along the inside of his left arm instead. She heard him curse in pained fury as the tip of her sword caught living flesh.

Jerking back, she steeled herself for the onslaught that would surely follow, almost weeping in mingled rage and frustration. She had come close, so close, but she had missed her chance. This man wouldn't make the same mistake twice.

Richard glared at the muffled figure, seething with rage at the base trickery that might have cost him his life. Was this cowardly specimen the man he'd spent the last four months freezing and hungering for? Was this the best his enemy had to offer? Why, the creature wouldn't even stand and fight! Somehow he had expected more of his enemy.

Lunging forward, he met the determined thrust of the Welshman's sword, sending it downward and away with the force of a shattering blow. His momentum carried him into his opponent, and the two went down heavily onto the frosty grass.

Richard held his panting adversary easily, his knee forced into the man's heaving stomach while he quickly jerked a dagger from the man's belt, pressing it against a slender throat. His shouting knights clustered round like a pack of ravening dogs gathering to tear at a wounded animal. "Light . . . bring me a torch!" Richard shouted irritably.

Two squires scuttled hastily forward. Richard turned to the man he'd so easily defeated, jerking back the fox hood still shadowing his face. Delicate features of an undeniably feminine cast met his astonished gaze.

"God's death!" he swore in utter disbelief. Throwing down the knife in disgust, he swung to his feet. "It's a woman! Christ's mercy, 'tis naught but a *woman*! While we lingered here with this foolish ploy, the real Fox of Wales has escaped us!"

Elen lay on her back, staring up into the ring of angry, hostile faces as she fought to get her breath. They would kill her now, no doubt most horribly. But she didn't care; hatred took her beyond fear. And her diversion might have helped some of her people escape. That knowledge would sustain her through whatever pain was to come.

Slowly, she eased herself to a sitting position, her eyes warily following the movements of her golden-haired enemy as he paced forward and back, obviously struggling for control. His stride was long and purposeful, his chest and forearms broad and well muscled from endless hours of carrying shield and sword—against her people, she reminded herself.

He swung about, abruptly halting before her. "The Fox has fled, has he not?" he bit out, his words icy with smothered rage.

She returned his stare with unwavering contempt, delighted at causing such fury.

Catching her arm, he jerked her roughly to her feet. In the reddish glow of torchlight, two determined gazes met and clashed as dangerously as their swords had earlier. Richard's eyes narrowed in surprise. This woman was no coarse-featured peasant. Even in the uncertain light he could see she was a beauty, no doubt the leman of the man he pursued. How else would she have come by that fox cloak and a horse of such value, especially in the confusion of the unexpected raid? She had to be sharing the man's bed.

Suddenly, he smiled in cynical appreciation of the trick that had duped him. "Good Christ, what a jest," he murmured. "And more what I should have expected from your canny Welsh Fox. Tricked by the master trickster of them all!"

Releasing the woman, he turned to his friend. "Giles, come and tend my arm. The invincible Richard has been wounded in battle by a woman. Our Edward is like to die laughing at the joke!"

Giles moved closer to cut away the blood-soaked material encasing Richard's forearm. Motioning the torchbearer nearer, he inspected the wound. "A deep scratch, but clean cut," he informed his leader. "You were lucky, Richard. Her thrust was so quick, I scarce saw it myself."

"Yes, it was, wasn't it?"

Richard's gaze strayed to the woman, who watched him with such a blaze of hatred in her heavily lashed eyes. Of a sudden, he wondered what color they were. It was impossible to tell aught but dark and light in the wash of torchlight. "My compliments, lady," he said mockingly as Giles bound up his arm. "I trust you found me a worthy opponent?"

The woman didn't blink an eyelash. Of course none of this savage brood understood good Saxon English. He released a weary sigh. "Speak to her, Giles," he said, nodding at the woman. "Ask her what she's called. I've a strange desire to know the name of those who seek to skewer me."

Giles moved a few steps nearer the woman, quickly repeating the question in her native tongue. The beauty maintained a scornful silence.

Turning back to Richard, Giles ran a hand through his curly black hair. "She's probably frightened out of her wits thinking we'll torture her for her attack on you, Richard. May I tell her you mean her no harm?"

"She doesn't look frightened to me, Giles," Richard responded with a wry grin. "She looks more apt to take that sword to the lot of us." He moved nearer, once more caught by the perfect symmetry of the woman's features. "Lord, the man must be a fool to have risked this prize," he muttered.

Without considering the consequences, he lifted a hand to catch the dark, heavy braid that hung over the woman's shoulder. Immediately, she lunged at him, curved fingers reaching for his eyes.

Flinging up a protective arm, he warded off her attack as two of his men leaped forward, roughly restraining her. "God's blood, it'd be a man's death to mount this one," one of the men remarked with a crude laugh. Two others then joined in with explicit suggestions as to how the difficult task might be accomplished.

Richard ignored the ribald comments. The woman didn't seem to understand them, and his men were disciplined enough to realize the folly of doing aught without his permission. Early in his command he had strung up a half-dozen soldiers for savaging the people of a harmless village. He allowed his men none of the brutal liberties taken by Hugh de Veasy's troops in the south. Edward would have difficulty enough ruling this hardy race without deliberately inflaming them to greater resistance.

Catching the woman's chin, he tilted her face toward him in the torchlight. She was young, far younger than he'd first thought, but she showed no fear. Her large almond-shaped eyes gleamed back at him with hatred—

the same hatred that had flamed in the gaze of a small, starving boy this afternoon. "Christ's wound, this people must be suckled on hatred!" he exclaimed.

"For their own kind, no," Giles responded. "But for us it's true, and oft with good cause, I'm afraid. If you'd grown up in the border lands of the Welsh Marches you'd have learned that fact early and well."

Richard glanced at his friend, then back down into the lovely, defiant face before him. God's truth, he'd fought and almost slain a child, a beautiful, half-wild child. Pity stirred in his heart, pity and something more—admiration. The girl had fought damned well. "Tell her I mean her no harm," he said, dropping his hand. "I don't make war on women and children."

Turning away, he called for his horse. He jerked several leather thongs from his saddle and pitched them to Giles. "Here, bind her wrists and ankles and hand her up to me," he ordered, swinging onto his horse. "Not so tight as to hurt her, but tight enough she can't get free. I've a purpose in mind for this lovely warrior."

Giles quickly followed his command, and the girl was trussed and lifted up across Richard's lap. She didn't struggle, but held herself straight and proud in his arms.

He thought of his own half-sister, Isabel, not so very much younger than this girl. Isabel was fragile and lovely as a spring violet and trusting as a newborn lamb. She would have been fainting in his arms if subjected to even half of what this girl had been through tonight.

But the sorrows of Wales bred strong children. "You've nothing to fear from me or my men," he said softly in French. "We mean you no harm."

The girl didn't speak. She probably didn't really understand the court language, had probably learned only a few choice insults for appropriate moments. Richard sighed heavily and turned his mount across the meadow.

This strange night was near done. The moon would be

setting in less than an hour, and he still had wounded men and prisoners to see to. Though he had been tricked into losing the Welsh Fox, all was not lost. He'd ferreted out and taken a major Welsh camp and captured or killed a great many of the enemy. And the girl he held might yet be turned to good purpose.

"Come, gentlemen, we must see to our prisoners," he called out to his men. "And pray God our comrades didn't find many more wildcats like this one!"

CHAPTER FIVE

$\mathcal{T}$he confused fighting in the Welsh camp was ended. As Richard's bay stallion picked his way through the scene of destruction, Elen held her breath against the powerful urge to retch. Everywhere, bloodied bodies lay sprawled in grotesque angles on the ground, while silent, stone-faced women knelt over their dead or held weeping children away from the sight. The attack had been short, but violent, the outnumbered English soldiers winning easily with the aid of their allies, darkness and surprise.

At the sight of their leader, Richard's men sent up a shout. A stocky, square-faced soldier broke away from a group guarding the prisoners and hurried across the ground. "You got 'im? You caught the cursed Fox?" he called eagerly.

Seeing the woman held tightly in Richard's arms, he drew up in dismay. "What's this, m'lord?"

"A long story, Henry," Richard responded grimly. His arms tightened around Elen as he drew rein. "Tell me, how did we fare?"

The guard captain stood gazing up at Elen in bewilderment. He came to himself abruptly. "Uh . . . naught but three dead, m'lord, and some six others badly wounded. Over a score dead among the enemy and some eight or ten others be hurt bad from what I can tell."

His gaze dropped sheepishly from Richard's to study the ground with an absorbed concentration. "Near the same number prisoners taken, m'lord. Some of the beggars got away into the trees when that devil-gray horse came a-gallopin' through the midst of us!"

"It's all right, Henry. I'm afraid I, too, was fooled. While this enterprising young lady masqueraded as the Fox, the real Fox slipped away from us."

Henry glanced back up, his expression turning into a fierce scowl. "Never you fear, m'lord, we'll get 'im. We'll get 'im next time!"

"Yes, Henry, we'll get him. He and I have something to settle between us now."

With a heavy sigh, Richard swung down, catching Elen's stiff body and lifting her down easily beside him. "Keep a close guard on the prisoners," he ordered. "I'll want to question some of them. And do whatever you can for the wounded. Theirs as well as ours."

"Yes, m'lord."

As Richard stared at the bodies scattered on the blood-soaked ground about him, his features hardened into the unfeeling mask he had cultivated for moments such as this. A waste, what a profane waste of brave men—on both sides. "Whom did we lose, Henry?"

"Beorn, Walter Seward, and John of Shrewsbury."

Richard nodded grimly. They were all good men and he would miss them, but he had really been incredibly lucky. This near foolhardy scheme to attack the enemy camp after stumbling along a moonlit trail in the middle of the night might well have been the end of all of them.

"What do you plan to do with her, Richard?"

Richard turned to his knights who had dismounted behind him. Giles stood regarding their young prisoner curiously.

With a challenging look, Richard shoved the lovely renegade into his friend's arms. "I don't plan to do anything with her at the moment. But you're going to make sure she doesn't brew further mischief. Keep an eye on her, Giles." He grinned. "Both eyes. If she gets away, I'll take it out of your hide!"

Giles's dark eyes met his. "Me?"

"Naturally. You speak that gibberish better than anyone else. Perhaps you can convince her to give us the information we want without resorting to any of the time-honored methods."

"But Richard . . ."

Ignoring his friend's imploring cry, Richard strode away to see to his wounded men.

Elen watched the enemy commander move across the camp, her heart almost bursting with grief and despair. Though she had seen men die violently, had even killed one of the enemy herself, she had never before been exposed to a scene of such carnage.

She stared about in horror. How, how could people do this to each other, she wanted to scream. Easily enough, came the ready answer. They hated in a way that made killing a pleasure, a way she was quickly coming to know.

She stared at a headless corpse, an armless torso. It was difficult even to put names to some of her friends. Was this how her father had looked, his carefree laughter stilled forever on bloodied lips? Was this how Enion and Rhodri had been slain? Owain had sworn they'd died bravely in battle, but somehow she hadn't imagined this!

"Come, lady. This is not a place for you," Giles said softly.

She stared at him, wild-eyed, despairing. "So many are dead," she whispered in a strangled voice. "So many . . ."

He nodded curtly. "It is war. There's little enough of honor and glory now. The broadsword and mace do their jobs pitifully well."

She swallowed back the bitter sickness rising inside, vowing not to show such a disgusting form of weakness. "May I help with the wounded?"

"I fear not. Richard would have my head if you escaped."

She studied her captor closely for the first time. His features were clean and bold with the fierce aggressiveness of a falcon, the lines of his face hard from the numerous battles he had fought. Yet compassion glowed warmly in his dark eyes.

"I give you my word I'll make no attempt to escape so long as I tend the wounded," she promised, and swallowed against the tight constriction in her throat. "I know something of healing. Mayhap my skill can keep others from dying."

He shook his head.

Drawing a deep breath, she bit her lip. "Please."

He stared at her in surprise. Such a word came at great cost. "You pledge your honor you won't escape? I have your word?"

She nodded, still holding his measuring gaze.

With one easy movement he drew his dagger, bending to slice through the thongs binding her ankles.

Now it was her turn to be surprised. "You take the word of a Welsh woman? You've not heard we're a treacherous race? A people little better than animals?" she asked bitterly.

He straightened, quickly untying her hands. "My father is vassal to the Lord of Clare. I grew up on the Welsh Marches dealing with your race. Like any other people, some are to be trusted and some are not. There are good and bad in all nations." He paused, gazing at her narrowly. "I'll be close beside you as you tend your people. Do not seek to prove me a fool."

With a curt nod, Elen turned away, refusing to look at the bodies in her path as she made her way to the line of English soldiers guarding their Welsh prisoners. To her relief, she saw Tangwen already moving among the injured, binding up wounds and distributing cooling draughts of water from a leather flask she carried. "Tangwen, thank

God you're alive!" she exclaimed, stepping forward to catch the woman's arm.

"Of course I'm alive. What sport to kill a worthless old hag like myself?" she asked dryly.

Elen clung to her bony arm, feeling of a sudden like laughing and crying at the same time. "Yes, we're both alive, though I fear to what purpose."

The old nurse squeezed her hand. "'Tis truly a dark hour, child. But God will reveal his purpose in his good time. For now we must do what we might to help these poor souls. Here, take this flask and see to the cleaning of Dylan's shoulder wound. I must go beg yon English dog to allow me to fetch my healing potions."

Elen glanced toward the shadowy shape Tangwen indicated. So her friend Dylan was alive. Thank the merciful Virgin Enid had been spared this night of torment. Enid. Had it really been only this afternoon she'd died? It seemed like years ago instead. And the babe—had that tiny, helpless babe survived the night?

Kneeling in the dirt, Elen put a hand on Dylan's arm. "How badly are you hurt, my friend?"

"Not so bad I won't take a few more of those devils with me before I die!"

Peeling back the coarse homespun of his rent tunic, Elen inspected the ragged wound on his arm where he'd caught a glancing blow. It would heal, she decided.

Gently she began cleansing the wound. "Dylan . . . I've been trying to think what best to do," she whispered. "Owain must be found and warned against trying anything foolish to aid my escape. I'm afraid what he might do when he hears the events of this night."

She studied his set face in the wavering torchlight. He had the dark, handsome coloring of so many of their race, yet his features were distorted with a bitter hatred visible in every line. "Dylan, do you think if I managed to get you a knife, you could escape from here and find Owain?"

His hand gripped her arm so tightly she winced. "Get me a knife and I'll do better than that!" he promised grimly.

"No! There's more at stake than the lives of the one or two Englishmen you might take before you died. Can't you see, Dylan? We must live to outwit them. They're too strong and too many for us now, but surely we can find a way to best them. Owain will think of something, and until he does, every live Welsh fighting man is a hundred times more important than one or two Englishmen killed for revenge!"

He sighed heavily. "You speak the truth. Help me win free and I'll gather the men hiding in the wood and together we'll find Owain." He glanced up, his eyes narrowing angrily. "But what of you? Your lot won't be pleasant with the Wolf and his men."

Elen dropped her gaze uneasily, remembering the ugly comments of the English knights with disgust and fear. "I don't think they'll kill me," she said shortly, "and they will pay soon enough. Tell Owain I'll find a way to escape. They cannot watch me every moment."

He nodded. "Have a care, Elen. I would not see you dead as my Enid, though the dogs will pay for that before I'm much older. They killed her," he added bitterly, "they killed her with hunger and cold as sure as the men lying there were slain by the sword!"

Elen touched his shoulder in a brief gesture of comfort. She had spent time with him earlier in the evening, and Dylan's grieving had been intense, painful to look upon. "I'll try to find Marared and see that your daughter is still well," she murmured. "The woman can suckle both yours and her own wee one."

"I've named the babe Enid," he said softly. "For her mother."

Elen bound up his arm, closing her mind to thoughts of the lovely young woman who had died that afternoon, and to all the dead lying scattered around them. She would survive, she promised herself fiercely. She had to, if only to see the one responsible for this nightmare made to pay. "Enid would have liked that," she said only.

Finished with her rough handiwork, Elen rose to her feet. "Now, you must do something for me, Dylan. You must see the prisoners all tell Richard the same tale when questioned . . . but none too readily."

He nodded. "The devils would be suspicious if they got information from us without torture."

"They are to hear the Welsh Fox is dark of hair and not much older than Richard of Kent. That he goes by the name of Rhys. That he is believed to be from Gwynedd, but none knows for sure," she continued. "And tell them he spends his time among the various camps in these mountains. That he trusts no one with news of his comings and goings."

She smiled grimly. "They already believe I'm his woman, so that fact may be given to lend credence to the tale. And tell the men to add aught else they wish to sound convincing."

Dylan frowned. "Owain will not like it."

"It doesn't matter what he likes. We must throw this Richard off the scent. Above all else, we must keep Owain's identity from them. He's our only hope."

"Very well. I'll spread the tale about."

Elen sighed with relief, the tightness in her chest easing slightly. "Good. I'll see what can be done to find you a weapon."

Getting the dagger was really far easier than she expected. The prisoners had all been searched, but the dead had yet to be relieved of their weapons. As she hurried across camp to refill a water flask, the first lifeless man Elen bent over still wore his knife in his belt.

As unobtrusively as possible, she slipped the dagger from beneath the body, quickly shielding it with the water flask as she shoved it into her left sleeve. Rolling the man over, she gazed at his face. Dyfed ap Cynan, a gentle giant who had oft helped the women and children about the camp. "Thank you, Dyfed," she whispered, gently closing the man's staring eyes. "God have mercy on you . . . and on all of us."

Unexpectedly, a strong hand closed about her right arm, jerking her roughly to her feet. "How did you get loose?" Richard bit out. "I told Giles to keep an eye on you!"

She stared up into the furious gaze of the tall knight, speechless with dismay. Had he seen her? Had he seen her take the knife?

"I set her free to tend the wounded," Giles remarked, stepping forward from a group of men several paces away. "She gave her word she wouldn't attempt to escape, and I believed her. Besides, I've been watching."

Richard snorted contemptuously. "You believed her? You think that after doing her best to put a sword through my heart, she'll keep her word not to escape?"

"Yes."

Elen's heart was beating so wildly she could scarcely breathe. Richard was holding her right arm, but if either of the men touched her left arm, they would surely feel the knife. She turned to Giles, doing her best to appear disdainful. "If your lord fears my escape, tell him I am not such a coward. I will stay of my own will so long as there are those who need me."

Giles quickly translated, and Richard's painful grip on her arm eased. She stared up into his grimy, blood-stained face, resisting the almost overwhelming temptation to lunge at his unprotected midsection with the knife. A better time would come, she cautioned herself. A time when she couldn't fail. If she had her way, Richard of Kent wouldn't leave Gwynedd alive, but the important thing now was to see that Dylan escaped.

Richard released her and scowled down at the body. "This man is obviously beyond her tender care. Get her back with the others where she can be watched."

Giles translated again.

Elen's gaze shifted to the ground. So they hadn't seen the knife. But would Richard think to search Dyfed now for his weapon? She drew a deep breath to ease the trembling deep inside her. "This man was a friend," she said, seeking to cover her actions. "I but sought to speak a prayer over him." Turning on her heel, she made a proud retreat toward the wounded, doing her best to appear not to hurry.

Without glancing to right or left, Elen made her way through the guards and back among her people. "I saw Marared," she whispered to Dylan. "She suckles your young Enid even as we speak. The babe seems healthy enough."

A small smile lightened his features. "Good." He glanced at the ring of guards standing with drawn swords several paces away. The smile disappeared. "Did you manage the knife?"

"Yes. When I bend over to tighten your bandage, reach into my left sleeve and slip it out," she whispered, suiting her actions to the words.

His rough hand moved over her wrist. She felt the chill of cold steel as the knife slid along her arm and into his hand. She had pledged her honor she wouldn't escape, but she hadn't said a word about not helping the others. "God protect you, Dylan," she whispered, moving away without a backward glance.

The moon had set, but the sun had not yet risen to lighten the shadowy recesses of the valley. Darkness hung over the camp, though it was a misty, gray darkness that heralded the coming day. Torches still smoked and flared. Several had gone out, and the grumbling soldiers hadn't relit them as they stumbled about the camp in exhaustion.

Elen huddled on the ground in her place with the other women, shivering with cold and fear. Though she was overwhelmingly weary, she couldn't doze as so many did. Her muscles felt like coiled springs, and sweat stood out on her brow despite the fierce cold of the early-morning air. Sometime soon Dylan would make his escape!

Wrapping her arms about her quaking shoulders, she forced herself to think. Dylan might be killed in the attempted escape, but what else could she have done? She had to get word to Owain to warn him away. At least with a knife, Dylan would have a fighting chance. Besides, they might all be slain, or worse, if even a few of the tales of English brutality she had heard were true.

Sudden shouts rang out, and the section of the camp holding the prisoners erupted in confusion. It was Dylan—it had to be! Leaping to her feet, Elen struggled against the urge to rush past her guards in an attempt to see what was happening. Please make it, please make it, Dylan, she begged.

Richard sprinted across the ground toward the sounds of trouble, roundly cursing these madmen of Wales. As he reached the circle of guards, his men fell back, silently allowing him into the center of confusion.

The sight that met his eyes was not what he had expected. One of the ragged Welshmen clutched a knife at the throat of Sir William of Hereford, the knight in charge of the guard detail. How in blazes had the man gotten a knife?

"Kill him, Richard! Kill the bastard!" William spluttered, struggling furiously against the Welshman's rigid death grip.

"Silence, Will. Be still!" Richard called. "I believe your friend wishes to bargain."

A deathly quiet fell over the men. "Giles, ask him what he hopes to accomplish by this mad act," Richard said evenly.

Giles moved forward and repeated the question, then turned to Richard as the Welshman shot back his answer. "He says he will slay your knight unless you allow all the prisoners to leave."

Richard frowned. The man couldn't possibly expect him to agree to such terms. "Tell him that is impossible, Giles.

Tell him unless he frees Sir William at once, I will kill not only him, but every man I hold in this circle."

Giles sent Richard a questioning glance, then obediently began translating his words.

The Welshman bit out a few brief words and began to back toward the woods, dragging Sir William with him.

"His own life for the life of the English dog," Giles repeated quickly.

Richard nodded. "His life for William's. We won't follow him into the trees. But tell him if he spills one drop of William's blood, every hostage I hold will die before the sun lifts over this mountain!"

Once again Giles translated.

Richard held his breath as the two men disappeared into the misty tree line. The middle-aged William was not only a good warrior, but a stalwart friend as well, and there were upward of thirty hostages in this camp, counting women and children. Richard spoke the most horrible threat that came to his mind, and he didn't want to think of the consequences if the desperate Welshman called his bluff.

About him, the men shifted uncomfortably, gripping their swords in impotent rage. They glanced at the dark forest, then back to him, nervously awaiting orders.

Richard stared intently at the wood, willing his eyes to pierce the dark pall. What in God's name was happening?

His nerves stretched as tautly as the silence. He couldn't send his men into the trees. The wily Welsh were probably just waiting to fall upon a few lone soldiers struggling through an unknown wood.

Then a familiar outraged bellow rang out. "Richard. God's death, don't you dare let this beggar get away! I can see where he's gone. Richard . . . I say, Richard!"

Richard gestured a handful of men toward the trees. "Bring him to the forest line, but don't venture into the wood," he ordered sharply. Drawing a quick breath of relief, he cupped his hands to his mouth. "William, get back here," he shouted, knowing full well the headstrong knight might take off after the Welshman. "*Now*, William!"

Moments later, the dark-bearded knight and several men-at-arms came toward him across the short space of open ground. "By the Holy Cross, Richard, you should hack off my spurs!" William exclaimed disgustedly. "To be taken like a downy-cheeked youth—a man with my experience!"

William shook his dark head in a fury. "You shouldn't have let the black bastard get away, but I'll wager he won't go far, wounded as he is. Give me six men, just six, and I'll bring him back. Or what's left of him!"

Despite his anger at what had occurred, Richard felt a grin tugging at his lips. William looked like nothing so much as an outraged bear. "Your life is too valuable for me to waste in such a fashion, Will." He lifted one tawny eyebrow. "Who could I beat at chess with such regularity?"

William's black scowl lightened considerably. "I'm damnably sorry, Richard! I swear the prisoners were all thoroughly searched and none left with weapons. I can't understand how it happened."

Richard frowned. "See they're searched again. And have every man, save the most seriously wounded, bound with his hands behind him."

William nodded. "And the women?"

"Leave them here. We'll move too fast to drag a herd of weeping women along."

"What of the men—those too wounded to keep the pace? Shall I have them slain, Richard?"

Richard's frown deepened. He could kill his enemy with ease in the heat of battle, but wantonly slaying an injured man helpless in his power was a thing he couldn't countenance. Yet his force was far too small to leave a band here guarding the wounded.

He closed his eyes, feeling the gritty dryness of too many hours without sleep. "No. Leave the dying."

When he opened his eyes again, William was staring at

him, bushy eyebrows half lifted in surprise. The men would think him grown soft.

Richard gritted his teeth. Well, let them! They'd soon learn differently. But even this savage country wouldn't turn him into a barbarian!

Turning on his heel, he made his way toward the hut where he had set up headquarters, signaling for Giles to follow. His men needed to eat and sleep a few hours before they moved out. But did he dare keep them here?

As he moved past the women, his eye caught that of the girl who had tricked him earlier. A knowing smile curled her full, pouting mouth and, in the pale dawn light, eyes of a surprising blue stared back at him triumphantly. He'd wager she knew how that man had gotten a knife . . . he'd wager his last farthing she knew exactly how it had been accomplished!

Richard halted so abruptly, Giles stumbled into his back. His fists clenched in frustration and his whole body heated with a deep, explosive rage. That girl was the embodiment of the treachery and defiance of this whole accursed land. Never in his life had he taken his hand to a woman, but now he ached to force that smile from her face.

Turning on Giles with a glare that had made brave men quail, he pointed to the girl. "Tell her not to look so damned pleased with herself till she learns her own fate!" he snarled. "She rides with us." He glanced up at the lightening sky. "On the hour!"

CHAPTER SIX

The brilliance of dawn broke over brooding mountain peaks, sending golden waves of light down the mountainside to the shadowy valley below. The morning air was crisp and still. In the Welsh camp, men beat their arms together to warm chilled limbs, and horses pranced and snorted, their warm breath sending plumes of steam rising into the frosty air.

Elen gazed at the frantic preparations for departure, trying desperately to keep her gnawing fears at bay. Richard of Kent was furious and taking no pains to hide the fact. As he strode about the camp, men leaped to nervous action at his low, clipped orders, while his green eyes blazed with an anger more terrifying for its icy restraint.

He knew! He knew she had given Dylan the knife. She swallowed nervously, wondering just what price he would exact for her deception. The Wolf of Kent was no fool, nor was he a man to be toyed with. She wasn't afraid, she assured herself hastily, but God forbid he take out his rancor on his helpless hostages.

A new and terrible thought crossed her mind. The wounded—what would he do with them? Her people were poor and had few horses, not nearly enough for all to ride. The answer came with a sickening realization that near brought her to her knees. Kill them if they couldn't keep the pace.

And what of her? What would Richard do to her? She stared blindly at her leather-bound wrists, remembering the crude words of Richard's men. They obviously thought her a common camp follower. But that was the way she must keep it no matter the price.

In those first terrible weeks after the flight from Teifi, Owain had told her again and again of her importance to her countrymen. She hadn't really believed him at first. How could one lone woman not yet seventeen be of any importance in this cursed war?

Yet the English were searching high and low for the wife and daughter of Aldwyn of Teifi. They had already seized the dead Llywelyn's daughter, a babe of only a few months whose English mother, Eleanor de Montfort, had died in childbirth. And Llywelyn's treacherous brother, Dafydd, had been deserted by his own men—a fitting reward for one who had betrayed both his brother and the powerful king of England. It was only a matter of time until he too was caught in Edward's tightening net.

She alone was left of the great warrior families her countrymen might look to, and the mighty Edward was determined to have her in his power. For so long as she lived and was believed to be free, her people might yet rally.

Edward had yet no legal claim to her lands. It was the English king's own laws that tied his hands, she reminded herself with a grim smile. By Welsh custom a woman could not inherit, but Edward had forced the hated English laws upon them after the failure of Llywelyn's revolt.

It was the king's one weakness. He would do everything according to his laws. In her case, however, it would be most convenient to his purposes if he could seize her and put one of his own knights to rule the lands of Teifi legally in her name.

But even more importantly, if allowed to remain free she

might marry and breed sons—sons to claim the crown of Wales that Edward swore to wear, sons to lead future rebellions in pursuit of their stolen birthright. Yes, so long as she remained free, a lone woman could be important in a war!

She smiled grimly, promising herself Richard of Kent wouldn't learn who he held. And if he did, he would die.

"Mount up."

The cry spread quickly throughout the camp. The English swung into their saddles, driving their prisoners before them on foot. Elen watched the men go by. The wounded weren't among them.

No one had spoken to her since Richard ordered her hands bound nearly an hour ago, and she had no way of knowing what he planned for his hostages. A sick feeling settled in her gut. He would kill them. What else could she expect from the Wolf of Kent?

As her guard tried to lift her onto a nearby horse, she twisted away. She couldn't just turn her back and ride out. Not without knowing what would happen to the women and children, the wounded men left behind.

"Now see here . . . none'a that!" the man exclaimed, jerking her roughly back toward the horse. Catching her about the waist, he swung her up toward the saddle, but she twisted in his arms, catching him in the groin with a well-placed kick.

With a violent oath, the man released her, dropping forward on all fours. Elen turned, searching desperately for the dark, compassionate face of the knight who'd helped her before. She hadn't taken two steps in his direction when the guard behind her set up a cry of alarm.

Richard glanced up from the instructions he was giving his knights. "God's mercy, what now?"

Seeing the chestnut-haired virago moving purposefully toward the wounded prisoners, he uttered an impatient oath and sprinted forward into her path. "What now? Do you think to arm them all against us?" he asked irritably.

Elen halted abruptly as Richard stepped before her. Staring up into his furious face, she searched for something, anything to turn him from his purpose. In the full light of morning, she could see his hair was the rich golden color of ripened wheat, and his eyes were incredibly green. Against the tanned skin of his lean face, his eyes gleamed the brilliant color of new spring grass.

Her own eyes widened in surprise. He wasn't what she had expected. He looked too young for so noted a commander, probably considerably less than one score and ten. And even in a rage he hadn't the look of a man who enjoyed killing. Yet his battle exploits were legend, and appearances were oft deceiving.

Turning from his angry glare, she gestured to the wounded men seated or lying about beneath a tall oak. "What will you do with them?" she asked in perfect French.

Richard bit back the sharp order he was about to snap out. So the girl did speak the language. He wouldn't need Giles to communicate with her after all. The thought was oddly pleasing.

His gaze followed hers, lingering on the prisoners. At his studied silence, she turned, lifting cool blue eyes to his. "I am sound of limb and have traveled many weary miles before this. I can walk. Give my mount to two of these who can't."

Richard's impatient anger melted away. The girl obviously thought he meant to kill his prisoners and was offering her mount to save whom she might. He had seen English knights who would not do the like for their own wounded men. Her words reawakened a grudging respect. "There's no need," he said. "These men will not be harmed."

A flash of anger kindled in her eyes, bringing an enhancing flush of color to her pale cheeks. "I'm no fool, sir!" she hissed. "Do you think to lead us all meekly away, then slay these men when none are by to see?"

Richard lifted one tawny eyebrow. "I think," he murmured provocatively, "that you have little choice in the matter."

Contempt flickered openly in her blue eyes. "Then the tales we've heard are true. You're no better than the animal for which you're named." She hesitated, her expressive eyes narrowing coldly. "But even wolves don't kill the helpless for sport."

Her contemptuous words touched him on the raw. His heavy lids dropped down, quickly hiding his irritation. "Perhaps not. But then perhaps you wish to save a man or two among them from the maw of the Wolf?"

"At what cost?" she asked, her chin lifting a fraction.

"Oh, a piece of information well and truly given."

For a moment they studied each other in strained silence. The girl looked as pinched and weary as he felt, Richard realized suddenly. Only her eyes were alert and watchful, clear blue as the restless western sea above the smudges of exhaustion beneath them.

"And what is this information you seek?" she asked at last.

A smile stole over his face. "You may recall from last night. I wish to know your name."

Elen's thoughts whirled frantically. He was toying with her, of course. But did she dare tell him the truth? The name Elen was common enough in Wales. Impossible for him to suspect she was Elen of Teifi in her filthy, bedraggled state. Besides, he'd already questioned several of his prisoners. Might he not already know her name and be seeking to trap her in a lie?

"Elen. Elen of Powys," she replied at last, hastily appropriating Enion's land.

He nodded. "Elen. Thank God it's not one of those impossible Welsh names my English tongue can't form."

He turned from her and gestured for her shame-faced guard, nervously holding two horses several paces away. "Is that all?" she asked incredulously, unable to believe the Wolf so easily appeased.

He glanced back. All trace of the smile was gone, and his face was suddenly so hard she decided she had only imagined it. "For now, yes. But I'll not have any of my men struck again or you'll suffer for it. One more bit of trouble from you, Elen, and you'll not only walk out of these mountains, you'll walk bound in chains all the way to meet Edward at Westminster!"

Her gaze never wavered. "And these men?"

"I told you before—they'll come to no harm. Believe me or not, as you will," he said impatiently. "There's nothing you can do in any case."

With a sharp warning to her guard to keep a firm hand on her mount, Richard was gone. Elen stood staring after him, scarcely daring to believe his words. Yet he was right. There was really nothing she could do, anyway.

"My lord, hold up a moment!"

Richard turned in the saddle as Giles cantered up alongside. His friend had ridden in the rear of the column for the last two hours, helping Sir William prod the weary prisoners along the trail.

Giles leaned nearer, his voice dropping so low only Richard might hear. "I know you're in a hurry to reach Beaufort before that damned Fox can ambush us. But if we keep this pace there are those who won't make it." He glanced down the line of men. "And not only among the enemy."

With the experienced eye of a commander, Richard looked over the column of his men-at-arms. Several reeled in the saddle like drunkards, while all slumped heavily in exhaustion. His men had been too long without sufficient food and sleep, and many were too proud to complain of painful wounds obtained in the vicious fighting last night. They needed a rest. With the rush of battle excitement long ended, he felt weary unto death himself. Besides, his own wounded arm ached with a vengeance.

"We'll stop a few moments then, Giles. Pass the word. This is as good a place as any." He glanced up. "Oh, and Giles, have Simon unpack the wineskins he carries in my baggage. See they're distributed among the men. I've been saving them for a moment such as this."

"Wine?" A grin stretched itself across Giles's haggard face. "Richard, I'd kiss your feet if I thought I could get down without falling on my face."

Richard gave a weary chuckle. "Pray don't, then. I'd be honor bound to pick you up, and I'm afraid we'd both end up in the dirt."

Giles glanced around. "Where is the lad?"

"Somewhere back to the rear of the train. I told him I wished to carry my own shield, and it offended his dignity so greatly he's scarce speaking to me. And I'm afraid I was a bit sharp with him this morning," Richard added sheepishly. "God's mercy, I was sharp with everyone when I learned the Fox had escaped me."

"Yes, but you snapped everyone's nose off, not just his. Simon knows you well enough to realize you don't mean what you say in a rage." As Giles stared at his friend, his dark eyes were thoughtful. "But you might think about speaking to the lad if you can spare a moment, Richard. I know you've more important tasks, but the boy worships you. It won't do to have him mooning about camp like a kicked puppy. By the way, did you know it was he who raced into the path of that gray beast last night and swung the torch?"

Giles smiled at the surprised shake of Richard's head. "The squires are all abuzz with their own importance this morning. It seems it's Simon we owe for the capture of that young woman you seem to prize so highly. And the boys managed to get her gray stallion back, too. He strutted into camp this morning looking for his mares. That animal alone is prize enough to justify the raid."

"I wonder Simon didn't tell me himself," Richard remarked, puzzled.

Giles swung his black gelding away. "Mayhap you weren't in the mood to be told anything," he called as a parting shot.

Turning to the first soldiers in the column, Richard gave the order to rest. As exhausted men fell out along the trail, he edged Saladin toward the rear of the train. He wanted to see for himself how the prisoners were holding up . . . and the girl called Elen.

When he first caught sight of her, the girl was leaning slightly forward over the pommel of her saddle, eyes half closed in weariness. But as the men about her leaped to attention at his approach, her eyes flashed open and she straightened stiffly to meet his gaze.

Pride. He knew her damned Welsh pride would keep her erect in the saddle if it killed her. "Help her down," he ordered, as he rode by. "Simon will bring wine for you all, but I want no less than two men guarding this prisoner at all times."

Reaching the end of the train, he dismounted, giving his horse to a young squire who raced to assist him. The boy offered up a cup of wine. Richard seized it and drank deep, welcoming the strengthening bite of the rich liquid.

Wiping his mouth against the sleeve of his leather jerkin, he gazed at the nervous boy in speculation, searching his memory for a name to go with the mop of reddish curls. The boy looked young to be a squire, but he remembered that William had taken in the twelve-year-old son of a kinsman. "Adam, isn't it?"

At the boy's pleased nod, he handed the cup back. "I thank you for your aid, Adam, you were quick to see my need. Now I have something further I wish you to do," he remarked with suitable gravity. "There is a lady near where Sir William's chestnut gelding stands. Take this cup and offer her wine. Don't be surprised if she refuses at first, but be patient with her. She's weary and frightened."

He smiled at the boy and was rewarded by seeing a grin

brighten the youth's face in return. "And if you see Simon, pray send him to me."

The boy made a quick, respectful bow. "Yes, my lord."

Richard frowned at the lad's retreating back. It wasn't like Simon to leave him to the ministrations of another. As personal squire to the commander of Edward's northern forces, Simon held the place of honor in the complicated hierarchy of squires. And he was jealous of his position as only a proud fifteen-year-old could be. Yes, something was definitely wrong.

With a weary sigh, Richard slipped his blade from its scabbard, placing it beside him before he eased himself to the ground. Leaning back against the trunk of a smooth-barked beech, he reached into a leather pouch inside his jerkin and caught up a handful of the moldering grain he had seized from the scarce supplies of the Welsh.

The grain was foul and unpalatable, but he forced himself to chew and swallow the two handfuls that were his portion. It was all he would have to quiet his protesting stomach until he reached Beaufort Keep. Pray God his men could get theirs down as well. They all needed the strength.

A short time later, Simon came hurrying down the path toward him. The boy was pale, but erect as he halted the correct two paces away.

"You sent for me, my lord?"

"Yes, Simon. It seems you and I have a problem between us."

The boy went a trifle paler beneath the fringe of flaxen hair falling about his face. Eyes of soft, light blue glanced painfully in his direction and then away. Squaring his shoulders resolutely, the squire came to attention. "If you would tell me in what manner I've failed to please you, my lord, I will amend my ways," he said stiffly.

"Yes. Well, as I've said, we have a problem between us," Richard repeated. "You have the misfortune to have a master who is dull of wit and sharp of tongue when his temper is sorely tried." His lips twitched slightly. "And I carry the burden of a squire who refuses to speak up when I'm behaving like an ass."

Simon glanced at him in amazement. "Oh no, Ri—my lord," he protested. "I'm sure it's me. I . . . I've done something wrong, failed in some way, I know, but I can't decide what it is for the life of me!"

Richard gazed up at the handsome boy, remembering his own days as a squire and his acute misery on those few occasions he had failed his master. "You've done nothing wrong, Simon," he said gently. "Though young, you bid well to be the best squire I've trained. And I'd tell you that more often if I didn't think it would swell your fair head so it wouldn't fit your helmet. Now sit here beside me," he added with a smile. "You make my neck hurt with the strain of gazing up at you. Don't you know you shouldn't frown down at your betters, boy?"

Simon's worried frown slid into a grin and he sank obediently onto the carpet of spring grass at Richard's side. "I . . . I couldn't help wondering why you left me in the wood with the younger boys last night," he said diffidently. "You didn't take me with you when you attacked the camp. I . . . I thought perhaps you didn't trust my swordplay, that you feared I might be a hindrance," he added in a rush.

Richard shook his head. One part of him hadn't wanted to expose the boy to the possibility of ambush by the deadly Welsh bowmen, but that hadn't been the real reason he had left his squire in the wood. "You're my squire, Simon, and you share in some measure the responsibility I bear for this mission. I half believed we were walking into a trap last night but felt it a risk worth taking to snare the Fox," he explained.

Keen green eyes bored into worshipful blue ones. "If anything had happened to me last night, I needed someone on the other side of that glen who could see to the safety of the other squires. Someone with the ability to elude the enemy and get to Sir Thomas at Beaufort with news of what had happened. I would have expected you to do that, Simon, if aught had gone amiss. Now do you understand what I think of you, lad?"

The boy was silent, obviously digesting Richard's words. "I'll do my best never to fail you," he murmured after a moment. "I . . . I'll practice even harder with my sword and lance, and I'll—"

"God forbid I should have a perfect squire," Richard interrupted, holding up one hand. "I'll go daft if I can find no cause to curse and beat you on occasion."

The boy's lips twitched. "You know you don't beat me, Richard."

"Hmm, perhaps I should. Calling me by name . . . insolent whelp!" Richard grinned. "I'd beat you here and now if I didn't owe you a debt for helping capture our young prisoner. The girl would have escaped if not for your quick thinking, lad. I'd have said something before, but I didn't know it was you until Giles told me."

Simon smiled but shrugged off the compliment. "It was really to no purpose, though, was it, Richard? I thought to help corner the Fox, but all we got was a cursed woman!"

"Quite possibly an important woman, Simon. I believe her to be the mistress of the man we seek." Richard took the near-empty wineskin from the boy and turned it up for a last swallow. Finishing off the contents, he handed it back, his shrewd green eyes deadly serious once more. "There's more than one way to snare a fox, Simon. Do you care to help bait the trap?"

Elen twisted her hands once again, gritting her teeth against the pain in her chafed wrists. Despite the hours of struggle, there was still no loosening of the leather thongs binding her.

Taking no chances on another mishap, Richard had inspected the bonds himself before lifting her onto her mount after their short rest. He had noticed the ugly, raw places on her wrists at once. "You give yourself pain to no purpose, Elen of Powys," he'd said with a frown. "I've no wish to harm you, but neither will I let you escape. When your usefulness to me is ended, you'll be set free. That's all I can promise you."

Now she stared murderously at the broad back of the golden-haired knight riding so tirelessly at the head of the column. Her *usefulness!*

The men about her had spoken openly, never dreaming she understood their tongue. Their precious leader planned a trap for the Welsh Fox using her as bait. And Owain would fall into it readily enough, she knew. He was always careless of his own safety where hers was concerned.

She bit back a groan of frustration, desperately trying to think of some way to escape. She'd die before she'd let Richard use her to bring Owain down. But at the moment, even that choice was denied her.

The party picked its way through the peaceful beauty of greening forests, then down through another winding mountain pass. Since her horse was led by one of her guards, Elen had nothing to do but hold to her saddle and search her mind for a way of escape.

With every mile they traveled, she grew more desperate. Though armed soldiers rode on each side, she continued her futile effort to work free. If she once ceased to work and plan, she knew she would be beaten. Unwilling to face the fact that there was little she might accomplish, even if she did get her hands free, she nursed her hatred for the renewing strength it brought.

Gradually the rocky path narrowed. Brooding cliffs of slate reared up about them and the distant roar of rushing water echoed through the chasm. Single file now, the column of English soldiers moved along a rocky ledge high above the churning waters of a mountain river, swollen to a rushing torrent by recent rains and the melting snows further up.

Elen gazed up longingly at the narrow ribbon of sky still visible beyond the steep mountain walls. She hated this dark cut in the mountains, hated the feeling of being shut away from the sun and sky in so melancholy a place. An apprehensive chill ran through her and she wondered if she would soon be locked away in a stone prison somewhere.

High above her a mountain eagle soared across the narrow slice of cloudless blue and she envied both his freedom and his flight. Her throat constricted suddenly and the fear she had held at bay so long came near to choking her. She couldn't stand being shut up. Dear God, if only she could fly!

Merciful heaven, her desperation was stealing her reason. Of course she couldn't fly! Shaking off the panicked thought, she stared down at the churning gray waters in the shadowy depths of the gorge, a daring thought taking shape in her head. She couldn't take the wings of the eagle and fly upward, but she could go down. It was a chance, perhaps her only chance.

She had traveled this dim trail on a half-dozen occasions and knew it passed close to the head of the cascading falls she could hear just ahead. The tumbling white spray fell nearly a hundred feet to a deep quiet pool of green-black water. No cowardly Englishman would follow her over that cliff.

She straightened in the saddle, trying to think. She knew the trail widened as it came abreast of the falls and her guards would be able to ride alongside her again. But she couldn't jump too soon, for the pool was deepest near the pounding waters of the falls.

Could she make that dive and swim to safety with her hands still bound? It would take Richard and his men at least a half hour to find the trail and descend to the base of the cliffs. Her breathing quickened with excitement and fear. With Owain's life in the balance, there was really little choice. If she didn't take the chance, he might die because of her. If she didn't make it . . . well, either way Richard of Kent would be deprived of a useful tool.

A *useful tool.* Her lips thinned to a bitter smile. Let him find out just how useful she was willing to be!

Rounding an outcropping of rock, they came within sight of the falls. Silver-green water spun downward in liquid threads, while far below small black birds danced in and out of the sparkling spray. To Elen, the sound of rushing water seemed to shake the stones beneath her, the roar deafening in the dark gorge.

She studied the guard ahead. He was urging his horse along the ledge with heels and hand, dragging her reluctant mount forward, the reins wrapped firmly about his fist. Glancing over her shoulder, she noted the man behind was fully occupied nursing his own nervous steed along the narrow trail. Neither was paying her any attention.

Catching the saddle with both hands, she swung herself down from her mount and ran across the trail in two bounds. For the space of a heartbeat, she stood poised on the edge. The swirling mists wet her face; the noise of rushing water drowned all sounds but its roar. She didn't dare look down.

Closing her eyes, she drew a deep breath and thrust herself out . . . out into nothingness.

As the trail widened, Richard drew Saladin to one side. Holding the stallion quiet, he watched his men edge along the cliff face. It was a dangerous stretch, and a nervous horse might easily spook, carrying his rider to his death. But the falls were a breathtaking sight. Grudgingly Richard admitted England had naught to match the beauty of this savage land.

His gaze came to rest on his lovely young prisoner riding so stiffly erect in the saddle. She was staring fixedly at the churning white water. He felt a moment's regret he hadn't taken her up on the saddle before him. She was obviously afraid of the roaring falls.

But even as he watched, she swung herself from her mount and leaped to the edge of the precipice. Before he could lift an arm or shout an order, she had flung herself from the rocks.

No! Christ's mercy, no! Richard raced back along the trail, ripping off his sword belt and his leather jerkin as he ran. The girl's hands were still bound. She wouldn't be able to save herself even if she did know how to swim!

The homespun shirt he wore under his mail followed his jerkin to the ground as he frantically searched the dark, frothing water below for the girl's head to resurface. Dragging off his boots, he moved to the very edge of the cliff, his heart hammering wildly with anger or fear, he couldn't determine which.

Sir William caught his shoulder, forcibly holding him from the edge. "Don't be a fool, man," Will shouted above the roar. "You'll be dead of the fall alone!"

Richard jerked himself out of his friend's hands. "See to your prisoners and leave me be. There . . . there she is!"

He gritted his teeth, not sure why he placed such value on the girl. But she wouldn't escape. By God, he wouldn't let another prisoner escape! Without daring to think, he flung himself out and away in a long, arching dive. *These Welsh were mad. All mad . . .*

Down, down, down, he felt himself falling. He sent up a hasty prayer the pool was as deep as it looked. He would rather drown than be smashed to death on the rocks.

Then the shock of icy water drove all prayers from his mind. He couldn't think, couldn't move as the pain closed over him like a giant, tightening fist crushing out his breath.

Hazily aware that he was floating upward in the dark, freezing void, he kicked feebly with legs that were becoming numb. His arms worked sluggishly, too slow for the command of his screaming brain. *Drowning . . . he was drowning in this godforsaken country because of a damned woman! Elen . . .*

The thought of the girl brought his spinning thoughts into focus. *Kick . . . kick harder!* The darkness above him was gradually growing light. *Fight . . . fight upward toward the light!* His head unexpectedly broke the surface, and he sucked great, choking gulps of air into his burning lungs.

Richard shoved a mass of streaming hair from his eyes, glancing frantically around. No bobbing chestnut head met his gaze. Damn! She could be dead by now in this icy pool! He cursed himself for keeping her bound on such a treacherous trail, suddenly realizing he would sooner see the girl free than dead at the bottom of this black devil's hole.

All at once, she surfaced some six or eight yards to his right, coughing and choking as she tried to catch her breath. He set out to reach her with long, powerful strokes, grabbing her shoulder as she went under again. She kicked at him, but he grabbed her heavy braid, ruthlessly dragging her with him toward a tiny crescent of beach where the pool narrowed to become a rushing river again.

Moments later, his feet struck the gray slate lining the river bottom. He clambered out of the tugging current onto the coarse shingle of the beach, dragging the girl's limp body with him. Her skin was cold as ice and she didn't appear to be breathing. Cursing Elen and all her race, Richard caught a fistful of the sodden wool of her tunic, rolled her onto her belly and pressed firmly against her back to force the water from her lungs. Nothing.

He redoubled his efforts. She wouldn't die, damn it! Not after all this trouble.

Then she began to cough. He eased the pressure on her back, holding her with hands that were suddenly gentle. With great heaving gasps, she choked and retched as if reluctantly giving up the quantities of water she had swallowed. Then with a last trembling gasp, she lay still.

Moving her onto the coarse gravel of the beach, Richard felt for a heartbeat. The rapid thudding beneath his hand was reassuring though her skin was cold and gray, her breathing ragged and shallow. He sank back on his heels, watching anxiously. For the first time he became aware of the chill wind whistling up the chasm and of the fact that he was cold . . . very cold. Pray God they didn't both take the fever and clotted lungs that carried off so many after a cold dunking.

He squinted up toward the summit of the falls. He could see his men moving about on the ledge. Giles was already directing placement of several scaling ropes over the cliff's edge. Someone would be down here soon with blankets and a tent to cut this cursed wind.

Glancing back at the motionless girl, Richard brushed a hand across her forehead. Her dark braid had come unbound and loose, wet hair now coiled about her shoulders past her waist.

He stroked the dripping hair back from her face. Cold . . . she was cold as death, and he was shaking like a leaf himself. He prayed to God his men got here soon.

A short time later Richard stood inside the protection of his hastily erected tent. Simon draped a blanket about his bare shoulders, then knelt, untying Richard's cross-garters and tugging the soaked woolen chausses down his master's shivering limbs.

Richard clutched the warm folds of the blanket gratefully about him. "Ah . . . that's better already, lad. By the time Giles gets here with the rest of the men and horses we can be on our way."

Simon nodded, rising to add another blanket to the one already warming his master. He glanced at the girl, lying in a sodden, unconscious heap a few feet away. "What about her?"

Richard frowned. "We must get her dried and warm. She's too important to let her take her death of a fever. Even if that is what she deserves."

Simon gazed back at him, wide blue eyes mirroring a

mixture of adult anticipation and boyish unease. Richard grinned. "Out," he ordered, jerking his head toward the tent entrance. "Just see that you fetch me in a half hour should I chance to fall asleep."

As the boy exited the tent, Richard caught hold of Elen's soaked tunic, tugging it over her head. Her sodden clothing would only hold the icy wet against her skin and keep her from getting warm. He removed her linen shift, leaving her slender young body naked.

His gaze narrowed appreciatively. She was painfully thin from a long, hungry winter, but her body was perfectly formed. Her small, girlish breasts were high and firm above a narrow waist, her hips gently curving into slender thighs and long, shapely legs.

His gaze lingered for a moment on the soft vee of dark auburn hair curling between her thighs. She was young, yes, but not too young for bedding, as the Welsh Fox must have discovered.

Dragging his eyes from the pleasurable sight, he caught her wrist and began briskly rubbing her hands and arms with a firm, downward motion to send her blood stirring. Methodically, he moved across her body and down her long legs. He stopped at last, with an anxious frown. Perhaps her skin had a bit more color. At least it didn't feel quite so cold and lifeless now.

With a heavy sigh he stretched out beside her, drawing her unresisting body full length against his. He was trembling from cold and exhaustion, but he smiled a little at the immediate stirring of his own blood with the feel of her against him. It had been a while since he'd had a woman.

Tugging the blankets snugly about them, he warmed Elen's cold flesh with his own. She would probably want to kill him for this, but sharing their combined warmth now would help them both. He tucked her damp head beneath his chin and wrapped his arms about her, finally giving in to the oblivion of exhaustion.

CHAPTER SEVEN

*E*len awoke from dreams shrouded with lingering mists of terror and death. She shifted her head, struggling to throw off the half-remembered fear of a blackness so cold and deep it had no end and of an echoing, watery silence so vast it terrified her. "Owain," she murmured, calling for the man who had soothed her fears since she was a babe. "Owain," she whimpered again, attempting to sit up.

At once a powerful arm tightened around her waist, drawing her back against a broad chest in an embrace of comforting warmth. For a few seconds she relished the radiating heat of a bare body molding the contours of hers, of a muscular arm wrapped protectively about her waist. There had been water, so much water, and the frightening sensation of falling, she remembered, trying to focus her spinning thoughts. Then it had been cold . . . incredibly cold.

Opening her eyes, Elen stared at her surroundings in astonishment. She seemed to be lying on the floor of a tent, of all things.

Suddenly, she came fully and furiously awake. *Richard!*

"No!" she hissed, twisting in her enemy's embrace. She dug her nails into his arm, striving to pry it away from her body. "How dare you!" she spat, jerking her knee up to get more leverage between their naked forms.

In a single quick movement that spoke of years of experience, Richard flattened her on her back, pinning her arms uselessly above her head while his powerful thighs captured her flailing legs between them. His weight pressed her down, but she continued to struggle, unwilling to give him the satisfaction of subduing her so easily.

"Look at me," he commanded, leaning over her so that his tanned face was a scant few inches from hers.

Panting slightly from her effort to break free, Elen stared helplessly into a pair of riveting emerald eyes blazing with flecks of dancing gold fire. The heat of his gaze took her breath. She had seen that look of wanting in Enion's dark eyes, but then it had been tempered by love and respect. Richard's look was tempered by nothing.

She could already feel the swell of his manhood against her leg, the urging of his taut body against hers. In a surge of desperation, she renewed her frantic struggle.

"Stop it, Elen! Lie still now, very still—unless you've a desire to start something between us I'm willing and able to finish," Richard bit out.

She caught her breath on a tiny sob of fear, immediately going limp at the threat in his voice. Forcing herself to meet his gaze, she shivered at the look of naked desire on his hard face.

"I'm going to let you go now and get up, and I don't want you moving an inch in either direction," he warned, his voice harsh with the effort to speak around his uneven breathing. "Do you understand? Not an inch!"

Their eyes met and held. Elen felt the rapid beating of his heart against her breast, the brush of his breath against her ear. Her enemy obviously wanted her, but he planned to take his time in using her. Choking back a furious retort, she nodded obediently, buying herself a few more moments to think.

Richard released her wrists, then rolled away and sat up, running a hand through his tousled blond hair. Turning

his back to her, he gazed irritably at the lowered flaps of
his tent, then back to her. "Don't move," he repeated,
rising on well-muscled legs to walk to the entrance. He
jerked back a flap. "Simon! Giles!" he called out.

Elen scrambled for the tangled blanket beneath her, jerking its frayed length to cover her bare body. The lewd
comments of Richard's knights echoed in her thoughts.
Holy Mary! Surely he wasn't summoning help to restrain
her!

At her hasty movement, Richard sent her a dark scowl.
Wordlessly turning back to the entrance, he shifted his
weight from one foot to the other, impatiently waiting for
his men.

When his back was toward her, Elen quickly scrutinized
her adversary, hoping for some sign of weakness of mind
or body. But she found little comfort in the stiff expanse
of Richard's back. Powerful muscles broadened already
broad shoulders and textured the long graceful curve of his
back to his narrow waist. Richard of Kent certainly had
nothing to fear from her wiry strength.

Feeling her eyes on him, Richard half turned toward her
and cast a wary glance in her direction. To Elen's surprise,
he wasn't nearly so hairy as the dark Welshmen she was
familiar with. A light whorl of golden hair dusted the center
of his chest, narrowing to a thin line that darkened in color
as it descended his flat abdomen, finally losing itself in the
dark bush between his muscular thighs. Only the slight
puckering of an old battle scar running from waist to hip
along one side marred the golden perfection of Richard's
body. The Wolf of Kent was a magnificent animal, she
admitted grudgingly.

Elen dragged the blanket closer around her shoulders,
fighting the instinctive urge to cower in a corner of the
tent. A man's naked form was no oddity to her. From the
time she was seven, she had helped her mother bathe and
tend the honored male guests that visited Teifi. It had only

been in the last three years that her father had excluded her from the customary duties performed by the ladies of the keep. More than one noble visitor had been embarrassed by his uncontrollable reaction to Aldwyn's lovely daughter.

No, Elen was no stranger to the sight of an aroused male, but the natural animal instinct that was merely amusing in the safety of Teifi Keep was something vastly different in the tent of her enemy. A shudder of revulsion swept her at the thought of a forced coupling with Richard, and she shifted her gaze from his intimidating body to the ground.

Moments later, Giles ducked into the tent. Elen clutched the blanket to her breast, her face burning with fury and humiliation as the dark knight took in her disheveled appearance with one appraising glance. "So you're both awake," he commented without preamble. "We've trout cooked and waiting for your dinner from the glut the men trapped in the shallows."

"Trout?" Richard repeated incredulously. "How long have I been asleep?"

"Just over three hours."

Richard began to curse in an impressive mixture of both English and French.

"The men needed food and sleep. They cannot drive themselves as you do, Richard," Giles remarked, interrupting his commander's tirade. "And don't rail at Simon," he added quickly. "It was by my order he didn't return to dress you on the half hour as you bade him. You're exhausted, hungry, wounded, and now like to take your death from that cold soaking you had." He frowned. "What will it profit Edward if you fall ill from fever and exhaustion?"

"I'm never sick!" Richard snapped. "And what will it profit Edward if the Welsh Fox overtakes us with men fresh and eager to avenge our raid? Christ, Giles, do you realize what you've done? If they can but outstrip us a half hour's march, they can easily slaughter us in an ambush on this cursed narrow trail. We'll never make Beaufort by nightfall now."

"One of the Welsh guides claims to know a rough path that will get us to Beaufort more quickly. It won't take us past the old keep where our armor is hidden, but he says we can make the castle by nightfall or soon thereafter."

Richard sighed and rubbed his beard-stubbled chin, the anger in his eyes slowly fading. "I suppose we could send a troop for the armor later. The important thing is reaching Beaufort. Do you believe the man speaks the truth?"

"Hywel has never deceived us before."

"Hywel? No, he has his own reasons for hating Llywelyn and his allies. His family lost lands to Llywelyn's ambition and that makes him trustworthy—as trustworthy as any Welshman can be." Richard shook his head, rubbing his aching left arm abstractedly. "God help England if this savage race ever stops fighting among themselves long enough to unite against us. Without Edward's allies in South Wales, this whole campaign might have gone differently."

Giles grinned. "I wouldn't mention that around de Veasy or Mortimer if I were you, Richard. They think Edward's victory all due to their own skill."

Richard's weary frown disappeared, his green eyes brightening with mirth. "No, Giles, I'll be careful around those strutting peacocks, so not a single feather will be ruffled. I haven't stood so close to Edward this last year to have all his lessons of diplomacy wasted. The man is a master at playing off the pride of one lord against another, yet keeping them all to a measure of peace. And I'm certainly not of the consequence to risk upsetting his hard-won balance."

Richard yawned, stretching his body without a trace of self-consciousness. "By the way, it's damned cold in here without a stitch to put on. I could use my clothes." He glanced around. "And weapons."

Giles nodded. "I sent Simon to fetch them when you called out. The girl's things needed to dry beside the fire, too, and we thought it best to keep your steel out of reach of the tent." He glanced at Elen, his lips resisting a smile.

"I was afraid your friend here might put the blade to good use if she were first to awaken."

Richard dared a glance at Elen, dismayed by the strong flash of desire returning to quicken his loins. Damn all women! Perhaps he should have taken the girl and gotten it over with. After all, despite her youth she was nothing but a camp follower, the mistress of the Fox. She might ease his need as well as his enemy's.

Still, he had no taste for rape, and she was sure to fight him. It would take time to bring her around, but the effort might well be worth it. He had discovered long ago most any woman could be bought if a man had enough patience and the right trinkets for bait. Some just came at a higher price than others.

Eyeing the girl critically, he took in the tumultuous fall of hip-length, deep chestnut hair framing her slender form. She was far darker than the angelically fair women he usually favored, and though she was certainly lovely in a wild sort of way, his taste never ran to willful, independent females. He had learned the kind of damage a bold, conniving woman could wreak firsthand.

But there would be time enough to decide about the girl when they were out of danger. Unaware he was frowning again, he turned to Giles, forcing his thoughts to the problem at hand. "Make sure the men are ready to ride," he ordered. "We'll leave as soon as I'm dressed. The girl and I can eat as we ride."

The last rays of the setting sun had long fled, but Elen had no idea how many hours of darkness had passed. She remembered being lifted from her horse to the damp ground for a short rest as exhausted men and horses waited for the rising moon to shed light on the unfamiliar trail to Beaufort. Then she had been helped back into the saddle where she continued, doggedly erect, willing herself not to groan aloud with every bone-jarring step of her plodding mount.

The thought of escape was now beyond her. Sooner or later the party would reach its destination, and she would find food, rest and warmth. Then she would be able to come up with a plan, she assured herself. The English soldiers would watch her closely at first, but her guards would grow lax if she behaved docilely enough.

The vision of Richard's powerful frame suddenly intruded upon her thoughts, but she was so weary and cold that threat scarcely frightened her. Men and women coupled freely in Wales, and though Enion had reluctantly agreed to take his rights only after the priest's blessing, Elen wasn't ignorant of what went on between a man and woman. She was fairly certain by now Richard wouldn't beat her as some men did their women, and she supposed she would survive the ordeal as well as the countless other females taken by the conquering English soldiers.

The jolting movement of her horse suddenly ceased, and Elen gazed up in surprise. They had reached the shadowy edge of the dense forest and she could see the palisaded wall and small, squat bulk of a simple tower fortress standing several hundred yards away across a moonlit clearing. That inhospitable-looking place must be Beaufort Keep, she thought.

The party halted and a rider set off toward the gates, prodding his mount into a tired gallop as he hastened to inform the garrison fellow Englishmen approached. After a few moments of confusion, the red flare of torches began to blaze along the wall and the great, creaking gates were unbolted and pushed ajar.

Richard eased his bay stallion out in front of the column and the entire band swung into motion. Elen's cold-numbed fingers clutched the warm fox cloak comfortingly about her as her horse moved eagerly toward the stable. No matter what awaited her at Beaufort, she could soon rest, Elen reminded herself as they trotted through the gates. And she could think no further at the moment.

In the smoky, hissing torchlight inside the castle bailey, servants and men-at-arms milled about, anxiously calling to comrades and carefully leading hard-used horses toward the stable lean-tos against the inner wall. Elen slid wearily from the saddle, her bound hands clutching the saddle for support as the flickering torches and shouting men began to waver and spin about her. She closed her eyes, hating herself for her weakness. *Holy Mary, Mother of God, not now. Don't let me faint now!*

A strong hand unexpectedly caught her elbow. "Take a deep breath and lean on me," a voice said in Welsh. "It will pass."

Too weak to do aught else, Elen did as she was bid, praying desperately not to humiliate herself by swooning before these haughty Englishmen. To her relief, the whirling ceased and she opened her eyes to find the dark-featured knight called Giles holding her erect.

Taking another deep breath, she straightened away from the man. "My thanks," she said stiffly.

He nodded toward the narrow door high in the wooden wall of the keep. "Do you think you can climb those stairs or must I carry you?"

Elen raised her chin, fixing him with a deadly glare. "I can walk."

"I meant no insult," Giles said softly. "You've already won my respect. God's truth, the only thing keeping some of us in the saddle was the fear of being shamed by falling out before a woman. This was a killing ride, even for a man. Richard doubted you'd last the distance."

Elen glanced across the bailey at the tall, golden-haired commander. He stood surrounded by his knights, giving orders for the bestowing of men, horses and prisoners. "You may tell your Richard I appreciate his concern," she said bitterly. "But if he thinks to break me, it will take more than a pleasant afternoon's ride."

"I will remind him of that," Giles replied gravely. "Now,

shall we go inside and get out of this cursed cold?"

Despite her brave words, Elen's knees almost buckled as she climbed the steep wooden stairs and passed into the smoky interior of the hall. A fire burned fitfully in a raised stone fireplace in the room's center, and Giles guided her toward its welcoming warmth. She held out her numbed hands toward its radiating heat, wincing at the pain of returning circulation. Nothing seemed important to her at the moment save driving the damp chill from her bones.

A short time later Richard entered the room, walking beside a slender, dark-haired man of medium height and knightly dress. Elen watched the two walk toward the fireplace, instinctively readying herself for battle.

At sight of the two men, hovering servants sprang forward, and the unknown knight began giving orders in the clipped voice of authority. "Hugh, bring food and wine for Sir Richard and his knights. And see you help Stephen get the bread and ale down to the barracks. Move now, do!"

A female servant stepped forward, hastily unclasping Richard's muddy cloak, then holding out a laver for him to wash his hands. She performed the same service for Giles, but pointedly ignored Elen, moving away to minister to the other knights who were beginning to enter the hall.

Elen kept her gaze proudly on the leaping flames. The woman had seen her bound hands and had immediately put her down as a person of no import. Noble prisoners were watched but usually left unfettered at their pledge to conduct themselves honorably until a ransom could be arranged. Elen might have won her freedom in the same way, but she swore never to give Richard of Kent such a pledge. In fact, she would plan her escape as soon as she was rested.

"What quarters do you have inside the keep here, Sir Thomas?" she heard Richard asking.

"I fear this miserable Welsh fort was built more for defense than comfort," the older man replied apologetically, "but I've made the upstairs solar as civilized as possible since

Edward sent me here. It's been ready and waiting for you since I learned you'd be stopping." A rueful smile lit his narrow, weather-lined face. "I don't think you'll find it too uncomfortable, and your men may sleep here in the hall with the rest of us. The place is so small there are no other private chambers available, I'm afraid."

Richard put a hand on his host's shoulder. "I'm not worried about myself or my men, Thomas. God knows we're so weary we could take our rest in the bailey and be comfortable. But I need a place secure enough to keep the girl from escaping." He nodded toward Elen. "At the moment she's the only link we have with the Welsh Fox."

Sir Thomas shrugged his shoulders. "You watched the prisoners put below. I'll warrant no man can escape that hole, not to mention a—"

"It's not suitable for her," Richard interrupted.

Sir Thomas frowned, his narrow black eyes moving thoughtfully over Elen's lovely countenance. "I suppose we could make a place for her in the first-floor storage area. It's cold and damp there, but I'll see what can be done to make her comfortable if that's what you wish. The area in the stable where the servants sleep is not secure enough."

"What of your solar? If she were put inside with a man to guard the door, would there be any possibility of her getting out?"

Sir Thomas shook his head, a knowing grin suddenly dawning. "Of course not, my lord. Even the master's chambers here are built like a fortress. My solar would be the best place to hold the girl. You'll find it snug as you could wish with a large hearth and anything else you might desire." He sent Richard a broad wink. "Including a stout bed frame and a comfortable straw mattress for your pleasure."

Richard ignored the wink, reaching for a wine cup a servant held out to him. He took two deep swallows, then stared coolly at his host. "I want the bolt inside the door removed, the shutters closed, and I'll have a man . . . no,

two men guard the entrance at all times. Make it very clear
to them, Thomas, if this prisoner escapes by any wile, no
matter how cunning, they'll wish they'd never been born."

Sir Thomas frowned at the insult. He had been successfully taking keeps and holding prisoners for near fifteen
years. "My men will have no difficulty holding the girl,"
he replied stiffly. Turning away, he snapped out the order
for a guard.

Richard finished his wine, then placed the empty cup on
a nearby table. Drawing his knife, he moved to Elen's side
and quickly cut the thongs binding her wrists. She tried to
jerk away, but he kept his hold on one arm, studying the
raw places she had rubbed in her efforts to work free. "I
told you, Elen, I would not allow you to escape, but I do
not wish that you suffer unduly," he explained in French.
His eyes lifted to her heart-shaped face, wary and defiant
even in exhaustion. "Giles will take you upstairs and I'll
have food and wine sent up for your refreshment. And if
you behave yourself, that is the worst that will happen."

The girl glared back at him, an angry fire smoldering in
the crystal depths of her luminous blue eyes. Where in God's
name had she gotten eyes that shade of blue in this land
of dark-eyed women?

Releasing her arm, he stepped back. "Have a tray of food
and wine sent upstairs for her, Thomas, along with some
mutton fat for her wrists," he added, returning to his native
English. "And Giles, get her upstairs now before she drops."

Nearly an hour later, Richard made the weary climb up
the steep, narrow stairs to Sir Thomas's third-floor solar.
He would just check to be sure all had been done as he
had ordered, then return to the hall to sleep with the rest
of his men. Before he retired for what was left of the night,
he wanted to make certain there was no chance of the girl
escaping.

With a low word to the two guards stationed outside the
chamber entrance, Richard swung open the heavy oak door

and stepped inside. The room was warm and dimly lit by the dancing blaze of a fire in the stone hearth. He moved farther into the room. The large bed was empty, but Elen had dragged a fur from its covering and lay huddled on the floor before the fire, the red fox cloak clasped tightly in her arms as if it were a talisman protecting her from harm.

He stood for a moment looking at her, a wave of unexpected tenderness sweeping over him. In sleep she looked even younger than her probable thirteen or fourteen years, and it was difficult to believe she had fought him so boldly and had tried to take his life. But the girl was a conniving trickster, a thing he despised, he reminded himself.

His eyes narrowed thoughtfully, as another part of him leaped unexpectedly to her defense. Elen was only what she had been raised to be, as all of the Welsh were. Theirs was a country small and poor, yet they had kept the might of England at bay for hundreds of years with a combination of fearlessness and cunning.

No, he couldn't condone treachery, but he didn't blame the girl for fighting in the only way she knew. Besides, what did women know of honor anyway? Giles had been the fool to trust her in the first place. And they had been damned lucky Will hadn't lost his life to the mistake.

He knelt on one knee beside her, drawn by the radiance of her hair and skin in the reflected glow of the nearby flames. She seemed so delicate he could break her with one hand, yet she had endured that journey out of the mountains as well as any man.

Touching the tangled silk of her hair, lifting it away from her thin, high-cheekboned face, he admitted he was intrigued by this girl, intrigued as he had not been by any female in years. She was naught but a child, but she had faced him with a man's courage, a man's determination.

He tried again to estimate her age using his half-sister Isabel as a guide. It was difficult. There had been that in her eyes this morning that spoke to him of a maturity beyond the burgeoning womanhood of her half-starved body. Oh, she was young still, but old enough to have learned a deep, festering hatred for all of his race.

He sighed heavily, wishing this futile war with Wales were ended. But there would be more pain and killing, more hungry women and motherless boys before it was done.

Catching hold of the fox cloak, he eased it gently from the girl's grasp, wrapping its warm folds about her slender body. "Sleep well, Elen," he whispered, rising to his feet. "Sleep well and perhaps tomorrow you and I will come to a better understanding."

CHAPTER EIGHT

*R*ichard awoke the next morning long after dawn to the rattling sound of the wind and the rhythmic beat of rain driving against the wooden walls of the keep. He rolled over with a muttered curse. The spell of good weather had finally broken. He had known it couldn't last long in this land of rain and mists, but had hoped to make Gwenlyn before bad weather set in again.

Sir Thomas de Waurin and his men were already up and gone from the hall, so he rose from his pallet with a muffled groan, stretching his stiff muscles. A serving girl approached with a tankard of mead and Richard took it, smiling his thanks.

Raising the cup to his lips, he took a deep draught of the sweet, smooth brew. Simon still lay curled on his pallet a few feet to his left, sleeping deeply as only an exhausted fifteen-year-old could do. There was no need to wake his squire, Richard decided. He would fend for himself this morning.

Carefully stepping around his sleeping knights and their squires, he made his way down the hall toward the narrow doorway where one trestle table was set up. The rough plank surface held the remains of a hasty meal: several rounds of cheese and the crusty remainders of three loaves of bread.

Sir Thomas had eaten a cold breakfast to keep from awakening his exhausted guests.

Richard took a hunk of cheese and the leftover bread, swallowing it down quickly to quiet his grumbling stomach. He had been so tired the night before he had eaten little, but the initial weariness blunted, he found he was ravenous.

The urgent gnawing in his belly reminded him of the hungry women and children he had seen in the Welsh village the day before yesterday. He had promised to send food, and it was a vow he didn't take lightly. Sir Thomas might well think him daft, but he would personally choose a healthy young heifer and a couple of sheep to be delivered to the wrinkled old crone in the village. It was a small enough payment to a boy for the loss of his mother, he told himself grimly.

With that decision made, he turned to the more perplexing problem of disciplining Simon. His squire had failed to obey his order yesterday, letting him sleep three hours instead of the few minutes he had commanded. As it was, no harm had resulted, but if the Welsh Fox had been in pursuit, that failure to obey could have meant death to them all. He would speak to the boy as soon as he could find a moment of privacy in this overcrowded keep. Simon must realize his master's word was law, but a public raking down would be unjustly humiliating.

Richard refilled his tankard from a pitcher left on the table. He needed to talk with Giles, too, about countermanding his orders. Giles Eversly had been his friend since they were both squires on Edward's aborted crusade in the Holy Land, and Giles was an excellent second-in-command on this campaign. But there could be only one leader on an expedition.

In his years as a fighting knight, slowly rising to prominence in Edward's army, Richard had seen more than one promising campaign destroyed for lack of discipline. He had sworn it would never happen to a troop in his command,

and so it wouldn't—even if both Giles and Simon had thought themselves acting for his good. He had worked too hard to win this chance to prove himself, too hard to win the respect of his men and not a few of the powerful barons surrounding the king.

Edward trusted him to break North Wales and it was a commission Richard took more seriously than any other in his twenty-six years. Several of the great, landed barons had been furious when he had been given this command. Who was this Richard Basset to receive such favor? A nobody from Kent whose only recommendation was skill with a sword. He had no wealth or land, no powerful family backing him up. And by the Blessed Rood, he was English, for God's sake, the barons had exclaimed, looking down their long Norman noses at Richard, sitting at Edward's left hand with an air of forced calm.

A soft smile curled Richard's full, sensual mouth at the memory of that day. The taste of triumph had truly been sweet. Edward had glanced about the table at several of his fuming lords. "And I am an English king," he had reminded them softly in the tongue he had caused to be spoken at court at least as often as the more fashionable Norman French. "And do any of you have more to say on the matter, you may take it up with me later." His cold blue eyes had flashed dangerously. "If you still care to."

Richard drained the last of his mead, rose from the table, and moved across the rush-strewn floor to a chilly window embrasure. Stepping into the alcove, he gazed out the window at the heavy storm-whipped clouds scudding before the wind. The narrow slit in the wall was only a few inches across, but the hall's second-floor vantage point gave him a clear view over the wooden palisades of the wall into the soggy meadow and mist-shrouded woodland beyond.

Edward was a careful ruler, Richard reminded himself as he stared out into the wild day. The king seldom showed favoritism or created new peerages even for those who, like himself, were steadfastly loyal. He had seen his nation torn by a bloody civil war and nearly wrested from his father over such capricious actions, and no doubt he had learned the lesson well. He trusted few people, realizing most swarmed about him for the benefits they hoped to receive. But if he had earned a reputation for being a cold and calculating sovereign, Richard knew better. He had glimpsed a side of his king few men ever saw.

A small puff of wind sent a gust of rain buffeting through the window to spatter against his face. The clean fresh scent of damp moss and bracken, of low-growing bilberry bushes swept over him with the refreshing wetness of the rain, and he drew a deep breath of the moist Welsh air. Edward had given him a rare chance to distinguish himself and Richard wouldn't let it slip through his fingers, he swore. He would fight this land, its people, and even this accursed weather until he broke the resistance in North Wales. And he would take the Welsh Fox no matter the cost.

Behind him the door to the hall swung open and Richard heard the stamping and clatter of men entering the room. Leaving the chilly alcove, he moved out of the shadows.

Thomas de Waurin threw off his wet cloak and smiled in greeting. "So, you're awake. I expected you to sleep till mid-afternoon at least."

Richard shook his head. "I usually rise early, Thomas. I've already wasted too much of the day as it is."

"And a foul day it is to be about," Thomas remarked, shoving his dripping hair out of his eyes. "Take my word for it, Richard, we're much better off in here by a cozy fire. I doubt even the damned, sneaking Welsh will be skulking about the forest on a day like this one."

"I must see to my men and our prisoners. I'll need to question some of them as soon as possible," Richard stated, frowning at the thought of the ordeal ahead. He hated to resort to torture, but it was often necessary to get information from the stubborn Welsh. And information concerning the leader of the Welsh rebellion was necessary to save English lives. He pursed his lips determinedly. "It's time we learned more about this elusive Welsh Fox."

Thomas nodded in agreement. "I've already been to check on your men and found them still sleeping. I left a servant to fetch food as soon as they wake. And I've taken a look in on the prisoners, too. One died in the night of his wounds, but the rest are like to remain alive, more's the pity."

"I'm surprised we didn't lose more," Richard stated bluntly. "That was a killing march. I wonder if I could have made it wounded and on foot." He shook his head. "One thing you must give our enemies, Thomas, they're a damned hardy lot—hardy and determined. If they had money for horses and weapons and were even a few thousand more in number, I wonder just how well we'd fare."

"They're savages," Thomas scoffed, "unable to think as we do, and fit only to serve us. I haven't run across a man of them I've found suitable for aught save the lowest servant's tasks."

Richard grinned. "That's because the fit ones are still hiding out planning to slit our throats! It's only the old and crippled they allow us to see. The men I faced two nights ago certainly weren't lacking in skill or energy."

"You may be right. God be praised, we've seen none of their fighting men here at Beaufort."

Richard's grin widened. "Think how mortifying if it took us this long to subdue naught but a few cripples and old women. I'd not dare show my face again at court."

Thomas chuckled appreciatively. "I didn't say they weren't fighters, Richard. But I don't hold with the treacherous, heathen way they conduct their raids. A man who waits in ambush and won't fight in the open isn't much of a man in my eyes." He glanced at Richard, eyeing him thoughtfully. "You met Llywelyn once, didn't you? Some say he was a noble prince despite the rabble he led."

Richard nodded. "I was at Worcester when his marriage to Eleanor de Montfort took place. He brought several allies to court, Aldwyn of Teifi, Cledwyn of Powys . . . a half-dozen others."

Richard frowned, staring at the floor, almost as if he could see that happier time when Llywelyn was a powerful vassal of England. "They're all dead now," he said slowly. "God, what a waste of men! Even Edward mourned the loss. He'd hoped to talk the northern Welsh princes into becoming allies as several in the south had already done."

He sent Thomas a rueful smile. "I don't think you'd have thought the Welsh savages if you'd seen those haughty lords at court, Thomas. If you ask me, they could have given a few of our own civilized nobles a lesson or two."

Thomas glanced around and motioned for a female servant who was standing nearby. "We're speaking of civilized men and I've yet to offer you aught to break your fast, Richard. You must be half starved."

Richard shook his head. "I ate the remains of your breakfast. It will suffice for now, but I could do with something more substantial later."

Thomas nodded. "I'll see to it. And what else may I offer you? I've not had visitors since taking command of this cursed place and I'm afraid my hospitality is rusty. Do you wish for a bath? I'll send Lyna here up to help you."

The thought of a hot bath after several weeks in the countryside was heaven. What's more, it would give him an opportunity to speak privately with Simon. "It would be good to be rid of the dirt and vermin I've accumulated," Richard replied. "But I'll not need the girl. My squire can do all I require."

"See water is carried above and a bath made ready for Sir Richard," Thomas ordered the girl. He turned back with a questioning look. "Do you wish for a woman afterward? There are several about who are young and fairly clean."

The vivid memory of Elen's bare body pressed against him, of her long slender limbs tangling with his suddenly intruded upon Richard's thoughts. Yesterday his desire had been sharp, and his host's offer would have been a welcome distraction. But today the thought of bedding some strange serving woman was vaguely distasteful. "I've no time for pleasuring today, Thomas. I'm anxious to learn what I may from our prisoners."

"And if you can get naught from them about the Fox? I'll wager the girl above could tell you much if you could persuade her." The older man grinned widely. "And you might find the questioning more to your taste."

Richard forced himself to gaze back evenly at his host. He had known men who enjoyed knocking a woman about, but he had always considered them something less than men. "The prisoners will talk," he said coolly, "but I'll question the girl as well. In any case, she's valuable just as she is. I've reason to believe the Fox will come for her. He'll come . . . or he's not the man I believe him to be."

The ominous noise of several pairs of tramping feet sounded from outside. Elen swung toward the door, her heartbeat quickening despite the vow she had made to remain calm. A key rattled in the latch and the door opened with a creak of poorly oiled hinges.

Two men entered, lugging a heavy wooden tub that had seen better days. Behind them, several more servants filed in, carrying pails of water that were set at once to heat on the hearth. A serving woman bent to put more peat on the fire, stirring the coals until the flames began licking at it greedily. Obviously, some great lord would have a bath.

Elen studied the servants closely. They were English, every one of them. No hope for her from that quarter. She could tell them not only by their features, but by their stooped shoulders and blank subservient stare. In England, the lower classes took their lowly status for granted, never even dreaming of being treated decently.

Such was not the case in Wales. There every man down to the poorest herdsman kept his dignity, and even women had honor. They were not owned as sheep or goats and could not be beaten or ill-used at some vicious husband's whim. They could even divorce with good cause.

She glanced miserably away. But the laws of England would change all that. If Wales lost its struggle her countrymen would become lower than the meanest servants in the eyes of their English masters. It was unthinkable that her people might be forced to such a life!

She thought of her beautiful home on the lush meadows along the Teifi River, wondering how her people were faring under English rule. Though Teifi would have belonged to her brother Rhodri, she had always nurtured a fierce possessiveness toward it. It was a feeling so strong, she would have been loath to leave her home even to become Enion's wife.

She smiled now at the memory of the many lively discussions she'd had about the matter with her father. She had begged and teased, flattered and cajoled until she'd won from him the promise that she would not be forced to take a husband until her seventeenth birthday—quite old for an unwed maiden.

Secretly she knew she was the light of her father's heart, and it hadn't been so very difficult to drag the promise from him. He hadn't wanted to give her up any more than she'd wanted to leave—even though they'd both loved the man who would be her husband. And they'd laughed together over her mother's dire prophecy that "those who waited too long to sup often found the bowl empty and the bone taken by another."

Her mother had been right. Enion had been taken from her by a much more powerful mistress. Death had stilled forever the flush of desire on his face, the sudden narrowing of his dark eyes when he looked at her, the huskiness of his voice when he spoke to her of love. She had held him off, changing the subject when he talked to her of the strength of his feelings.

Not that she was indifferent. She loved Enion desperately. He was every bit as dear to her as Rhodri. It was just that life was good and she was enjoying herself far too much to become a wife. And there was plenty of time. To the spoiled, fourteen-year-old daughter of the most powerful prince in Mid Wales, there was always plenty of time. But like the grains of sand in a glass, those carefree moments had slipped away, and now she would never have the chance to make Enion happy.

The overwhelming pain of regret cut through Elen and she dropped to her knees. "Oh, Enion, I'm sorry," she whispered, fighting the tears that rose, quick and burning, to her eyes. "God, I'm so *sorry!*"

If only she could go back. She missed him—she missed all of her family so desperately. At times it almost seemed those happy years growing up in Teifi Keep had never been, as if the months of cold and hopelessness in the mountains were the only reality and all else naught but a happy dream saved to relive when the present became unbearable.

She clasped her hands together, praying desperately for Enion's soul—for the souls of all of her family. She had neglected her prayers of late, but she would do better, pray harder. Perhaps the Holy Virgin would intercede. Perhaps the Queen of Heaven would even have mercy on her.

So intent was she on her prayers, Elen failed to hear the sound of approaching footsteps. When the door swung open, she leaped to her feet in surprise, whirling instinctively to place the tub between herself and the doorway.

Richard took two steps into the room, then halted abruptly. The girl before him stared back like a startled animal, poised to flee at his slightest movement. He extended one hand reassuringly. "I see you approve of the idea of a bath," he remarked with a smile.

Elen glanced down at the water as if she were seeing it

for the first time. For a few moments at least, the pain of her memories had overcome her fear of the present. She backed away uncertainly.

Richard advanced into the room, Simon following at his heels with an armful of fresh clothing. The girl was intrigued by the tub, Richard decided with another glance in her direction. He guessed the Welsh, like the lower class English, seldom bathed save for the occasional summer dip in river or stream. Perhaps she could be encouraged to enjoy the refreshing novelty of a bath when he was done.

"I'm sorry to invade your sanctuary, but there's no place else to go for my bath," he said easily. "I fear I've the accumulated filth of weeks of living on the march." He smiled again. "And the vermin I've picked up make life miserable for a man in armor. I confess, I've been looking forward to the pleasure of a hot bath almost as much as that of a hot meal."

Elen said nothing. The man before her would soon be looking for more than the pleasure of a bath, she thought cynically.

Simon stepped past her, placing his master's fresh clothing carefully on the bed. Then the boy moved to the hearth and began transferring the steaming buckets of water into the tub. After the last bucket was emptied, he knelt and began unwinding Richard's leather crossgarters in preparation for removing his chausses. "I'll see these are cleaned for you, my lord," he said, glancing up.

"Later," Richard replied, transferring his thoughts from the girl to his squire. "Sit with me while I bathe, Simon. I've some questions to put to you."

Simon nodded obediently, moving to help his master remove the rest of his clothes. Neither man paid any attention as Elen pointedly turned her back and moved past the bed to the window alcove.

With a deep groan of contentment, Richard eased himself into the steaming waters of the tub. "Heaven," he sighed, gazing at his squire through half-closed lids.

Simon grinned at him impudently. "Better than a woman?"

Richard sent an arc of water splashing playfully at the boy. "That depends on the woman . . . and how long a man has been without."

"Without what—a bath or a woman?"

Richard chuckled and leaned back against the rim of the tub. "Perhaps I'll tell you that someday when you're older and wiser. Or perhaps I'll let you tell me. Now fetch me that soap before I lesson you for your laziness."

Handing him the soap, Simon stared over his shoulder at the girl across the room. "What of her, Richard? Do you think she's pretty?"

Richard glanced sharply at the boy. Here was a problem he hadn't foreseen. Simon was a handsome boy on the verge of manhood. But as far as Richard knew, the lad was still innocent. Yet he and the girl were suitably close in age, and Simon was staring at her now with a painful mixture of longing and suspicion struggling for supremacy on his youthful face.

The boy was obviously smitten and doing his best not to show it. He would have to keep a close eye on Simon lest he be betrayed into doing something foolish on the girl's behalf. The boy might be the elder in years, but if Richard was any judge, Elen was far superior in knowledge of the ways of the world.

"Oh, pretty enough," Richard responded in a casual tone. "But I've not found many of the Welsh women pleasing to my taste. And take my word for it, Simon, a willing, eager woman is much to be preferred over a kicking, scratching enemy in your bed."

The boy met his eyes evenly. "I don't mean that, Richard. I know that's not your way."

"Nor yours either, I hope."

The faintest hint of a blush suffused the boy's face. "Of course not. I . . . I just think she's pretty. That's all."

"I approve your taste."

Simon smiled self-consciously and dragged a stool near the tub. "You said you had questions for me," he prompted, shifting into a more normal tone.

Richard nodded. He often spent hours drilling his squire on armaments, battle strategies and all manner of matters a full-fledged knight should know. And it was a part of his duty to teach the boy all the knowledge of leadership he could impart.

"Yes. Today I need advice on matters of discipline among the men. If you were the knight in charge, what would you do about the disagreement between Hugh of Sussex and Ranulf de Presteigne?" he asked, slowly working the strong soap across his grimy body.

The boy thought for a few moments, then gave him a carefully worded opinion. Richard nodded in agreement. It was exactly the action he had already decided upon. The boy was learning his lessons well, and Richard felt a thrill of pride in his protégé.

They talked on for some time, with Richard putting forward both real and imaginary situations requiring the judgment and swift action of a firm leader. "So you are agreed with me, are you not, Simon, that there can be only one leader among a troop of men?" he said at last. "That his orders must be obeyed unquestioningly for the good of all, and that the soldier who disobeys a direct order must be punished severely."

Simon nodded. "Anything less might result in confusion and loss of life, especially during a battle or an unexpected ambush. Men must respond without hesitation to their leader's command," he recited dutifully.

"And do you think me a capable leader?"

Simon grinned. "Of course."

"Then why did you disobey my order yesterday?"

The boy stared at him aghast. He hadn't suspected what Richard was working toward. "I . . . I didn't . . . I was afraid," he floundered helplessly. "I thought you might fall ill and—"

"But it wasn't your duty to think, was it, Simon?" Richard interrupted ruthlessly. "It was mine. My duty is to make decisions and give orders and yours is to listen and obey. And you must obey without question, for there won't always be time to explain. If the Welsh had been in pursuit, that long delay you caused would have been disastrous. We'd have been killed to the man because you failed to obey a simple order. And the Welsh seldom make death easy. Would that have been a pleasant thought to take to your grave, Simon?"

Simon shook his head miserably but didn't drop his eyes from Richard's compelling gaze. "The difference between tragedy and triumph is oft a small one, Simon. I've seen the outcome of a battle turn on smaller mistakes than the one you made yesterday. Were we in England, it would have been a small offense, something we might have laughed about together. But we are in Wales, lad, in enemy country! The land of an enemy is brutally unforgiving of small mistakes. Learn that quickly so you will live."

Richard's voice took on a firmer note. "Learn too that I demand absolute obedience in the men I command... more than that from those I trust."

"I'm sorry, Richard. I did wrong, I know, but Gi—" Simon bit off his words, suddenly stiffening in his place on the stool. "I did wrong, I can see that now. I'm ready for whatever punishment you order."

Richard shook his head. "I'm not through discussing the matter, Simon. In your defense, you were given a conflicting order by my second-in-command, an excuse any other squire would plead." A faint smile crossed his face. "I'm glad to see you did not. Rest assured, though, I've already spoken with Giles on that subject. And to be truthful, I'm as much to blame as you, for I shouldn't have fallen asleep in the first place."

"No, the fault was mine. You trusted me to wake you as you ordered," Simon repeated woodenly. "What is to be my punishment?"

Richard sent him an appraising look. "Nothing save knowing your unthinking action might have caused the death of all of us. Knowing you, I believe that to be punishment enough . . . perhaps even too much." He smiled again. "Next time, I know, you'll follow my orders even if Edward himself says you nay. Now ready that towel, for the water grows chill. I'll be out in a moment."

While Simon warmed the towels by the fire, Richard submerged his head in the water, scrubbing his hair vigorously with soap and rinsing it. Then he rose from the water and took the heated cloth Simon held out to him.

Stepping from the tub, he wrapped the towel about his dripping body. "There's one more thing we should speak on, Simon," he added, frowning, "and it's a difficult matter for a man to judge. Despite what I've told you, there are times a man must consciously decide not to follow an order. Unfortunately, there is no guide I can give for making that choice."

He caught the boy's shoulder. "In your life you will serve under many leaders and not all will be wise. In fact, some will be unbelievably foolish. It may be necessary to choose not to obey. But I warn you, Simon, choose those occasions with care for you will live with the consequences for the rest of your life."

Simon gazed up at him with a troubled look. "Have you ever disobeyed an order, Richard?"

"Yes. And on at least a half-dozen occasions it has saved my life and that of others about me." Richard stared at him thoughtfully. "You will see some men, Simon, who seldom obey anyone. They don't make good soldiers and most end up outlaws. You will see others who always obey. They make good soldiers, but rarely become leaders. The trick to it, lad, is in gaining the wisdom to know when to do each."

He gave the boy a gentle push toward the bed. "Help me dress now, and be quick," he admonished fondly. "Even with the fire, it's damned cold in here."

From her place beside the hide-covered south window, Elen frowned thoughtfully. Though the conversation between Richard and his squire had been in English, she had followed it with ease and had been surprised to find herself unconsciously comparing it with the gentle way her father had of correcting her and Rhodri. Always careful of their pride, her father had yet kept them striving to please him, for to fail to live up to Lord Aldwyn's high expectations was a fate neither had cared to contemplate.

Troubled by the unwanted comparison, she glanced over her shoulder at her enemy. So Richard didn't plan to bed her, didn't bother the women of his enemies. She frowned. The Wolf of Kent was a complex man and wise in many things other than battle. And he was obviously capable of kindness. It was easy to see there was real affection between Richard and Simon. Certainly there was trust. No, Richard Basset was not the devil she had believed him to be, but his wisdom made him a far more dangerous opponent than she had originally thought.

Her intense study drew Richard's gaze. Across the distance of the room, questioning green eyes met brooding blue ones. She had underestimated him before, but she would not continue to do so, Elen decided. Richard of Kent would be a very difficult enemy to defeat.

CHAPTER NINE

Elen didn't have long to brood. Shortly after Richard and his squire took their leave, the servants returned with buckets of fresh water to heat. After draining the tub, then half filling it with fresh water, they too disappeared.

Sir Thomas de Waurin must be planning a bath. There was no other man in the keep who would demand such a luxury, she thought irritably. Now, she'd be forced to stomach the prattle of another Englishman.

Moving closer to the tub, she gazed longingly at the clean water. It had been months since she'd had a real bath. Hot water and washing belonged to that other life in Teifi that seemed so long ago. Bending over the rough wooden rim, she ran one hand through the water. Richard was right about one thing. A hot bath would be heaven.

Moments later, a hesitant knock sounded against the wooden door of the solar. With a protesting creak, it swung open a few inches and Richard's squire put his head round the panel. "Pardon, lady. My lord sent me to see you had all you desire."

Elen stared at him, uncomprehending.

Simon took a step into the room and closed the door. "Richard sent the water for you," he explained in French, gesturing to the buckets heating beside the fire. "Do you wish me to fill the tub?"

A bath . . . for her? Elen stared at the boy suspiciously. What would it profit Richard to send her such luxury? He must have some deep purpose in mind. "Tell your master I am clean enough," she snapped. "I do not choose to bathe."

Ignoring her shrewish comment, Simon moved to the hearth and began filling the tub with buckets of steaming water. "You need not fear the water," he said over one shoulder. "Washing won't make you ill as some believe. At least not if the room is warm and there's no danger of taking a chill," he amended. He grinned engagingly. "But I don't guess you're afraid of water. Not with that jump you made."

He paused in the act of emptying the last bucket. "You don't seem to be afraid of much. Richard's like that, too. My friend Sir Giles says it's like to get him killed, but I notice he's always first to follow my lord into a tight corner."

Elen was suddenly aware that the boy admired her. Perhaps he could be useful if she could gain his friendship. Not that he would knowingly betray his master, but it might be possible to glean important information from his chatter. Besides, he obviously thought she was pretty even in her present filthy, disheveled state.

The idea brought a smile. "How long have you been with your lord?" she asked in a milder tone.

"Not quite a year. I'm just turned fifteen, but already Richard says I'm the best squire he's trained," Simon boasted. His elation dimmed suddenly as the memory of the talk with Richard washed over him. Ducking his head, he fiddled uncomfortably with the bucket. "Of course, I still make mistakes sometimes," he added diffidently.

In spite of her prejudice, Elen's heart went out to the boy. Somehow, she couldn't see him as an enemy. He reminded her too much of the delightful young men of good family who gathered at Teifi Keep when Lord Aldwyn held court. Proud and boastful in the exuberance of youth, they became shame-faced and despondent over any real or imagined failing as they strove above all else to rush headlong into manhood.

"At fifteen it's difficult always to know what is right," she remarked, holding back a smile. "I'm sure your lord doesn't expect perfection. Each year brings its own wisdom."

Simon nodded. "That's what Richard says." He glanced eagerly up at her. "How old are you?"

"Near seventeen." She shrugged. "Perhaps I am already. I do not even know what month it is."

Simon stared at her incredulously. "Seventeen!"

Elen could no longer hold back her smile. "Yes, old by your standards, I'm sure. My birth month is Ebrill . . . your April," she added.

"B—but you're so . . . so thin," he stammered. "And Richard said you were naught but thirteen or fourteen."

A flush of annoyance warmed Elen's face. So Richard didn't even think her a woman. "If I am thin and weak, it is because I do not dine so well as you," she snapped. "You English sit out the winter in our keeps, warm yourselves with our furs, dine on our grain, slaughter our herds." She paused, the bitterness and resentment of the conquered for the conqueror spilling into her voice, making it throb with passion. "You will not see a fat Welshman, boy, unless he be a traitor!"

Simon straightened indignantly. "You Welsh started this. We didn't! By Christ's bones, it was Llywelyn himself who slunk down in the dead of night and massacred the men at Rhuddlan and Flint. And on Palm Sunday, for God's sake!"

"It was not Llywelyn!" Elen corrected vehemently. "It was his brother Dafydd. And he only did what he'd learned in league with his precious English allies a few years earlier. Your men suffered only what they taught by example! I've not enough fingers and toes to mark the times you've slaughtered men, women and children in such attacks."

"That only shows how little you know about it," Simon

responded, belatedly recalling the cool dignity befitting the squire of so important a personage as Sir Richard Basset. He put down the bucket he was brandishing in one hand. "Bathe or not as you will, woman. It matters little to me."

Elen watched the flaxen-haired boy stalk through the door and slam it resoundingly behind him. She bit her lip in frustration. She had certainly not made the most of that encounter. Richard's squire was the only one in this whole place disposed to think well of her, and now she had alienated him in an argument neither could win.

And the truth was, they were both right. There had been countless acts of cruelty and betrayal on both sides of the border, and doubtless it would continue. And if she hoped to be alive and free to see any of it, she had better keep her wits about her and come up with a way to escape.

Moving to the tub, she ran her fingers through the water. Its silken warmth slid across her hand and up her arm, sending a shiver of pleasure along her spine. There was nothing she could do to improve her situation at the moment. And merciful heaven, it would feel good to be clean again even if Richard of Kent had suggested it.

Dragging the worn, dirty tunic over her head, she tossed it on the floor. God send all Englishmen to the devil, she thought defiantly. She would have a bath!

Richard moved carefully along the wet, slippery path through the bailey. The morning storm had spent its fury, leaving heavy clouds and lingering mists hovering dismally above the rain-darkened tower of Beaufort. He lifted his face to the mizzling damp, willing it to cleanse him of the clammy feel of the earthen dungeon below.

He had done his duty, he reminded himself now. Despite his own feelings, he had wrung what information he could from his enemies. But such work always left a sick churning in his gut.

He passed an arm across his forehead, taking a deep

breath to steady himself. Cold as it was, he was sweating profusely. He was ashamed of this womanish weakness, yet he drove himself to be present whenever prisoners were questioned, both to protect the men from a too-eager jailer and in the hope he would become hardened to the necessary task. He had never discussed his feelings with another soul, yet he knew Giles understood his problem—even shared his feelings somewhat.

Fortunately the Welsh had talked more readily today than in times past. The long weary march and the hours in the tomblike blackness below ground must have broken their spirits. Praise God, he had learned what little they could tell him fairly easily.

Richard frowned thoughtfully. Though the Welsh Fox remained a mystery, now at least he had a name to put to the man. A name and a vague description—Rhys ap Iwan of Gwynedd, a dark-haired man of thirty or so, an enemy of cunning and determination who seldom revealed his plans even to his own men. And of the womenfolk of Teifi, he had discovered little beyond what Edward already knew. Nothing had been seen of them since Builth. It was believed they were safe in France.

He had also learned the locations of two Welsh camps, though he suspected the information was worthless. Past experience had taught him the camps would be deserted by now. The Welsh always moved out whenever any location was discovered or prisoners taken.

Would Elen know more? He paused on the first step of the narrow stairs to the keep entrance. Exactly what did the girl know? Not a girl, but a woman, he corrected himself. Simon had indignantly repeated the argument with their prisoner, including the surprising information that she was older than he had guessed.

Seventeen. He had been far off the mark, fooled by the girl's starved body and the grimy, ill-fitting rags she wore.

There was something more, he admitted. For once in his

life he had let his feelings get in the way of his judgment. Something about the girl had attracted him from the start, something beyond her wild, youthful beauty and the fascinating appeal of her slanted, sapphire eyes.

But she was his enemy and he had consciously chosen not to respond to that attraction, making the decision easier by telling himself she was too young for such thoughts. He had always preferred older, more experienced mistresses, and by linking the girl in his mind with Isabel, he had almost convinced himself she was naught but a child to protect. But now he knew without doubt she was a woman—his enemy's woman—and the thought was strangely unsettling.

Entering the keep, he searched in vain for Giles. He had already laid his plans to trap the Fox, but he wanted to discuss the ambush with his knight before he went over the final details with Sir Thomas.

His gaze took in the stairs at the back of the hall. The room above was the only place he would be able to speak without fear of being overheard. There were a few Welsh servants about and it never hurt to be careful. Until he decided what information his enemy should hear, he would keep his plans among those he could trust. Besides, he still needed to discover what Elen could tell him.

After sending Simon in search of Giles, he climbed the stairs to the third-floor solar. What information could the girl give him and, more importantly, how could he trick her into divulging it? Still pondering the problem, he swung open the door and stepped inside.

Across the room, Elen stood atop a stool she had dragged to the south window. Her back was toward him, her face turned longingly toward the misty woodlands beyond the wall. She had managed to tear down the scraped hide covering put up to block the window in winter, and light and cool, damp air flooded into the smoky interior of the room. Richard's eyes traveled downward. The red fox cloak loosely enveloped the girl's body, leaving her bare feet and ankles peeking beneath its hem. "I doubt even so skinny a maid could manage to slip through that hole," he commented dryly.

The girl swung about with a revealing flash of pale shapely leg beneath the swinging folds of the cloak. She was obviously naked save for its covering, and despite her earlier refusal she had bathed and washed her hair.

His eyes slid over her in admiration. The silky fox fur set off her coloring to perfection. She held the cloak's edges together loosely at the curve of her breast, while her shimmering chestnut hair, now unbraided, cascaded over her shoulders in dark harmony with the primitive richness of the fur.

Richard caught his breath at the sight. How had he ever convinced himself this lovely, wild creature was a child? Already a night's sleep and a few good meals had removed the sunken hollows from beneath her eyes. Soon the rest of her body would round out just as nicely, he realized.

She swept him with a haughty glance before turning back to the window. "Skinny I may be, but I am not a lackwit," she said pointedly. "I but sought to see the sky."

He moved toward her. "You will be cold when the wind and rain sweep in."

She threw back her head with a bitter laugh. "You forget. I've spent all winter outside, thanks to you."

He had forgotten. Here was no fragile, swooning female like the ones he knew at court. She had stayed with her man through the killing winter in the mountains of Gwynedd, even risking her life to lead their enemies astray when the camp was discovered. And now he hoped to make her betray that man.

He stared up at her, noting the long seductive expanse of her pale throat, the wide, generous curve of her mouth. All at once he wanted to taste the passion of those full lips, to see her spread naked among the furs as he bedded her,

her long hair tumbling about them in glorious disarray.

The strength of the urge shook him. Drawing his breath in sharply, he reminded himself of the reason he had come. "Step down. I would speak with you."

Elen jumped lightly down beside him, her eyes wide and wary. "I doubt we have aught to say to each other."

"Oh, but we do. We could speak of your friend Rhys," he remarked, watching her expression closely.

The girl showed no surprise at his use of the name. "We could—but I do not choose to. Besides, it's obvious you already have the information you desire." At that she crossed the room and knelt before the fire to turn her woolen tunic, which was laid out to dry. "My thanks for the water," she said changing the subject. "I haven't washed since before the snows."

Richard moved to a rough wooden chair positioned beside the fireplace and sat down. He frowned at her bent head. "You must realize I'm going after him. I know where he is now," he stated softly.

She glanced up from the ragged cloth in her hand and sent him a serene smile. "I think not."

He leaned toward her, ignoring the bewitching curl of her lips, the hint of creamy breast he could see as she bent forward again. "Your friends below were most helpful. With a small amount of persuasion they talked readily enough."

The hand clutching the fur to her chest tightened convulsively, but Elen's eyes held no fear as they met his. Instead they blazed with contempt. "Does it please you to give pain to others? Does it make you feel a mighty warrior to hear the screams of your helpless victims? Oh, you are a brave man, Richard of Kent," she taunted. "Will minstrels now sing of your valor, of your triumph over a few dozen beaten, starving men and one woman?"

Richard kept his face expressionless. He had to discover what she knew. "No, it doesn't please me to force the truth from brave men, Elen, nor do I need the praise of others to measure my courage. I know exactly who and what I am, and I take the course that leads most surely to my goal. I fight for my land as you fight for yours. And I think each of us might respect that in the other."

He saw her swallow uncertainly then look away. "What would your people do with me if our situations were reversed?"

"Find out what they could from you by any method, then kill you when they were done," she answered honestly.

"So you see we are alike—alike except for one small detail. I have no plan to put your people to death. But I will take the Fox, Elen, no matter where he hides."

"Will you English take to your feet, then? Will you leave your great war-horses and follow him into the mountains where your mounts cannot climb?" She stared up at him triumphantly. "Will you meet him with longbow and sword on his own terms?"

So the Fox would move higher into the mountains. There had been no plan then to raid Beaufort or any of the English keeps in the valleys. "If I have to," he replied.

Elen cocked her head slightly to one side and studied him thoughtfully. "You do not fear death, Richard of Kent?"

"I wish for death no more than any other, but neither do I flee from it. I will do the task I am sworn to and nothing will interfere with my duty."

Elen shrugged her shoulders lightly. "Then go after him with my good will."

Richard leaned back in his chair. Obviously the girl did not fear his moving out to search for her lover. "Perhaps I will let him come to me after all," he said easily.

Elen's eyes were downcast, but he noticed the slightest tightening of the muscles along her jaw. "He will not come. He is not such a fool."

Richard was satisfied. He had learned what he wanted to know. "Oh, I think he will. Your friends below seem to think he is quite fond of you."

She shook her head, her hair tumbling wildly about her shoulders. "They do not know. Besides, no man would risk his life so foolishly. I am nothing more to Rhys than any other woman. He will not be lonely, I assure you."

From out of nowhere, Richard felt a stab of jealousy, as unexpected as it was unsettling. Just what did the man mean to her? Suddenly it was of the utmost importance that he know. Seizing Elen's wrist, he jerked her closer, one small, rational part of him realizing that he was giving in to the overwhelming urge to touch her.

She stumbled against him, catching herself against his thigh. "What is he to you?" he bit out. "Tell me!"

She stared at him defiantly. "Nothing!"

He caught her shoulders, pulling her closer across his knees. "Nothing? You risk your life, risk capture by your enemies for a man who means nothing?" He leaned forward, eyes searching hers, overwhelmingly aware of her full, half-parted lips only inches from his. "Now why do I find that so difficult to believe?"

Elen's heart thudded so wildly she could scarcely think. She sought to gather the wits Richard's abrupt move had scattered. What did this man want of her and what in God's name should she say? "I . . . I couldn't know I'd be thrown," she stammered, "didn't realize the risk I was taking with that trick."

One side of Owain's cloak slipped from her hand and she sought to draw the edges together over her chest. But Richard's grip on her shoulders tightened painfully. His gaze shifted slowly over her, his nostrils flaring, his pulse beating visibly in the hollow of his throat. Her bewilderment changed to fear. "Y-you're hurting me," she cried.

For a moment Richard continued to hold her in the awkward position. Suddenly, he seemed to come to himself. His grip on her shoulders eased and she slipped from his lap, drawing the folds of the fox cloak protectively around her.

"Richard?"

They both jerked self-consciously toward the door. Giles was standing just inside the room, his dark face inscrutable. "Simon said you wished to speak with me."

Richard felt a flush warm his cheek. Rising to his feet, he moved across the room, ashamed of the lack of control he had just exhibited. "Yes. I wanted to discuss my plans for taking this Rhys ap Iwan," he said, shifting hastily into English so that Elen wouldn't understand. "I knew no other place to speak without fear of curious ears."

Elen stiffened as Richard's words effectively drove all thought of his unsettling behavior from her mind. Keeping her eyes downcast, she moved to the window pretending no comprehension of what the men discussed. But the pretense grew more and more difficult as Richard unfolded his plan.

First, it would be put about that she was an ill-used prisoner. That would be easy enough, as Sir Thomas suspected the local Welsh servants were spies. He seldom allowed them into the keep, forcing them to the roughest work outside the walls. But this time he would be sure they had duties about the stable. They would easily hear the talk bandied about concerning the pretty leman of the Welsh Fox.

In another day or two, the news would leak out that Richard was making up a supply train of ox carts to head for Gwenlyn, and that he was taking the girl for his amusement. The tale would be readily believed, Elen knew. The Wolf of Kent had come into this region on his way to garrison the great stone fortress farther west. She and Owain had discussed the fact at length.

She leaned against the wall for support, the whole hideous plan playing out in her mind's eye. Owain would be quick to avenge any hurt to her, but instead of bags of grain and supplies beneath the oiled cloth covers of the carts, the attacking Welshmen would find soldiers. Instead of easily dispersing the helpless serfs walking alongside the supply train, they would meet armed knights carrying weapons concealed in their loose peasant dress. Richard would strip the entire garrison from Beaufort to take part in the charade, and when Owain swept down to rescue her, Richard's trap would be sprung.

"There's one weakness in your plan, Richard," Giles was saying. Elen turned, straining desperately to hear. "What if this Rhys doesn't follow you? With most of the men gone, Beaufort will be defenseless against attack. You must make sure the bait is strong enough to draw the Fox."

"It's a gamble," Richard agreed, "but I believe he'll come for her." He turned to study Elen. "She told me as much before you came in."

Feeling Richard's eyes upon her, Elen forced herself to move casually to the fire. Kneeling, she made a great pretense of checking her drying clothing.

"She showed no fear when I told her we would go after Rhys, so she must know we have no notion where to look," Richard continued. "But she was frightened when I said I might wait here. She obviously believes he will come for her—and so do I. In a week's time, we'll have the Welsh Fox, Giles. And we can all go home to England."

Elen stared into the dancing, orange flames, seeing instead the massacre of what was left of her people. She counted each breath, concentrating on breathing deeply and evenly to manage her panic as Rhodri and Enion had taught her when she was a child.

The dreadful plan would be successful, but not for the reasons Richard believed. He had no idea of her identity, or of why Owain would willingly give up his life for her. But the results would be the same in any case. If she didn't find a way to warn her old friend, Owain would die.

Closing her eyes, she bit down hard on her lip. There had to be some way to stop Richard. Sweet Mary, Mother of God, there had to be!

Suddenly her eyes snapped open. That was it! She could stop Richard. Certainly with his leader dead, Giles wouldn't go on with the planned ambush. Why, the whole garrison would be thrown into confusion.

Her eyes narrowed now with a determination stronger than any she had ever known. She must find a way to kill Richard before he could put his plan into action.

She glanced at her enemy from beneath lowered lashes. He sat on the fur-covered bed, talking easily with Giles. She noted with interest that he had removed neither the great sword at his side nor the dagger that rode at his belt. He always wore them when he came into the room. If she could just get her hands on one of those weapons. . . .

Her thoughts returned to his earlier behavior. He wanted her. Despite his feigned indifference in front of his squire, Richard had made it quite obvious that he desired her.

The two men were concluding their conversation. She rose to her feet along with them. "Richard?"

He turned to her in surprise.

She moved toward him, halting a few inches from where he stood. "Y-your tunic," she began nervously. "The cloth is rent and has been poorly mended. Here," she added, lifting her hand to caress the frayed brown cloth at his shoulder. Raising wide innocent eyes, she forced herself to smile. "I could mend it if you desire."

Richard went painfully still at her touch. He frowned but made no move to thrust her away.

"I'm judged skillful with needle and thread," she continued. Dropping her hand, she shrugged one shoulder. "But then perhaps you've some other woman to see to your needs."

Suspicious green eyes stared into hers as if he sought to uncover the dark secrets brewing in her soul. "A few days ago you sought to end my life," Richard said slowly. "Why this concern now?"

Elen was ready. "Because you have used me well. Then

I feared for my life, but you are not as others have made me believe. You have not been unkind."

With a fleeting glance to see how this speech was received, she dropped her gaze, hoping desperately Richard wouldn't suspect the deception. She was new to this game, but if she failed to play it well, Owain and the rest of her people would pay the price. "Do not seek information from me, for I will not betray my race," she continued in a soft, earnest voice. "But I must look to my own well-being now."

Richard caught her chin, lifting her face toward him. "I do not ask you to betray them," he said, his voice softened with an understanding that made her feel vaguely uncomfortable. His fingers lingered along her cheek with a gentleness she hadn't expected. "Simon will bring you the clothing—and needle and thread if he can find it in this place."

Elen swallowed uneasily. Richard gazed at her as a man who desired a beautiful woman. She forced herself to return his look. She would fight Richard of Kent with the only weapon at her disposal—the weapon women had used against men from the beginning of time.

CHAPTER TEN

The long, gloomy afternoon slowly waned, but nightfall brought no sound of firm, familiar footsteps outside Elen's chamber. Inside, she paced the narrow confines of her prison room, nervously awaiting the next battle in her war with Richard of Kent. He would return, tonight, if she was any judge of the matter. And she must be ready to play the whore, ready and skillful enough to distract him until she could put his own blade through his heart.

An apprehensive shudder ran through her. She pictured Richard as he had looked smiling down at her in those last few moments before he left this afternoon. Somehow, knowing a man made it infinitely more difficult to consider taking his life. Not that it mattered with Richard, she reminded herself. The Englishman was her enemy, a man sworn to destroy everything she held dear. And the fact that he was a capable soldier, easily able to follow through with his murderous plan, made it all the more necessary that he be permanently removed from the game.

Climbing atop the stool below her window, Elen leaned her cheek against the rough, timbered wall and stared out into the darkness. The night was damp with a heavy blanket of fog shrouding the heavens. A light breeze blew fitfully against her face, occasionally stirring the clouds so that a shaft of moonlight gleamed along the log palisades, streaking the puddles in the meadow beyond the wall with sparkling silver.

Elen breathed deeply of the cold wet air, indulging the melancholy thoughts that had plagued her all afternoon. This might well be the last night of her life. Her small part in the battle for Wales would soon be over, for it would be check and checkmate when she took Richard's life. If she were successful, his men would kill her in reprisal. The action was only to be expected and she faced the fact bravely. She had no desire to die, but Owain was now far more valuable to the Welsh cause than she. And if it were her life for his, she would gladly pay the price.

But Holy Mother of God, she didn't want to die yet....

It was one thing to risk her life on a brave impulse during the heat of battle. But she had learned it was something else entirely to sit pondering certain death through the endless hours of a lonely afternoon. She swallowed heavily and closed her eyes, willing herself not to think of her mother's narrow grave high in the Welsh hills where she had painstakingly erected a cairn of gray stone. It was enough one person she held dear had died because of her willfulness. Owain would not be another.

Suddenly Richard's golden image swam before her mind's eye. She recalled the straight, proud way he held himself, the effortless way he swung his heavy sword, his tirelessness on that long trek yesterday when she was weary unto death herself. For all that he was her enemy, a man like Richard of Kent deserved to die honorably on the field of battle, not in bed at the hand of some treacherous jade.

She jerked away from the window and jumped down, angrily resuming her narrow pacing. She despised herself for the part she was about to play but there was no other way.

Richard touched his spurs lightly to Saladin's sweating sides. He was annoyed by his eagerness to return to Beaufort but strangely unwilling to curb his headlong pace. Elen's abrupt overture of friendliness yesterday had surprised him, and he had found himself thinking of little else on this trip to the Welsh village. In fact, he had been so intrigued, he would have delayed the journey by at least one night if he hadn't already given his men the order to march.

But the brief expedition had served several purposes, and now it was almost done he was glad he hadn't postponed it. He had retrieved his armor and had delivered two barrels of beans and corn, an excellent milk cow, and a pair of sheep to the astonished people of the tiny village. But he had also ridden in force with an extra contingent of men from Beaufort, the ferocious red boars of his coat of arms waving proudly on the banner Simon displayed. For once in his life, Richard meant to make as much show as possible. He wanted those who acted as eyes and ears for the Welsh Fox to be fully informed of his whereabouts.

Glancing back along the line of his men, he frowned at the woman riding in the empty supply cart. The beautiful Margaret of Chester had begged to return to Beaufort with him, insisting that her life would be worth little if word of her treachery leaked out. And she was right. The Welsh memory was long. These people seldom forgot or forgave an injury.

With that his mind spun full circle and he was back to thoughts of Elen. After fighting him so fiercely, why had she suddenly softened? He had expected her to continue to resist him as staunchly as ever.

But then he found he couldn't think clearly where the girl was concerned—just the memory of her hand lightly touching his shoulder, of her blue eyes gazing up at him with a mixture of uncertainty and invitation sent his blood coursing through his body in a way he couldn't control.

But had her look truly held invitation or had he seen only what he desired? Had the lovely child-woman merely been trying to thank him for his kind treatment—or was she offering something more?

That question had kept him twisting and turning uncomfortably in his blankets last night long after everyone else in camp was asleep. It was simply a woman he needed—any woman—he told himself irritably. The girl held no special fascination for him.

Yet if that were the case, he could have taken Margaret. The woman was young and attractive and had offered herself to him openly and honestly in exchange for his protection. But to his own surprise he had found himself making excuses to send her away.

He scowled at the bobbing bay head before him. Was that what Elen was seeking—a protector? What manner of land was this that a woman must sell herself to one man in exchange for protection for her life and virtue from others? He gripped his reins with a mailed fist, realizing the answer to that question at once. Wales was a land at war, and if they wished to survive, the weak sought protection from the strong.

Saladin stumbled on the rough trail and Richard steadied his mount, muttering a low curse at his own inattention. If he didn't keep his mind on what he was doing, he wouldn't live long enough to ask any more questions, much less find the answers.

But Elen's last words returned to plague him. "I must look to my own well-being now," she had said. Perhaps she thought she must please him to insure continued good treatment. No doubt she had been raised on blood-chilling tales of English brutality. But he had offered her no harm. Surely she no longer feared him.

Of course, the girl's words could be taken another way. A cynical smile curled his lips as he remembered his past mistresses. Every woman he had ever known had sought gain from her relationships. Naturally, Elen would hope to better her position by seeking his favor now that the Welsh cause seemed hopeless.

He shrugged off the surprisingly sharp disappointment

the thought brought him. Somehow the girl didn't seem the type to sell herself for a bauble or a length of velvet cloth. But if that's what she wanted, he would surely pay the price.

A short time later, the wooden stockade of Beaufort came into sight. Richard touched his heels to his stallion's sides, cantering easily across the meadow and into the open castle bailey. Swinging down from his sweating destrier, he gave his reins to one of the waiting lackeys.

Sir Thomas came down the narrow stairs of the keep. "By God's grace, Richard, I didn't expect you back before nightfall! Come inside and refresh yourself. My people have yet to remove the midday meal."

Richard glanced up. "I saw nothing in that godforsaken place to cause me to linger, de Waurin. And with things as they are, I thought it unwise to leave you poorly manned for longer than necessary." He stared down at his hands, carefully removing his gauntlets. He longed to ask after Elen, but wisely avoided it. "Any trouble here?" he inquired instead.

Thomas shook his head. "It's been near quiet as the tomb."

The two men entered the keep and Richard washed his hands and face from a laver a servant brought him. With thoughts of the girl plaguing him he hadn't even realized he was hungry, but now the smells in the hall made his mouth water in anticipation.

While servants hurried to bring fresh trenchers and goblets of wine, Richard and his knights helped themselves to bread and cheese that were quickly passed among them. Sir Thomas seated himself beside Richard with a broad smile. "A courier rode in last night with news from my brother-in-law Henry St. Sanson. There is little noteworthy in the letter, mostly communication from my sister." He grinned and shrugged his shoulders. "Women's talk," he added disparagingly. "But there was a bit that will interest you. Your brother Philip is in South Wales. Henry saw him at Chepstow Castle. It seems he's taken service with Hugh de Veasy."

Richard stiffened. So Philip was in Wales. And naturally the boy would have sought service with a man like the Baron of Ravensgate. He reached for a goblet of wine a servant held out, thankful for the interruption that gave him a moment to collect his thoughts. "Philip will see little action of any import in the South," he finally said, taking a sip of wine.

Across the table, Sir William of Hereford snorted derisively. "So the young whelp finally found a man fool enough to knight him. More's the pity, but he and de Veasy should get along well!"

Richard sent his old friend a heavy frown and Sir Thomas glanced from one man to the other in confusion. "I thought you'd be pleased."

"My half-brother and I are not on the best of terms, Thomas," Richard explained. "Our opinions differ on everything." He smiled painfully. "Everything, that is, except the fact that we wish to see as little as possible of each other."

"Oh, I . . . I didn't know."

Richard reached for a steaming platter of roast venison. "It matters little, Thomas. The injuries are old and long forgotten, but Philip and I avoid each other whenever possible."

Giles smoothly offered another topic of conversation and the talk of the men veered off on another course. Richard ate in silence, willing himself not to think of their last meeting over two years ago when his half-brother had petulantly sworn to see him dead.

But the painful memory wouldn't leave him. Philip was naught but the product of his upbringing, Richard reminded himself; the only son of a spiteful and manipulative woman who vowed her own child would have his elder brother's birthright. From the cradle, the boy had learned to despise his older brother and to look on the Basset holding of Waybridge Keep as his own. But he didn't plan to oblige the boy by dying, Richard thought wryly. And he knew well enough how to hold what was his.

Still, he was irritated at the news that had set old wounds throbbing. Between them, Philip and Jeanne had made what little time he spent with his father at Waybridge a misery. Yes, Jeanne had ruined the boy, he told himself, spoiling him. By all rights he should feel sorry for Philip. But somehow he didn't.

Having finished his meal, Richard pushed back from the table, suddenly wondering what mischief his brother might be planning. The fact that the boy was in Wales at all was amazing. He liked luxury and easy living too well to enjoy the rigors of camp life. But whatever it was that brought Philip there, it probably boded ill for him.

Richard smiled darkly. Just let the young pup try to cross him! He'd show him how men fought. He'd send the boy running for cover behind his mother's skirts—and he'd enjoy doing it.

The sight of a serving woman descending the stairs at the back of the hall suddenly distracted him. The woman carried a tray with the remains of a meal. *Elen . . .*

Richard stood up abruptly, embracing the thought of the girl with eagerness, a welcome distraction from the pain of his recent musing. When he had drained the last of his wine, he placed the heavy goblet on the table. He might as well find out what the girl had intended yesterday.

"If you'll excuse me, gentlemen," he remarked, gazing fixedly at the stairs. "I've some unfinished business to see to."

Elen flung herself onto the bed in despair, frantically wondering what was happening beyond the walls of her chamber. Had she misunderstood Richard's plan yesterday? Had she stupidly mistaken his guttural English words?

Richard hadn't come in to her last night and as the hours passed, she nervously recalled the confused sounds of men and horses gathering in the courtyard yesterday afternoon. At the time she had paid little attention to the noise, putting it down to a routine patrol making ready for a foray. And since the north window overlooking the castle bailey was still tightly boarded with heavy shutters to hold out the winter wind, she hadn't been able to satisfy her curiosity. But what if Richard had ridden out after Owain yesterday? What if the trap had been sprung this morning and Owain was already dead?

She tried to tell herself the idea was ridiculous. No one could have put such an elaborate plot into effect in just one day. But as the long hours of night dragged by, her panic had multiplied with the darkness until all reason eluded her. And she didn't dare ask the stolid-faced guard who brought her breakfast where his master had gone. The English men-at-arms spoke neither French nor Welsh, and Elen dared not reveal she spoke their own crude tongue.

The sound of returning men and horses a half hour earlier had flooded her with fresh fear, sending her tearing frantically at the sturdy wooden shutters until the fingers of her right hand were bloody and sore. But she couldn't remove the bolt and had succeeded in breaking off only one tiny corner of the barrier.

Suddenly the sound of approaching footsteps caught her attention. It was a man's tread. She sat up, straining her ears. If Owain were dead, she couldn't bear it!

A sharp, impatient knock sounded, then Richard swung open the door. Elen rose anxiously to her feet, regarding the tall knight with a fierce scrutiny. At least he didn't appear to have fought recently. Clutching her hands together, she took a deep breath. "You have been gone," she stated flatly.

Richard studied the girl before him in surprise. Her voice was curiously breathless, her face taut and anxious. If he didn't know better, he would think she was afraid. "Yes. I had business to see to."

A flicker of pain crossed her face and he felt more bewildered than ever. "Has something frightened you, Elen?" He crossed the floor toward her. "Has anyone harmed you?"

She shook her head, searching for some excuse for her obvious unease. Richard must not guess the real reason for her fear. "You left and I didn't know if you meant to return. I . . . I didn't know what would become of me here."

Her halting words touched him as did the frightened look in her wide blue eyes. What an unfeeling bastard he'd been to have left her helpless and shut away like this, with no key to her future save the memory of old brutalities practiced between his race and hers. No wonder she was afraid.

Taking her arm, Richard drew her down beside him onto the fur-covered bed. "Let me tell you what will happen then, Elen, so you will have no need for fear," he said quietly. "No one here will harm you. My word is law and I've given certain orders concerning you. And if anything should happen to me, Giles would take command. He would see you came to no harm."

The girl was staring down at her clasped hands and Richard followed her gaze. He noticed her bloody fingers with surprise. "What's this?" he inquired, taking her right hand in his.

She tried to pull away but he held her wrist firmly. "It's nothing," she said nervously. "Pray, don't regard it."

"How came you by this?"

Elen lifted her eyes to his, knowing the truth would answer better in this case than a lie. "I tore my hand trying to force the shutters from the window. I . . . I can't stand to be closed in."

Richard's eyes narrowed and he curled her fingers protectively in his large hand. "I will have them opened for you, then, if you're certain you won't be cold."

She glanced away uncomfortably. His kindness was the last thing she wanted now.

Taking her injured hand, Richard blotted her fingertips gently against the forest-green cloth of his tunic. He lifted them to his lips, slowly kissing the back of her hand and then each individual finger. Something about this girl moved him to an unexpected tenderness, and despite the many impatient hours of wanting her, he now felt no haste.

At the warm touch of Richard's mouth against her skin, Elen's eyes flew to his face in surprise. His head was bent near hers, his eyes regarding her impassively. Her hand warmed to his touch and she sought to draw it away, but his fingers held hers securely.

They studied each other wordlessly, then Richard's hand moved to her chin, lifting her face toward him. His fingers strayed to her unbound hair, stroking it in a way that sent a warm shiver of pleasure down her backbone. "In answer to your words yesterday, Elen, I have no other woman to see to my needs," he said quietly.

The hand slid to her neck, gently cupping the back of her head, holding her face toward him. His mouth lowered slowly to hers, so close she could feel the soft brush of his breath against her cheek.

Instinctively, she closed her eyes. His lips caressed her temple, then brushed against her mouth, feather soft, gently urging instead of rough and demanding as she had expected. "But I desire something more from you than a woman to mend my garments," he whispered against her closed lips.

Elen took a deep breath. Not now, she thought wildly. It couldn't be happening now! She'd been so afraid for Owain she hadn't even thought of her plan to kill Richard in hours. She needed time to ready herself, time to steel herself for a task that was growing increasingly distasteful. No, she thought frantically. Not now!

Richard's lips grazed her closed eyelids then returned to

take her mouth. The pressure was light and strangely pleasing . . . and somehow compelling. She put one hand against his chest in mute protest, and he ceased his tender aggression at once.

Elen's eyes snapped open and she stared up at him in bewilderment. She hadn't expected this pleasant feeling his touch evoked. He slid his fingers through her hair, moving his hands until he cupped her face gently between both palms. "I make no secret of the fact that I desire you, Elen. But I'll not force you to come to me against your will." He stared down at her so intently she lost all ability to look away. "You will continue to be treated well—even if you refuse me."

Elen felt the warmth of each separate finger against her face. She had not counted on this kindness from the Wolf of Kent, and it left her strangely shaken. Suddenly she wished he would beat her. It would make her task easier to bear.

Richard's overwhelming nearness sent her heart thudding painfully, his gaze capturing her own so that even her thinking was disjointed. Never had she felt so helpless to plan, to decide. Richard desired her. This was exactly what she had wanted, what she had planned for yesterday afternoon. Yet now she felt a frantic urge to flee. "But . . . but we are enemies!" she blurted out in protest, more to herself than to him.

Richard smiled. So he had been wrong about Elen yesterday. There had been no calculated invitation in her eyes, no plan to use him for gain. The girl seemed genuinely surprised by his proposal—surprised and afraid. He could feel her pulse leaping wildly beneath his fingers, see the panic in her eyes. His hands slid to her shoulders, gently drawing her closer. He wanted her, but he wanted her willing. And something told him he could make her so.

"We do not have to be enemies," he breathed against her mouth. His lips moved over hers once more, his tongue sliding temptingly along her full lower lip, urging her to open to him. "We could share a truce. At least in this room," he whispered, finally lifting his head.

Elen struggled to catch her breath. The fire in Richard's eyes kindled something deep inside her. Fear, she told herself, hastily struggling to conquer it. She was afraid she couldn't do this thing—perhaps she really wasn't equal to the task.

But her father had always told her she could do anything.

Her father . . . Enion, the host of other friends this man had slain. The thought steadied her, reminding her of her purpose. Despite his gentleness with her, Richard was responsible for the deaths of all her family. She could kill him, and she would. Her dead cried out for vengeance. But first she had to find out where he had gone. If Owain were already dead . . .

Her hands moved to clutch Richard's shoulders and she held him slightly away. "Do you come to me with fresh blood on your hands? Did your business take you to war on my people?"

Richard met her accusing gaze with an innocent smile, refusing to think of his damning plot to capture her lover. Thank God he had nothing to hide this time, at least. "Even you could find no fault with my business, Elen. I rode to take food to a small Welsh village northeast of here. The people are starving and there are only women and children and a few old men. I doubted feeding them would endanger the English cause."

Some strange emotion shone fleetingly in her eyes. Pain or regret, he thought. But that was impossible. Her grip on his shoulders relaxed and he drew her full against his chest, thrilling to the feel of her slender body in his arms. She didn't struggle when his mouth moved over hers. Her lips relaxed against the pressure of his, opening to let him explore the velvet softness of her mouth.

Richard felt a white-hot excitement building within him.

Elen would come to him willingly now. There would be no more nights of wanting. He bent her back onto the bed, the upper part of his body pressing eagerly against the soft curves of hers. Stroking her hair, tangling his fingers in the rich cool silk of her dark chestnut tresses, he wondered how he had ever thought he favored fair women. All his past mistresses seemed but pale, faded images when compared to Elen's fiery loveliness.

He shifted closer to mold his hips against hers, already imagining the exquisite pleasure he would seek in her body. But the awkward bulk of his sheathed broadsword came between them.

Impatient annoyance gave way to a smothered chuckle and he rolled away from the girl. She had him so eager, he hadn't even thought to remove his weapons. He was acting like an awkward boy with his first woman, for pity's sake.

Rising on one elbow, he smiled down at her. "My wits have clearly gone begging, Elen." He brushed the hair back from her flushed face, her slightly parted lips silently pleading for one more kiss. Bending, he took her mouth once more, slowly, thoroughly, scarcely able to bear the thought of stopping, even for a moment. "I doubt we can get on satisfactorily with this damned thing between us," he whispered, touching his sword.

Elen lay on the bed staring up at the man above her in surprise. Her thoughts spun crazily and she was vaguely aware of her own breathless excitement, of a strange disappointment that his heady, drugging kisses had ended. She had been kissed scores of times, but never like that, she thought dazedly. Englishmen were certainly different from the men of her race.

Richard slid to his feet, his hands moving quickly to unbuckle his sword belt. He removed it hastily, and it dropped to the floor beside the bed with a noise that shook her out of her bewilderment.

Her enemy was removing his weapons! Blessed Saint Dafydd, when should she take his life? All at once, the thought was incredibly repugnant, but she thrust the cowardly feeling aside. When . . . when was the best time? Not now—Richard was still too aware of what was happening.

Richard removed his dagger, tossing it onto the bedside table. His eyes held hers, and a slow smile spread over his face, a smile that sent a strange, aching emptiness uncoiling in the pit of her stomach. "Perhaps we should both get a bit more comfortable," he suggested. With the words, he slipped his tunic over his head, quickly stripping off the homespun shirt beneath it. He emerged bare-chested, his powerful golden body bared to her gaze.

Easing one knee onto the bed, he caught her shoulders and raised her to a sitting position. "Your turn, sweetheart." His hands were firm but gentle against her flesh. There was no painful haste. Not even Enion had been so tender in his treatment, Elen caught herself thinking.

Lifting her arms, Richard tugged the worn brown tunic over her head. Then his mouth sought hers unerringly, his tongue slipping between her lips, touching, teasing, filling her with a mass of dizzying sensations that sent her world reeling. His hands caressed the length of her back, slipping beneath the tattered hem of her linen shift to rest against the curve of her hip.

At the warm feel of his hands against her bare skin, Elen flinched. The situation was almost beyond her control and she still wasn't certain she knew what to do. Yesterday she had planned how this would be, how *she* would be the aggressor, seducing *him* to carelessness. But her enemy had unexpectedly turned the tables.

Richard eased her shift over her head. She made one frightened grab for the protective covering but he held her gently, rubbing his cheek against her hair. "I want to see you, Elen," he whispered against her ear. "Don't hide yourself. We need have no secrets between us."

She forced herself to focus on Richard's bare chest, willing herself not to think of what he was doing, reminding herself she must decide exactly where to put his blade. She would get only one chance with this man, and she would have to move quickly. His dagger was well within reach. With a half roll, she could have it in her hand. An uncontrollable shudder ran through her and she closed her eyes against the vision of Richard's golden body running red with blood. *Dear God, could she do it?*

Richard heard her deep sigh, felt her tremble in his arms. She was afraid of him and he was probably going too fast for her. Despite the fact she was no virgin, he had the overwhelming feeling she wasn't all that experienced either. Perhaps the Welsh Fox was a poor lover, he thought with a satisfied grin.

Easing Elen down on the scattered furs on the bed, he let his eyes range over her bare body. She was tall and leggy like a prize colt, but incredibly well put together in spite of her thinness. Her pale flesh gleamed with a translucent whiteness against the background of dark fur, and it was all he could do to keep from ending his torment at once. He rested one hand on her belly, slowly moving it along her ribs until he cupped one small, perfect breast, teasing its pouting nipple with the pad of his thumb.

With a tiny, smothered gasp, Elen half rose against him, her blue eyes wide with outrage and bewilderment. He bent his head and took her mouth, teasing her lips open with more insistence than he had done before. His hands began to move, his fingers encircling the tight, hard bud of her nipples while his tongue explored her mouth with a rhythm that wrung a low groan from her throat.

Shifting forward, he moved over her, parting her thighs easily with his knee and fitting his body between them. There was nothing stopping him now save the thin fabric of his chausses. He was thankful he still wore the garment else he'd not have been able to control his desire. And he wanted to take his time making love to this woman. She had been through hell, and as a soldier bound to further war on her people, he had little to offer in exchange for the use of her body save her own pleasure. Sliding his hands along the graceful curve of her back, he lifted her slender hips against his aching loins, swearing before he took her she would know this same fierce need that burned through his veins.

Elen felt the weight of Richard's eager body pressing her down onto the bed. He showered kisses across her bare shoulder to the warm hollow of her throat. She stifled another groan as his lips explored lower, gently nuzzling the suddenly sensitive crest of her breasts. Why didn't he get it over with? This wasn't the hurried act of coupling she had heard crudely described. It wasn't the primitive rutting of animals she had seen. She gritted her teeth against the strange warmth spiraling through her. Why didn't he just take his pleasure and be done so she could do what she must?

Richard's mouth took possession of hers once more, his curiously knowing hands moving over her in a way that nearly robbed her of thought. She hated Richard, hated him, she repeated in a frantic litany that was the only steadying anchor in a sea of confusing feelings flooding over her. He had killed Enion and he would kill Owain too. And he was using her in a way no man should dare!

She swallowed hard and tried to shift away from the exquisite torment of his hands, but Richard pulled her on top of him, molding her tightly against his body in a way that left her aching for something she didn't dare think about. She couldn't let him continue this, she told herself wildly. She had to end it now while some measure of will remained to her.

Wrapping her arms around Richard's broad shoulders, she let one hand stray over his head, feeling desperately for the table. There! Her groping fingers found the dagger and she shifted her hand upward until the handle fit her palm. She must do it now. There was just no other way.

Opening her eyes wide, she stared down at Richard's golden body, feeling a sudden overwhelming remorse. He didn't deserve to die like this—not like this!

Owain . . . think of Owain. For a second more she hesitated. Owain or Richard—her choice which would live.

But there was no choice. Closing her eyes, she brought the blade down with all the force of her arm.

Richard caught the flash of descending steel out of the corner of his eye. Through a haze of building passion he had felt the sudden change in the woman in his arms, his battle-trained senses responding to the tensing muscles of an opponent preparing for a blow. As his instincts took control, he thrust himself sideways before his mind even registered the thought.

Elen was trying to kill him!

The knife buried itself harmlessly in the straw mattress beside his shoulder. Richard swung from the bed with a low snarl of rage, but the girl was up, too, the dagger a flash of deadly silver between them.

"Bitch! You lying, treacherous bitch!" he bit out furiously.

Elen held the knife low and close in, like one trained to use it. Her eyes were wide and desperate, her face devoid of all color. Richard fought the impulse to rush forward and simply jerk the weapon from her hand. Elen wasn't just any foolish woman with a knife. She would cut him to pieces if he took that mad course.

Snatching up a fur from the bed, he caught it between both hands, holding it before him as a shield in case she rushed him. He could call the guard outside the door, but that would be too easy. She had made a fool of him and he'd be damned if he'd get help to subdue her. No, he wanted to break the lying jade himself. She would be begging for mercy before he was done!

He feinted once, twice, three times with the fur, the fourth time swinging it over her head to entangle her right arm. Elen ducked back, but he dove for her midsection, hurling her backward into a wooden table that careened across the floor to shatter noisily against the wall.

They went down in a tangle of wildly thrashing limbs, every muscle straining with furious, deadly purpose. Richard caught her right wrist, squeezing down with a bone-crushing grip to make her release the weapon. He could feel the pounding of her heart, hear the sound of her harsh breathing as they struggled desperately for the weapon. He knew her strength was no match for his, but she stubbornly held on.

With a vicious oath, he struck her arm against the floor seeking to knock the knife from her grip. She rolled sideways, shielding the weapon from him with the bulk of her own body.

Richard dragged her arm back, not caring now if the delicate bone snapped beneath his weight. Christ, he'd kill her if she kept this up!

Elen flung herself away from the relentless pain in her wrist just as Richard forced back on her arm with all his strength. Her arm gave way, the power of his thrust jerking the blade down along her thigh. It slid sickeningly through her bare flesh, a searing pain that blotted out all thoughts, all sensations save the fiery ache burning through her.

With a gasp, she released the weapon. Through a red haze of pain, she heard Richard curse as he rolled her over to inspect the wound.

Instinctively she knew it was bad. Without opening her eyes she recognized the warm feel of blood gushing down her leg to puddle wetly beneath her body on the cold floor. Richard's hands were rough and impatient, a far cry from the gentleness he had shown such a short time ago. Yet they felt strangely competent, too, as they pressed strips torn from the bed linens against her flesh to stem the flow of blood.

Elen kept her eyes tightly closed, unable to face the implacable hatred she knew she would read in Richard's gaze, unable to watch her own life's blood spending itself on the floor. She had tried to do what was necessary, but it wasn't enough. She had failed.

Her determination began to ebb as the pain intensified, filling every inch of her world with a bright, throbbing hurt. She would die now, but she didn't care. At least the pain would be no more.

Richard swung to his feet and padded across the floor. She heard him open the door and bellow for Giles. With a concentrated effort, she opened her eyes and sat up. The room spun before her, and her stomach churned weakly with nausea. An uncontrollable chill shook her and she felt burning hot and freezing cold at the same time. The blood welled from her leg in a crimson stream, but strangely enough, it didn't seem to belong to her.

"Sorry, sweetheart, but you weren't quite quick enough. Too bad you missed . . . and for the second time now too."

Richard had returned. She lifted her head to speak, to try to explain, but her mind refused to translate her Welsh thoughts into French. And it was just as well. What could she say to him anyway?

Richard studied the beautiful girl before him. Any other woman and not a few of the men he knew would be groveling on the floor after such treachery, begging for their lives. Elen just gazed up at him without a whimper, the glazed look in her wide blue eyes the only hint of her pain.

The look sent his insides tightening with dread. He had seen that look in the eyes of countless wounded in the aftermath of battle. It boded no good. For God's sake, where was Giles? He would know what to do to staunch this flood of bleeding.

Another chill shook the girl. Richard grabbed up one of the furs and wrapped it around her shivering body. She looked so pathetic huddled on the floor. He shifted forward impulsively to take her in his arms, then drew back with an oath. Christ, she'd almost killed him. He was more of a fool than he'd realized. "Don't think I'm going to let you die now, sweetheart," he said coldly. "I need you alive— at least for another week."

"Richard! For the love of God, what's happened?"

Richard glanced up. "We had a small scuffle over a knife," he said bitterly. "She lost."

Giles took in the situation at a glance: the rumpled bed-covers, the naked girl and his near-naked lord. Going down on one knee beside Elen, he spoke soothingly to her in the Welsh tongue.

"I saw at once I couldn't stop the bleeding," Richard explained as Giles lifted the blood-soaked linens he'd wrapped about Elen's thigh. "The wound's too deep and more than the span of my hand."

Giles nodded and looked up. "You know, then, what we must do. She's like to bleed to death else."

For a moment the two men looked at each other, then Richard turned on his heel and retrieved his knife. Moving to the fire, he bent and forced the blade deep into the glowing bed of embers, his own flesh cringing at the thought of holding it against Elen's shapely thigh. "You do it," he snapped, his back still turned toward his friend. "I might enjoy it too much."

In a few terse Welsh sentences, Giles explained what they would do. But his words were unnecessary for Elen. She had seen Owain seal a wound on more than one oc-casion. She met his worried gaze. "I understand," she said softly. "I will not struggle."

Minutes ticked by. Elen watched as Richard rose from the fire and moved toward her, the glowing blade held gingerly in one hand. This wasn't real. It couldn't be hap-pening. Holy Mary, help her to be brave.

Giles frowned and took the knife, biting his lip in con-centration. "I don't want to frighten you, but I must hold your leg flat with my weight, Elen." He gazed at her steadily. "If you jerk away, the knife might slip and we'd just have to do this again. Do you understand?"

She drew a shaky breath. At least it would be over quickly. "Do what you must. I'll not move."

Richard sat down beside her. "She won't move, Giles. I'll make sure of that," he said harshly. "Just get this over with."

Elen's tongue flickered out over suddenly dry lips. She watched in grim fascination as Giles moved into position. Richard caught her shoulders, his painful grip holding her so tightly against his side she could scarcely breathe. Her eyes flashed up to his expecting hate, triumph.

His gaze narrowed with a strange, unreadable expression. "Don't look," he whispered, drawing her face against him. "It'll be over in a—"

The searing pain arched through her, jerking her upright against Richard's bare chest. Her nails dug into his shoulder as she fought back the scream of anguish rising from her soul. The smell of burning flesh filled the room, and mercifully, Elen fainted.

CHAPTER ELEVEN

Time passed slowly in a near-oblivion of nightmare days and nights, but Elen could scarcely distinguish one from the other. Why was she so thirsty, and what was this fierce, burning pain in her leg? She realized vaguely that a dark familiar face bent over her from time to time, lifting her to ease some sweet drink between her parched lips. But who was this man with the gentle, strangely accented voice, and where was Papa? And by the mercy of all the saints, where was Tangwen? Tangwen and Papa would make her feel better if only they would come. She wanted them—she wanted them now!

By the morning of the third day, Elen awoke from a restless sleep, still groggy from the drugged wine she had taken so liberally. Her head ached and her throat was dry and sore. Lifting herself up from the bed, she reached weakly for the basin of water on a table near the bedside. Holding the dipper, she drank long and deep, grateful to whoever had drawn the table within her reach.

But where was she? The room spun dizzily before her eyes, and she eased herself back down, trying desperately to remember where she was—what dreadful thing had happened to make her feel so wretched?

Then the memories came flooding back. Her father was

dead and God alone knew where Tangwen might be. And she was imprisoned in an English fortress at the mercy of her enemy, Richard of Kent—a man she had just tried to kill.

With a low groan, she rolled onto one side, slowly pushing herself back to a sitting position. Raising her shift, she inspected the neat linen bandage around her right thigh. There were no red streaks running from the wound, no stench of dying flesh. She would live, if only so that she might be tortured to death for her attack on an English knight.

But Owain, was there any chance of saving Owain? Her head throbbed with a vengeance as her fears came rushing back. Should she throw herself on Richard's mercy? Try to bargain with him somehow? There must be some way to prevent him from springing his trap. Merciful Father, how much time had she already wasted in useless sleep?

Moments later, a murmur of voices came to her from outside the door, and the surly woman who brought Elen's meals stepped into the room. The woman carried a bowl of steaming gruel and a pitcher of fresh water. With a disapproving frown, she placed both on the bedside table.

Elen stared at the woman hopefully. Her harsh-featured face was tightly framed by the concealing folds of a dingy wimple, her thin mouth set in dour lines. Surely the English woman couldn't be as forbidding as she appeared. Marshaling her wits, Elen spoke first in French, asking the woman how long she had slept.

The woman merely gave her a disdainful glance and began moving toward the door.

"Wait! Please." In an intentionally halting performance of both English and French, Elen thanked the woman for bringing her food, then asked her question again.

The woman held up the fingers of her right hand, then tapped them off. "Three days it is now, you've been feverish. And lucky you be, Richard Basset didn't leave you die as you deserved." Swinging open the door, she crossed herself. "God protect him and us from you treacherous savages."

Three days. Elen stared at the retreating woman in disbelief, scarcely hearing the remainder of her words. How could it possibly have been that long? Carefully unwinding the bandage around her thigh, she studied the knife wound. The flesh was pink and tender but already showing signs of healing. *Three days. Dear God, it must be true!*

Easing from the bed, Elen dragged herself to the south window, pulling herself up onto the stool to gaze over the ledge. Beyond the palisade wall, the empty meadow rolled away like a carpet of green velvet, dew-kissed and sparkling in the golden morning sunlight. There were no knights or men-at-arms engaging in warlike exercises in sight. She cocked her head and held her breath, listening for the telltale sounds of soldiers and servants moving about Beaufort. But the tiny fortress was eerily silent.

The hours dragged by, and Elen strained her ears for the sound of Richard's voice, for the noise of his footsteps outside her door. But few sounds of any kind filtered up to the third-floor solar. By nightfall, she could no longer hide from the truth. Richard had put his plan into action. He had taken the garrison of Beaufort and gone after Owain.

Strangely enough, she did not weep. She was beyond that comfort. She ate because she had to and slept because her battered young body demanded it. And she spent hours on her knees imploring the Holy Trinity and all the saints in heaven to spare Owain's life.

Slowly two days passed, then another faded into nightfall. By the afternoon of the fourth day, just when she thought she must go mad with the waiting, the noise of horses brought her to the boarded north window.

Breathlessly, she listened for sounds rising from the bailey. She could hear horses, many horses, and the rumbling noise of carts. In desperation she began struggling with the stubborn wooden shutters covering the courtyard window. Owain might be down there. She had to see what was happening!

But the boards remained tightly in place. Gazing frantically around the room, she noticed the stool standing in its accustomed place across the floor. Grabbing it up, she wedged one leg beneath the edge of the window board, throwing her weight against it. Nothing. She tried again, this time jamming the leg against the window ledge for leverage and forcing it back with all her strength.

With a protesting groan, one of the boards gave way, splintering noisily from its iron bracket to fall to the floor with an alarming clatter. Elen beat the stool against the remaining piece of board until it, too, fell to the floor. At the noise, a nervous guard, one of Richard's men, rushed into the room, gesturing for her to move away from the window.

Elen ignored the man. Dropping the stool to the floor, she stepped onto its now-wobbly surface and stared out. The narrow bailey was rapidly filling with soldiers and horses, and one by one, the heavy, oxen-drawn supply carts were rumbling through the wide wooden gate. Horses nickered and oxen lowed tiredly for their stables. Men called to men and occasional laughter rang out. Everything was turmoil, but it was the happy confusion of a victorious campaign.

Elen felt a sick dread spreading through her. Gripping the window ledge with a white-knuckled fist, she strained her eyes for the sight of a golden knight, taller than most men. A flash of red caught her eye as Simon swung down from his gray gelding, still carefully holding Richard's banner proudly aloft.

The boy moved in the direction of one of the carts and Elen's heart skipped a beat. Richard was standing at the rear of the cart personally directing the removal of the wounded. Several men moved forward, carefully lifting an inert form wrapped closely in a bloodstained blanket.

Elen closed her eyes and leaned against the wall for support. Owain . . . it was Owain they had below in the bailey. And even from this distance she could see he looked wounded unto death. Why had they even bothered bringing him back? Why hadn't they just finished him off after the ambush?

The memory of that midnight raid when she had been mistaken for the Welsh Fox flashed before her. Edward of England wanted the Welsh Fox alive. He wanted to make an example of the leader of this rebellion.

The sickness in her gut intensified. She had to talk to Richard. She must find out if he knew Owain was the Fox. She would deny it with her last breath, would swear Owain was her uncle. Richard would believe her—he had to!

Drawing a deep breath she rounded on the unsuspecting guard, still babbling on about the broken shutter. "I have news for your master. News of great import. I must see him at once!" she interrupted in English.

The hulking soldier stared at her in amazement. "You . . . you speak our tongue?"

Elen nodded impatiently. "Take me to Sir Richard. I must speak to him."

The soldier began to shake his head. "An I take you from this chamber, it's lucky I'd be to get off with a hundred stripes for my back. My lord will see ta you in his good time."

Elen was used to dealing with servants. With stupid ones like this, fear was often the best goad. "Fool!" she snapped. "Your lord will give you worse than the lash when he learns you kept important information from him. If you wish to save your tongue as well as your skin, you'd better take me to him now!"

The man shook his head again, but now he looked nervous. Richard of Kent was no man to cross. "Mayhap you could give me this news. I'll see if m'lord be interested."

Elen glanced down into the bailey. The men were moving Owain's motionless body toward the keep door. Time was of the essence. She gazed coldly back at the soldier. "The words are not for your ears, but those of Sir Richard. If you fear I might overpower you and escape, then fetch your lord here to me. Only do so without delay."

The man moved toward the door. "I'll see to it," he muttered sullenly. "But don't be pullin' the place down about our ears. Sir Thomas won't be pleased."

As the man left, Elen stepped down from her stool to pace the floor in an agony of apprehension. What if Richard knew about Owain? Her old friend would never leave here alive. And Richard might even know her identity. There were a handful of individuals who knew she was Elen of Teifi, but they could be trusted. Of course, even the strongest man might break under torture.

The minutes crawled by. Gradually the noise and confusion in the bailey subsided. Elen tried not to think what might be happening to Owain. Even now his life might be slipping away.

After what seemed like hours, she recognized the sound of Richard's footsteps in the corridor outside. Strange, she thought abstractedly, that one man's tread should be so different from all others, that after even this short time, she should know his step well.

Richard swung open the door and moved a few paces into the room. He was dirty and bloodstained and a scratch the width of three fingers marred his tanned cheek. He had removed his hauberk and gauntlets, but it was obvious he had come to her without bothering to wash.

Elen searched his face for any sign of the gentleness she had seen a week ago, but the search was in vain. Richard's mouth was compressed in a hard line, and his eyes were dark and cold as the ice that forms in the deepest mountain pools during the bitterest winters.

He came to a halt in the center of the floor, arms crossed

before him, legs half spread as if bracing himself for battle. "I find you a woman of many talents, Elen," he remarked coldly. "I wonder when I shall cease to be amazed. Soldier, whore, and quite the consummate actress . . . oh, did I forget to commend you on your most convincing performance last week? You were magnificent. I almost believed you were as innocent as you pretended."

He paused, his green eyes raking her contemptuously. "And now Hugh tells me you speak English as one born to it. I wonder what might be so important you reveal this secret now. What pressing news must you impart?" One hand swung down to caress the hilt of his dagger. "Tell me, was last week not enough, or did you lure me here to have another try?"

Elen didn't flinch from the caustic bite of his words. She had to discover what Richard knew. Only then would she know what to do . . . if there was anything left to hope for. Ignoring his question, she motioned toward the window. "It appears your trap was not successful. I see no sign of the notorious Welsh Fox." She studied Richard carefully, searching for any flicker of emotion betraying his thoughts. "Did you really think our Rhys would fall for such a ploy? I warned you he was no such fool."

Richard shrugged. "No, we didn't take the Fox. I believed he might think you worth saving, but obviously he knew you better than I. You spoke the truth when you said you were nothing to him." He turned and walked to the fire, bending to stir up the dying coals. "But my men and I found good sport just the same. We were attacked by a ragged bunch of Welshmen."

Straightening to his full, commanding height, Richard turned back to her with a dark smile. "Your people were a bit surprised, though, by the reception they received. They say in my country that the only good Welshmen are corpses. If the words be truth, we left many a good Welshman behind."

Elen pressed her sweating palms against the rough wool of her tunic. God, how many more of her friends were dead? She could well imagine that scene of carnage after Owain's ambush, but she dared not allow herself to think of it now. Richard obviously didn't know who Owain was, but he was enjoying baiting her. She had roused his ire and he would probably see Owain dead now if only to spite her. He would teach her the folly of her effort to best him and enjoy doing it.

"I sought to take your life and you are angry . . . and rightly so," she said softly. "Use me as you will. Punish me. But by God's mercy don't take out your anger on the man you have below."

Richard felt a sudden flicker of interest. He gazed narrowly at Elen. Her blue eyes were pained and anxious. She tugged nervously at a strand of hair, then shoved it over her shoulder with an impatient movement of her hand. It was obvious she cared for his prisoner—she cared a great deal. It was a weapon he had not counted on.

His thoughts turned bitterly on how he might use the knowledge. He had returned from this short campaign still furious with both himself and the girl. He had been far too soft on her, allowing himself to let down his guard with an enemy he should have distrusted instinctively. And she had used his softness and his desire, playing him for a fool. She was as treacherous as the most conniving of her race, only far more dangerous because of her seductive beauty.

She was just like Jeanne. His beautiful stepmother had used her face and body to bewitch his father until the man could see naught save what she desired him to see. He hadn't even noticed the bitch was destroying his own son.

Richard's fingers clenched convulsively. He had been a boy determined to succeed, and that boy had prevailed. He had triumphed in spite of Jeanne and his greedy half-brother, or perhaps because of them. They had driven him to harden himself, to become stronger than they. But God, he hated devious women!

He stared at Elen, determined she would find him soft no longer. "That man led the ambush yesterday," he said harshly. "He attacked me with the ferocity of ten demons. Though not the prey I sought, he is a rebel leader and I was pleased to take him." He shrugged his shoulders as if suddenly bored by the conversation. "But this discussion is pointless, Elen. The man's wounds will most likely be his end. And if they aren't, I'll be pleased to show you how I reward rebels."

Staring at Richard's impassive countenance, Elen faced the final, full bitterness of defeat. She could not fight Richard—God had cursed her with this frail woman's body that could not match her enemy for strength—and there were no more tricks to try. She moved across the floor toward him, swallowing against the tight constriction in her throat. If she had to beg, she would do it. Let Richard mock her if he chose. There was nothing left to do.

"The man you hold. He . . . he is my uncle," she got out. "He has helped care for me since I was a babe. If he heard the story your men put about, he would have risked all to save me. He is no danger to you. By the mercy of God, let him live!"

Richard lifted his eyebrows in wry amusement. "No danger to me? You've obviously not seen the man with a sword, Elen. He's a bit more proficient with the weapon than you."

He was mocking her and she longed to strike him. Instead, sliding slowly to her knees, she bowed the head she had always held so proudly. Praise God her father had not lived to see her thus! "Please, Richard . . . I beg of you."

Richard merely stared at her, unmoved.

She took a deep breath, swallowing hard. "M-my lord. Grant me the life of my uncle, I beg of you." The words were difficult—she thought she must choke on them, and a burning ache in her throat warned of pressing tears. "At least let me see to his wounds. I will ask for naught else, I'll cause no trouble. Anything you ask of me, I will do, I swear . . . *anything!*" she cried out. "Only grant me his life."

Richard frowned. A moment ago, he had wanted to see the girl beaten and begging before him, had thought of little else these last few days. But now the sight of her pleading touched him. Merciful heaven, what did he want?

The answer came on a wave of unreasoning anger. God help him, he still wanted her. He was more a fool than any man he knew! "Get up," he snarled. "*Get . . . up!*"

Grasping Elen's arm, he jerked her roughly to her feet. "A convincing performance, but pray pardon me if I don't believe you this time. You gave just such a performance last week, and I near lost my life!"

Jerking the girl close, he forced her chin up with unrelenting fingers. "You forget, sweetheart, you have nothing to bargain with. You will do exactly as I wish because you must—because you've no other choice. I can force you to my bidding any time, and I suggest you remember that. My mistake came in showing you the same courtesy I would offer a civilized woman of my own country. I forgot you were simply a beautiful savage. But I won't make the mistake again."

He slid one arm about Elen's narrow waist, drawing her hips to press suggestively against him. How in heaven's name could he still ache for her? How could he still desire this woman so he could think of little else even now when he was so weary with fighting and blood his very muscles screamed with exhaustion?

The answer to his dilemma was simple enough and any other man would have sought it long hence. The girl was an enemy who had twice sought his end. She deserved to die for her treachery, but he would be merciful. He would simply enjoy the use of her until the fire left his blood, then send her from his sight. She had no hold on him save that of thwarted desire.

He twisted her face up closer to his. "You see, Elen, I don't have to ask anything of you. From this time on, I will simply take what I want without regard to your feelings. Do you understand?"

Elen felt the hate rising up inside her like a physical ache. Richard's arms tightened around her, crushing her against him. His mouth lowered slowly to hers and the kiss was far worse than she'd expected. He did not tease her into acceptance this time, but coldly forced her lips to part for his in a vivid demonstration of his power to use her.

She forced herself to stand straight and unresisting in his arms. If she struggled, she told herself, he would only enjoy hurting her more.

The kiss continued—brutal, punishing, a pledge of his treatment to come. But from nowhere, the memory of the intensely pleasurable way Richard had kissed her before swept through her and the threatening tears crowded close against her lids. There was no comparing Richard's treatment today to that incomprehensible thing that had happened in his arms before.

When he finally lifted his head, Elen felt bruised and shaken. Slowly she opened her eyes. "I hate you, Richard Basset," she whispered, staring up into his sun-bronzed face. "I will hate you with the last breath in my body. And never will you make me beg for anything again! Never! If there is a God in heaven, I will see you pay for what you've done."

"You're confused, Elen," Richard remarked coldly. "The payment must be yours. And you are about to render up a full accounting for your treachery."

"My treachery?" She shook her head. "You dare speak to me of treachery?" She gave a near-hysterical laugh. "My father and brother are dead because of you—murdered at Builth at the hands of English soldiers so mad for blood, they couldn't content themselves with simply killing their enemies. No! They must needs hack brave men to pieces and behead helpless corpses!"

Her voice rose shrilly, and she realized she was rapidly

losing control. "My mother died after Builth from cold and
starvation in the mountains where we fled. The mountains
where you drove us to hide out like wild animals. And my
friend died in childbirth there, unable even to scream out
her agony because we stuffed rags between her teeth, fearing
her cries would bring you down upon our camp.

"And this month . . . this month I am turned seventeen,
Richard," she continued in a flood of bitter words she could
not stem. "This month I would have wed a man I have
worshiped for so long as I have memory. But you ended
that dream—you, Richard! You took his life at Builth!"

Elen had lost the battle for composure and tears coursed
hotly down her cheeks in a torrent she made no effort to
restrain. Catching Richard's powerful hand, she pressed it
to his sword hilt. "With this hand and this sword you ended
everything I dreamed of a lifetime ago. Go on, finish it!"
she shouted. "Let Owain die untended in a dark hole in
the earth. Go on, make an end of us all. Punish me for my
treachery if that's what you want! I cannot fight you any
longer. You have proven your might. Go on, it's easy for
you! So easy for a *brave, honorable knight* of England."

Jerking away from Richard's loosened grasp, she moved
blindly away from him to the opposite wall. "My God, you
sicken me! You English all sicken me," she bit out. Then
the last vestiges of control slipped away, and she crumpled
to the floor in a flood of hysterical sobbing.

Richard stared at Elen and then at his hand. He was
stunned by the hatred that had spewed from the girl, but
he was even more amazed by her tears. Elen had never
wept, not even when Giles had held a burning knife to her
flesh.

Moving slowly across the floor, he bent and lifted Elen
into his arms. She tried to push away. "Leave me be," she
choked. "For God's sake, either slay me now or leave me
be!"

"Hush," Richard murmured. "Hush now. I'll not hurt

you." He strode to the bed, easing her down onto one side so that she lay facing him. Her gaze held his, her great tear-filled eyes brimming with accusation, her sweet, ripe mouth red and swollen from his bruising kiss. Remorse filled him. He had come perilously close to being the savage he so despised in others, to treating her as the women of his own people had once been treated by conquering Norman soldiers.

Reaching out one hand, he stroked the damp tangle of hair back from Elen's face, suddenly wishing he had met her earlier, that they might have known each other before so much lay between them. With a heavy sigh, he drew the bed fur around her shaking shoulders.

"We are at war, Elen, your people and mine, and I am only a man—not a god," he began softly. "It is difficult to judge right and wrong in war . . . impossible in the heat of battle. All my life, I've been trained to fight and kill, and I'm judged good at it. And may God forgive me, I even enjoy the testing of my strength and wit against another. I make no apologies for what I did at Builth. I killed many men who strove to kill me. If they had been stronger, I would have fallen and you would not now be cursed with me." He drew a deep breath. "But when I found men mutilating corpses, Elen, I hanged them. That I promise you. When the battle is over, honorable men forget their savagery."

His right hand rested against her throat, his thumb gently caressing her tear-stained cheek. "No, Elen," he repeated, "I make no apology for Builth. But out of my own misplaced pride, I have wronged you now. Forgive me if you can."

He stared at her a moment, but the girl didn't speak. Suddenly he longed to be away from the hatred and accusation in her eyes, to be outside in the cleansing wind and fresh air. With one last glance at the huddled figure on the bed, he hurried from the room, ignoring the curious stares of the guards outside the doorway.

When Richard entered the hall a few moments later, his men were busy eating and more than a dozen still sat waiting to have their wounds tended by the overworked castle leech. He moved through them in a daze, his mind still wrestling with what had happened above.

From his youth, he had prided himself on being fair to his enemies, on refusing to take advantage of those weaker than himself. But wound his pride and he could descend to the status of savage as quickly as the lowest soldier.

Giles caught his arm. "Richard? What is it?"

Richard shook his head, barely taking note of his friend. "Let be. I'm going outside for a walk."

"A walk? You're so exhausted you're stumbling now." Giles's grip tightened. "It's the girl, isn't it? The wound isn't healing. Don't tell me you found her worse than before!"

Richard shook off his friend's hand. "No. I suppose it's healing. I didn't think to ask." Turning, he headed once more for the door. Simon sprang up to follow, but Richard gestured him away. "No. I desire no company. But Giles..." He looked back at his friend, and pointed at Owain, saying, "Have *that* wounded prisoner carried upstairs. And see the girl has anything she needs to tend him."

Frowning, he ran a weary hand through his hair. "The man's name is Owain," he told Giles in a strained voice. "And I only pray he lasts the night."

CHAPTER TWELVE

$\mathcal{F}$or some time after Richard left, Elen continued to sob out her grief. All the months of pent-up bitterness and frustration, the fears she had tried so desperately to hide, came pouring forth in a torrent of soul-cleansing tears. She was alone, so terrifyingly alone.

And no matter her determination, she was utterly helpless. She had done naught to help her people nor could she move Richard concerning Owain's plight. And now she couldn't even control her own wretched tears. She was ashamed of such weakness, especially before her enemy. Her father would have laughed at her for one of those "weepy-eyed females" he so despised.

But what did it matter? Her father was dead, and soon Owain would be too.

Slowly Elen's sobs spent themselves. She stared up at the low-beamed ceiling, heavily blackened by years of smoke from the hearth and burning rushlights. Was there anything left to hope for, anything even to try?

Where there was life there was hope. The saying was a favorite of Owain's, and comforting somehow. He had repeated it to her on so many occasions when her spirits were lagging and victory seemed impossible. As she shoved the damp hair out of her eyes, her thoughts went back to Richard. He held Owain's life in his hand—but just what had Richard said about his prisoner? He had been surprisingly gentle after her tears, but had he left her any hope? She tried to remember.

Suddenly she sat bolt upright. Had she told Richard too much? Had she said aught in that frightened, furious tirade that could betray Owain or herself? Was that the reason Richard had grown so thoughtful, so kind? Jesu forbid! The last thing she wanted was to fall into Edward's hands. Even Richard of Kent was preferable to the King of England. Holy Mary, Mother of God, help her guard her foolish tongue!

The realization that she preferred Richard to Edward was staggering. Richard of Kent was her most hated enemy—Enion's murderer. She had even sworn a blood oath to see him destroyed. So why should she now think of him as any less a devil than Edward?

Because he was just.

Just? She could expect no justice from an Englishman, she told herself furiously. Richard led a force of foreign invaders bent on conquering Welsh soil for the simple reason that they were strong enough to do it. They burned and slaughtered without remorse, without quarter. And Richard had just bragged about it, she reminded herself. He had told her he had no apology to make for Builth.

But he had not slain his helpless prisoners as most men would have done. And he had not punished her, even though she so richly deserved it, a small nagging voice reminded.

Footsteps sounded outside. Elen dashed a hand across her eyes and slid from the bed.

The door swung open and the dark knight called Giles stepped into the room. Three men filed in behind him, supporting Owain's unconscious form. Elen's eyes widened in disbelief. A miracle!

* * *

Richard sank wearily onto his narrow cot in Beaufort's great hall. The fire in the raised central fireplace had already been banked for the night, and all about him, men were making ready for bed or were already slumped on straw pallets in exhaustion.

"Richard, hand me your sword and I'll give it a quick cleaning. I fear it grew damp when you were out this afternoon."

Richard glanced up at his squire. Simon was a good lad, scrupulous in his duties. And the boy was right. Steel rusted quickly in this wretched climate.

Richard slid his sword from its leather sheath, staring narrowly at the cold, glittering steel. The sight reminded him of Elen and her furious accusations this afternoon. Just how many men had he slain in the last twelve years? He had no idea.

He turned the sword in his hands, watching the play of firelight on fine metal. This blade had served him well, and he felt no real regret. He had lived his life as honorably as he was able, allowing his enemy quarter when he could— bringing the end swiftly when he could not. And even the worst of his detractors at court admitted he was a fair man . . . sometimes foolishly so.

He pursed his lips thoughtfully. But now Elen had reminded him that corpses were men. They had mothers and sweethearts who grieved, wives and children left alone and unprotected by their deaths—dangerous thoughts for a fighting man to dwell on.

Recalling his actions at Builth, he sought to conjure up the hoard of faceless enemies he had fought. Which had been the one dear to the girl, and how in God's name did she know it was he who had taken the man's life? Surely she had not been present at that scene of destruction.

The battle had been bloody, for of all England's enemies, the Welsh were the fiercest. And even Edward's usually sleeping Plantagenet temper had been roused by Llywelyn's unprovoked rebellion. After the battle, when the head of the fallen Welsh prince had been brought before him, Edward had coolly ordered the grisly prize planted on a pike to frown down at the English from the Tower of London. A crown of ivy had been placed upon the bloody head, further mockery of the ancient prophecy that a Llywelyn would wear the crown of all Britain.

No, Richard didn't blame the girl and her people for hating him and all his countrymen. In some perverse way, he respected her for it. If their positions had been reversed, she would have fought for Edward with the same dogged determination. Elen's loyalties were those of a soldier for his lord—something Richard understood well. But it was the first time he had happened upon such sentiments in a woman. Save for Edward's queen, Eleanor, Richard's experience of females had led him to believe the weaker sex had few such noble sentiments.

"Richard?"

He glanced up at Simon in surprise. He'd almost forgotten the boy. "Sorry, lad. I was just . . . thinking."

Simon nodded and reached for the proffered sword, his blue eyes filled with concern. "I'll just be a minute. I'll put it back here by your side when I'm done. Don't wait. Go on to sleep now."

A wry grin lightened Richard's face. "I look as bad as that, eh? Well, don't be long. I'll wager you could use some sleep as well."

Simon headed across the hall, and Richard lay back in exhaustion. He couldn't remember ever being so tired—in body or spirit. No doubt that was the reason Elen's words bothered him so. He was sorry for the pain he'd brought her, but what matter the feelings of one insignificant woman? England would conquer Wales—Christ's blood, had already! And he would finish the task he was sworn to, no matter his growing sympathy for a beaten people who refused to admit defeat.

Closing his eyes, he forced himself to relax, slowly releasing the tension from days of constant battle alert. The sooner he ended the Welsh resistance, the better, he reminded himself. Once this rebellion was over, a lasting peace might grow between the countries. Edward promised to do well by his enemies who put down their swords. He was not a vindictive ruler save when his temper was roused. And for all their mutual hatred, his country and Elen's might someday be at peace. Yes, he decided, even in the midst of war, a warrior might hope for peace.

With the thought, sleep claimed him.

"M'lord."

Richard was instantly awake and grabbing for his sword.

The man touched his arm. "No cause for alarm. 'Tis only myself, sir."

Richard stared up at his burly guard captain in dawning recognition. For a moment he had thought himself under Welsh attack. He drew a steadying breath and glanced around the room. It was dark in the hall, but the faint gray light sifting through the narrow window slits and the sound of servants stirring behind the pantry screen told him day was dawning.

Henry Bloet cleared his throat. "Pardon, sir, for wakin' ye, but I dared delay no further. Robert of Sherbourne"— he jerked his head toward the stair—"de Waurin's man above, says the girl's been askin' for ye this hour past."

Richard rubbed the sleep from his eyes with a clumsy fist. "I suppose the Welshman died in the night. I thought he'd not last."

Henry shook his head. "The man lives still. Leastways he did near an hour ago when Robert woke me."

Richard glanced up in surprise. Why would Elen send for him? After yesterday, he'd have thought she'd leave him be.

"I . . . I hated ta wake ye, sir, seein' the sleep was on ye so heavy," the older man continued apologetically. "I told Robert I'd see to it at first light and no sooner. And I'd not be disturbin' ye now if I'd not heard Sir Giles say ye had interest in the prisoner."

"It's all right, Henry. I've slept enough. But fetch me a mug of ale from the buttery."

Henry nodded and moved away, threading a careful path through the maze of sleeping knights and squires toward the partition screening the darkened pantry and buttery at one end of the great hall. Richard reached for his boots, then buckled his sword into place.

"What's afoot?" Giles asked softly.

Richard glanced down at his friend. Giles had raised himself from his pallet on one elbow, but in the dim light Richard couldn't make out his face.

"Elen wishes to speak to me. I suppose I should go."

Giles sat up and reached for his sword. "Then I'm coming too."

"If I need you, I'll call. For Christ's sake, Giles, get another hour of sleep while you can."

Giles frowned. "Richard, on the Marches we speak of Welsh blood feuds. Have you heard of them?"

Richard nodded.

"It's warfare on a different level from ours—something the Welsh take quite seriously. When a kinsman is slain, it's up to a family member to avenge the death. I've seen them wait years, generations even, to exact their revenge. But they always do, Richard, they always do—even after seeming to live in peace with the enemy for lengthy periods." Giles rose from his pallet. "From what you told me earlier, Elen holds you responsible for the deaths of her family. And that's something you'd best think on."

Richard slipped his dagger into his belt. "Would you have me afraid of a woman?" he snapped irritably.

"No, but I'd have you remember who she is." Giles hesitated a moment, then stared at Richard pointedly. "With a woman like that it's too easy for a man to forget."

"I won't forget. To my sorrow, I've already learned that particular lesson." Richard turned thankfully from his friend to take the mug of ale Henry had returned with. He drank it down in a few swallows, then handed the mug back. Without another word, he moved to the open hearth and grabbed up a stubby tallow candle. Lighting it in the sluggish fire, he made his way across the hall and into the darkness of the stairway.

When Richard reached the upstairs solar, he hesitated, then swung open the door and moved inside. The room was well lit by the blazing fire in the fireplace and a pair of rushlights burning near the bed. Elen had dragged the single heavy chair to the bedside and was slumped against its back, her forehead resting on her hands, her chestnut hair a shimmering silken curtain reaching to the floor. At his entrance, she rose to her feet.

Richard blew out his candle and moved stiffly across the floor. "I was told you wanted to speak to me."

"I . . . I didn't think you'd come," she said softly. "I asked for you hours ago."

"My men are overzealous of my welfare. They only now awakened me."

"Oh." Elen turned back to the bed, her eyes anxiously tracing the features of the unconscious man before her. "Without the proper care, my uncle will die . . . perhaps even with care," she began hesitantly. "He's lost much blood and the wounds fester. I need herbs and roots, certain potions I can mix to draw the poison from his body and help him rest. But I've little with which to work."

Richard stared down at the wounded man lying so pale and still on the great bed. The man, Owain, was beyond help, but Elen refused to acknowledge it. Despite Richard's effort to remain untouched, he felt a stirring of pity. The man had been a valiant fighter and was obviously dear to the girl. But perhaps it was best this way after all. At least the Welshman would die a warrior's death rather than pine away in some hellhole of a dungeon. "I doubt there is aught anyone can do to save him now, Elen," he said gently, "but I will send up the leech if you desire it."

She swung around to face him, her blue eyes desperate, beseeching. "But it might not be too late, Richard! With the right care, Owain may yet live. I've skill with healing—more so than your leech. Give me leave to fetch what I need outside the wall. I can gather what I require in the nearby woodland and marsh in scarce an hour or two. I'll even use my skill to care for your wounded if you wish it."

Richard frowned and shook his head. Elen must think him little wiser than a babe. She knew the man was dying and thought to use this ruse to escape. There must be little sincere feeling in all her treacherous heart, yet how convincing she appeared. "You've tricked me before, but don't think to do so again," he said curtly. "You'll not leave Beaufort until I allow it, so think no more on ways to best me."

Elen stared up at him, her eyes wide and earnest in the pale oval of her face. "This is no trick, Richard, I swear it on my father's honor. I need rock moss and sage, leaves of rowan, and another half-dozen ingredients if I can find them. If I thought your people would fetch the right thing, I would ask that you send them. As it is, I must go myself. But come with me if you suspect a trick," she added desperately. "Bring the whole garrison if you wish! Only give me leave to save the only kinsman I have left."

Staring down at the girl, Richard felt a ridiculous urge to give in to her pleading. The Welshman would probably die no matter their efforts, but at least he could feel he had done all in his power to treat the girl fairly. And he could accompany her to make certain she didn't simply disappear. "I put little faith in your father's honor, even less in your own protestations," he said dryly. "But I do have men who might benefit from your care—if your promise to help can be believed." He gestured to the coffer. "Fetch your cloak. It'll be chilly outside at this hour."

Elen closed her eyes briefly, her rigid body relaxing with his words. When she opened her eyes again they shone up at him through a suspicious sheen of tears. "Thank you. I swear you'll not be sorry." Moving across the floor, she caught up the fox cloak. "Could someone stay with my uncle until I return? He may need something."

Richard nodded grimly. By the look of matters, the only thing the Welshman needed was the last rites.

Elen followed Richard from the solar, and in a short time they were outside the castle palisade in the damp morning air. Away to the east, the sun was just lifting above the gilded forest roof in a stunning blaze of crimson and gold, while all about them the meadow grass was decked with dew-bejeweled webs that looked for all the world like priceless necklaces fit to dower a queen.

She drew in great lungfuls of the damp, fresh air, reveling in the freedom of wide gray skies and an unobstructed horizon. And in spite of her worries, her spirits began to rise. Richard had been obliging, far more so than she had dared hope. And, praise God, Owain was still breathing. With skill and care he might live.

She glanced at the man who walked by her side, the man who had struck Owain down, then made it possible for her to tend him. She wondered anew at his forbearance. He had ordered near three dozen men out of their warm beds to guard her on this ramble. Richard obviously didn't trust her, but she couldn't blame him. After all she had done, he would be a fool to do so—and Richard of Kent was certainly no fool.

"You must think me very fierce," she remarked, glancing back at the heavily armed men moving behind them.

"I put some value on my own life, and I've no doubt you've friends out there in the trees," Richard replied lightly. "I wouldn't put it beyond you to be leading me into an ambush even now."

Elen smiled. If only she did have men waiting! "Not that

I know of," she remarked, matching his own wry tone. "But one might always hope, I suppose."

Richard grinned. "You've no idea what comfort you give me, Elen, but I think I'll keep the escort just the same."

"Well, I promised I would not trick you," she reminded him. "Nothing more."

"Yes, and so you promised Giles the night of our raid. And before I knew what was happening you'd armed your friend and I was like to lose one of my best knights. I'm fast learning how you Welsh keep a pledge."

Elen shook her head. Why was it so difficult for these English to understand? "I swore I would not escape and I kept my word—though I could have done it easily enough in the confusion that night. I said nothing about not helping the others." She raised her chin in a haughty gesture. "I keep my word, Englishman!"

Richard's grin widened but he said nothing.

"Besides," she continued, "your knight was never in danger. The man was naught but a messenger I used to send word to my uncle and warn him away." Her face darkened for a moment. "I feared he might do something foolish to save me."

"As he did?"

She glanced up, frowning. "Yes . . . as he did."

The party entered the edge of the woodland where lingering night shadows still darkened the forest floor. Elen slowed her stride, reminding herself why she was here. There were certain plants that held healing properties and she had often helped Tangwen seek them out for the folk of Teifi. Focusing her eyes on the ground, she began to search for the necessary items.

Richard followed her in silence. He watched as she knelt to pluck some leaves or scratch up a root, placing them carefully in an earthenware bowl a servant had fetched from the kitchen.

"How came you to speak my language so well?"

The words were unexpected. Elen almost dropped the bowl.

"You speak both English and French fluently . . . and not with any coarse mannerisms either. Almost as one educated at court," Richard added thoughtfully.

Elen knelt to inspect a plant she knew had no healing properties. "We Welsh are not such ignorant savages as you believe," she replied, buying time by studying the leaves. "My father was one of the Prince of Powys's men, so we were often at Powis Castle where Englishmen came and went. The priest there discovered in me an eager pupil and delighted in teaching me. My learning pleased my father and so I continued." That, at least, was true. She rose to her feet and met Richard's gaze. "There is no mystery in it. I even read a few phrases in Latin, though not so well as I would like," she added, taking a chance.

Richard nodded, still appraising her intently. "You surprise me, Elen. You are not like other women."

Elen's arched brows lifted. "Oh? And do you know so many other Welsh women?"

"No, not Welsh women," Richard admitted with a smile. "But tell me. Do your countrywomen all read Latin and handle sword and dagger so well as you?"

Elen stared down at her hands, hands that were red and work roughened, hands that reminded her suddenly of all the grief of the year past. Her voice took on an icy edge. "They do if they must. Need is a stern master and we have few men left to assist us. You have seen to that."

The brief truce between them was obviously at an end. "I see," Richard replied, disappointment sharpening his voice.

They continued in strained silence, but Richard was thankful when the girl had all the ingredients she required and they could return to the keep. Giles was right—he should stay away from her. Somehow Elen's beauty made it difficult to keep thought of Welsh blood feuds uppermost in mind.

CHAPTER THIRTEEN

"*F*or mercy's sake, Elen, cease this foolish scheming!"

Elen bit off her words and stared at Owain in surprise. He had closed his eyes, and his pale, weathered face was etched with weariness. And he looked old, far older than she remembered. Perhaps she had talked too long. After all, his fever had broken just yesterday, and he was still weak. But after these past days of worry, she was so buoyant with the knowledge he would live, she had unwisely prattled on the entire morning.

She leaned forward over the bed, tenderly stroking the dark, graying hair from Owain's lined forehead. "I'm sorry, my friend. I fear in my happiness my tongue runs on wheels. You are still much too weak to plot with me today."

Owain's gray eyes opened wide, and he lifted a hand above the covers to catch Elen's wrist. "I'm weak, yes, but my mind is not affected." He brought her hand into his own, twining his rough, callused fingers around her slender ones. "We must face the truth, Elen. I've never known you to hide your face from it before. Even if our enemies don't know I'm the Welsh Fox, my life is forfeit. I led an attack on an English commander and that fate deserves the harshest of punishments. The Wolf has simply spared me a few last hours to spend with you. A boon I thank God for."

Elen shook her head stubbornly, unable to believe the resignation in her old friend's voice. In all their years together, she had never known Owain to give up. He was as persistent as a battering ram, her father had always said, and nearly as single-minded in purpose. "You're alive and we must work to keep you so. I'm not so certain Richard will have you put to death, but if that is his intention we'll simply escape before he can do so." Her fingers tightened about his. "We can do it, Owain. We'll make it to France. You know, together we've always been able to do anything we set our minds to!"

Owain shook his head. "Not this time, Elen. I'm sorry to fail you, but I've not the strength of a lamb. Even if we could overcome the guards with one of your tricks, I doubt I could make it down the stairs, much less find a way over the wall to safety. For once an impossible thing you ask of me is truly beyond both my body and will."

He took a deep breath as if gathering strength. "I'm not afraid to die, Elen. 'Tis a thing a fighting man learns early to face. My only regret—my only real fear is in leaving you without protection. I've failed in my pledge to your lord father. I've not taken such care of you as I should have liked."

He gazed up at her, one hand lifting to touch her cheek. "You were the daughter I never had, you know. Since you were old enough to toddle about your father's keep, I've looked on you as my own. And it's a bitter thing to leave you in the hands of our enemies." His arm fell helplessly to his side. "Christ, I'd rather see you dead by my own hand than in Richard Basset's power!"

Elen clasped his hand between both of hers, searching for words of comfort. "It's not as you think, Owain. Richard of Kent is not as the tales of him have led us to believe. He . . . he seems an honorable man."

She hesitated a moment, trying to put the conflicting images of their enemy into words. "Oh, he's a powerful soldier, true enough. And he can be harsh," she added thoughtfully. "I've seen him so. But he doesn't kill for the joy of killing as so many of the English do. And after a battle, I've seen him show mercy. He can even be gentle at times. I thought him only foolish at first, but that is far from the truth."

She frowned and bit her lip, conjuring up the tall English knight in all his recent moods. "And he hasn't harmed me though I've goaded him beyond what most men would bear. I've tricked him at every opportunity and twice tried to kill him. Any other man would have put me to death for such treachery."

Owain snorted. "No man in his right mind would put a woman such as you to death, Elen. I find little reassurance in such mercy as that. You're right, Richard Basset is no fool!"

"Very well, then," she responded, meeting his cynical gaze coolly. "Though I know he desires me, he has not forced me into his bed. He has treated me honorably even though he thinks me naught but a camp follower and the leman of this imaginary Rhys."

"You think highly enough of the man," Owain accused. "Are you forgetting the misery he's caused? Merciful Father, I've seen him at work. He lays waste our people like a veritable fiend!"

"No, I don't forget what he's done. How could I?" Elen snapped, stung. "I don't defend him and I will never forgive him Enion's death. Never!" She drew a deep breath, seeking to compose her unsettled feelings. "I'm only saying he's given me reason to hope he might spare your life. He doesn't seek to wipe us off the earth like some plague to be destroyed. And I'll not let him put you to death. I won't!" she added vehemently.

"Elen, don't be a—"

The sound of footsteps outside the door halted Owain's words. The door swung open and a serving woman entered with a tray of food. Richard's golden head ducked through the low doorway behind her. He walked toward them, halting as the woman placed the tray on the bedside table. With a quick glance at the impassive knight, the woman curtsied from the room.

"I see your attentions have been rewarded, Elen. Giles told me your uncle was much recovered." Richard hesitated. "I don't know that it will please you, but the men you tended below are also doing well. Sir William sends his thanks for easing the pain of his shoulder so quickly."

Elen nodded. For some inexplicable reason her earlier defense of Richard had made her uncomfortable. "I kept my part of the bargain," she said stiffly.

Richard shifted to study the man on the bed. "Does your kinsman speak English?"

"Owain speaks French and some limited English, though not so well as I."

Richard sent her a hard look, one tawny eyebrow quirking upward questioningly. "And is that the truth?"

She blushed angrily. "Yes, it's the truth! What profit a lie in this?"

"I haven't the slightest idea. You seem to make up the rules as you go along." Without another word to her, Richard addressed himself to Owain in French. "I am Richard Basset, knight of your sovereign lord, Edward of England, and commander of the English force in Gwynedd. You have committed a grievous crime in taking arms against England, and for this act I now hold you prisoner. You are obviously a leader in this rebellion, and it is within my rights to put you to death. What say you now?"

Elen began to protest, but Owain silenced her with a single sharp word. Richard waited, arms crossed, as the Welshman slowly raised himself against the bolster.

"I am Owain ap Cynan, man of Ald—" He glanced at Elen. "Man of the late Lord of Powys. I yield myself as your prisoner and recognize your right to take my life—as I would take yours if the fates had ruled differently." His hard gray eyes held Richard's unwaveringly. "But I will never recognize Edward of England as my king. No true Welshman would do so. Now do as you will with me for I am grown old in service to my lord and have already lived to see things I've no wish to. I request only the mercy of a priest before my end."

Elen's hand crept out, clasping Owain's fingers nervously. Her eyes lifted to Richard's. "What will you do with him?"

Richard's green eyes narrowed, but whether in anger or thought, she couldn't determine. "To be truthful, I haven't decided," he replied slowly. "It will depend on a great many things. If your uncle continues in this vein, however, I will have little choice."

Elen slipped to her feet, speaking rapidly in English. "Would you put a mother to death for defending her child . . . a father for protecting his daughter? Owain has stood in place of both to me for a long time. You put out the tale I was ill-treated here. It is you who are responsible for his attack! What kind of man would sit idly by without lifting a hand to protect his family? Would you, Richard? Would you stand by and let an enemy abuse your wife or mother or sister?"

Richard said nothing and Elen studied his dark face. Her voice dropped. "I think not, Richard," she said softly. "I think you would fight to the death for those you loved."

Owain said something in Welsh, but Elen bit him off with a few sharp words in the same tongue. Despite the seriousness of the moment, Richard smiled. It didn't appear Elen was an obedient female even in her own family. "I will think on it, Elen, that is all I can promise you now. My decision will depend a great deal on your uncle himself."

He turned and moved toward the door, pausing a moment as he lifted the latch. "On tomorrow next we leave for Gwenlyn Keep, so be ready to travel. I've delayed too long already over this affair and our supplies grow short."

"You . . . you will take us with you?"

Richard nodded. "Yes. I haven't yet decided what to do—with either of you."

Closing the door behind him, Richard made his way down the narrow twisting stair. Just what did he intend to do with the man and the girl? The man deserved to die. And so he would if he couldn't bend to the will of his new sovereign. But Elen's words had touched him. In truth, Richard had brought Owain's fierce attack upon himself by putting that story about. Only it was another enemy he had hoped to snare in the shadowy Welsh woodlands. And could he really put a man to death for attempting to rescue his kinswoman? The answer was no if that was the man's only crime.

And what of Elen? He wasn't about to release her, not yet. He had held her barely a fortnight and the Welsh were known to be patient. But what if he continued to hold her? Might not the Welsh Fox grow impatient and come for her? After all, it must rankle with Rhys to know his mistress was in the keeping of his enemy.

But that was the only reason for his decision, Richard assured himself. He took no personal interest in the girl beyond the simple need of a man long without the pleasure of a woman.

The vision of Margaret of Chester rose before him in all her blond loveliness. The woman was as different from Elen as day and night—far more like his past mistresses. Yes, he'd been too long without a woman, he admitted. But that was a condition he would remedy soon enough.

Elen winced as the rough supply cart jolted over a ridge of rock and shuddered into another mudhole. She had forgotten how uncomfortable a plodding trip by ox cart could be, and her leg still hurt a great deal. Owain gave a low groan as two men-at-arms put their shoulders to the iron-bound cart wheel and wrenched it free from the sucking muck. She leaned forward and touched his arm. "We're almost there," she whispered. "Giles told me we should reach the English fortress by nightfall. Can you stand the pain till then? It should be only a few more hours."

Owain smiled mirthlessly. "Have I another choice, little one?"

Despite her worry, Elen smiled at the use of the old pet name. "No . . . not unless you wish me to toss you over the side of the next cliff."

"A happy prospect." Owain closed his eyes wearily. "Let me think on it."

Elen leaned against a sack of grain at her back, trying to find ease from the jolting motion. It had been a miserable five days of travel, a journey made more daunting by the bone-chilling rain that had drenched them both yesterday and the day before. And the party had made even worse time today than on all the days before.

The mounted soldiers about them had fretted openly at the slow travel, but they dared not leave the valuable supply train until it successfully negotiated the mountain passes near the coast. It was just the kind of opportunity the Welsh would be waiting for.

Elen frowned as she caught a glimpse of Richard's banner far ahead through the misty green of new-leafed trees. He was riding Moroedd this afternoon. He was actually riding her horse! And the knowledge of her helplessness to stop him had fanned the flames of her bitterness.

Moments later, as if to further goad her temper, Richard flashed by on the narrow trail, the gray stallion straining at the bit and occasionally kicking up as he sought to get the better of the unfamiliar rider on his back. But Richard held him in easily, curbing the animal's natural exuberance and forcing him to a controlled canter.

Under her breath, Elen cursed the Englishman and all his ancestors, calling on her favorite saint to send the man sprawling in the mud. How she would laugh at the sight!

And she wouldn't even care if Richard beat her for it. Surely any good Welsh saint would sympathize with her prayer.

But her fervent petition went unanswered. Richard controlled the restive stallion as only a born horseman could do, and Elen felt somehow betrayed to see the animal settling down and performing at his best. Moroedd had rarely been so tractable for her.

The afternoon waned, lengthening shadows edging out the golden spring sunshine on the valley floor. The carts bumped and strained as the trail grew more treacherous, winding upward through a last range of mountains before reaching the coast.

Suddenly, Elen's cart gave an unexpected lurch, upending and sending her sprawling against the side. A sharp pain stabbed her middle. Then she was rolling over and over in a headlong tumble down a steep embankment to the right of the trail.

She came to a painful stop on a bed of loose shale. Opening her eyes, she gazed at a patch of blue sky overhead, trying to breathe around the constricting ache in her chest. What in God's name had happened? One minute she was sitting in the cart admiring the desolate beauty of the dark Welsh mountains and the next she was staring at the snow-capped peaks upside down.

A scramble of rocks sounded above, and all at once Richard was bending over her. "Elen! Elen, are you hurt?"

She shook her head, still trying to draw air into her lungs. "No. I . . . I don't think so."

Richard's eyes were dark with concern. His hands moved over her, gently but impersonally checking for injuries.

As Elen's breathing steadied, so did her whirling thoughts. She pushed Richard's probing hands away, struggling to sit up. "Owain! Merciful heaven, Owain may be hurt!"

Richard caught her shoulders, forcing her to remain seated. "Giles is with him. Your uncle was thrown from the cart but didn't go off the trail. You can see to him, but first be certain you've nothing broken."

Elen sent him an impatient look. "If you'll release me, you'll find I can stand on my own. Nothing is broken."

Richard nodded and sat back, still eyeing her closely. "There's blood on your tunic. Here," he said, fingering a narrow rent at her waist.

Elen glanced down, suddenly aware of a stinging pain across her middle. She gingerly parted the torn cloth and touched her bleeding flesh. "'Tis naught but a scratch. I must have fallen against the side of the cart as I went over."

She sighed as she brushed the dirt and leaves from her tattered garment. Her serviceable woolen tunic was torn in several places and had already been so oft mended it was something beggars would scorn to wear. She sighed again, thinking of the fine clothing that had filled her chests at Teifi. No doubt the English had it now, she told herself angrily.

Richard rose to his feet, holding out a hand to help her stand. Ignoring his outstretched hand, Elen stood abruptly, but regretted her hasty action at once. The blood drummed loudly in her ears and the scene about her spun and dimmed. She caught Richard's arm, closing her eyes and breathing deeply to steady herself. "I . . . I stood too quickly. I'll be all right."

Richard didn't hesitate. Swinging her into his arms, he turned and began carrying her up the rocky hillside toward the cluster of people on the trail above. Elen protested, but Richard's arms only tightened around her. "Hush!" he admonished. "Do you wish to reach your uncle or not? You don't seem like to do it on your own strength."

Elen subsided into mutinous silence, holding herself as stiffly erect as she could. She could feel the beat of Richard's heart against her shoulder, the warmth of his body insinuating itself into hers. The feeling of being carried in his arms was oddly comforting, but she refused to relax against him. It would serve him right if he tripped and they both went sprawling back down the hillside!

When they reached the crest of the embankment, Richard lowered her to the ground. Elen gazed at the scene of chaos. Scattered bags of grain littered the ground, and the wooden cart still leaned at a crazy angle, its shattered wheel askew. "She's unhurt," Richard replied in answer to Giles's questioning look. "But that wheel is beyond saving. Bring up the next three carts and distribute this grain among them."

Elen pushed away from Richard, fighting an unexpected urge to linger beside him. The fall must have shaken her more than she'd thought. She dropped to the ground, covering her weakness by leaning over Owain to determine if any of his wounds had reopened. "Is the pain bad?" she asked anxiously, satisfied there was no new bleeding.

Owain smiled ruefully. "The ground is not so soft as I remember from my younger days. Still, it could be worse. As I recall, you did threaten to toss me over a cliff."

Elen smiled back in relief. "Yes, and I'm justly rewarded for my threat. It was I who went sliding down the mountainside."

Moments later, the carts were reloaded and Richard mounted the fretting gray stallion. At his order, Owain was lifted into a cart that already contained several passengers. Elen rose gingerly to follow but a sharp ache in her side triggered another wave of dizziness. Catching the wooden sideplanking, she leaned against it for support.

Richard nudged his mount close beside her. He was still shaken from that terrible moment when he had seen Elen tumble over the edge of the embankment. Today's experience along with the memory of her daring leap into the mountain pool set him thinking. One never knew what mischief might be brewing behind the girl's wide blue eyes, and he didn't plan to take such a risk again.

He leaned down, catching her up onto the saddle before

him, one arm holding her securely against his chest. "Margaret, watch over the man and see to his needs," he directed a young blond woman seated in Owain's cart. "If he grows restless or complains of pain, send one of the men ahead to inform me."

Elen fought against Richard's hold, twisting to stare at him in amazement. "But I can see to my uncle's needs far better than a stranger," she protested. "It's my place to stay."

Richard turned Moroedd down the trail away from the cart. "I should think you'd had your fill of riding in ox carts. The rest of the way you ride with me."

"Why?"

Richard frowned. He really had no reason he could name. "Because I wish it."

Elen jerked away from the seductive warmth of his arms. Richard only wanted to show his power. He would humiliate her before Owain and give his men more cause for talk. "I prefer the cart," she said coldly.

Glancing down at the dark chestnut head beneath his chin, Richard's lips twitched into a smile. "I shall remember to ask your opinion—sometime when it matters."

"Oh, as you did before stealing my horse?"

"Your horse?" he repeated dryly. "I would rather imagine your Rhys stole him from some English knight. Besides, as I recall, you seemed to have some difficulty remaining mounted the last time you rode him."

"Moroedd is my horse," Elen snapped, swinging around to regard Richard indignantly. "He was stolen from no one. He belonged to my father, and after Builth I took him for my own. And I suggest you try riding him without a saddle during the middle of a midnight raid. You might find yourself in the dirt as well!"

Richard's green eyes narrowed in surprise. "Your father owned an animal so valuable as this? He must have been a wealthy man. This horse is beyond a whole year's wages even for a man such as myself. Tell me, Elen, exactly who was this father of yours?"

Elen stared at him in dismay, horrified by what she had thoughtlessly disclosed. Moroedd was far too valuable for a mere fighting man to own. "I don't wish to discuss my father," she replied. "He is dead because of you and that is enough."

"Very well, I'm sure your uncle will talk—with a little persuasion."

Elen frowned and bit her lip. Having said so much, she needed a plausible tale, else Richard might become suspicious enough to seek her true identity. And if that happened, she and Owain would never reach their refuge in France.

"Gwenwynwyn," she said, hastily grasping at the name of one of Enion's powerful friends. "His name was Gwenwynwyn. He was a great man in Powys."

"I know the name," Richard replied. "But to my knowledge, the man had no daughter."

"He was not married to my mother," Elen said, embroidering the tale.

"Oh." Richard's arm tightened about her. So the girl was baseborn. He was suddenly ashamed he had forced her admission. "I'm sorry. I'd no right to pry."

"Bastardy is no shame in Wales. 'Tis common enough and bastard children share equally in inheritance with the lawful born," Elen remarked pointedly. "I took my share in a swift mount in the confusion after Builth."

"This is no horse for a woman, Elen. I'll find you another mount, but I have plans for this devil. Your Moroedd is a war-horse. With a little more training he'll be a suitable gift for a king. And Edward has a great liking for gray horses."

It took several moments for Richard's words to sink in. Elen swung to face him, blue eyes blazing. "You would give my horse . . . *my horse* to Edward of England? I would sooner see him dead than a gift to that spawn of Satan. Holy Christ, I would take a knife and hamstring Moroedd myself!"

Richard's tanned face went rigid. "You go beyond what even I will allow, Elen. I've been patient with you in respect for your troubles, but you'll not speak of my king in such a fashion." His voice dropped. "Remember that, Elen. If you do so again, you'll be sorry."

Elen was breathing heavily, every muscle tense with outrage. Yet something in Richard's tone gave her pause. For once, she dared provoke him no further. He meant what he said.

She turned her back on him in an icy rage. "I beg pardon, *great lord,* for daring to speak my thoughts. I keep forgetting my place. After all, you own my land, my horse ... even my life. And you've already slain most of the people I know. Yes, I must thank God for your great patience and good will."

Richard sighed heavily. "Did anyone ever tell you you've the tongue of a shrew, Elen? I begin to see why at seventeen you're still unwed."

"It was not from lack of offers," she snapped back. "I won a promise from my father that I'd not be forced to wed until my seventeenth birthday. He honored that pledge."

"Then it wasn't a love match you were promised in?" Richard rejoined quickly. "You didn't relish the man who died at Builth?"

Richard heard her sharp intake of breath. "T—that's not true! I've loved him all my life. When I heard he was dead, I wished my own life was ended. I—" She broke off, as if the memory were too painful to contemplate. "It is not fitting to discuss him with you," she added with a quiet dignity. "A man such as you would never understand."

Richard said nothing further and the silence stretched between them for nearly two hours. They had been steadily climbing during that time and now they mounted the final crest of the mountain pass into a last blaze of golden twilight.

Richard drew rein, gazing down at the vast sweep of rugged, mountainous coast stretching out below them. It was a breathtaking sight. In the distance, the great fortress of Gwenlyn sat impregnable on a rocky cliff, her towering curtain walls tinted pink by the brilliance of the dying sun. Above the castle, all the colors of evening were painted across the sky, while far below the blue haze of night crept silently over the mountain valleys.

Elen shivered and Richard instinctively tightened his arms around her. "I suppose that is Gwenlyn," she said in a voice curiously devoid of emotion.

He bent his head. Elen was afraid, but he would not let on he sensed her fear. He rested his cheek against her hair for the space of a heartbeat. "Yes," he said softly. "That is Gwenlyn."

CHAPTER FOURTEEN

*R*ichard turned Moroedd up the last long hill toward Gwenlyn's gates, and Simon followed close on his heels. The castle was obviously expecting him. Dozens of torches flamed along the walls, and the messenger he had sent had already seen that his banner hung over the heavily fortified stone gatehouse.

As they approached the castle drawbridge and the great iron portcullis of the outer gate, Moroedd flung up his head, arching his neck and shying sideways in mock fear. Richard curbed the stallion's playfulness, sending him plunging across the echoing drawbridge and into the outer bailey where a milling crowd of English men-at-arms had gathered to cheer them into the castle compound.

As eager soldiers crowded around them, the stallion reared and lashed out, excited by the noise and confusion of the crowd. Richard brought him down sharply, amazed at the animal's spirit. No one attempting to control the beast now would believe the weary miles he had traveled this day. Moroedd was truly a mount for a king. He would be a fitting token of Richard's affection for his sovereign.

The great horse eased into a tight turn and traversed the outer court, passing once more through a tall stone gatehouse with raised portcullis and into the inner bailey.

Gwenlyn was one of the impregnable stone castles designed by James of St. George, Edward's master of castle defense and construction. It was designed on revolutionary new lines with double curtain walls and numerous self-contained defensive towers at regular intervals along the walls.

Though it might be taken by prolonged siege and starvation, Richard doubted an army would ever breach Gwenlyn's vast walls. And the Welsh had neither the men nor the time to mount such an assault.

But the king was taking no chances. The stone castles he was building in North Wales would spell the end to all hope of resistance.

Drawing Moroedd to a halt in the center of the courtyard, Richard swung down, then lifted Elen to the ground beside him. Simon immediately stepped forward to take the stallion's reins.

"Richard! Before God, I'm glad you're here! There's been skirmishing in the mountains and I was beginning to count you lost."

Turning, Richard moved across the cobblestones toward the deep, familiar voice. Sir Roland Denbeigh, the knight who held Gwenlyn now, was an old battle companion from years gone by. Richard grinned in response to the wide, welcoming smile that split the older knight's craggy face. His arm shot out and the two clasped hands. "And I was beginning to think you'd moved Gwenlyn five leagues west just to spite me," Richard responded. "We'd no trouble save a cursed rain that turned every inch of soil between here and Beaufort into a bog."

Roland shook his head. "Aye, the rain. I feared it might be a hindrance. By the Blessed Virgin, I've seen so much this past six-month I'm surprised I've not webbed feet!" His gaze drifted past Richard, halting at Elen in surprise. "But come, I forget my manners. Introduce me to that lovely creature you've brought with you."

Richard glanced back at Elen, his smile fading. "She's

Welsh—the woman of Rhys ap Iwan, the Welsh Fox. I took her in a raid."

Roland's dark brows shot up and he gave a low whistle. "You strike your enemy a painful blow, Richard." He glanced at the younger man with a grin. "And find sweet solace for yourself too, eh?"

Richard shook his head. "Don't be deceived by that angelic face. She's twice tried to kill me . . . and damned near succeeded too. And you should know she speaks English and French as well as Welsh."

Roland spat disgustedly. "Bah! These Welsh are all alike. Damned treacherous cutthroats, the lot of them. I work a few dozen in the castle by day, but won't have 'em sneakin' about after nightfall. Any Welshman I find within the walls after sundown I string up for a rebel." He paused, glancing over his shoulder at the congested movement of ox carts and men through the crowded courtyard. "Not that way, you fools!" he exploded. "Christ! If I don't get them straightened out, we'll have overturned carts and the devil of a mess. Excuse me, Richard."

As Sir Roland moved away to direct his men in the bestowing of the wagons, Richard frowned at his friend's harsh comment. Were the man's actions based on the true temper of the countryside or his own personal feelings? Sir Roland had good reason to hate the Welsh. He had lost both a brother and a promising young nephew in an unexpected Welsh raid several years back. But Roland had ever been an honest soldier, if sometimes harsh. Richard frowned again. He supposed he would have to wait to judge the situation here for himself.

"So you are Richard Basset, knight of Kent. The man we've all been hearing about."

Richard turned quickly toward the deep, lilting Welsh voice. A black-robed priest moved out of the shadows, halting a few paces before him. Eyes so dark they shone black in the torchlight regarded him intently from a sharply angular wedge of a face. "I've long pondered how you would be," the man continued in flawless French, "but I'd not dreamed you'd be so young."

Richard's eyes swept down the man, identifying him as one of the Welsh clergy. He was dressed in worn sandals and a tattered, much-mended robe with a crudely carved wooden crucifix hanging about his neck. His dark hair fell shaggy and uneven about his ears, yet for all his air of poverty, the man held himself proudly, commanding instant respect. "I cannot know what you've heard of me, Father, but I am the man," Richard replied.

"Oh, I've heard much." The priest's austere expression lightened somewhat, and his thin lips turned upward in a smile, crinkling the deep lines about the corners of his eyes. "But I promise I've disregarded at least two-thirds of it."

Richard shifted uneasily. Something about the man's intense scrutiny made him feel he was being judged. And no telling what a Welsh priest had heard of him!

"You! You, man, what are you doing here? I know I've thrown you out at least once today!"

Richard glanced up in surprise as Sir Roland stalked toward them.

The priest didn't flinch. "I told you I would see Richard Basset," he said quietly. "And so I am here."

"Well, not for long. Walter! John! Take this pesty priest beyond the walls and see he doesn't return," Roland directed. "And you've my leave to be as convincing as you like!"

Two burly guards stepped forward, laying rough hands on the priest. "Hold!" Richard turned to Sir Roland in disbelief. "You would treat a priest so violently? I fear you go too far, my friend."

"Humph! If he is a priest," Roland scoffed. "'Twould not be the first time these devils have donned priestly garb to mount a spying expedition. And what matter even if he is. Half the Welsh clergy took up arms in this last revolt.

You know the Archbishop of Canterbury has defrocked a vast lot of these un-Christian beggars."

"Do you know that he is a rebel?"

"No, of course not. How could I know that?" Roland responded irritably. "But it's of little matter one way or the other. I've already written the Bishop of St. David's requesting an English priest be sent here as quickly as possible. And I'll not have this man inciting the rabble in the village. We've enough trouble here without that!"

Richard turned back to the priest. "Are you a churchman in good standing?"

The man's dark eyes held his unwaveringly. "Yes."

Richard nodded in satisfaction. "Then you may sleep here tonight if you will, Father. A room will be made ready."

The priest shook his head. "I would sow no discord between you and your friend. Besides, I'm sore needed among my people. There are plenty of roofs eager to house me down by the docks." His eyes suddenly narrowed and he took a step toward Richard. "But I would seek audience with you as soon as possible. And I ask leave to visit among the prisoners you've brought."

Roland snorted in protest and, in the wavering torchlight, Richard searched the priest's gaunt face suspiciously. After all, blasphemous as his old friend's actions appeared, Roland could be right. This dark, earnest-looking man could easily be a Welsh patriot. "I will see you as soon as possible, but for now my prisoners will see no one save their guards." He hesitated a moment, still seeking to judge the man's intentions. "And where can you be found when my duties allow?"

"Put it about you've time for Father Dilwen." A narrow smile touched the priest's face. "And I will find you." Without waiting for Richard's reply, the priest moved away, losing himself quickly in the milling crowd of soldiers and servants.

Richard watched the dark-cowled figure disappear before

turning back to Sir Roland. His friend's lean face was stormy with anger. Richard let out his breath in a long sigh. "Forgive me, Roland, but I couldn't let you imperil your soul and mine by attacking a priest. Sweet Jesu, I've not the silver for buying such an indulgence as that!"

Roland nodded stiffly. "You were within your rights. After all, you're in command here now, not I. I'll be leaving in a few days to return to England, praise God, a land of civilized people who aren't seeking to cut a man's throat every moment!"

Richard studied his friend's closed face. It must be hard for the old knight to see a young whelp he had helped guide through his first battles now take precedence over him. "I hope you'll stay a while. I visited Gwenlyn with Edward only once, and there is much I must learn from you concerning the castle's fortification." He grinned in attempted lightness. "I've ever been better at attack than defense, while you were always a wily dog at both arts."

The man's expression thawed slightly. "I suppose I could stay a few days if you've need of me."

Richard put his hand on Roland's shoulder. "You know I need you. Besides, we've lots of catching up to do. How is your Lady Blanche?" he asked prudently.

"I've not seen her in near a six-month, but she's happy enough, I'll warrant, lording it over those grandchildren of ours. We've seven now, Richard. Five fine, lusty boys, and but two girl-children." Roland expanded visibly. "Come into the hall. I've a choice Gascon wine I've been saving, and we'll get a hot meal in your belly. We've plenty of time to talk without standing about out here in the damp."

Richard nodded. "That's all I could wish. But first, have you a room fitted up where we might safely keep this woman?" He glanced at Elen, still waiting impatiently beside Simon. "I'd see her comfortably bestowed before I relax and sup with you. The room must be secure with a guard for the door. I can't chance having her slip away."

"Certainly. Bring her inside and I'll fetch a guard," Roland responded, hastening to mount the stairs leading up to the keep.

Richard glanced back at Elen, hoping she wouldn't choose this moment to defy him. He was tired and hungry and growing unutterably weary of dealing with difficult situations. But with Elen there was no telling. "Come," he said, jerking his head toward the stairs.

Elen moved across the space separating them, her chin lifting angrily. "Don't you fear your friend may string me up?" she asked sarcastically. "After all, it is after sundown and I am most assuredly Welsh!"

Richard smiled. The girl was much like the gray stallion. Despite the damp and cold and the long miserable hours they had traveled, she refused to be completely subdued. And regardless of the trouble it caused him, he couldn't help admiring her spirit.

Catching her wrist, he drew her along up the stairs beside him and into the arched stone doorway of Gwenlyn. "It's Welsh *men* Sir Roland despises," he leaned down to remind her, his accent heavy on the word "men." "Knowing Roland, I'm sure he has no argument with having a Welsh *woman* or two in his keep after sundown."

A mile from Gwenlyn in the narrow stinking streets that wound through the impoverished harbor section of the village, a slender figure moved steadily forward, the stiff sea wind whipping his long black robes about his wrists and ankles. The man moved forward fearlessly, glancing neither right nor left as he passed along the dangerous stretch outside the town wall where the dispossessed Welsh crowded together in simmering resentment of their English neighbors inside.

Making his way past the dock, the man headed toward a ramshackle lean-to at the far end of the muddy street. A shadowy figure stepped around the corner of the building. "Well, what news? Have you seen him?"

The man halted, the wooden crucifix he wore catching a sudden gleam of moonlight. "Yes. I have seen him."

"What say you, then? Are you with us?"

The black-robed figure was silent for a moment. "It is too soon to know," he said at last. "I must see him again. But I pray all may still be as we hope."

CHAPTER FIFTEEN

$\mathcal{G}$rabbing the reins, Richard vaulted lightly onto Saladin's back. The bay stallion sidled fretfully in the cool morning air. "Easy, my lad, no need to show off for me," Richard crooned. He nodded to Simon and the boy released the bridle, stepping away from the animal's head.

Richard held the impatient stallion in tightly while his squire swung onto his mount. "Saladin's jealous," Simon remarked with a grin. "You've spent too much time training that big gray. He must think he's about to be replaced."

Richard turned his mount toward the gate, and his armed guard hastily clattered into position in his wake. "No chance of that," he called over his shoulder. "Saladin's like his master—just impatient to get outside these walls. I've studied food and weapon stores, maps and troop numbers with Sir Roland till I'm near blind with eyestrain!"

"A knight should never cut short his study of important details," Simon intoned in a pious voice.

The grin Richard sent his squire was one of a schoolboy kicking over his traces rather than that of a seasoned commander. He touched his spurs lightly to Saladin's side and the animal leaped forward across the drawbridge onto the springy green turf along the roadside.

It was good to be out in the warm sunshine. Despite the

uncomfortable scene with Sir Roland the night of his arrival, Richard had managed to salvage something of the old relationship with his friend. And other than a few hours spent in slumber and a few in working the mettlesome gray stallion, he had passed most of the last three days learning all the facts about Gwenlyn the old campaigner could teach.

And he had studiously avoided Elen; it was best that way, he decided. Giles reported on her uncle's improving condition and had even fetched Elen some female clothing Richard and Sir Roland had unearthed in a storeroom. Roland had grinned at Richard's extravagance, but for pity's sake, Elen's brown tunic was so tattered it was indecent!

Richard frowned, recalling his thoughts when they opened the heavy chest. A garment of a rich golden silk had caught his eye, and though experience told him it was out of fashion for court wear, his mind had leaped ahead to thoughts of Elen clothed in the becoming fabric seated beside him at Edward's court.

His frown deepened. The girl was in his thoughts entirely too much. He had even feared her influence on his decision to spare the Welshman. But Richard's own instincts spoke for Owain as well. The man was a natural leader, would be a powerful ally if his loyalty could be won. The task would take time and wouldn't be easy, but it might well be worth the effort in the end. And he doubted Owain would be going anywhere. The Welshman wouldn't be anxious to escape so long as Richard held Elen.

"Did you wish to take a look at Ruthlin today?" Simon asked.

"What?" Richard shook himself out of his absorption. "Oh, the village. Yes, we might as well see it. Roland assures me we've a good harbor to receive supplies from the granaries on the isle of Anglesey and additional troops from Edward's castle of Rhuddlan should they be needed. There's even a growing population of tradesmen transplanted here from the settlements along the English coast. Edward granted them land and tax concessions for braving the hardship of living in this godforsaken place." He gazed out over the rugged countryside. "But first we'll check on the spring planting. Roland says it's not gone forward as it should."

"Sir Roland says the Welsh are lazy."

Richard glanced at his squire. "Do you believe that?"

"By God's grace, I see no sign of laziness when they fight us," Simon replied with a grin.

"Keep that in mind," Richard responded dryly.

Bypassing the road, the party made its way across country, swinging south beyond the village to assess the narrow rocky tracts of farmland outside. But what they saw was even worse than Richard had expected. There were few fields either in the common village tract or the portion set aside for the use of the English keep that had been readied for planting. And fallow fields now would mean starvation for them all come winter.

Richard completed his survey in less than an hour. Guiding Saladin along the imposing town wall built to protect the English settlers from the Welsh, he led his men slowly down the muddy road past the scattered makeshift buildings that huddled outside the wall.

A small crowd was gathering before a squat stone building that doubled as village warehouse and Welsh church. At sight of Richard and his men, the people shifted about, muttering angrily in Welsh. A few fists were raised in threatening gestures.

In the center of the crowd, Richard could see a score of men from Gwenlyn's garrison. Their swords were drawn. He pushed Saladin toward the soldiers but didn't dismount. Though well armed and in mail, he would be foolhardy to be afoot if the ugly mood of the crowd turned to violence. "I am Richard Basset. What trouble is this?" he called out.

The knight in command strode forward. "I am Sir Gifford de Bay, and we've no trouble, my lord. 'Tis naught but two poachers in need of punishment."

De Bay gestured to a soldier who had forced two unfortunate Welshmen to their knees in the dirt. "They were caught with snares and two dead hares between them," he continued, giving one of the men a shove with his foot. "As Sir Roland's forester, I've decided punishment according to English law. The thieves will lose both hands. With these two as examples, perhaps the rest of these beggars won't be so quick to go hunting. I warrant we'll miss little more of Gwenlyn's game."

Richard leaned over Saladin's neck, gazing down at the two Welshmen. Their hands were tightly bound and they bore the marks of a vicious beating. The sight made his insides tighten with anger. "I didn't know Edward had extended his forest law to Wales," he remarked coldly, "nor that he had granted a charter of private chase to Sir Roland. But if that is the case, these men must be tried and punished by a royal forest eyre as established by the Forest Charter." He glanced at the knight, adding sarcastically, "Certainly as Sir Roland's forester you are aware of the law, de Bay."

The knight shifted uneasily. "We've no actual charter as yet nor any real officials. But as Gwenlyn is a royal keep, I thought—"

"Then I'd say you've no real authority to punish these men," Richard said, swinging down from his horse. He bent over one of the prisoners, and lifted the man to his feet. The Welshman gazed back at him with hatred, though one eye was so swollen from the beating it would scarcely open.

Richard swore under his breath. What could Roland be thinking to order forest law here? Even loyal Englishmen hated the law declaring huge tracts of forest land off limits for hunting save to those assigned by the king. And Richard knew for a certainty Edward had no intention of enforcing the bitterly contested law among the starving populace of Wales.

He touched the man's bleeding cheek gingerly then turned to de Bay. "You and your men have been most zealous in your duty, but I fear I must take a hand. You'll seek out no more poachers while I am lord of Gwenlyn."

"But my lord," the knight protested, "Sir Roland let it be known no game was to be hunted. Yet these men were caught in open defiance of that order. What would you have us do? Let them go free?"

Drawing his knife, Richard cut the thongs binding the battered prisoner's hands. "Did you take game from Gwenlyn's forest?" he asked.

The prisoner stared up at him sullenly, a flicker of comprehension in his eye telling Richard the man had understood. "As you value your life, answer me," Richard ordered.

"My crops was burned last year, my sheep and pigs slaughtered or run off by soldiers," the man replied in broken French. "My folk live by what bits I glean from yon wood." He nodded about the circle of faces then turned the full force of his hatred on Richard. "Me an the rest here eat what we find. Now kill me for that if you will, Englishman," he snarled. "An God curse your black soul!"

Instead of the swift blow the man obviously expected, Richard ignored his outburst, moving to cut the other prisoner free of his bonds. He turned to regard the angry crowd. "Hear me now," he said loudly in French. "I am Richard Basset, he you call the Wolf of Kent. I tell you there are no forest laws in Wales, nor will there be while I rule here."

A few in the crowd must have understood his words. They shifted in surprise and began to whisper among their neighbors. "I hold Gwenlyn for Edward, King of England, and so long as I am here, no man will be killed or maimed for taking game to feed his family," Richard repeated, hoping to make them understand.

A few feet to Richard's rear, the surly prisoner began a halting translation of his words into Welsh. The muttering of the crowd increased in volume, then subsided as the people waited for him to continue.

Richard studied the ring of pinched, suspicious faces. These people were starving and didn't really believe conditions would get better. "You may hunt where you will, both deer and small game. You may take what fish you can from river and sea. But I tell you this, no man will be idle. Your fields are barren now when they should be sprouting spring crops. Tomorrow I expect to see them being readied for planting."

"We've no grain for eatin' much less plantin'," the prisoner interrupted. " Them what had a bit of seed put back had it taken from 'em by our new neighbors." He spat disgustedly on the ground, inches from Richard's feet. "Have a Welshman complain about the thievin' ways of an Englishman an see where it gets 'im."

"We've seed grain aplenty at Gwenlyn," Richard responded, ignoring the remainder of the man's angry words. "When the fields are ready, come to me for what you need." He studied the bruised, disbelieving face before him. "You will be in charge of organizing these people. Bring one man from each family to receive his share of seed. You may work your own plots till the fields are planted, but I'll expect each man to work his share on Gwenlyn's fields when that is done."

"And when harvest time comes. What then?" the man asked bitterly. "Will we watch our fields ruined, our crops taken by Englishmen who never did a day's work to raise 'em?"

"Each man will eat his own harvest save the tithe he owes the church and that he owes the lord of Gwenlyn. That I promise you and I swear to make it so," Richard said evenly. He turned from the man and once more surveyed the crowd. "The fighting is done and England has won," he said loudly. "You do not like it, but it is so. I rule this place in Edward's name and I tell you you will find in me a just master if not an easy one. The law will be obeyed by Welsh and English alike, and you need not fear to ask justice from me—even against an Englishman. You do not believe it now, but you will soon find it so."

Turning away from the crowd, he took his reins from Simon and swung onto his mount. The prisoner moved forward and caught his stirrup. "You promise well," he sneered, "but I've yet to see an Englishman keep a vow to one of my race."

Richard ignored the man's insolence. Leaning forward, he regarded him coolly. "What is your name?"

"Heffeydd Sele."

"Well, Heffeydd Sele, you may live to see much you've not yet seen . . . if you correct that insolent tongue."

The man spat again and rubbed his swollen jaw. "Don't think we'll kneel in the dirt and fawn like dogs just because you've tossed us a bit of a bone. We've no more love of your kind than you have of ours."

Richard raised one tawny eyebrow. "Have I asked you to kneel?"

The man shook his head.

Richard settled back in the saddle, his green eyes narrowing dangerously as they locked with the dark eyes of the Welshman. "Well, I promise if I ask it, you will do it . . . or you will do nothing else in this life!"

The man dropped his eyes and shifted away, releasing his hold on Richard's stirrup. "Aye. I'll have the people to their plots this very day. Barley'll grow here and beans too."

Richard barely controlled a smile. The man was daringly rebellious, but shrewd enough to know when he had pushed too far. "Come to me when the fields are ready. You'll have your seed." With that, he swung Saladin about and the muttering crowd fell back. Simon followed at Richard's left, and the rest of the troop joined in behind.

"Do you think the Welshman spoke truth?" Simon asked.

"Do you?" Richard countered.

"Well, they looked hungry enough."

"Yes, I believe he spoke truth. A man doesn't risk his

life for a bit of game unless he has no other choice. And we've just seen the fields. There's not even a leek growing there."

"I'm glad you stopped it, Richard. Cutting off those men's hands, I mean. It seems a poor way to discipline."

Richard nodded again. "Take a man's life before you take his limb," he advised. "By maiming a man you make an enemy for life. If he deserves so grievous a punishment, then slay him outright. Don't leave him to fester and spread hate like some running sore."

"Do you really think they'll ready the fields—theirs as well as ours?"

Richard was silent for a moment. "Yes. They wish to feed their families and for now they realize they must do as I say. And I've no plans to make them desperate. A desperate man is a dangerous enemy to have, Simon," Richard commented grimly. "Dangerous, because he has nothing left to lose."

From her place in the sumptuous Queen's Chamber of Gwenlyn, Elen watched Richard and his men ride into the bailey. Richard wore no helmet today and the warm spring breeze ruffled his straight blond hair, making it gleam in the sunlight like burnished gold. She sank down onto the cushioned window seat, studying his profile. Her enemy was truly a man who was good to look at, she mused.

She studied the width of Richard's shoulders beneath his surcoat and hauberk, the play of trained muscles as he lifted his arm to point out something to one of his men. All at once the memory of the afternoon they had almost made love swept over her, and she recalled the feel of those muscles rippling beneath her fingers, of the sleek power of his golden body stripped bare before her gaze.

She sought to put the image from her, but her treacherous mind dredged up more disturbing thoughts. The memory of Richard's searing kisses warmed her, and her body suddenly ached from the remembered pleasure of his caress. He had brought some unknown part of her to life that day— a part she had fought to forget.

Elen rose to her feet and paced nervously about the room. What was it about Richard that made her feel so restless and aching and longing to be in his company even when they did nothing but fight? Her ungovernable thoughts returned to that day and the remembered feel of his arms about her, of the exquisite pleasure of his flesh against hers. She had never felt like that before—not even in Enion's embrace.

The realization fueled a bitter sense of betrayal that caught her up short. Enion . . . had she truly loved him?

She swung away from the window with a gasp of outrage. Of course she'd loved Enion! She'd loved him all her life. The restless excitement Richard evoked was naught but the remembered thrill of danger she was recalling, a danger that had heightened every sensation of pleasure. She had known her life was at stake the moment her enemy walked into the room. She had wondered if she could take his life or if she would lose hers. That was all.

She moved to the window, peering down into the bailey once more. The inner court was empty now and she felt vaguely disappointed no tall blond figure met her gaze.

Annoyed, Elen told herself she didn't really wish to see Richard. It was only the boredom of being pent up inside. Even the sight of her enemy was a longed-for distraction, their frequent clashes the only diversion she was allowed.

She paced about the room for what must have been the thousandth time, finally pausing beside the bed where the gowns Giles had brought her were piled. The dresses were too short for her unusual height, but the hems could be let down several inches to hide her ankles. And since there was nothing else to do, she might as well continue her sewing, she told herself dispiritedly.

With a deep sigh, she ran her hands appreciatively over the soft gown of blue wool she wore. It was good to wear fine clothes again, if only for a little while. Naturally, she would take nothing with her when she left Gwenlyn. She had mended her old brown tunic as well as she could, and it would do far better service in the mountain wilds than these rich fabrics. Settling herself resignedly on a stool, she took up one of the gowns and began letting down its hem.

Some time later, the sound of familiar footsteps came to her from the corridor. She took a deep breath. Would Richard stop or pass by?

The footsteps halted. A knock brought her to her feet, and she nervously smoothed the folds of her gown. "Yes?"

Richard strode into the chamber. His eyes traveled slowly over her, coming to rest on her face with a warm look of approval. "I see you've made use of the clothing. I've no notion to whom it belonged, but it's my wish that you keep it." An engaging smile flashed. "I was growing quite weary of brown."

Elen fought the urge to smile in return. How could she even think of making pleasant conversation with the hero of Builth? "I can't see why I should wear such grand garments," she said stiffly. "Surely you'll not keep me here much longer."

This bedchamber was one held in readiness for Queen Eleanor's visits. Richard gazed pointedly at the tapestried walls, the other rich appointments. "This room is fit for a queen. Do you tire of luxury already? I thought women enjoyed such things."

"No woman tires of luxury such as this. But I tire of prison, Richard, no matter how luxurious," Elen said earnestly. "And I tire of wondering what will become of me and those I care for."

Richard moved across the floor, pausing at the window to gaze down into the bailey. "So you are weary of your prison," he repeated. "I do not blame you, so too am I.

While I cannot set you free as yet, I've no desire to keep you a close-held prisoner unless you force me. You are free to come and go within Gwenlyn as you wish—if you give me your word you'll not attempt to go beyond the walls."

Elen stared at Richard in amazement. She wasn't sure what she was expecting, but it certainly wasn't this.

Richard swung around. "Well, what say you? Will you swear an oath to remain in Gwenlyn?"

Her eyes rose to his. This was her chance. Richard had said nothing about pardoning Owain, but once out of her room it would be simple enough to learn where the Welshman was held. An easy trick for a few slow-witted guards and she and Owain could be on their way to France.

"You've told me you keep your word," Richard reminded. He was smiling again. "Well, prove it. We might both benefit thereby."

A dozen conflicting thoughts spun through her. Yes, this was a chance, a chance for freedom for Owain and herself— but dare she foreswear a vow? She might lie to Richard, for among her people a lie to one's enemy was no dishonor. But she couldn't break an oath, not even for such purpose as this. And Richard had treated her well, so well in fact, she was more than a little ashamed of her past treachery. "No," she said abruptly. "I cannot give you such an oath. You must know I'll do all in my power to leave this place as soon as I might."

"I see." Richard leaned against the wall, his dark face thoughtful. "That bit of honesty just cost you a great deal, did it not, Elen? I thank you for your truth, and I would offer you something in return. I'll give you your freedom for a time of two days if you give me your word for the same time. You may be quit of this room without making so binding a vow."

A rush of gratitude swept Elen. Richard understood. But she was surprised he would make things so easy. "You would do that?" she whispered incredulously. "You would trust me?"

"Not overly so, but I will try. Is it agreed?"

"Yes," she said quickly. "Oh, yes!"

Richard smiled. Things were going far better than he had hoped. The hatred was gone from Elen's face, the bitterness from her voice. It was a small victory but, perhaps, a beginning. "Since that is decided let us speak of your uncle. I talked with him last evening and again this morn. I made him the same offer of freedom about Gwenlyn I just gave you. But your uncle is a wise man. He took the offer. Though he'll not swear allegiance to Edward, he's given his oath not to raise steel against the men of Gwenlyn or attempt an escape."

"Y-you'll spare him?" Elen inquired breathlessly.

"I've thought long on your words, Elen. If your kinsman fought only for your honor, I'll not fault him." Richard sent her a swift, slanted glance. "As you said, I would have done the same. If he keeps his oath and abides here peacefully, I'll hold nothing more against him. But I warn you as I did him. If he violates any detail of his oath, his life is forfeit."

"Oh, Richard . . ." Elen took an impulsive step toward him, reaching out to catch his arm. She had hoped and prayed for this, but some small part of her had been terrified Owain would be taken from her. She stared up into Richard's hard, handsome face, feelings of surprise, relief, profound gratitude, washing over her. "I . . . I cannot thank you enough. You've been kind, so much kinder than I ever expected!"

Richard gazed down into the lovely, heart-shaped face turned up to his so eagerly. This was only the second time Elen had touched him voluntarily, and her hand on his arm sent all his good intentions scattering to the winds. How simple to bend his head and make that wide, sweet mouth his, to take Elen in his arms and forget their enmity in pleasure.

He bent toward her. One kiss, one taste of that sweet

mouth. One kiss . . . and then he'd let her be.

Elen saw the sudden change in Richard's face, knew he wanted to kiss her. And she was shaken by the realization that she wanted it as well. They had kissed last in anger. It had been punishing, intentionally cruel. But she felt no fear of Richard now, only an inexplicable sensation of loss, a terrible disappointment that there could be nothing between them—nothing but hate.

Her hand tightened on his arm and she held him away. "No, Richard," she said low. "Don't . . ."

Richard caught himself. His eyes narrowed, and he straightened at once. Elen's hand fell back to her side, and she stared uncomfortably at the floor.

"What? No kiss of thanks?" Richard asked cynically. "A small price for a man's life, don't you think?"

Elen's eyes rose to his in wordless appraisal. She had lived all her life in the company of warriors. She knew the braggarts, the cowards, the honorable men. And she knew beyond doubt which type stood before her. "You didn't decide to let Owain live because of me, nor will my refusal now bring him harm," she remarked with a quiet assurance. "I am grateful, but that is all. That is all there can ever be."

Richard took a deep, slow breath, struggling to keep command of himself. He was angry, unreasonably so—and he wished he were as certain of his reasons for sparing the Welshman as Elen seemed to be. "I suppose I should go, then. I'd not strain your gratitude," he said coolly. "Forgive me for troubling you."

As Richard strode from the room, an unexpected feeling of sadness swept Elen. She took one impulsive step toward the door, then stopped, shaken by an urge stronger than any she had ever known.

Merciful God, she had almost called him back!

CHAPTER SIXTEEN

$\mathcal{T}$he morning sky was filled with swirling mists and intermittent rain. Elen stared down into the bailey, listening to the sonorous tolling of Gwenlyn's chapel bells. Father Dilwen had been given permission to hold mass this morning. Giles had told her the good news last evening when she had discovered her guards were gone and had hesitantly ventured from her room.

She had gone at once in search of the Welsh priest, but he was busy in the village so she had yet to talk with him. Still, it had been enough just to be outside her chamber, to take a turn in the garden and see the evening sky overhead . . . to realize Richard had kept his word regarding her freedom to roam about Gwenlyn.

Richard Basset, Wolf of Kent, the man she had hated above all others. It had come as a surprise these last weeks to learn he was a man of honor, a man it was growing increasingly difficult to hate. Pactum Serva, Keep Troth, was the motto of Edward, King of England—but Giles had told her Richard had taken it for his own as well.

She frowned thoughtfully. What would Richard do if he learned she and Owain were living a lie? Oh, he would continue to treat them with proper English justice. She didn't doubt that. But English justice was a terrifying matter if one were Welsh . . . a deadly matter if one were the Welsh Fox.

Reaching up to catch the shutters, Elen swung them in and locked them, shivering in a sudden chill that had little to do with the weather. Richard was her enemy, she reminded herself. Despite his kindness to an unimportant Welsh woman and her kinsman, his mercy didn't extend to battlefields, or to rebels who continued their fight against England.

Turning away from the window, she moved toward the door. The church bells had ceased their tolling. If she didn't hurry, she would be late for mass.

Richard stared grimly over the carved oak balustrade of the balcony, watching the movements of the priest as he began the familiar litany of the mass. Edward had built the small withdrawing room so that the royal family might celebrate mass without mingling with the castle folk. And today Richard was thankful for the solitude.

He scanned the crowd below thoughtfully. What was this black mood that had overtaken him? There was no reason for it. The campaign in Wales was going well. He had not yet captured the Welsh Fox, but Rhys's fierce depredations on the English had ceased. Richard's men were pressing the rebels mercilessly and they appeared to be scattered and disorganized. They had not attempted a raid in weeks.

His thoughts shifted to an inventory of more personal matters. Morale was high and even Roland was in good spirits preparing for the journey home. The people of Ruthlin were making headway in readying the fields for planting. One villager had even spoken respectfully when Richard rode out yesterday with his bailiff and two teams of oxen to aid them in preparing the soil. Yes, everything was going well, so why this feeling of discontent?

His eyes wandered slowly over the crowd of knights, soldiers and castle folk gathered in the chapel below, finally coming to rest on a bright chestnut head. His fingers tightened on the railing and he leaned forward slightly. If he were honest, he would admit Elen was at the root of this feeling. But what made her so different from the other women he had known? Was he grown so high in his own conceit that one woman's scorn could thrust him into this black mood? The whole idea was ridiculous! He should be laughing about the matter with Giles over a flagon of choice wine. But he had seldom felt so little like laughing.

Elen's words came back to him. Gratitude . . . was that all she felt? Well, he'd show her gratitude! He didn't need the gratitude of some half-savage Welsh bastard.

His eyes narrowed angrily as he recalled the times she had spurned him. Had he no pride? Why keep panting after a woman who had sworn to hate him with her last breath?

But did she still hate him? Recollections danced teasingly along the edges of his memory: a gesture, a glance, a hint of desire on her face when he had bent to kiss her yesterday. For just a moment, Elen had wanted that kiss as much as he. So why her pretense?

Richard frowned thoughtfully. In his world a man took a mistress, and it was an honorable enough estate. Elen must know he wanted her, must know she would be far better off in that position. She would have her freedom, a place of honor at Gwenlyn, and whatever material possessions he had at his disposal. Any other woman of her station would see the advantages to be gained and jump at the chance.

But Elen wasn't any other woman, a small voice reminded. And if he understood anything about her at all, it was that she was fiercely and passionately Welsh. She might not be completely indifferent to him, but they were enemies and that was enough. She would fight any developing relationship between them with every weapon she could command. And if he wanted things differently, it was up to him to make them so.

With a start, Richard realized the mass was over and Father Dilwen was giving a final blessing to the people. He swung on his heel and vaulted down the stairs, hurrying to find Elen.

As he reached the door to the hall, Henry Bloet caught up with him. "My lord!" the man called out. "My lord, there be a persistent dog of a Welshman outside a-askin' for ye." Henry paused to catch his breath. "I told him ye was at mass, but he said as how ye'd best be hearin' him out, the insolent scoundrel! That it'd not be him what'd suffer if ye didn't."

Richard nodded impatiently, intent on catching Elen before she left the hall. "Yes, tell him to wait and I'll see him after breakfast. I've something else pressing now."

Elen walked slowly through the crowd of people leaving the chapel. She hated returning to her chamber, but she had no reason to linger below. She felt an outcast among the English. The servants treated her like a leper and save for Simon, Giles and William, she didn't dare speak to Richard's men.

She moved into the spacious hall, critically appraising the fine craftsmanship of the stone walls, the great vaulted ceiling and carved stone fireplaces at either end of the room. Above the lord's table, a canopy of crimson silk embroidered with the leaping golden lions of Edward Plantagenet shifted slightly in a draft, making the animals appear to flex and stretch in the uneven light.

To Elen the grandeur of the richly appointed keep seemed a deliberate contrast to the relative poverty of even the greatest Welsh princes. She had thought her lofty oak-beamed home at Teifi wonderfully built, but she couldn't help thinking the arrogant English king would find the wooden keep a hovel.

Well, let the English have their stone castles, she told herself defiantly. Owain and Dylan would pull this magnificence down about their ears. And if she had her way, it would be soon!

She turned her back on the splendor, watching forlornly as servants scurried about dodging well-dressed knights and common men-at-arms as they hurried to put away sleeping pallets and set up trestle tables for the breakfast following mass. Suddenly, her mind registered a familiar face beneath the lowered cap of a struggling servant—a face that belonged to the mountain wilds of Wales. Her eyes widened in astonishment as she watched the man lift a heavy plank across its trestle. Dylan . . . by the love of heaven, what was the Welshman doing here?

He caught her eye, then quickly glanced away. She stared intently at the man working beside him. Dylan and Gruffydd! And if they were here, other friends might be in Gwenlyn as well.

Her heart began a wild, excited throbbing, but she maintained enough presence of mind not to stare. That would be sure to draw attention to the men. Perhaps she could manage to whisper a message if she walked by.

Her mind began to churn with possible plans, but the sight of Richard moving across the floor toward her caught her up short. Damnation! She'd forgotten their bargain. She had given her word she'd make no effort to escape and Richard trusted her.

But freedom was precious, too precious to hang on her oath to an enemy. If a chance came, she should take it—anything else would be foolish beyond belief.

"Good morning, Elen," Richard said, coming to a halt beside her. "I trust you enjoyed the day's mass."

She nodded, forcing herself to speak calmly, to appear unconcerned. "Yes. It's been months since I've heard mass. It was kind of you to allow me to go."

"I would have you attend anytime you wish. And I would have you take your meals with us here in the hall." He gestured toward the high table. "My knights grow weary of their own company. If you would consent to join us, we would be honored."

She glanced toward the table in surprise. Richard's men were already gathering. "Oh, Richard, I don't think—"

"You've but two days of freedom," he interrupted, his eyes holding hers. "Let's make the most of it." Taking her hand, he lifted it briefly to his lips, then tucked it into the curve of his arm. "Shall we . . . my lady?"

Not wishing to make a scene with every eye in the hall upon them, Elen allowed Richard to lead her across the rush-strewn floor and up the three steps to the table. Simon stepped from behind Richard's chair to seat her, his well-trained face betraying no hint of surprise at the altered arrangements this morning. And though there were many curious glances, Richard's knights stood courteously while she was seated and served. The lord of Gwenlyn was treating her as a lady and they could do no less.

Elen felt more than a few pangs of guilt. By according her such courtesy before his household, Richard had set a pattern for the way she would be treated. And he would look more than a little foolish when she and Owain escaped. She frowned into her ale cup. Dylan would think her a fool when she told him they must wait—but she had been called worse before. After all, she had given her word.

They were halfway through breakfast when Henry Bloet thrust open the side door and moved quickly toward Richard. "My lord," he exploded, coming to a halt before the table. "I must speak with ye."

Richard shot his man a sharp glance, but he knew Henry wouldn't disturb him for a trivial matter. Dipping his fingers in a basin Simon held, he wiped them on his napkin and rose to his feet. "Very well." He nodded his apology to Elen, then caught Giles's eye.

The two knights joined Henry at one side of the hall. "That dog of a Welshman outside be still insisting on speech with'y, m'lord," Henry spluttered. "He said if ye didn't come

at once, he'd not be believin' any more 'a yer fine promises
. . . and a great deal more besides."

He glanced sharply at Richard. "He'd give no name, but
said his words are for your ears alone. I don't like it, sir.
Let me come with ye at least."

Richard was staring at the floor, eyes narrowed thoughtfully. "Never mind, Henry. I think I know who it is. Where
have you got the man, and what precautions have been
taken?"

"Near the garden wall in the outer court. I'd let the
scoundrel nary a step further," Henry growled. "I've sent
young Walt to bring up a second guard on the battlements.
The least sign of trouble an' they're to rain arrows on any
bastard hintin' at mischief. Be sure ye keep close to cover."

Richard nodded in satisfaction. "No cause for alarm, but
I'd like some men ready as a precaution." He glanced at
his friend. "Giles, stay close to Elen. This Welshman could
be the bait sent to lure me from the hall. Our friend Rhys
may be getting a bit impatient for my blood."

"Certainly, Richard. Rhys could come with my good
will."

Richard smiled coolly. "And mine as well. I'm growing
most anxious to meet our Fox."

With another low-voiced order, Richard was out of the
hall and moving across the bailey into the outer court. The
rain had stopped, but the drifting fog curled wet, clammy
fingers about his body, dampening his face and shrouding
the far corners of the bailey in white obscurity. He frowned.
It was a good day for treachery.

A heavily cloaked figure stepped out of the mist. Richard
moved forward across the empty courtyard, more curious
than worried. By now Giles and Henry would have men
posted at every doorway and arrowslit as well as any number
waiting to rush from the barracks to his assistance. If treachery were planned, he had only to defend himself a few
seconds and the entire courtyard would be swarming with
his men.

As he drew near the dark figure, the man lifted the frayed hood of his cloak away from his battered face. "Well, Heffeydd Sele, I thought it must be you," Richard remarked.

"Aye, I thought my persistence would bring you. But I'll swear, I know not whether to be pleased or sorry that you came."

Richard said nothing. The Welshman chewed his lip a moment, then took a deep breath. "I've no love of you, Englishman. God knows I'd as soon see yer whole race perish from the earth. But you've given me a problem I've no easy answer for." He frowned, then shifted uncertainly on his feet. "You did me a good turn . . . and likely saved a host of others as well. That's a thing no Welshman forgets."

He glanced up, an arrogant jut to his bruised jaw. "Not that we can be bought, mind you, but you seem a sight easier to stomach than the last two vermin what held this cursed keep. Not that you won't forget all yer promises in the wink of an eye be it convenient," he added sourly.

"I won't forget," Richard responded. "But I still have no idea why you brought me out in this cursed wet."

The Welshman grinned. "Aye, your fine feathers be a bit damp." The humorous glint in his eye dimmed and he sobered at once. "But tell me this, Richard Basset, Wolf of Kent. Be you a vindictive man like the rest of your race?"

"No more so than you, Welshman."

The man shrugged, acknowledging Richard's words. "What I mean is . . . if you learned of something, something to your displeasure, that is. Would you punish a whole village? Even people innocent of the plot?"

Richard's eyes narrowed. The man obviously had news but couldn't make up his mind to spill it. "I make it a point to punish the guilty, Heffeydd Sele, and I give little quarter in that respect. The innocent I do my best to protect. I would think you, of all people, would realize that."

The man gave a curt nod. "Then hear me out. There's

a plot afoot . . . a plot to make an end of you and free the prisoners you hold in Gwenlyn."

Richard didn't move. "Go on."

"I know little more than that. And by Our Lady, I'd of spent an easier night had I not heard so much!" The Welshman sent Richard a long look. "It's not the local folk, but some men what came out of the mountains these last weeks. And I can give you no time. Only that I've heard they'll move soon. That some be already within Gwenlyn."

Richard pursed his lips thoughtfully. Already inside Gwenlyn—he would have to act quickly. "Is that all?"

Heffeydd hesitated. "I've a notion there's a woman involved."

A woman. Richard cursed himself suddenly for ten kinds of a fool. Rhys's men were already in Gwenlyn and he had played into their hands by allowing Elen out of her room. Not trusting her completely, he had alerted the men at the gates to be on watch, but he should have had her followed within Gwenlyn as well. She had probably already made contact with the rebels. He gazed down at the Welshman. The man had obviously gone against his better judgment by bringing word of the plot. "My thanks for the warning."

The man nodded. "We're even, Englishman."

For a moment, Richard considered offering a reward, but the proud Welshman might think the offer an insult. "You owe me nothing nor I you," Richard agreed. "But you'll still get justice from me, Heffeydd Sele."

The man sent him a measuring look. "If you live long enough."

Richard smiled coldly. "Oh, I'll live. But can you tell me how you gained knowledge of this plot?"

The man gave an eloquent shrug of his shoulders, his voice dropping to a mysterious whisper. "News in Wales be spoken on the winds and waters if you've the skill to hear."

"I see," Richard commented dryly, realizing he would

get nothing more. "No doubt Englishmen haven't the skill."

The man drew the hooded cloak up close about him. "I'll be leavin' now. If anyone be askin' after our talk, you tell 'em I came to beg mercy for a clumsy village boy what lamed one of Gwenlyn's oxen."

"Is one of the beasts injured?"

"No." The Welshman grinned. "But I can make it so if need be."

Elen lifted the spoon to her lips, forcing herself to swallow another mouthful of the thick pottage Simon had ladled into her cup. What was happening outside the hall? She'd seen no sign of Dylan or Gruffydd since breakfast was served. Had they been taken? Had they somehow lured Richard outside into a trap?

She was surprised to find both ideas upsetting. Richard was her enemy and she wished him gone from Wales with all her heart. But the idea of him walking unsuspecting into a trap out in the mists somehow sickened her.

By carrying on an absentminded exchange with Giles, Elen forced herself to continue the appearance of real conversation. And she was quick to note Giles made a pretense as well. His voice was light, his motions well controlled, but his eyes turned frequently toward the door with a wariness she couldn't mistake.

It was with great relief that Elen watched the lord of Gwenlyn return to the hall. Richard smiled down at her as he seated himself. "It was as I suspected, only a small problem in the village. One of the oxen I loaned the men has turned up lame. They fear I'm like to flay them alive simply because the beast can't work for a few days."

Elen tried to settle her unsteady breathing. Surely Richard wouldn't appear so relaxed if he'd just seized two Welsh rebels in his own keep. "What will you do?" she asked.

"I told the man to bring the creature here to be tended. That I would send another."

The meal continued and Elen toyed with her food, glancing covertly about the hall in search of her two friends. Richard lingered over his ale talking amiably with Giles and Sir William. Finished with their repast, the soldiers on the floor below rose and Richard dismissed them to the bailiff for a change in duties.

From the back of the room, servants began moving forward to remove the tables. Elen's eyes nervously searched for her two friends. They were wisely remaining on the other side of the hall, far from the chance notice of anyone at the high table.

Without warning, Richard rose and sauntered across the floor, pausing to speak to each of the diligently working servants. Elen caught her breath. What had induced the master of Gwenlyn to take notice of his servants on this of all days?

Richard's zigzag path took him alongside the laboring Welshmen. Dylan turned his back, ducking his head and working with pretended zeal, but Gruffydd glanced at Richard, then across the hall to where the last of the soldiers were disappearing through the doorway.

The temptation to destroy the most hated man in Gwynedd was suddenly too great. At once, a length of glittering steel appeared in Gruffydd's hand and he swung the dagger at Richard's unprotected back with all his strength.

Gruffydd . . . Gruffydd, no! Elen opened her mouth to scream, but Richard had already wheeled sideways. The arching blade swept past Richard's shoulder with a force that put the Welshman squarely in front of him. Richard's own weapon flashed out, and he dealt the astonished man a crushing blow to the wrist with the flat of his sword, sending the dagger skittering harmlessly away across the floor. The Welshman turned to flee, but the point of Richard's blade caught him in the throat, bringing him up short.

Dylan didn't hesitate. Catching up one of the table boards, he swung it broadside into a half-dozen heavily armed men who had suddenly sprung from behind the pantry screen. The first two went down in a tangled heap, thrashing limbs and weapons effectively blocking the others. With his path cleared, Dylan darted through a rear doorway and out of the hall.

The entire episode had lasted only a few seconds. Somehow Elen was on her feet and staring at the confused scene in horror. She took a step away from the table, but Giles caught her arm. "I doubt you're needed, Elen," he said in an icy voice. "Richard has the matter in hand."

Elen glanced up into a pair of dark accusing eyes. Giles's grip cut painfully into her arm and she stared at him in amazement. "Surely you don't think I had aught to do with this!"

"Bring her here!"

Giles glanced up at Richard's order. He spun Elen about, shoving her unceremoniously toward the crowd of soldiers.

Richard lifted his sword, pointing it toward the Welshman. "Do you know this man, Elen?" he snapped. "You had better tell me true."

Elen exchanged a look with Gruffydd, then glanced at the circle of murderous English faces. "Yes, I know him," she said evenly. "He's a good man and a fine warrior, and I have long called him friend." She sent Richard a look of entreaty. "And in spite of what he's done, he doesn't deserve to die like a dog, Richard."

"Oh? And just how do I deserve to die, Elen?" Richard bit out. "Perhaps you can tell me. Perhaps you can even tell me what little surprises I might next expect from your friends. An unexpected ambush . . . a knife in the back . . . poison perhaps. By Our Lady, I wish I'd the stomach to force the truth from you," he ended disgustedly.

"You think I knew of this?" Elen asked in amazement. "I recognized the man this morning, yes. But I swear, before God, I knew naught before that. I've not even spoken to him yet. How could I?"

"Perhaps not to him, but I've just learned Father Dilwen begged jobs for him and the other one who ran from my steward." Richard stared at her coldly. "And you did speak to the priest, I'm told."

So Richard hadn't trusted her after all. "You should speak to your spies. Their information is faulty!" she snapped. "I did go in search of Father Dilwen but he wasn't here. He'd returned to the village to see a sick child."

"That's true, Richard," Giles said quickly. "Elen came to me seeking the man. By the time she was downstairs, the priest was already gone."

Slowly Richard's anger began to fade. Perhaps Elen wasn't a part of this plot. He drew a deep breath and sheathed his sword, surprised at the intensity of relief that swept him. "Giles, see this fellow lodged below with our usual hospitality. And his companion should be along soon to join him if Henry and his men didn't get carried away."

Giles nodded and stepped forward to lead the prisoner away. But before the soldiers could move, Gruffydd had slipped a second knife from his tunic and was lunging toward Richard.

It all happened so quickly, Elen scarcely realized what was going on. Richard dodged and reached for his sword, but Giles's blade was already up and swinging in a deadly arc that caught the desperate Welshman full across the midsection. Cloth and flesh connected with naked steel and an agonized groan tore through the room. Gruffydd stumbled back, then crumpled to the floor.

For one second of frozen horror, Elen didn't move. *Gruffydd . . . Dear God, no!*

She sprang toward him, but Richard caught her against his chest, swinging away to shield her from the sight. She struggled in his arms. "Let me go, Richard. For pity's sake, let me go!"

"No, Elen. Elen, stop it!" he commanded as she continued to flail at him. His arms stilled her fight. "Think a moment, Elen. Think!" He waited until she quieted, until her eyes met his. "He's beyond all human aid now," he added softly.

Slowly the words sank in. Elen ceased her struggle, burying her face against Richard's chest, closing her eyes as the image of Giles's powerful stroke played through her mind. "Merciful God," she whispered, clutching the soft wool of Richard's tunic convulsively. "Sweet, Merciful God . . ."

As Richard continued to hold her—his embrace a welcome sanctuary now from the grisly scene in the hall—she clung to him, finding strange comfort in his arms.

After a moment, Richard moved away. "Simon, take her upstairs and fetch her some wine. Then return to me at once."

The boy stepped forward and Richard handed Elen into his squire's arms. She went quietly, without looking back, and Richard watched, frowning, as Simon led her toward the stairs.

"The Welshman's dead, Richard," Giles said unnecessarily. "I'm sorry we can't make him talk."

Richard glanced down at his friend. Giles knelt among the fouled rushes, his bloody sword in hand. "Considering the circumstances, I'm glad you didn't hesitate," he responded dryly.

"Do you believe the priest is involved?"

"Before God, I don't know." Richard ran his fingers through his hair and sighed heavily. "I like the man, even our own soldiers like him. And he seems a man of God. But that's just the trouble—the Welsh can seem to be anything they choose if it fits their purpose. I've sent Henry to fetch him. I'll have to question him."

Giles nodded in agreement. "A pity. I like him too."

Richard's gaze shifted to the stairs where Elen had just disappeared. Yes, he'd talk to the good Father, and then he'd see Elen. But he feared he hadn't the right questions for one nor the necessary answers for the other.

A half hour later, Richard found himself hesitating outside Elen's chamber. He had questioned Father Dilwen, but the priest claimed no knowledge of any plot against the English. He had sought only to find work for Welsh herdsmen, men who had lost their living when thousands of sheep were slaughtered last year to feed Edward's armies and starve out the Welsh.

Richard frowned. He wasn't entirely convinced, but what could he do? Put a priest to questioning with the knife? On this scanty evidence? Others would have done it in the hell of these wars, but Richard's whole being revolted at the thought. No, he would settle for having the man closely watched. If he proved a rebel, he would be executed, Richard promised himself grimly.

He nodded to one of the guards that once again stood to attention outside Elen's chamber. He knocked, but there was no sound from within. Opening the door quietly, he stepped over the threshold.

Elen lay on the bed staring blindly at the canopy of cream and gold brocade above her. A goblet of wine sat untouched on a coffer chest near the bed. He crossed the room slowly, easing himself to a seat on the mattress at her side. Still, she didn't move or speak a word.

Lifting the wine, he took a steadying draught. "I've given orders the man's to have a proper burial," he said at last. "You may go if you wish."

"And the other one?" she asked woodenly. "Is he dead as well?"

"No." Richard placed the goblet deliberately on the coffer. "He got away in the fog."

"I'm glad."

"I know."

Elen shifted her head to look at him. "Gruffydd was not so many years older than I. When I was a child, he used to carve blocks of wood into toys to amuse me. And he played the harp and sang. He sang with a skill my father said could make the holy angels weep for joy."

"And he just tried to put a dagger in my back," Richard added sardonically.

Elen simply stared at him, her slanted blue eyes twin pools of frozen grief.

"What do you want of me, Elen?" Richard asked softly. "They came here to kill me. Would you have me say I'm sorry they didn't succeed?"

She shook her head. "They came here to free me, not to kill you. And now an old friend lies dead because of me. One more," she added, turning miserably away. "One more to mourn."

Richard turned her back to face him. "Oh, they planned to free you all right, but their goal was to kill me as well. I just encouraged them to show their hand sooner than they intended." His voice hardened. "And two of my men were slain out there in the mist by your gentle friends. Those men also have friends and families who mourn."

Elen sat up. "Richard, you don't understand. If you would just let me go, this all would be ended!" She leaned toward him. "Richard, for the love of God, let me go!"

Richard caught her shoulders with both hands, his face scant inches from hers. "Tell me, Elen. Make me understand." He gave her a rough shake, his eyes searching hers. "Just how many lives are you worth? Rhys must value you highly indeed to continue risking men on these raids to free you?" His eyes narrowed suddenly, his fingers digging into her arms. "Just who are you, Elen?" he asked harshly. "Are you his wife?"

"No!" Her answer was sharp, almost panicky. Taking a deep breath, Elen closed her eyes, seeking to lead the conversation away from such dangerous ground. "I could never make you see, Richard. You English don't wish to understand us. You never have." She opened her eyes, forcing herself to speak in a deliberate tone. "Just let me go and this pointless bloodshed will be ended."

"You know as well as I that would not end the bloodshed. And you are wrong, Elen. Some of us do seek to understand you. I've been trying for weeks now, sometimes, I think, successfully." Richard's grip on her shoulders eased, his hands lifting to cup her face. "Besides," he added softly, "I've no wish to let you go. Not now."

In the second before Richard's mouth covered hers, Elen knew she should stop him . . . knew but didn't care. His arms slid around her, drawing her into an embrace so warm, so comforting, it released the frozen grief inside, bringing tears to her eyes in a way the earlier horror she had witnessed had not. She was tired of bearing it all alone and Richard offered strong arms and a warm shoulder, an instinctive understanding that both pleased and surprised her.

His lips moved over hers, gentle, compelling. There was no pain this time, no punishment in his embrace. There was no sense of mastery or subjection, only the reassurance of no longer being alone, of being swept along on a turbulent course she had no will or wish to change.

Her lips parted beneath the pressure of his, her face turned up to accommodate the sensual movement of his mouth over hers. Her fists opened against his shoulders, wrapping around his neck, losing themselves in the thick golden hair that curled over his tunic.

"This is only the second time I've seen you cry," Richard murmured, brushing a tear from her cheek with his thumb. "I regret it always seems to be my doing."

Elen dashed the back of her hand across her eyes, her heart aching with the knowledge that Richard had almost been killed—and that she was thankful he hadn't. But Gruffydd . . . how could she be thankful Richard lived when Gruffydd did not?

"Elen," Richard began earnestly. "I'm as tired of the bloodshed as you—"

A sudden, frantic pounding sounded against the chamber door. Richard glanced up in irritation. "Yes?"

Simon swung into the room, out of breath and a little nonplussed by the intimate scene he'd stumbled upon. "Richard, t-there's a messenger arrived from Edward," he stammered. "He calls you to a conference at Chepstow. He says he's been delayed by weather and we'd best make haste!"

Richard released Elen and slid to his feet. "Has he letters?"

The boy nodded.

"Then have him wait in my chamber. Ask Giles to stay close—I'll need to leave orders. Tell the grooms to ready the horses and see to my packing."

Simon nodded. He was used to Richard's rapid commands.

Richard turned back to Elen. "And tell the messenger I'll join him in a moment."

The soft noise of a door closing echoed in the silent chamber. Richard touched Elen's hair, tracing one finger gently along her cheek. "I must go now," he said softly. His hand fell back to his side. "You'll be safe here, and I'll return as soon as I'm able."

He waited, but she didn't speak. She turned her head away, the moment of intimacy between them obviously gone. With a heavy sigh, Richard moved toward the door, silently cursing the luck that called him away just now.

He hesitated on the threshold; the picture Elen made in the middle of the great curtained bed was one he would keep for the long ride to Chepstow. There was so much he wanted to say, but she wasn't ready to hear it now. And besides, there wasn't time. Edward had called.

He forced a light smile. "Be a good girl and don't slay any Englishmen while I'm away."

And with that he was gone.

CHAPTER SEVENTEEN

$\mathscr{A}$ small fire burning quietly in the hearth made soft comforting sounds, adding to the peaceful atmosphere in the cozy chamber. Richard lifted the silver goblet in his hand and took a swallow of fine Bordeaux wine. He gazed at his queen, an amused smile tugging at his lips. "Now, tell me true, Your Grace. Why did you bring me here? This nonsense about my opinion of a new jeweled chaplet is ridiculous. You know I've little sense in such matters."

Eleanor of Castile's dark eyes twinkled up at him, and she lifted the circlet of cunningly wrought topaz and gilt leaves to rest against the snowy linen of her wimple. "Well, don't you think it's becoming? I'm sure I shall set a fashion."

"You could wear blacksmith's iron and set a fashion, Your Grace, as you know well," Richard said dryly.

"Oh pish, Richard, you can do better than that!" Eleanor's eyebrows lifted provocatively. "My ladies tell me you can be extremely gallant when you choose. And from the rumors, some should know."

Richard grinned. "I'm sure—like their mistress—your ladies talk a great deal of nonsense."

Eleanor settled into a velvet-cushioned chair with a muffled rustle of silk, gesturing for Richard to seat himself on a nearby stool. "Well, they do gossip a bit," she conceded.

"And I admit, I've encouraged them to talk on you of late."
She leaned toward him, her face suddenly serious. "Tell
me, Richard, has no woman caught your fancy enough for
you to think of taking a wife?"

At the sudden shift in conversation, Richard glanced up
in surprise. "A wife? No." He searched for something to
keep the moment light. "The only woman I've interest in
is already wed." He lifted his shoulders helplessly. "And
alas, I fear, I've little to offer the Queen of England."

Eleanor sent him an exasperated glance. "Yes, and the
Queen of England is old enough to be your mother and has
borne her lord a quiverful of children besides. Now be serious, Richard, do. You're of an age to be well married. Edward
and I'd been wed ten years by the time he was your age."

"Yes, and he had a great deal to offer you too." Richard
met her frowning gaze calmly. "I'm a soldier, Your Grace,
making my living with my sword. I've little to offer any
woman of rank. You know my situation. Without part of
my pay, Waybridge would scarcely support my father, much
less any family I might take. And I dare not wed some sweet
child and leave her with my stepmother while I go off
soldiering. What would become of her if aught should happen to me? No, Eleanor, I've no thought of marriage, at
least at present. Besides," he added with a wry smile, "who
would have me?"

"Any woman of sense," Eleanor snapped. She lifted her
chin and pursed her lips thoughtfully. "Any woman of
sense," she repeated, "especially if she already has such
wealth that your lack doesn't signify." She lifted the jeweled
chaplet in her hands, twisting it absently between her ringed
fingers. "Do you remember my goddaughter, Alicia de
Borgh?"

Richard searched his mind for a face to go with the well-
known de Borgh name. He had a faint memory of a summer
two years ago when Edward had summoned him to Leeds
castle. He had spent several hours amusing a lovely blond

waif while he waited for Edward. "I remember the girl," he said after a moment, "but surely she's no more than a child."

"She's fourteen and has finished her training with the nuns at St. Mary's. And she has fond memories of you, Richard." Eleanor's eyes narrowed reflectively. "Her parents are looking about for a desirable husband for the girl. They've an inordinate wish for her hap—"

"Your Grace, don't even think it!" Richard interrupted, the thought of marriage oddly distasteful. "Ranulff de Borgh would drive me away from his gates with a whip if ever I mentioned such a notion. And what's more, I wouldn't blame him. The idea is preposterous!"

"Not if Edward backed your suit."

Richard shook his head. "Edward has more important matters to attend. Besides, it would create dissatisfaction among a host of powerful families I could name. And the King doesn't need that just now. I know you mean well by me, but I beg you not speak of the matter."

"But you know very well you're one of Edward's favorites." Eleanor smiled indulgently. "Even though he claims not to have them."

Richard shook his head. "No, Your Grace."

"Don't say no to your queen, my man," Eleanor ordered, lifting her expressive brows with feigned haughtiness. "Are you forgetting I was with him after Acre? I saw what you did at the tournament and I shall never forget it!"

"I did nothing any other Englishman wouldn't have done. By Our Lady, your lord husband is the King of England. He owes me naught for being a loyal subject."

"Humph! Some Englishmen don't give a fig for loyalty, Richard. But that's not the point. I know Edward wishes to do something to advance your fortunes."

"He already has. He's raised me higher than I ever thought to climb. Now forget this idea. It's impossible."

Eleanor tapped her slender finger impatiently against her chin. "Oh, very well. But tell me this. Have you a fancy for any particular woman? Is your heart taken?"

Richard hesitated. A sudden image of a fiery chestnut beauty bloomed in his mind, but he thrust the memory aside. That wasn't the type of fancy Eleanor meant. "No, Your Grace. Of course not."

"Good, then I can—"

The queen broke off. Richard glanced over his shoulder, following her gaze. Edward had entered the solar. In the outer chamber, the queen's ladies leaped to their feet, then dropped into low curtsies. Richard and Eleanor rose as well.

Edward nodded in greeting, then moved through the women toward the queen's bedchamber. "What mischief are you two brewing?" he inquired, leaning his massive six-feet-two frame against the ebony marble of the fireplace. "Richard, I think it best to inquire into your business when I find you closeted in this secrecy with my wife."

Eleanor lifted the jeweled circlet, sending Edward the radiant smile she saved solely for her lord. "I was showing him the present you gave me. He says I could wear blacksmith's iron and still be fashionable."

"And so you could, my love." Edward glanced at Richard, his drooping left eyelid lowering even further in the suggestion of a wink. "I wonder I didn't think of that. The metal would be a great deal less dear."

"But then all the women would be bent on having it and there'd be none left for our horses," Richard interposed in a serious tone. "So perhaps the gold is just as well."

"You are both impossible and I see, between you, I'm to have no peace," Eleanor remarked, motioning to a servant. "May I offer you wine, my lord?"

Edward shook his head. "No, I came to borrow Richard if you've done with him. I finished the dispatches from this afternoon and we've matters to discuss."

Richard tossed off the rest of his wine and glanced at Edward expectantly. "Matters pertaining to the north?"

Edward nodded. "If you'll excuse us for a short time, my

love," he added, turning to Eleanor. He motioned Richard toward the door, staying behind a moment to talk privately with his wife.

Richard moved through the queen's ladies, scarcely noticing the interested looks sent his way. A pang of envy pierced him. Edward and Eleanor had a harmonious union such as any man might desire. He knew Edward was faithful to his queen, while any fool could see Eleanor's devotion to her husband.

It was a combination one rarely saw in marriage. But of all the women Richard knew, Eleanor of Castile was one who might achieve such a triumph. She was generous, witty, brave, and near single-minded in her devotion to Edward. She followed her warrior husband on his campaigns about the country, untiring and unprotesting, preferring the rigors of camp life to separation from Edward.

But Eleanor wasn't merely a woman, she was a queen, Richard reminded himself. And perhaps it was too much to expect such qualities in other women. He had certainly never found them in another . . . at least until Elen.

The thought was ridiculous, but the comparison had nagged at him since he had arrived at Chepstow. How could the girl possibly remind him of the queen? There was certainly no physical resemblance between the two women. Yet something in Elen's proud bearing, in her dogged determination and her unflinching devotion to those she loved brought the English queen to mind.

Richard rubbed his chin in perplexity, glancing up as Edward emerged into the corridor. "The dispatches brought good news, I take it?"

"Yes, news I've been anxious for. Dafydd ap Gruffydd is surrounded and holed up in some wretched stockade with no chance of escape. After months of harrowing the traitor through every bog and thicket, it seems we have him at last. And by God's sword, his own countrymen betrayed him to our men!"

Richard turned to follow his king down the hall. "Most Welshmen didn't take kindly to Dafydd's plotting with you these last years to overthrow Llywelyn. There was certainly no love lost between Gruffydd's two sons."

Edward paused before the small, comfortable room he used as an audience chamber. He glanced at Richard. "No, I didn't take kindly to his betrayal of me either." The king's blue eyes hardened suddenly with an icy expression Richard knew boded ill for his enemies. "A little matter he'll soon pay dearly for."

They entered the chamber and, at Edward's invitation, Richard seated himself at the king's right hand. " Dafydd's capture has been a foregone conclusion since we sealed off the coast at the first of the year, but there are others I'm concerned about," Edward continued broodingly. He glanced up. "Have you still discovered nothing of the family of Aldwyn of Teifi?"

Richard shook his head. "I've questioned every prisoner I've taken and spread your silver about with the promise of more. But I've heard nothing save that the two women are in France which you know already."

"I don't believe they sailed to the continent," Edward responded. "I've had men searching there. The women would have surfaced in France by now were it true."

"Why this concern? They're only women."

"Women bear children," Edward remarked dryly. "The family claimed a distant relation to Llywelyn which makes them dangerous. I didn't cut off the head of one snake to have it grow a half-dozen more." He rose and paced restlessly about the table. "No . . . I learned my lesson with Simon de Montfort. I thought that trouble ended when he was slain at Evesham, only to have his daughter marry Llywelyn and see every discontented de Montfort adherent in England flock to the Welsh banner. I'll leave my sons a greater hope for peace than that!"

Richard nodded grimly. The scars of England's bloody

civil war went deep in his sovereign and he knew Edward was determined there would never be another such episode in England's history—at least in his lifetime. "We'll find them. No one can hide forever." He grinned. "Most especially a woman."

Edward came around the table and sat down. For a moment he poked absently at a stack of parchment, then his piercing blue eyes lifted to Richard's. "That wasn't all I wished to say to you. Hugh de Veasy arrives tomorrow and your half-brother Philip with him."

Richard didn't blink. It was only natural that Hugh de Veasy would be called to Edward's council on the Welsh problem. The Baron of Ravensgate was one of the most influential men in the south and a good fighting man for all Richard didn't care for his tactics. But he was a little surprised the haughty nobleman would bring a green lad like Philip with him. "That's nothing to me," he said, keeping his voice neutral.

"Your brother has been most unwise, and it hasn't escaped our notice," Edward commented, shifting to the royal we, a sure sign that he was troubled. "He has talked loud and long about his supposed misfortunes at your hands... oh, and a great deal more besides. We would have you be on your guard, Richard. There's to be no trouble here."

Richard's lip curled up in disdain. "The empty braying of an ass. I don't concern myself with Philip's noise."

Edward shifted the paper before him thoughtfully. "An ass perhaps, but an ass that has attached himself to a most powerful master. A master who bears no love for you, Richard."

"De Veasy and I bear no love for each other, but neither are we enemies. We even respect each other in our way."

"De Veasy wants North Wales. Christ's bones, the man wants all Wales!" Edward exclaimed impatiently. "His ambition knows no bounds. And make no mistake, he would discredit you if he could. I say again, Richard, I want no trouble between you two. De Veasy has alliances with half the families in the south. The last thing I need now is some feud to upset the uneasy balance I've achieved for England."

"You've given me a job to do in Wales. It's a temporary duty and de Veasy should find little to upset him in that. I'll be back in England before long. But let him scheme how he will, he'll not undermine my work."

Edward's eyes narrowed thoughtfully and the ghost of a smile touched his lips. "Good. You know I make it a practice not to interfere in petty squabbles among my nobles, but I thought you might need a hint, Richard. And as for leaving Wales soon, don't be in any hurry. I need good men and true to hold for me, especially in the north. I'm pleased with the progress you've reported, and once you take this Rhys ap Iwan, I want you to stay on to administer my business until the land is stable. I can't risk another rebellion there with trouble brewing in Scotland."

Richard's face fell. Stay on in Wales . . .

"And now that we understand each other, I've other matters to see to before I take my rest. I'll speak with you further after the conference tomorrow."

Richard forced a smile to his face and took his leave of Edward. Wales. He was going to have to stay on in Wales.

But as the dismal thought registered, another took its place, soothing him with an unexpected feeling of contentment. Elen was at Gwenlyn awaiting his return.

Richard shifted his weight in the saddle, slowing Moroedd with the slightest tightening of his reins. This was the last time he would exercise the big gray before turning him over to Edward's head groom. The king had been absurdly delighted by the gift, but Richard felt a vague qualm at thought of Elen's reaction. Still, the restive stallion was no mount for her. It was only God's mercy she hadn't broken her neck on the brute already.

His gaze drifted from the road to the tranquil beauty of

the river Wye flowing past the high walls of Chepstow Castle. Above the river, the pale limestone cliffs gleamed white in the summer sun while the water swirled past in a constantly shifting pattern of silver and blue—a blue as deep and changeable as the color of Elen's eyes.

Richard frowned in exasperation. Why did everything here remind him of Elen? She was just a woman, for pity's sake. Beautiful, yes, but no more so than others he had known. Still, she filled his thoughts far more than he liked, the memory making him more easily reconciled to Edward's plan to keep him in Wales. But after this morning, he might have to fight for that privilege. Hugh de Veasy wanted Richard's command and was making no secret of the fact.

Richard's hand tightened involuntarily on the reins, making Moroedd sidle nervously and shake his head. Christ's blood, de Veasy had already worked out elaborate plans for subjugating all of Gwynedd—plans that would incite every hotheaded Welshman to further hopeless rebellion. Fortunately, Edward hadn't listened this morning despite the urging of the Marcher lords bent on punishment for the conquered country.

Richard bit his lip thoughtfully. Edward was right. The Baron of Ravensgate wanted Wales at any cost. And if he could discredit Richard in the process it would make the victory that much sweeter.

A sudden image of hungry, hopeless faces encircling two beaten prisoners flitted through Richard's head. De Veasy would crush all of Gwynedd beneath his heel and enjoy doing it. And Elen . . . what would he do to a woman like Elen? The thought made his stomach churn, made him suddenly anxious to get back to Gwynedd. No, Hugh de Veasy would take Gwenlyn over his dead body!

Turning Moroedd away from the river, Richard eased the big gray into a canter, checking only as he passed through Chepstow's gate and into the bailey. As he swung down from the saddle, he handed his reins to a servant, then walked toward the hall.

Near the stairs, his eye fell on a familiar figure. His half-brother Philip stood nearby inspecting a horse a young groom held. The boy had grown up in the last two years, Richard decided, eyeing Philip critically. He still had the dark good looks of his Norman mother, but for the first time, Richard detected some look of their father in Philip's slim, muscular build.

Rejecting his first impulse to enter the keep from another doorway, Richard made his way toward Philip, uncertain what he would say or even if he truly wished to speak with the boy. "A fine-looking animal. Is he yours?" he tried, coming to a halt.

Philip glanced up, then fell back a step in surprise. "I . . . I, yes he's mine. Bought and paid for," he muttered defensively. "But what have you to say of the matter?"

Richard felt his brother's hostile stare burn over him. He slid his hand along the deep-chested roan gelding's powerful shoulder, certain now the coin he'd sent his father for improvements at Waybridge had gone to purchase this costly steed. "Only that you have good taste," he said mildly. "This fellow looks to carry you easily on most any campaign."

He glanced at his brother. They hadn't seen each other in over two years and what was past was done. He might at least try to bridge the gap between them. Besides, Edward wanted no trouble. "I'm glad I see you well, Philip. And I hear you deserve congratulations. You won your spurs at Walmsley. I was pleased to hear of your knighting."

A flush of surprised pleasure warmed the boy's face. "I doubted you'd heard. It was an unlooked-for piece of good fortune. I unhorsed two opponents at the tournament and was successful in the melee as well." He shot a suspicious look at Richard. "Not that it can compare with your glorious record, brother."

"I should hope not!" Richard stroked the nervous roan once more, then turned to Philip with a low chuckle. "I can remember being tossed on my backside on more than one occasion in my early days."

A slight grin eased the tightness around the boy's mouth. "How I'd have loved seeing that."

"I'm sure you would. I'm just thankful few remember those days save myself. By the way," Richard added, "how fares our father?"

The boy's face hardened unexpectedly. "Well enough, I suppose. And able to talk of little save your successes, brother. What a shame he'll soon hear of your loss of command in Wales."

Richard's hand fell away from the roan. Philip had been lapping up de Veasy's poison as a cat laps cream. "No man sees the future, but I feel safe in saying there'll be no immediate change in command. Your information is faulty, though I can guess the source."

"Well, well . . . what a touching sight. One might think Cain and Abel reunited."

Richard glanced up with a heavy frown. Hugh de Veasy and his host, Roger Bigod, Earl of Norfolk, were bearing down upon them. "Philip, be a good lad and fetch my squire here to me," de Veasy continued, waving a languid hand in Philip's direction. "I can't imagine where the boy's got off to."

Philip sent Richard a hostile look, then glanced at de Veasy. "Certainly, my lord." He gestured to the groom to take his horse inside. "I'll be quick."

De Veasy paused a few paces from Richard. "It's my good fortune to meet with you here instead of sending my boy on a search for you, Basset. My courier just rode in from Tintern Abbey with messages from Gregory Vespain. Oddly enough, the bishop sent a letter for you."

Richard studied the face of his enemy suspiciously. De Veasy's black hair curled back from his forehead, his dark eyes surveying Richard with poorly concealed disdain. The baron held out the bound parchment, his lips curling above his beard with more than a hint of mockery. "If you've trouble with the reading, I'll be pleased to offer assistance."

The thinly veiled slur on Richard's upbringing brought a bark of laughter from Bigod. It was well known Richard had had none of the fine tutoring afforded to noble households.

Trouble, Edward wanted no trouble, Richard reminded himself, forcing a smile to his lips as he took the letter. "I appreciate the offer, my lord, but I've no need of your help . . . in this matter or any other." He turned pointedly away from the man, giving his attention to his host. "Let me compliment you, Norfolk, on the building here at Chepstow. Few men thought to see your father's plan improved, but you've done it. The work is magnificent."

The earl cleared his throat and glanced shamefacedly at de Veasy. "Why, thank you, Basset. It's been long in the planning."

Richard nodded. "If you'll excuse me now, gentlemen, I've pressing business to see to." He sent de Veasy a cool smile. "My thanks, de Veasy, for fetching my messages. I'll send for you if I've a reply."

With that parting shot, Richard entered the hall, and quickly tore open the surprising missive. His eyes skimmed eagerly down the tight lines of flowing script, his mind racing ahead of the genial words he read.

So the Bishop of Lanwort had heard of Gwenlyn's need of a priest and, by a strange coincidence, he had just the right man. Richard smiled grimly. He just bet the old fox had the right man, but the right man for whom? It was well known that Gregory Vespain and Hugh de Veasy were hand in glove in their quest for power. No, he would sooner take a man from Lucifer himself than from the Bishop of Lanwort—but how to refuse without causing a fuss?

Suddenly, Richard chuckled. By all the saints, he didn't need a priest—he already had one! For all he knew, Father Dilwen was a Welsh rebel, but in this instance, at least, the man was a godsend. He could refuse the bishop without giving offense.

When Richard broached the matter to Edward that night,

he wasn't surprised to find his sovereign in agreement. "Any man Gregory Vespain sent would be on the lookout for news for de Veasy if nothing worse," Edward said thoughtfully. "But are you certain you've not a Welsh spy in your midst with this priest?"

"I'm certain of nothing as yet, but the man's been a help in the village. He seems devout and, for all he's Welsh, more learned than most priests of my experience. He gives the appearance of caring for men from both sides of the border with no thought for the bitterness he encounters. Besides," Richard added cynically, "if I discover he's a spy for this Rhys, I can feed him what information I choose . . . before I hang him."

Edward nodded. "I leave it to your judgment. And when all's said and done, it may be a shrewd move. If the man's no rebel, his appointment to such a post might keep the locals content. I've seen it work before. In any event, do as you think best without stirring up a hornet's nest around Vespain. The man has powerful friends in Rome.

"And speaking of friends . . ." Edward leaned forward, studying his well-shaped fingers intently. "How many years is it you've served me now, Richard?"

"Nigh on ten, my lord."

"And in all that time, you've asked for naught. I'd almost forgot the passing years."

Richard glanced up in surprise. "You've given me more than I can measure. I've had no need to ask."

"What? A war-horse here, a suit of armor there, gifted to you after important campaigns won." Edward's shrewd eyes studied Richard assessingly. "In my father and grandfather's day you'd have been an earl thrice over. Do you never wish for such?"

"In your father and grandfather's day, England was nigh given away," Richard remarked evenly. "You'll not hear me complain of my lot, Edward. I value the command you've given me and the chance to prove myself."

Edward smiled. "I could leave it at that, but I fear Eleanor would give me no peace. She feels we should do better by you and I'm inclined to agree. Perhaps a suitable marriage arrangement can be made. I shall look about me for some rich widow or heiress."

His eyes narrowed thoughtfully. "Ranulff de Borgh is casting about for a husband for his only child—though that may be flying a bit high. Still and all, his interest is in finding a fair man with a strong hand to rule his lands after him. It might answer at that."

Richard's mouth tightened in consternation. Damn Eleanor's meddling! "This is the queen's scheming, and I told her the idea was ridiculous," Richard said lightly. "She promised not to broach the subject, but I should have known she's not so easily driven from the scent."

"Oh, she kept her promise. Eleanor'll not be foresworn. She led me, quite skillfully mind you, to think this whole thing my own idea. Now I see I was naught but a pawn." The king laughed. "Take my advice, Richard. Marry some sweet guileless child you'll not spend your days trying to outguess."

Some guileless child. The idea was overwhelmingly distasteful. "Take no further thought to the matter, Your Majesty. I've no mind to marry. The queen should never have bothered you with her matchmaking schemes."

"Well, I make no promises, Richard, but I shall look about with you in mind. After all, I can't keep you exiled in Wales and expect you to find a suitable match on your own, now can I?"

Richard started to protest, but Edward rose to his feet, signifying the audience was ended. "I shall be busy on the morrow and won't see you again before your departure. Take care, my loyal Richard, and bring me the hide of a certain Welsh Fox!"

CHAPTER EIGHTEEN

"*S*ir Richard! It's Sir Richard's party coming up the coast road!" The excited soldier waved his arms and hurried across the hall. "The men can make out his red boar banner plain from the tower."

Giles rose from his seat. "Excellent! Have men see to the horses." He turned to the servant who had appeared at his elbow. "Get two barrels of ale up from the storerooms and fetch me wine from the buttery for Sir Richard."

Elen set down the harp she had been absently strumming, and her heart suddenly leaped to a fast staccato beat. *He was back.*

She took a deep breath to steady herself against the nervous tensing of her stomach, against the ridiculous urge to rise and flee the room. She had spent the past few weeks steeling herself against this moment, telling herself she knew her mind, knew her duty. Yet three little words easily destroyed what peace she had found. He was back.

While Richard was away, it was easy enough to remind herself of the many reasons she had for hating him. But the very knowledge that he would soon be with her again sent all her hard-won determination crumbling. The memory of their last meeting rose up to haunt her along with the lingering tenderness of his kiss. No, she didn't want to see Richard. In very fact, she was afraid to see him.

She rose stiffly to her feet and turned to Giles, keeping her voice deliberately cold. It was easiest to be strong when she pretended to be angry. "I'd better return to my chamber. Your master will be ill pleased to find me loosed from my cage."

Giles gazed at her thoughtfully, the suspicion of a smile lurking in his dark eyes. "You've no need to go. Richard doesn't grudge you your freedom about Gwenlyn."

"I bow to your superior knowledge of the Wolf, but I prefer to go upstairs. I've no wish to remain below now."

"Very well." Giles called to her guard and the man moved to the doorway. "Richard will want to see you, you know."

Elen continued her dignified retreat toward the door. "I've no desire to see him. You may tell him that for me."

"Coward."

She turned indignantly but Giles was already halfway across the hall.

A short time later Elen found herself facing the master of Gwenlyn across the floor of her chamber. She had forgotten how well he held himself, how the smile spread from his lips to warm the emerald depths of his eyes. He was taller than she remembered, his hair more golden, his face more bronzed from his hours in the summer sun. Her memory didn't do him justice, she realized with a pang.

"Giles tells me he's done his best to keep you entertained while I was away," Richard remarked easily.

Elen shrugged and moved toward the empty fireplace, struggling to avoid the irresistible draw of his gaze. "Yes. He's allowed me to visit my uncle's cell. As I recall, you did promise to give him his freedom about Gwenlyn. But that was weeks ago." She glanced up, deliberately baiting him. "I suppose with so many Welshmen to kill, your memory deserted you."

Richard's eyes slid over her, brightening with a glint of amusement. "I can see you've kept yourself busy while I was away, fashioning me into a monster. Actually, I found no Welshmen to slay in all my journeys these past weeks. I fear I shall get out of practice."

She sent him a look of exasperation and he moved to stand beside her. "Perhaps you'll remember, we had some trouble here before I left, Elen. I freed no prisoners. I didn't wish Giles to run more risks than necessary." He leaned against the fireplace, continuing to study her. "I shall see to my promises now I've returned.

"And you may not be pleased," he continued, "but it looks as though I'll be here longer than we believed. With the rebellion over, Edward wishes me to see to the administration of Gwynedd. I'd like your help."

Elen gave a bitter laugh and shook her head. So Edward believed the resistance was finished . . . the more fool he! "Do you really think I'd betray my people, Richard? You'll wait a long time for help from me."

He shrugged. "Suit yourself. Giles is teaching me the speech of your people, but he doesn't know all of your customs. It's my intention to combine Llywelyn's civil law with the criminal codes of England. I hope to find the right blending of both, but it will be difficult without Welsh help."

She stared at him in amazement. "You would consider our ways?"

"If you'll explain them to me," he answered quietly.

She studied Richard's face, scarcely daring to believe her ears. The English had always run roughshod over ancient Welsh custom and law. Merciful heaven, it was the very reason for Llywelyn's revolt last spring! "You have the king's permission for this?" she asked dubiously.

Richard nodded. "Since you read and write we'd not have to summon the priest for every item we put down. And you could explain the system once it's put into practice." He searched her face. "Will you help me, Elen?"

She lowered her eyes, not wanting him to see her excitement. If he were serious, such a chance to temper English law with familiar Welsh ways would be of great benefit—at least until her people drove Edward's army from Wales. "I'll help," she said, after a moment. And then, so he'd not think her softening, "It will be interesting to see what an Englishman's version of justice will be."

Richard allowed the insult to pass. He moved to the window and glanced out. "Come, Elen. There's something I wish you to see."

She studied him suspiciously, but did as he bade. In the courtyard below, Simon held a lively black mare at the end of a short lead. The animal was sleek and delicately built, showing signs of judicious mixing of Eastern bloodlines with sturdy English stock—easily one of the finest she'd seen in years.

"Do you like her?"

She glanced up. Richard was so close she could see the gold flecks in his green eyes, the tiny lines of weariness etched about his mouth. "She's lovely," Elen said truthfully. "You've knowledge of horses at least."

Once again a flash of amusement warmed Richard's eyes. "I'm gratified by the compliment. She's yours."

It took a moment for his words to register. Perhaps he meant the mare was hers to ride. "You would let me ride?" she asked, incredulous.

"If you give me your word you'll make no effort to escape—at least for the time outside."

A feeling of thankfulness surged up inside her. She would be willing to swear to almost anything to be outside these walls for a few hours!

"But that isn't what I meant, Elen," Richard added. "The mare is yours to do with as you will."

Elen felt a glimmer of doubt. "Why . . . why would you do this?"

"Because I promised." Richard hesitated. "And because enough has been taken from you already."

The words were surprising, but not nearly so disturbing as the tender look that went with them. Somehow Elen found her breath. "She is mine? I . . . I may take her with me when I go?"

"Yes." Richard's eyes held hers. "One day, Elen, you will come to believe I mean what I say."

"Yes, I know, Richard," she murmured. "Pactum Serva."

"Keep Troth. I'd forgotten you know Latin," he said lightly. He stepped away. "I'll tell you something more so you'll not be suspicious of my every word. You are not the only spring in the desert, Elen. There are other women who do not find me so lacking as you." He sent her a slanted glance, heavy golden lashes veiling his expressive eyes. "I doubt we shall trouble each other further."

It was impossible to mistake his meaning. She made a pretense of studying the mare below. No doubt Richard had found some woman at Chepstow and brought her back—some lovely, half-witted Englishwoman who would defer to his needs and bow to every whim. Well, if that's what he wanted, she wished him joy of the creature. She turned with a biting remark, but Richard was gone.

It had rained in the night. Elen walked to the window and gazed at the clearing sky, feeling a breath of cool, damp air touch her cheek. Layers of mist still crowned mountain peaks to the east, but the clouds above Gwenlyn had thinned and the golden warmth of the sun slanted through. It would be a beautiful day for a ride.

She glanced down into the bailey, watching Simon bring Saladin and her mare, Ceiri, to the front stairs. Richard must be ready.

She caught up the light cloak Giles had found for her, throwing it across her arm. She had devoted the last week to discussing Welsh justice with Richard. They had spent hours together. He had established a local court hallmote, allowing the familiar Welsh law to govern in most instances, but reserving the right to hand out English justice himself.

They had argued heatedly on occasion, cursing each other roundly in a mixture of French, English, and Welsh. But during their time together, Elen had grudgingly come to admire Richard's determination. What he said he would do, he did, and nothing would turn him from his goal.

Now, Richard was waiting for her at the door as she came into the hall. He stood bareheaded, his hair tousled from the wind outside. He wore no steel hauberk or surcoat blazing with his coat of arms today, only the heavily padded doublet of a simple man-at-arms. He looked younger somehow, less the infamous Wolf of Kent.

"Good, you brought a cloak. The sun's broken through the mist but it may be cool in the wood."

Elen nodded, an inexplicable joy bubbling up inside her, threatening to overflow. She had a whole morning free of the castle and it was a lovely, high summer's day. For a few hours, at least, she would forget she was Elen of Teifi. For a morning, someone else could shoulder the sorrows of Wales. "Where will we ride today?" she asked eagerly.

"Just a little way up the coast," Richard replied, smiling. They moved outside to the horses and Richard helped her into the saddle. "We won't go far. I've no desire to take a whole troop of men clattering about with us today."

The horses crossed the drawbridge, prancing into the open country outside the gates. After the dimness inside Gwenlyn, the sun-bright day was blinding. Elen lifted her head, watching bits of wind-driven cloud send shifting patterns of sunlight and shadow over the patchwork of hills beyond. It was good to be out.

She took a deep breath. The sun was hot on her back, the breeze cool and fresh with the summer scents of vetch and rain-washed bracken. She had a good horse beneath her and an entertaining companion for a morning's ride. And she wouldn't let her thoughts wander beyond these simple joys of the moment.

Taking the coast road, the riders turned off the track onto the narrow beach below. Richard urged Saladin into a canter along the foaming tidal margin, sending up sparkling crystal droplets in a rainbow spray behind him. Elen sent her nimble mare alongside, splashing through the shallows like a graceful black bird skimming the water's surface.

Richard broke into a laugh as the cold spray showered them both. Elen joined in, the sound of their mirth rippling out above the splashing of the horses and the rhythmic drumming of hooves on wet sand.

Laughter. It had been months—a lifetime—since she had laughed like that. It felt good. She couldn't find it in her heart to feel even a moment's guilt for this joy.

They drew to a halt, dripping and giggling like two impetuous children. Richard lowered his eyebrows in mock displeasure. "I'm near soaked through! I should toss you into the sea for wetting me so."

Elen leaned forward to stroke her mount's glistening neck. "Ah, but could you catch me on Ceiri? She makes me think the tales of winged horses who fly on the wind are true. She's wonderful, Richard." Her eyes met his. "Thank you."

Richard smiled. "I'm pleased she suits you. And yes, she is fast." His smile widened. "But to preserve your soul from temptation . . . you should know Saladin can catch her. I made certain of that before I brought you outside the gates."

"Now why do I have the feeling you've no trust in me?" Elen remarked with an innocent look.

Richard grinned. "Let's just call it a healthy respect for your nimble mind."

Elen began to laugh. "I like that far better, Richard."

Turning the horses off the beach, they climbed a winding path through a tumble of scattered boulders and twisted, storm-bent trees. Drawing rein at a rocky outcropping, they gazed at the view below. From this angle, the narrow ribbon of beach was hidden by an abundance of tall salt grass. It bent before the wind in shimmering patterns of silver and green while the ocean beyond glittered in the morning sun.

"Beautiful, isn't it?" Richard remarked. "Wales in the sunlight is certainly different from Wales in the mist."

The air was moist and cool, fragrant with gorse and the heavy sweetness of honeysuckle. Elen drew a deep, appreciative breath. "No. They are one and the same. Living here year round, one learns to appreciate both." She glanced back at him. "And for all the damp, I couldn't imagine being anywhere else."

Richard nodded. "My people say your land is a grim, inhospitable place . . . a land of black magic, of demons and spirits and people who thrive in the dark and the wet." He gazed out over the brilliant green of the birch forest, the azure-blue of the ocean. "I begin to think that it's a tale some shrewd Welshman dreamed up to keep Englishmen away. I'm ashamed to admit it, but I think I'll miss all this once I'm gone."

Elen smiled. "Take care, Richard. Some of the infamous Welsh magic is at work. You're falling under our spell."

Richard gazed at the bewitching girl at his side. He was falling under a spell all right, but it wasn't Wales he was thinking of.

The horses climbed higher, breaking out of the silver and green of the birch wood into a sunlit meadow. A mountain stream widened into a pool where leaf-dappled water lay deep and still, shadowed by a thick canopy of ash and alder.

"'Tis an enchanted place," Elen whispered, gazing about in delight. "The Tylwyth Teg must live here."

Richard dismounted and sent his horse across the grass to the edge of the pool. He stepped over to Elen swinging her to the ground beside him. "I doubt the fairy people will mind if we intrude for an hour. I promised to gift them with wine and cheese if they'd leave us be today."

Elen smiled at Richard's whimsy. He seemed different

today—like a boy on holiday. "Oh? And just what's so special about today?"

He had taken a blanket from the straw hamper Saladin carried and was spreading it out in the shade near the pool. "Today happens to be my birthday."

"Oh." She hesitated, not sure what to say. "I wish you joy of the day."

Richard moved across the clearing, tethering the horses where they could crop the lush grass. He returned with wine and food, kneeling to spread it out on the blanket with a flourish. "Not a great feast, I'm afraid, but enough for a celebration. As I recall you've had a birthday too."

Elen's eyes met his. Yes, she'd had a birthday—her seventeenth. And it should have been her wedding day. But she didn't wish to think of Enion now. Today would be her holiday as well—from a host of painful memories.

Richard poured two cups of wine. Holding one up, he invited her to sit. "This isn't much of a birthday for you," Elen remarked, searching for a neutral subject. Taking the wine, she settled herself on the blanket with a smile. "I fear I've no gift."

"I've no need of gifts," Richard said easily. "I learned early not to expect them." He reached for a leg of roast fowl, and with a deft movement, slit the meat from the bone, offering it to Elen.

They ate and drank in companionable silence, listening to the birds and the rushing water. Finishing her third cup of wine, Elen lay on her back and closed her eyes. Bees droned busily in the tangle of grass and flowers, and the heady fragrance of mountain gorse was almost overpowering. "I wonder if heaven's like this," she murmured dreamily.

"Churchmen say it's golden cities with gates of pearl."

"Hmmm . . . this would be better."

Richard rolled nearer, pouring himself more wine. "Heresy . . . but I agree."

Elen glanced at him thoughtfully, then closed her eyes. "What were birthdays like when you were a boy?" she asked softly.

"Oh, wonderful when I was very young. My father was seldom about, but Mother would make honeyed fruits and allow me to eat my fill for once. And she always had a toy she'd had a tenant make. Often there was even a fine new suit of clothing."

Elen smiled at thought of the child Richard must have been—a small towheaded youngster with dancing green eyes. "Does she still make you honeyed fruits?"

"She's dead," he said bluntly, "of a fever when I was seven. My father remarried within the year and his new wife didn't wish me about. I was packed off out of the way."

Elen turned to study Richard's profile. He was frowning up at the interlacing branches above them. "Why?"

"I suppose she hated the thought that she was second in the house. That her child would never be my father's heir," he replied thoughtfully. "When she bore a son a few months later, she made my life such hell Father sent me away to achieve some peace. She and my half-brother have spent the years since praying to all the saints for my death." He laughed harshly. "I've yet to oblige them!"

Elen leaned up on one elbow. "Your father should have beaten her within an inch of her life!" she snapped, the wine and the comfortable intimacy of the moment making her temper flare in Richard's defense.

"He was besotted with the woman and it made him a fool," Richard said bitterly. Taking a deep breath, he glanced away. "But he did what he could for me, I suppose. His Norman overlord owed him a favor and he convinced the man to take me as a page. And when I came of age, he mortgaged part of our lands to purchase a decent horse and armor for me." A look of pain swept his face. "Yes, I suppose he did what he could."

Elen touched Richard's arm. "I'm sorry," she said softly. "And I wish I had a gift for you this day."

Richard turned, his eyes meeting hers. "It doesn't matter," he murmured. "It all happened long ago." He lifted her hand from his arm, brushing her fingers against his lips. "And this is the best birthday I can recall in my lifetime."

The words lingered in the air between them. His eyes held hers. Elen found herself wondering if he were going to kiss her—wanting it long before his mouth lowered to cover her own. Their lips joined, then parted, then melded again in a long, slow, deeply satisfying kiss.

Richard eased back on the blanket, drawing her down to rest in the curve of his shoulder. One slight tug of his fingers unloosed her thick braid. His hand raked through her hair, caressing her with slow, mesmerizing strokes.

Elen drew a deep, shuddering breath, willing herself not to think, not to move as she savored the feel of Richard's arms around her, the radiating warmth of his body against hers.

Unexpectedly Richard's arm clamped tightly about her, his whole body tensing in alarm. Elen sent him a bewildered glance, but then she heard it too—a low grunting noise coming from the clearing beyond.

Richard eased to a sitting position and then got to his knees, drawing Elen with him. Across the meadow, they spotted a huge wild boar. It had broken through the undergrowth, and was rooting about at the foot of a rotting log. The animal halted, four-inch ivory tusks slanting upward wickedly as his sensitive nostrils tested the wind.

Elen held her breath. Boars were aggressive and unpredictable, and among the most dangerous animals in the forest. But they had notoriously poor vision. She swallowed nervously. "P-perhaps he won't see us," she whispered.

Richard had already drawn his sword. "Get up," he ordered softly. "Slowly. Walk to the horses and mount up. But don't make any sudden moves." He was easing the blanket into his arms as he spoke. "I'll keep his attention while you get mounted."

"No!" Elen caught his shoulder. "Keep still. Maybe he'll go back into the wood without ever knowing we're here."

Richard hadn't taken his eyes from the beast. "He already knows, Elen. He can smell us. The wind is from the west. Now go!"

There was nothing Elen could do but obey. Rising, she moved slowly toward the horses. The bristly monster was watching her. He tossed his pointed head as if uncertain in which direction to attack.

Never had a walk seemed so interminable. Elen's heart began to pound; her breath came unevenly. She glanced over her shoulder at Richard. He was moving deliberately toward the boar, his path taking him in a direction opposite her. He sent her an encouraging look, then shook out the blanket and swung it about his head.

At sight of the flapping blanket, the boar pivoted toward Richard. Its sharp little hooves tore impatiently at the ground. Lowering its heavy head it grunted, preparing for a charge.

Elen darted the last few steps to her mare. Richard faced the beast with his broadsword, a pitiful weapon for such a purpose. Even the long, stout spears used on boar hunts weren't always protection enough. The reinforced bar above the handhold sometimes shattered with the shock of three hundred pounds of slashing, savage fury. She had seen the bodies of men mauled by boars. It was a horrible sight.

Throwing herself into the saddle, Elen swung Ceiri about and headed the startled animal directly for the charging boar. She had ridden on boar hunts, but only to watch. She had never attacked an animal and knew she hadn't the strength for a kill even if she had had a weapon. Her only hope now was to distract the beast. Boars were known to savage anything that moved—and she was going to show plenty of movement!

Tearing her cloak from the saddle, she whirled it wildly alongside. She shouted Llywelyn's war cry, hoping the noise would further confuse the animal.

And her ploy was successful. The capricious beast checked his stride, veering to meet her. As the boar swung sideways, Elen hauled on her reins, jerking the mare back onto her haunches in an effort to escape the fury of those slashing tusks.

Ceiri slipped and scrambled for her footing and Elen held her breath. The nimble mare righted herself and dashed on, but Elen brought her up short, turning about for one more pass at the furious boar.

From across the meadow, Elen could hear Richard shouting, but she paid him little mind. All of her attention was focused on the dangerous beast she faced. Once more she sent the game little mare directly at the boar. Turning aside at the last second, she leaned far out over the boar's hairy back. She was so close she could hear the animal's heavy breathing, so close she could see the rage in its little red eyes. With an effort, she flung her billowing cloak over the animal's head, and the creature turned, slashing and trampling the clinging enemy that gripped it.

In that moment's grace, Elen galloped past, drawing to a sliding stop beside Richard. He grasped the saddle, swinging pillion behind her, as she kicked the mare for a dash into the safety of the sheltering trees.

They drew up in a thicket of sweet-smelling spruce, both breathing heavily from the narrow escape. "Don't ever do anything like that again!" Richard bit out. He caught Elen's shoulders, twisting her around to face him. "You fool! Don't you realize you could have been killed? I've seen a boar bring down a horse in mid-flight then turn and tear the rider to bits!"

Elen's overwrought feelings exploded. "Oh, so I'm to watch you torn to pieces instead? Next time I will!"

Richard jerked her into his arms, crushing her against him. "You could have been killed," he whispered. "God, don't ever frighten me so again!"

Elen clung to him, still trembling. Richard might have

been ripped apart by the animal. It could have happened so easily. If she'd been a few seconds late in reacting . . . if the mare had stumbled . . . if . . .

"At least we've settled one thing between us," he added slowly. "I'll no longer spend my days wondering if you plot to see me dead."

All at once the enormity of what she had done washed over her. Elen buried her face against Richard's chest, closing her eyes against a world where nothing made sense anymore. "Don't say anything," she whispered. "Please . . . just take me back."

CHAPTER NINETEEN

$\mathscr{A}$ week had passed since the terrifying attack by the boar; a week since Elen had saved Richard's life. The incident had caused a subtle change in their relationship. They were bound together now by a memory of shared danger, by the knowledge that each might owe his life to the other. And they were bound by something else as well—a memory of shared tenderness and passion, and the intriguing question of what might have happened if only they had not been interrupted.

When Elen learned Richard was leaving Gwenlyn she felt almost relieved. He was off in pursuit of Welsh raiders plundering near Beaufort. And when he came to say goodbye, she took refuge in the old familiar anger. Richard was riding out against her people . . . again.

But for the first time, Elen was forced to admit the strong physical attraction Richard held for her. Never had she ached for a man as she did him. Never had the memory of a kiss so spoiled her days. This, then, was that powerful evil the priests spoke of—the thing called lust.

She would ask Giles permission to seek out Father Dilwen. Perhaps she could find a measure of peace in a long overdue confession.

• • •

Late one afternoon after Richard's departure, Elen entered Gwenlyn's chapel. The sun slanted through the narrow stained-glass window, painting a rich pattern on the cool tiled floor. She knelt on the steps before the high altar earnestly reciting her confession to the priest.

Father Dilwen gazed down at her, a gentle smile lurking in the depths of his dark eyes. "This is quite a formidable list, child, but to be understood in light of what you've been through this year past. The English soldier whose life you took. You say he sought your own?"

Elen nodded.

"Then you have not the sin of murder on your soul. It is still a serious matter, but take heart—we may absolve you. It is more the festering of hate in our hearts our Lord condemned. Had you sought to harm one who'd done no wrong to you, the condition would have been far worse."

Elen squirmed uncomfortably and lowered her eyes. She had not been entirely honest with Father Dilwen. "I . . . I have done this, Father. I sought to lead a man to death by deceit. I would have slain him if I could, but he escaped me. . . ." Her voice trailed off. "Twice."

The priest was silent a long moment. "I see." He put a gentle hand on her shoulder. "Are you certain that is all, child? You seem troubled."

Elen bit her lip. "No. No, that's not all. I have—" She took a deep breath. "I have desired a man," she got out miserably. "I have sinned the sin of lust."

Father Dilwen eased himself down to a place on the steps beside her, his gaunt face on a level with hers. "We are all subject to sins of the flesh, Elen. You are a lovely woman and beauty can be its own curse, especially in this unsettled time. Yet God has formed you for a purpose—to love and be loved and bear children that are blessed in his sight. And perhaps you have a purpose even greater than—"

Love? Her eyes flew to his indignantly. To even suggest she loved an Englishman was betrayal of all she knew. "I don't love the man!" she interrupted.

The priest's dark eyes probed hers. "Are you quite certain, my child?"

"Of course! It was naught but lust—a grievous sin, Father." She rose and paced before the steps, unwillingly recalling the tenderness and peace she had found in Richard's arms . . . and then the pleasure. Richard would be returning any day and now, more than ever before, she longed to be gone when he arrived. She didn't dare remain, not with the memory of that afternoon between them.

"I must leave," she cried in rising agitation. "Can you help me, Father? I've none else to turn to."

"Have you asked for God's guidance?"

"I've prayed night and day, but God doesn't hear me."

The priest frowned but didn't offer the rebuke she expected. "Are you certain he doesn't hear you, Elen? Or do you just not like his answers? Ofttimes his plan for us is far different from that we would choose."

Elen clenched her fists helplessly at her sides. Father Dilwen didn't understand, but she could tell him nothing further. "Just tell me what penance I must do," she said bitterly. "I must hurry. My guard is like to grow impatient."

The priest studied her in silence, then rose to his feet with a heavy sigh. "Very well."

Elen listened impatiently as he began the list of penance she must perform. But before he was done, a servingman hurried into the room. "Father! Father, please come at once!"

The priest glanced up.

"Sir Richard just rode in. There be wounded in the party and one needs last rites."

Father Dilwen nodded, gathering up his threadbare robe. "Tell the men I'll come." He glanced back at Elen. "I must go, child, but we will speak on this again." He touched her shoulder. "Compromise is not the weakness you believe, Elen. Ofttimes it requires a strength difficult to find within ourselves. Search your heart and mind and think on my words." He hesitated, his dark face impassive. "The Englishman from Kent is a good man."

"The courier waits below, Richard. He's ready to ride."

Richard glanced at his squire, then stared thoughtfully at the roll of sealed parchment in his hand. The letter was short, but the few terse words had cost him most of the day. He tossed it to Simon. "Have Watt give this into Ranulff de Borgh's own hand. I doubt there'll be a reply, but bid him wait if there is."

Simon nodded.

Richard frowned at the floor, unable to believe he was throwing away the most incredible chance at good fortune he had been offered in his lifetime. True to his word, Edward had put him forward as a husband for de Borgh's daughter, and the proud baron hadn't been offended. He was, in fact, willing to consider the match and had requested a meeting to discuss possibilities. But Richard couldn't bring himself to pursue it.

He ran a hand through his hair, telling himself the careful reply he had framed would buy time. But he wasn't a fool. The excuse he was too busy with the unrest in Wales was nothing less than a polite refusal of Ranulff's overture. He only hoped he had not made an enemy.

"Richard . . . is there trouble?"

Glancing up, he discovered Simon still hovering uncertainly in the doorway. Richard smiled reassuringly. "No, lad, no trouble. But I begin to wonder if some blow I've taken over the years has addled my thinking."

Simon grinned. "I'll let you know."

"Yes, and I'll give you the backside of my hand!"

Simon grinned again and turned to go.

"Simon, did Giles fetch Elen down to the hall? It's near time for supper."

Simon glanced back, his eyebrows lifting expressively. "She wouldn't come. Not even for Giles."

"Did he tell her I ordered it?" Richard snapped.

The boy gave an eloquent shrug.

"Then deliver a message to Her Grace. Either she comes down now or I'll have Henry drag her down. Enough is enough!"

Simon nodded once and disappeared, and Richard was left staring at the stack of parchment on his desk in perplexity. Shoving the work aside, he frowned at the door. What should he do about Elen? Their relationship had changed that afternoon at the pool in a way he hadn't expected. Without knowing how, he had let the girl grow more important to him than he'd ever planned.

As if realizing the danger, Elen had rebuilt the wall he had patiently battered down these last weeks, and since his return yesterday, she had been as ridiculously difficult as in the beginning. Behaving like a veritable shrew when he tried to talk with her, she claimed to be angry because he'd fought the Welsh again. But Christ, he and his men had been ambushed! He was lucky the attempt was a clumsy one. His men had routed the enemy and gotten off with the loss of only one man.

He rubbed his chin thoughtfully. No, there was something more troubling Elen, and he was certain it had to do with the developing relationship between them. He had tried to be patient, knowing hers was not an easy choice. But his patience was at an end. By the blessed rood, you'd think a man and woman had never desired each other before!

He thought once more of the letter, wondering at his own distaste for the de Borgh match. A man didn't whistle his fortune down the wind because of lust for a pretty Welsh bastard. Marriages had naught to do with such. They were made to unite fortunes or families in powerful alliances, and ofttimes the bride and groom had never met. There need be no warm feelings on either side for a union.

But he wanted something more.

Something more than a fortune? he asked himself grimly.

Something more than a tractable young bride and a respected family backing him up? Something more than an accepted place in a society that had scorned him the better part of his years? He must be a raving lunatic!

When he reached the hall, Richard was relieved to find Elen seated at the table in her accustomed place beside his. Perhaps she'd become reasonable. But one glance at her stormy face told him the hope was vain. "I'm pleased you've deigned to join us at last," he remarked.

"How could I resist such a courteous invitation?"

Simon stepped forward to serve them and Richard leaned back in his chair, his temper rising despite his effort to curb it. "I dare not guess. You've done more foolish things than that since I've known you."

Elen stared at him coldly. "Yes, at least one I can think of."

Richard sent her a measuring glance. She had already told him she regretted saving his life. But he didn't believe her. And he was about to call her bluff. He had been patient beyond belief, but he was about to put her pretense to an end.

"M'lord!"

Richard glanced up as one of his men hastened forward.

"A large party approaching, m'lord. A messenger just reached the gates. It's Sir John Basset and his lady with your brother and the Baron of Ravensgate."

Richard jerked to his feet. "What?"

"Uh . . . your family, m'lord, and Sir Hugh de Veasy. They'll be at the gates in a moment. Shall we let them in?"

Richard nodded dumbly. His father and stepmother here?

Giles rose and called for the steward. More food must be prepared and wine brought up from the storerooms. Bedchambers must be readied and room made for the men-at-arms.

Richard sank back into his chair, thoughts of Elen banished by the unexpected news. What scheme brought de

Veasy north in company with his family? And what, in God's name, were they doing here at all?

A short time later the travelers were announced into the hall. As he watched, Sir John advanced across the floor, and Richard noticed the drag of his left leg was more pronounced than he remembered. It was a grim reminder of the Battle of Lewes; the years had not been kind to the old warrior.

Gazing at his aging, once-powerful sire, something twisted in Richard's heart. He rose and hurried down the steps, then dropped to one knee. "I'm glad I see you well, Father," he murmured.

Sir John caught his son's shoulders, lifting him to his feet. "And you my son. You're a sight to gladden these old eyes." His fingers gripped Richard convulsively. "Aye, a proud sight, Richard."

Richard turned to the attractive woman standing a few paces away. His gaze slid over her lovely, dark features and he gave her a curt nod. "Jeanne."

She inclined her head. "Richard."

"I . . . I hope we've not inconvenienced you, Richard," Sir John began hesitantly. "After learning my wish to visit Wales, my lord de Veasy kindly offered to escort us. We owe him our thanks. We'd never have mounted such an expedition on our own."

The Baron of Ravensgate handed his cloak into the keeping of a servant. De Veasy turned, his gold neckchain and surcoat of crimson cloth gleaming richly in the torchlight. "Well, why wouldn't I help the parents of my young friend here?" he remarked, smiling at Philip. "Besides, I'd a desire to see Edward's Wolf of the North in action."

"You're welcome, of course, though I fear there'll be little action to entertain you." Richard gestured to the table, keeping his expression carefully blank. "But come and refresh yourselves. My men will see to yours, Sir Hugh."

He led the way to the high table, sending Elen a quelling

glance. "Father, I would make you known to the Lady Elen of Powys." He searched for a polite explanation for the girl's presence that was not too distanced from the truth. "She is a hostage I hold against the good behavior of Welsh rebels in the district."

De Veasy's dark eyes slid over Elen appreciatively and he sent his host a lazy smile. "What a charming hostage you chose, Richard. No wonder you were in such haste to get back to the north. And they say you've no taste for conquest."

Elen returned his look coldly. The Baron of Ravensgate was known the length and breadth of Wales, the raven banner he flaunted more hated even than Richard's dreaded red boar. It was a shame someone hadn't got next to *him* with a knife.

Richard ignored the comment and turned to his father. "The Lady Elen has helped me to understand the customs and practices here. With Edward's approval, we've produced an acceptable mixture of both English and Welsh laws for local use. On the morrow, I can show you if you've an interest."

As the travelers were seated, Elen made a quick study of Richard's family: the tall, silver-haired man with the martial bearing she would have known at a glance was Richard's father. And the cold, dark-eyed woman was the one who had made his boyhood such hell. Elen's eyes traveled over his half-brother, Philip. The boy was handsome in a dark way but with none of Richard's golden beauty or rugged strength. And he had taken up with the wrong master. He aped de Veasy's manner and dress in a way that was ridiculous.

"With your leave I'll retire now, Richard," Elen announced, her curiosity satisfied. "You'll have much to discuss with your family."

Richard gazed pointedly at the untouched food on the trencher they shared. "You've not yet finished your meal,

Elen. You may go above when you've eaten."

She sent him a rebellious glance, not caring that Hugh de Veasy watched the exchange with interest.

"After you've eaten," Richard repeated with a challenging look.

She was tempted to refuse, but thought better of the idea at once. Given the mood Richard was in, she decided not to press her luck. "Of course. I only thought to give you time alone with your family."

As the talk rose about them again, Elen picked at the food Simon served. The conversation was carried mainly by Richard and his father with Jeanne joining occasionally.

How little she knew about Richard, Elen realized as she listened. He had spoken little of his lands in Kent, his home at Waybridge. She had not even known of his half-sister, Isabel, of whom he was obviously quite fond. The girl was residing at a convent near London and Richard hoped to see her when next he was at court.

"And is this Isabel of marriageable age?" Hugh de Veasy asked. "Perhaps I should look about me for some suitable young men."

Elen felt Richard stiffen beside her. "My thanks, Sir Hugh, but we've no need of your help. In any case, Isabel is much too young."

"She's thirteen. None too young to be beginning to think of such," Jeanne put in. "As you'd know, Richard, if you took a proper interest in your family's affairs."

Richard sent her a scornful glance but remained silent.

"Speaking of marriages, Richard, I heard word of yours before leaving Ravensgate," de Veasy remarked into the sudden quiet. "If the tale's to be believed, we'll soon be wishing you joy of a most advantageous alliance. What truth to this talk you're in the midst of contracting for the de Borgh heiress?"

Richard smiled coolly. "And do you also believe in children's nursery tales, my lord?" he countered.

"Come, Richard, you can tell us. We're friends and family here," de Veasy persisted. "Don't be modest—how did you manage the feat?"

"There's no truth to the rumor I've contracted with de Borgh. The man would be out of his mind to consider any settlement I could make."

"But it's said the king put you forward," Jeanne said, leaning eagerly over the table. "Certainly he owes you something. Why, when I think of what such advancement could mean for Philip and Isabel, I—"

"Well, don't think of it, Jeanne," Richard interrupted coldly. "Edward owes me nothing."

"But—"

"Enough of this," Sir John said bluntly. "Richard says there's no truth to the gossip so there's an end to it."

Married. Richard was negotiating to be married. Elen lifted her wine cup and took a deep drink, hoping it would ease the sudden tightening in her chest. It seemed she knew very little about Richard Basset, very little indeed.

She placed her cup on the table, holding her face to a carefully set smile. The knowledge that Richard wanted her in his bed while he maneuvered for a rich wife was far more bitter than she had expected. But just what had she expected?

Nothing, she told herself furiously. Nothing but this. A man didn't discuss such details as his marriage with every wench he sought out for a tumble—most especially an English knight with a woman he thought a Welsh bastard.

But though she tried to reason away the pain, the knowledge still hurt. It was just that she had grown accustomed to honesty from Richard, had even begun to rue her own deceit. Well, Richard would get his surprise soon enough. After her escape she would send him a letter—a letter signed Lady Elen, late of Teifi.

Hugh de Veasy excused himself to see to his men and Philip followed him from the table. Richard motioned a manservant to show the men their chambers.

Jeanne gazed fondly after her son. "You could do much for him, if you would, Richard," she said softly. "A word to Edward and Philip's fortune might be made."

Richard glanced sharply at his stepmother. "The king is no bag of good fortune I may dip from at will. He has his own affairs to see to—as Philip must see to his."

Jeanne turned on him angrily. "You will scoop gain for yourself, but not for others of your family, eh? Well, you can't fool me, Richard. Ranulff de Borgh wrote your father of a possible alliance as is fitting he should before proceeding further. You forget—Waybridge is not yet yours to contract away!"

"I doubt Sir Ranulff is interested in Waybridge," Richard said dryly. "Or my dinner companions in hearing family grievances aired. I say again, there is nothing to the rumor." He rose to his feet, abruptly ending the conversation. "And as you've finished, I'll have you shown your chamber. I'm certain you're weary after your journey."

The group rose, and Elen came to her feet along with them. She had no desire to linger after the others departed. Any conversation with Richard could only end in a quarrel, a quarrel she felt strangely unequal to now. "I wish to retire as well."

Richard nodded. "I'll see you above."

"Don't trouble yourself. Simon may serve as my guard."

Sir John touched his son's arm. "I did have something to say to you, Richard. Stay a moment if you will."

Richard sent Elen a thoughtful glance. "All right, Father, I've a matter to discuss with you as well."

Elen didn't look at Richard again as she followed Simon from the hall. Was Richard really to be married? She took a deep breath. It made no difference to her, of course. He could take as many wives and mistresses as he chose.

As they reached the corridor leading to Elen's bedchamber, she became aware of the sound of footsteps behind them. A smooth voice called for Simon to wait.

She felt a touch of irritation as Hugh de Veasy caught up to them. Simon glanced up at the man, suspicion hardening his gaze. "Have you lost your way, my lord? If you'll wait here a moment, I'll see you to your chamber."

"No, thank you, boy. I've discovered my way quite well. You may be off about your business—I'll see the lady the rest of the way."

"You're a guest, sir. I couldn't think to let you wander about here alone. Sir Richard would have my head."

"And I'll have the hide from your back if you don't take yourself off. Now do as you're bid and be gone!"

Simon made a curt bow. "Certainly, my lord, if you're sure you know the way." He sent Elen a quick glance, then disappeared down the hallway.

De Veasy turned to Elen, his dark eyes gleaming in the shadows like polished jet. "My lady . . . shall we continue?"

"Your purpose in this, sir?" she asked, studying him warily. "I'm certain you have one."

"Ah, a woman who wastes no time reaching a point." De Veasy took her arm, leading her down the corridor. "I'm finding we have much in common, Lady Elen. You intrigue me no end."

She longed to jerk her arm away, but decided to humor the man instead. "Word has it the Baron of Ravensgate is a man who follows his purpose to completion. I ask again . . . what has that to do with me?"

De Veasy's dark eyebrows rose consideringly. "Very well. I'll be honest with you in hopes we'll deal better together. It didn't escape my notice you bear little love for Richard Basset. And I've already learned he keeps you here against your will. Perhaps something could be arranged to help you go where you would."

Elen's heart began an unsteady beating. She must move carefully, very carefully. "Oh? And what must I do for this 'arrangement,' as you call it, to take place?"

"I'm not certain of that as yet, but one never knows what opportunities may arise." De Veasy smiled darkly, drawing her to a halt in the shelter of an empty doorway. "I'd have you know I can be generous to those who aid me."

Elen veiled her contempt with a downward sweep of heavy leashes. The man thought her a fool and she would not disabuse him. "I can't imagine you should need help from anyone, sir."

He chuckled. "You play the game well, sweet. I can see why Basset won't let you go." He leaned his shoulder against the door, effectively blocking her way. One finger touched her cheek, then trailed slowly down her throat and across her breast. "Think on my words, Elen. Sir Richard may not always be master here. As I said, I could be generous . . . very generous to a woman like you."

In the hall below, Richard drew his eyes reluctantly from the doorway where Elen had just disappeared.

"I know you're wondering why we've come, Richard."

He forced himself to attend to his father.

"The truth is, I've been ill. So ill the leech doubted my recovery."

Richard leaned forward with a frown. "How is it I wasn't told?"

"You've more important problems than the health of an old man. And I'd not blame you if you'd little concern at that," Sir John admitted with a wry smile.

Richard started to protest, but his father shook his head. "Hear me, Richard. I've much on my mind and have traveled far to speak some part at least. I've long wished to see you but you've avoided Waybridge." He glanced up. "Not that I blame you. But since my fever, I've feared my days might be short. This blessed hope of your marriage and de Veasy's offer to escort us here seemed an answer to my prayer."

Ignoring the comment on his marriage, Richard raised

his eyebrows sardonically. "Yes, I wonder at de Veasy's sudden interest in my family." He rose and paced the floor. "He can have Philip with my good will, but he'll have no say in any suitor put forward for Isabel. Sweet Jesus, he'd find the worst brute in England just to spite me!"

"Sit down, Richard," Sir John said dryly. "I'm aware there's no love lost between you two. You've contributed at least half of Isabel's dower settlement over the years. You'll have your say in choice of her husband."

Richard hesitated, staring suspiciously at his father. "You swear it? Even if Jeanne urges differently."

Sir John sighed. "Yes, Richard. I swear it."

The older man waited as Richard returned to his seat. "Like you, I've no liking for the baron's influence on Philip. It was good at first. The boy came out from behind his mother's skirts, acted the man at last. But now..." Sir John's green eyes narrowed. "Now, what I see I don't like. And when I try to talk to him, Philip puffs up like an angry goose."

Richard shrugged. "Philip will become a man in his own way. I doubt there's aught you can say now to change his course."

"True. But perhaps you could, Richard. Despite the trouble between you, Philip has long looked up to you."

Richard gave a bitter laugh. "You know little of your own sons, Father."

Sir John shook his head. "When Philip was small, he idolized you, but you'd have naught to do with him then. It was his mother's jealousy that filled his mind with foolishness." He broke off with a frown. "Well, that's done now and no use thinking what might have been different. But I ask you to take an interest in him, Richard. I'd like to think things might be different between you someday."

"I've nothing against Philip," Richard said slowly, surprised to find the words actually true. "I'm glad to see him accomplish something. He won his spurs at Walmsley and acquitted himself well at a skirmish or two in the south, so I'm told."

"Then tell him that. He'd never admit it, but praise from you means a lot to the boy."

Richard shrugged. "I make no promises, but I'll do what I can."

"Good." Sir John clasped his large, square hands on the table, sending his son a sidelong glance. "There's another matter I would speak of for I've a need to set things right in my family."

He hesitated. "I know I've not been the best of fathers, Richard. In some ways I've been a rare fool. When you were young, I spent the years fighting for Henry. I thought there'd be time to know my son later. But when your mother died, I realized I'd lost something—something I longed to recapture." He took a deep breath, as if gathering strength. "I loved her, Richard, I loved her with all my heart though you may not believe that."

"So much so you sought sweet solace before the year was out," Richard remarked cynically.

Sir John's eyes rose to the unforgiving gaze of his son. "I don't expect you to understand, Richard. I don't even ask it. You've not yet learned what it is to love and lose what you hold most dear. The world was a bitter place for me then. I was fighting for honor when it was denied those of our blood. I was fighting to hold my land and keep bread in my family's mouth. And suddenly, I'd lost all that made the fight worthwhile."

Richard held his breath, suppressing the painful ache that cut through him even now. "But you had a son."

"Yes, I had a son. A son I loved dearly, though I thought it foolish to tell him so. I'm a soldier, an unlettered man. I'm no good with words—was even worse then." Sir John paused, but Richard didn't speak.

"Then Jeanne came along and gave me another reason for living. She saw to my needs, saw to my household." He sent Richard a keen glance. "You see only the bad in her, Richard, but there's much good there too. She's been a fine wife to me and, if not always wise, a loving mother to her own children at least. She gave me peace and comfort."

He glanced away sheepishly. "And yes, a pleasure I never thought to know again. I was away much of the time and I suppose I closed my eyes to your unhappiness, your need. I told myself you'd be better off in de Erley's household, that it was a heaven-sent chance such as I could never provide." He leaned forward. "Tell me I wasn't wrong."

Richard glanced away. "You weren't wrong. Gifford made a man of me."

"No. The man was in you, my son. Gifford just gave you a chance to show it." Sir John's voice dropped. "And I'm proud of you, Richard. I'll say this now—now that it's probably too late. You've ever been first in my heart. It's why I've been easy on Philip, could deny him and his mother little they asked."

He sighed heavily, suddenly looking very old and tired. "I fear I've wronged him more deeply even than you. Can you—" He stared at his hands. "No, I'll not even ask."

A long silence stretched between them. Richard thought of the days he had lived in dread of the tall, stern man he had scarcely known as his father. But why punish them both for a past long since done. Perhaps it had all worked out for the best. "A child sees only his own needs, feels only his own pain," he said slowly. Reaching out, he touched his father's arm. "But men may understand each other."

Sir John caught his son's hand and Richard covered the gnarled fingers with his own.

"Richard! Richard, come quick!"

Richard glanced up with a start. Simon was bounding across the floor toward him. Releasing his father's hand, Richard jerked to his feet. "What, lad?"

"De Veasy!" Simon got out breathlessly. "He caught us

in the hallway before the stair to the eastern gatehouse. He sent me away . . . insisted on seeing Elen alone."

Richard was already moving toward the stairs.

"I thought it best to fetch you," Simon panted beside him.

"You were right. Stay here."

Richard swung up the stairs two at a time, cursing as he went. Hugh de Veasy considered any woman fair game, but he'd cut the bastard's throat if he touched Elen!

He raced along the maze of corridors, finally reaching the hallway Simon had mentioned. As he hurried along, two shadows disengaged and stepped from a doorway into the light. He halted, every instinct roused for battle.

"Ah, and here's the master of Gwenlyn now. We were just speaking of you, Richard," de Veasy remarked smoothly.

Richard's eyes flew from Elen's flushed, indignant face to the blandly smiling one of the baron. "My squire follows my orders. And when I give an order, it's carried out or I know the reason why." He took a step forward, itching to draw steel on the man, reminding himself Edward would have his head if he did.

Hugh de Veasy grinned. "Such bother over my wish to walk a lady to her door!" He shook his head. "A man isn't even allowed to be a gentleman these days—but then I'd not expect you to understand that, Basset."

"I understand you perfectly. Far better than you'd like." Richard glanced at Elen. If she said one word, made one accusation, he'd have it out with the man here and now.

Elen held her breath as the men faced each other. A moment ago, she had longed for a knife to put between de Veasy's ribs, but she didn't want Richard fighting the man. The Baron of Ravensgate was near as renowned in battle as Richard himself. Besides, Sir Hugh might help her escape, though she would have to tread carefully. She wouldn't trust Hugh de Veasy if the Holy Virgin herself stood surety.

De Veasy was bowing gallantly over her hand. "Lady Elen, I relinquish you to my host, though grudgingly." With a nod to Richard, he strode away.

Elen studied Richard in silence. These men were enemies, deadly enemies. "Richard," she whispered impetuously, "have a care. He means you no good."

"Did he touch you?"

She thought of de Veasy's hand trailing over her, of Richard's cold fury now. "No."

Richard moved to stand beside her. "With de Veasy and his men here, it's not safe for you to be about alone, Elen. I know I'd dispensed with your guard"—he hesitated, gazing at her keenly—"until these last few days, that is. But I'll order one now for your safety. Do you understand?"

His words were a reminder of all that lay between them. Richard might want her for a quick tumble in some grassy meadow, but it was a wealthy Englishwoman he would wed. Turning away, she strode determinedly down the corridor, the angry hurt throbbing with each step. "Certainly I understand," she said, throwing his words back at him. "I understand far better than you'd like!"

Richard caught up to her as she reached her doorway. Seizing one arm, he turned her about. "We must talk. You know that as well as I. We can't continue like this."

"I've nothing to say to you," she returned.

"Tomorrow," Richard continued, ignoring her words. "We'll discuss this tomorrow."

Elen stared at the chessboard with pretended interest, striving to make sense of the complicated strategy Giles was executing. She shifted her piece of carved onyx forward. His move, then her move, then his move again. Something like her life played out on a small scale. Only she had no more moves to make. She was backed to the edge of the board, and Richard had all the options.

She stared broodingly at the carved stone pieces as Giles

studied the board. Richard certainly had a host of options. She wondered now if he had planned to bring his bride here all along. Probably not. Highborn English ladies didn't thrive among the savages of Wales. No, he wouldn't bring his pale, long-nosed lady here. And that was the reason he needed a mistress.

She frowned. Was that what Richard planned to discuss with her today? Little wonder he thought it a possibility after her unpardonable behavior at that cursed pool. Well, he could think again. And if a chance came to leave Gwenlyn, she would take it—oath or not!

But it would be easier to escape if Richard were away. "I suppose Richard will be leaving soon to see to his bride," she remarked in what she hoped was a conversational tone. "Is she truly so wealthy as Sir Hugh hinted?"

Giles glanced at her shrewdly, then turned his attention to the board. "Alicia de Borgh is heiress to a large estate and lovely into the bargain. All Richard's friends would be pleased to see the match come about."

"Oh." Elen shifted restlessly in her chair. No doubt Richard would be a tender husband. He certainly knew the ways to win a woman's trust. "Is she . . . is she young?" she asked, curiosity pricking her.

"Fourteen . . . and godchild to the queen." Giles deftly took the chess piece she had moved. "She's a sweet child and worthy of a man such as Richard."

"Oh." Elen averted her eyes, concealing her feelings by pretending avid interest in the game. From across the hall came the noise of several people entering the room. She didn't look up. Probably Richard and his father returning from their morning ride.

She heard Richard call for wine and the preparation of another bedchamber. Giles rose to his feet, a look of surprise lighting his face.

Elen shifted about. A tall, gray-haired man had entered the hall, arm in arm with Richard. He was rumpled and travel-stained, his clothing heavily powdered with dust. But something about the man was strangely familiar.

He swept off his traveling cloak, handing it to a servant. Elen caught her breath. *No . . . dear God, no!*

She swung to her feet. Sir Robert Grandison—the one representative from Edward her father had been pleased to call friend. Her eyes flew to the door. Was there any possibility of reaching it before she was noticed?

From across the room, the Englishman's eye caught hers. With an exclamation of surprise, he broke away from Richard. "Elen! Lady Elen, by Our Lord Savior, what a relief!"

His long strides ate up the space between them. "Christ, but I'm pleased to find you here safe!" He took her hand, carrying it to his lips. "I'd heard you and the Lady Gweneth were in France. Obviously the rumor was false."

Elen gazed at the man in stunned silence. As if from some great distance, Richard's voice sounded in her ears. "You know this woman?"

"Certainly. I was a frequent visitor at Lord Aldwyn's in Teifi. Elen and I are old friends."

Elen's eyes swept past Sir Robert to where Richard stood a few paces across the floor. The lord of Gwenlyn was staring at her as if he had been turned to stone, while behind him Hugh de Veasy leaned against a table . . . laughing.

CHAPTER TWENTY

"*So* it was a lie. Everything you told me a lie. Everything calculated for deception from the start. And I never even suspected it, would never have believed a lady of rank would live in the wilds with a band of rebels like some... some—" Richard broke off.

"Serf... whore? Just what were you about to say?" Elen inquired coolly.

Richard didn't answer, didn't even turn around.

"I'm Welsh, Richard, not English. Your rules do not apply."

He turned from the window and gazed at her coldly. "Before God, you've played me for a fool! You might as well make a clean breast of it. Where is the Lady Gweneth? By all the saints, I swear to turn Wales upside down to find her if I must."

"Then you'll have to move more than this earth," she responded. "My mother is dead as I told you. To my sorrow not everything was a lie."

"Then why don't you tell me what is truth?" he snapped. "I've given up trying to sort your stories. You've more tales up your sleeve than a wasp has stings!"

Elen tensed nervously in her chair. It was the moment she had dreaded most since Sir Robert had discovered her.

Richard's suspicion was roused, and she was terrified he would put the facts together and come up with the Welsh Fox.

Since Owain's capture, the damaging raids of the Welsh had ceased. True, there had been a few disorganized strikes and one clumsy ambush, but even Richard had laughed and wondered where his old friend Rhys had got off to. And now he knew she was Elen of Teifi, would Richard wonder if the Fox had stayed close to guard her? Would he wonder if Owain might not be the man?

She gazed into Richard's angry face, knowing she must maintain this fiction of Rhys even though she longed to admit the truth and be done with living a lie. "What information do you wish?" she asked.

"Why don't you just start at the beginning? You're such a gifted storyteller, I'm sure to be entertained whatever you choose to say."

Elen clasped her fingers together in her lap. Why not tell him? It mattered little now. Haltingly, she began her story the day of the English victory at Builth. She told how her father's trusted captain, the man Richard knew as her uncle, had taken her and her mother and fled north, how they had joined a host of terrified Welsh fleeing Edward's army, hiding their true identities from all save the handful of people from Teifi. She told how famine had stalked the camp, more feared than the hated English soldiers, and how her mother had grown ill and died, broken more by loneliness and despair than the harsh winter. She even told how she and Tangwen had struggled to tend the wounded, how they had fought to keep women and children alive, begging God in his mercy for a plenteous and early spring.

When she was done, Richard was silent for several long moments. He turned to her at last, the scornful look in his eyes gone. "And Rhys?" he asked softly. "What of him?"

Elen stared at her hands, hating the lie. "I will tell you nothing of him."

"You must know I'll find him, Elen. I've had men searching for months. The Fox heads the rebellion and it won't be finished until he's taken." He sighed heavily. "I've no other choice."

She didn't respond.

Richard sent her a sidelong glance. "Tell me this one thing. Do you love him?"

She hesitated, thinking of Owain. "Yes."

"I see. A foolish question, wasn't it? I had hoped—" He broke off abruptly.

She dared a quick look up. Richard was staring broodingly into the empty fireplace, head low, shoulders slumped. She had a sudden urge to go to him, to explain the best she could.

But what could she say? She dared not speak of Owain. And besides, Richard had had men searching the length of Wales for Elen of Teifi while she had been safe in his keep all along. She had made a fool of him before all of England. "I . . . I'm sorry, Richard," she said, surprising herself as much as him. "I'm sorry if you'll bear Edward's wrath because of me."

A rueful smile lit his face for an instant. "Oh, de Veasy will see I'm a laughingstock for a while, but I've been the butt of Norman wit before and doubtless will be again. The king will understand when he reads my letters." He shrugged his shoulders. "After a good laugh at my expense, he'll be pleased to have you at last."

Elen studied him in surprise. Few men would so easily dismiss being made to look a fool, especially by a woman. "Will it—" She took a breath, forcing herself to form the question. "Will it affect your marriage negotiations with this Ranulff de Borgh?"

"There are no marriage negotiations. I put an end to them last week by refusing to meet the man."

Last week. He had ended it last week. Her heart quickened painfully. "Why?"

His eyes met hers, then shifted away. "I think you know the reason."

For her? Impossible. She'd be foolish to think such a thing. But that look would be difficult to forget.

"My concern now is for you, Elen," Richard was saying. "You're Edward's ward—your future at his disposal."

She forced herself to attend to his words. "And what does that mean?"

"Your blood is the best in Wales. He'll find a man of sufficient rank, someone he needs to weld more closely to himself, someone who can rule your lands and wring a tithe for England." Richard hesitated. "Someone politically expedient to be your husband."

"Well, I won't agree! He can't marry me off without my consent. In Wales—"

"Welsh law no longer applies," he interrupted. "Edward rules now, Elen, and you'll have no choice. And I beg you, do not anger him with your tricks. He's a just king, but he has the temper of all his ancestors. I'd hate to see you ill used."

She gazed at him rebelliously. "Well, I won't go along. I'm no slave to Edward! I'll go to a nunnery. Surely that would please your saintly king."

Richard shook his head. "You'll have no choice."

"But Llywelyn's daughter, the infant Gwenllian," she protested. "Edward placed her in a nunnery."

"She's a babe. You're much too valuable to waste in such a way. According to our law, your father's lands go with you to any man you wed. It's my guess the lords of the Welsh Marches will be seeking your hand for themselves or their sons by the time this news is at court a full day."

Elen stared at him, obviously torn between fear and fury.

She was young in so many ways, Richard thought. And she could never even pretend to fit into life at the English court. He would have to make Edward understand that. Perhaps he could even convince the king to let her remain here until she was wed.

Until she was wed.

The thought was bitter as gall, making his voice harsher than he intended. "I'll do what I can for you, but I fear it won't be much."

Elen's eyes widened in alarm, but she made no further protest. He moved to stand beside her, the memory of those moments between them at the forest pool painfully vivid. He longed to take her in his arms, to make love to her just once before she left him forever. But that would be foolish beyond belief. It would only make the parting more painful.

"I must go now," he murmured. A wisp of chestnut hair had escaped her heavy braid. He pushed it behind her ear, thinking it a shame such hair would soon be covered by a wimple. "Sir Robert brought messages from Edward and I've business to see to." His fingers lingered along her cheek and she didn't pull away. His gaze dropped to her mouth, the hunger to taste it once more almost overpowering. Her lips trembled, then parted. "Richard . . ."

Duty, think of duty. Elen was Edward's ward! Spinning about quickly, Richard strode through the door before he lost all thought of honor. Elen would soon belong to someone else. He only hoped to God he would be gone from Wales long before that day!

Day followed endless day, finally merging into a week and then two. Richard arranged many pleasantries for his guests, but his heart wasn't in them. And though he avoided Elen as much as possible, he couldn't get her out of his mind. She had taken possession of near every waking thought and even his dreams were fired by her image.

And now that all hope was denied him, he faced a disconcerting fact. He was in love with Elen of Teifi and had been for some time. He didn't know how or when the feeling had crept upon him. He had told himself all along he had naught but a powerful desire for the girl. Yet it was a desire that couldn't be quenched by other women. And the thought of never seeing her again, or worse yet, seeing her at court as wife to some English earl, left him shaken and unexpectedly rebellious.

He reached for the flagon of wine Simon had fetched and almost upset a guttering candle. Love—a foolish word for a foolish emotion. In the past he had scorned all thought of the feeling, telling himself it made men weak and witless. Women were a pleasant enough diversion, but his father had been a fool for a pretty face and he'd seen the weakness destroy others. Yet Edward loved his queen and she him, and theirs was no weak or foolish union.

But Edward was a king, Richard reminded himself. And what was he save a near-penniless knight who would inherit naught but a small holding of overworked land—if he lived through Edward's wars to enjoy such a dubious future. He gripped his wine cup angrily, the bitterness of his position almost overwhelming him for the moment.

"Richard?"

He glanced up. Simon was standing in the doorway.

"I knocked, but you didn't hear," the boy added, still hesitating. "I hate to intrude, but a man's come from the village. He speaks little but Welsh gibberish, and I can't find Giles. I think there's trouble at Ruthlin."

Richard put down his cup and swung to his feet. Even his squire had hesitated to trouble him of late. "I'll come," he said, buckling his sword belt into place.

He followed Simon down the spiraling stone stairway of Gwenlyn's western turret. Two rushlights still burned in the chill hall but the servants were rolled up asleep on their pallets at the back of the room. Richard squinted in the dim light. A stocky man in a dirty homespun smock paced restlessly before the fireplace.

The man hurried forward at once, anxious words tumbling out like a river in spate. Richard raised one hand. Christ, where was Giles? "Hold . . . I understand less than one word in three. Speak slowly for I'm new to your language."

The man took a breath and began repeating his story.

Richard's features shifted into grim lines. "Simon, wake Henry!" he snapped. "Have him bring a dozen men and horses to me in the bailey."

"I sent a servant to fetch him. I knew you'd need men if there was trouble."

Richard sent the boy an approving glance. "Good lad." He shot out several questions to the Welshman, but before the man had time to reply, the burly guard captain and two dozen soldiers came clattering into the hall.

"What's amiss, m'lord?"

Richard sent his man a scowl. "This man tells me four English soldiers are tearing up half of Ruthlin—the Welsh half. They've raped a girl and beaten her family. And he says a fight broke out just as he came for me."

Henry swore a vicious oath. "The bloody bastards'll be wishin' they'd not been birthed when I'm done. Drunk, most like. I'll handle it, m'lord."

"No, I'll handle it," Richard corrected coldly. "They've had orders making that quarter off limits. This is exactly the kind of trouble we don't need."

Henry nodded. "Our mounts be ready."

Richard started for the door. "Wake the rest of the garrison. There's always the chance this is a trick."

"But Richard, you haven't your armor," Simon protested.

"Then fetch it to me at Ruthlin," Richard snapped. "I've no time to waste."

In the wavering torchlight, the castle bailey was awash with dancing shadows. Horses shifted nervously as men swung into their saddles. Richard rode Saladin across the courtyard through the narrow front gate, kicking the stallion into a dangerous gallop down the steep road.

But something was wrong. He took a deep breath of the chill night air. The moon rode high overhead so they carried no torch to light the roadway. They should have left the odor of pine and tallow behind in the bailey, but the acrid smell of burning hung heavy on the night wind.

"Holy Christ!" Rising in his stirrups, Richard turned. "They've fired the town," he shouted. "Send for the garrison and all the barrels you can find!"

Shifting low in the saddle, he touched his spurs to his stallion's sides. The animal leaped forward, settling into a run. God help those men when he found them!

Moments later, the party rounded a hill that had been blocking the village from sight and the full horror of the scene burst upon them. Fully half the buildings in the Welsh quarter were ablaze; their thatched roofs sent garish orange flames leaping across the midnight heavens in a scene that could have come straight from hell. Men dashed about in the streets, beating helplessly at the spreading blaze, while great clouds of choking smoke billowed from the burning thatch, making breathing an agony.

Saladin reared, but Richard brought him under control, forcing him forward into the smoke. The heat was intense in the narrow street and bits of burning rubble and soot rained down like brimstone from heaven.

He swung from the saddle, thrusting his reins into the hands of one of his men. "Forget these buildings!" he shouted to the soldiers crowding around him. "They're already gone. Try to save the rest!"

The men leaped to obey the orders he snapped out, moving forward to assist the rapidly tiring Welsh. He sent soldiers to help the hoard of women and children slopping pails of water from the town stream, organizing them into an efficient line to move water.

Hurrying through the twisting street, he noticed a black-robed figure struggling with a women in the doorway of a burning hut. The woman was heavy with child, but it was obvious she was fighting to go back into the building. Richard darted forward, catching her up in his arms and carrying her back from the structure. "What is it, Father?" he shouted above the roar of the flames.

"Clothing and blankets she'd made for the babe," Father Dilwen shouted back. "Little enough, but all she owned."

Richard set the woman on her feet. He tried to quiet her, but she was weeping hysterically. "For God's sake, Father, tell her I'll replace the loss," Richard promised recklessly. "Just don't let her near these buildings. They'll go like straw in the wind!"

The priest nodded and Richard hurried on. Ordering the Welsh to fall back to soak the buildings not yet burning, he was amazed to find they obeyed him. But he didn't stop to think—there wasn't time.

Suddenly, there were soldiers everywhere. Teams of snorting, terrified horses drew carts filled with barrels of water, and English and Welsh worked side by side, soaking the smoldering thatch of the buildings adjacent to the ring of fire. And slowly the spreading blaze came under control.

After nearly an hour of the struggle, Richard paused to rest. The fire had burned much of the Welsh quarter and had even laid waste a few of the English buildings inside the wall. But now it was nigh out. He took a cooling drink from a bucket Simon brought. It felt good to his parched throat. Cupping his hands he splashed water over his face, easing his weariness and ridding himself of his accumulated soot and sweat.

"My lord, I must speak to you."

Richard glanced up. Father Dilwen was standing a few paces away. He handed the bucket to Simon. "What is it?"

"Something you must see," the priest responded grimly.

Richard motioned to his squire and they followed the priest to the doorway of a neat structure of wattle and daub near the churchyard. "My home," Father Dilwen murmured.

Richard ducked through the low entrance. The room was bare of furnishings save two stools and a rough-hewn table. A small fire burned in the center of the dirt floor and a muffled female figure lay weeping softly on a pallet alongside it.

The priest knelt beside the girl and spoke, but her answer was lost in a torrent of fresh sobbing. Richard moved toward the figure, already sensing what he would see.

The priest eased the blanket back, exposing the girl's naked body. Richard felt the gorge rise in his throat. She might have been lovely once, but the girl had been used abominably by the men who had taken her. Her supple young body was beaten and bloodied and a dozen angry red welts rose across the white flesh of her buttocks.

Kneeling beside her, Richard gently replaced the blanket. "Who did this?" he ground out.

"We have the soldiers," Father Dilwen said low. "They were taken in the riot and are now in the church guarded by village men. It was all I could do to prevent murder."

Richard nodded. Turning back to the girl, he searched his mind for the proper Welsh phrases, wishing the language came more easily. "You'll be taken to Gwenlyn and cared for by the Lady Elen," he explained softly in Welsh. "She's a woman of your race and knows much of healing. The men who did this will be punished. I swear it."

He turned to the priest. "Simon will send round a cart. Take her to Gwenlyn and bid Elen see to her."

"I've a man outside who can carry her there. I'll stay with you," Father Dilwen answered in an odd voice.

Richard nodded again and rose to his feet. He led the way across the churchyard where angry villagers were already gathering, his fury mounting with each step. He had seen this before, of course—some men were animals—but that it could happen to people under his protection was unthinkable!

When they reached the church entrance, the priest stepped away. Richard pushed open the heavy oak door and went in. Numerous pine torches flamed in rough brackets along the walls and the smell of hate was near as strong as pitch. He moved into the room, blinking in the sudden light. A solid wall of stocky Welshmen blocked his path.

All held clubs or tools, but he was too angry even to be afraid.

Heffeydd Sele stepped forward. "You once said we need not fear to ask justice of you against an Englishman." His dark eyes gleamed dangerously. "Well, Englishman, the time has come."

Richard made an impatient movement of his hand and the men fell back. In the space before the altar, three of de Veasy's soldiers sat bound hand and foot, but a fourth was on his feet pacing nervously. The unbound man glanced up. *Philip. . . .*

It took a moment for the sight to register. Then a wave of rage swept Richard that left him near speechless. "You bastard!" he snarled. "I should kill you where you stand!"

Philip stumbled back a step. "I . . . I, we didn't mean to cause this trouble," he stammered. "We came down here for some sport, b-but it got out of hand."

Richard stalked forward into the torchlight. "Sport? Is that what you call what you did to that girl?"

Philip squirmed before his brother's obvious rage. "Well, for Christ's sake, Richard, she's naught but a Welsh serf. She'll be no worse for it in a couple of days."

Richard struck the boy hard across the face, knocking him to his knees. "Did you touch her? Did you?"

Philip glanced up, fear replacing the feigned arrogance in his voice. "Yes. Yes, I took her, Richard, but she was fine when I left. I didn't hurt her any. I swear it!"

"When you left?"

Philip nodded miserably. "W-we'd been drinking and were out of ale. I went for more. Richard, I swear on the surety of my soul, I didn't know what they were doing!"

"You left that girl alone with these wolves of de Veasy's? For Christ's sake, Philip, when you unkennel a pack of dogs on the countryside you must at least stay by to bring them to heel!"

Philip was shaken but trying desperately to keep his composure. "We'd been drinking and wanted a woman. I knew you'd be angry if we took any at the keep, s-so we came here."

"And?"

Philip took a deep breath. "We found the girl in the first hut we entered. I was drunk, I admit. I used her, but I didn't hurt her any, Richard, I swear it." He hesitated a moment. "Afterward, I was hot. I went outside to find something to drink. By the time I got back, they were at her." He shook his head miserably. "I . . . I didn't mean for that to happen."

"Oh? I'm sure she'd be pleased to hear that," Richard remarked sardonically. "And the fire? How did it start?"

"Someone must have heard us and gone for help. Before we knew it a score of men with clubs were trying to kill us. In the fighting, w-we torched a couple of huts."

Richard said nothing. For several long moments, no one moved. Finally, he grasped his brother by the neck of his tunic, jerking him to his feet. "Do you realize what you've done? In one thoughtless hour, you've destroyed everything I've done here in months. And you've put an innocent girl through hell. By the blessed rood, you sicken me," he added contemptuously. With a quick movement of his hand, he jerked a chain of gold from about the boy's neck. Turning, he held it out to the priest. "See this is given to the girl's family. It's little enough."

A murmur of surprise went round the room. The priest took the gold, the single ornament more valuable than all the miserable huts that had burned.

"You can't take that," Philip stormed. "It's mine!"

Richard turned back to his brother. "Oh? I've a notion it was bought with my sweat and blood—with coin sent to replenish the flocks at Waybridge. Besides, it may just buy your life. I should leave you here, but I don't suppose I can condone the killing of my brother, no matter how deserved."

"Half-brother," Philip snapped.

"Yes, thank God!" Richard glanced at the waiting Welshmen and jerked his head toward the prisoners. "Take them outside."

He stalked out into the night. The air was heavy and acrid from the fires. His men and the villagers waited quietly in the churchyard—waited to see what he would do. "Hear me," he began loudly. "These men of violence came into your village. They used one of your women and set fire to your town. They are no men of mine, yet they are guests in my keep. Since they answer not to me, I cannot deal with them as they deserve. Yet they will be punished."

He turned to Henry Bloet. "Bind them to the church wall. They're to have twenty lashes meted out by the kinsmen of the girl."

Philip caught his arm. "A knight beaten by a peasant? Not even you would dare that!" he sneered. "Besides, you can't put me to the lash like these common soldiers. I'm a knight, for Christ's sake!"

"If I had my way, your spurs would be hacked off this night. Take him," Richard ordered coldly.

"You son of a Saxon bitch!" Philip hissed.

Richard caught his brother by the throat. "One word . . . one more word, Philip, and there'll not be enough of you left to put to the lash!"

Philip held his tongue, but his dark, furious eyes spoke volumes. Richard released him, watching as the struggling soldiers were stripped and bound to the wall. Philip went quietly, holding himself erect as the fine clothing was torn from his back.

The whip snaked through the air—twenty lashes laid on with a vengeance. Richard held himself rigid as he watched the knotted cords bite into his brother's back. Philip didn't move or make a sound. At least he took his punishment like a man.

With each hissing bite of the lash Richard's rage ebbed,

a weary hopelessness rising to replace it. Philip would never forgive him this, but had he had another choice? His people had asked for justice—a justice he had promised. And it was little enough he could give.

Eighteen . . . nineteen . . . twenty. Silence. Richard moved forward into the sudden quiet, motioning Henry to follow. Drawing his dagger, he cut the thongs holding Philip upright. "Take him back to Gwenlyn, Henry. See his back's cared for properly."

Philip closed his eyes. "I don't . . . want . . . your help."

"Don't fret, m'lord. I'll see to the boy."

Richard nodded and turned away, overcome with an exhaustion that had little to do with the past hour of physical struggle. Philip would never forgive him this and his father might not either. But there was naught to be done now, and he told himself he didn't care.

Ignoring the scores of hostile eyes, Richard moved toward the horses. Taking his reins, he swung into the saddle, moving off slowly through the still-smoldering street.

The noise of returning men brought Elen to the window. It was dark below and she couldn't see if Richard was among them. Certainly he would be safe, she assured herself. Simon and Giles would have seen he came to no harm.

She glanced at the girl sleeping quietly in the great bed. She had bathed her and tended her wounds, soothing her into rest with the aid of wine laced with poppy. But the experience had had a strange effect on Elen.

Such could easily have happened to her. If Richard had been another kind of man, if she had been taken by beasts such as those who had used this girl, it might have been her. And it still might, depending on the husband Edward chose for her.

She closed her mind to the thought, focusing instead on the memory of Richard's tenderness. She had never valued him highly enough, had never really appreciated all that he was. And now she needed his reassurance, needed it as she did the air to breathe.

She moved to the door, persuading her guard to accompany her downstairs to the hall. But angry voices reached her long before she entered the room.

"You'd no right! Those were my men."

Elen peeked through the doorway. Richard stood beside the fireplace with his father while Hugh de Veasy faced them furiously from several paces away. "I'd all the right I needed," Richard said tiredly. "For God's sake, man, they started a riot with the Welsh and burned half the town! Twenty lashes is little enough for the offense."

"Baugh! They enjoyed a Welsh slut and torched a few miserable huts," de Veasy scoffed. "Nothing of value was lost. You've gone too far in your foolishness this time."

Elen stiffened, but she wasn't prepared for the cold fury that possessed Richard. "Those people are under my protection!" he bit out. "And I remind you, de Veasy. You and your men are guests here. You're welcome to stay if you like, but your men will follow my rules or suffer the consequences. As will you."

There was a moment of stunned silence and Elen held her breath. "I suppose I might expect any audacity from a man who'd put his brother to the lash for minor foolishness," de Veasy said finally. "But let me warn you, my friend—do not meddle with me. You'll find me less easy to cow than Philip."

"Let me warn you," Richard repeated. "Don't meddle with me or mine."

De Veasy smiled darkly. "Your warning is well taken. But I wonder how men of honor will look on your dealings with a belted knight. You took much on yourself, Richard."

Sir John put a hand on Richard's shoulder. "My youngest son did wrong. Perhaps he has an explanation, but Richard only did what he thought needful."

Richard shrugged off the hand. "I was within my rights,

as you both know. If you'll excuse me now, it's been a long night." He motioned to Simon and the boy sprang from his seat in the shadows, following Richard toward the stair.

Elen shrank back from the doorway. Philip! It was difficult to believe he had been part of such a thing.

Richard saw her as he came through the door. He paused. "How is the girl?"

"Sleeping." Elen studied him anxiously. Richard looked weary unto death, and he had several burns that needed tending. He looked nigh overcome in spirit as well. The night had taken its toll.

"I didn't know what to do save send her to you," Richard remarked. He took a deep breath, shoving a hand through his hair. "I'd have you go above now. De Veasy's in an ugly temper and it's not safe for you here." He hesitated as if he wished to say more. "Let me know if you need aught else," he added. With another glance, he brushed by her and started up the stair.

Elen caught Simon's arm. "Your master needs tending. I'll get my things and come."

Simon nodded. Turning, he, too, dragged wearily up the stair.

A short time later, Elen paused outside the entrance to Richard's chamber. The door was ajar but she hesitated on the threshold. Richard sat on a low stool in the center of the room. He was stripped to the waist, and Simon was cleansing several angry scrapes across his back.

Elen moved forward and both men glanced up. Taking the cloth from the boy, she sponged it gently across Richard's bare shoulder. "I will see to him," she said softly. "Go now." Richard's eyes lifted to hers and neither noticed as Simon slipped quietly out, closing the door behind him as he dismissed the surprised guard.

It was Richard who first found his tongue. "You shouldn't be here."

"Hush." Elen dipped the cloth into the basin of water,

easing it once more across Richard's back. He sighed with contentment as the soothing water did its work. She traced the rippling contours of his back, watching in fascination as the muscles flexed and smoothed beneath her hand. It had been a long time since she had seen Richard unclothed.

As the burns and scratches were cleansed, she worked a small amount of mutton fat mixed with herbs into the wounds. She smiled as Richard closed his eyes. He was so weary, he would be asleep where he sat in a few moments.

Dipping the cloth in fresh water, she dropped to a kneeling position before him. She drew the cloth gently down his arms, bending her head close to search for any bits of wood imbedded beneath the skin. Such tiny pieces could fester and poison a man's whole system, she had learned.

Richard shifted uncomfortably, the powerful muscles of his forearms tensing beneath her hands. She leaned against his thigh, reaching up to wash his chest. He suffered her ministrations for several seconds, then caught her hand, holding it firmly away. "You shouldn't be here," he repeated.

She kept her eyes even with his chest, not daring to look up. She was overwhelmingly aware of his closeness, of the warmth of his body next to hers. She wanted him to hold her, wanted to be in his arms. Suddenly she wanted it more than anything else on this earth. "But I wish to be," she said softly.

Richard said nothing and she held her breath. His chest rose and fell unsteadily. All at once, his arms curled around her, drawing her tightly against him. "Elen," he groaned. "Oh, my God, Elen . . ."

She pressed her face against his chest, her own arms sliding up to clasp him close. He sagged tiredly against her. "My brother . . . my own brother," he whispered, pressing his face against her hair. "Everything I've worked for, everything I've tried to do . . . gone. Up in smoke in a couple of hours. They'll never trust me now."

"That's not true, Richard." Elen pushed back and gazed

up at him earnestly. She had never seen this weary hope-lessness in his face, had never seen him other than confident and controlled. "After this night the people of Ruthlin will trust you more than ever. They'll see you didn't even spare your own brother."

He closed his eyes. "And Edward will have me recalled," he muttered darkly, as if he hadn't heard. "I'm in disgrace enough and de Veasy will see he hears the worst."

Elen stood up, dragging him to his feet with her. "That's nonsense! Come to bed, Richard. You're three parts asleep already. Things will look different in the morning."

She drew back the bed covers, smiling as Richard collapsed onto the mattress with a weary groan. Easing to a seat beside him, she brushed the tangle of hair back from his forehead. At that moment, the Wolf of Kent looked more like a small boy in need of mothering than King Edward's mightiest warrior.

Richard opened his eyes. "Don't go."

"No," she whispered. "I won't go, Richard. I'll be right here. Now sleep."

He closed his eyes and she rose and put out the candles. Stepping around the weapons he had dropped beside the bed, she slipped into a chair, tucking her feet comfortably beneath her.

For a long while she sat in the darkness, listening to the deep regular intake of Richard's breathing. She stared across the room. The window was a rectangular slash of gray in the wall. In another hour it would be dawn.

Strange, she thought, three months ago she would have given anything for this chance at Richard's unprotected throat—Richard Basset, the Wolf of Kent. He had destroyed her family and was sworn to take Owain as well. And he had shattered her peace in a way she had never expected.

All at once Elen closed her eyes, facing the bitter truth at last. She was in love with Richard of Kent. She had been for some time.

CHAPTER TWENTY-ONE

Elen shifted her head sleepily and slowly opened her eyes. A shaft of sunlight streamed through a high rectangular window across the room. From far away came the steady, rhythmic wash of the sea. This wasn't her room.

Flexing her stiff muscles, she twisted to gaze at the man sleeping in the great bed beside her. Now she remembered. She had stayed with Richard last night, stayed because he had asked . . .

And for another reason as well. She hadn't wanted to leave him.

Easing her cold, cramped legs from the chair, she watched Richard's slumber. He had so many sides, this Englishman from Kent. If only she could have seen that from the beginning instead of hating so blindly.

But if Richard were an honorable man, there were certainly Englishmen who weren't. She frowned as she considered her future. If Richard were to be believed, she would soon be wed to some man of Edward's choosing. She already knew a number of the border lords, by reputation at least. And she would rather be dead.

A familiar angry rebellion rose up inside her. She wouldn't do it! Edward couldn't make her. And he wouldn't have to—not if she came up with an acceptable alternative.

She thought of the convent her father had endowed not far from Teifi. Perhaps, just perhaps, Edward would let her take the veil. It was the only future that seemed even remotely bearable now.

She glanced at Richard, then quickly away, refusing to give in to the overwhelming desire to touch him. Yes, a nunnery it would have to be. Nothing else was acceptable. And she'd better leave here now before Richard awoke.

Returning to her bedchamber, Elen found her guard waiting outside the door. Obviously the man hadn't known what to do when she'd stayed all night with Richard. Since her patient was still sleeping off the effects of the drugged wine, Elen quietly checked her medicines, noting several were almost gone. She needed to fetch more mutton fat and thought it best to get it before the girl woke up.

A short time later Elen entered the hall. It was early yet and most of the men were still abed after their exhausting night. To her surprise, Owain sat alone at a trestle table, nursing a tankard of mead and a slab of dark bread.

She sent a manservant to the kitchens to fetch what she needed, then made her way to her friend. "What news of the girl you tend?" Owain asked by way of a greeting.

So he'd heard of that already. Elen seated herself beside him, frowning at her hands. "I suppose most would say she was lucky. She took no lasting hurt." Elen raised her eyes to his. "I doubt the girl would agree, though."

Owain's fingers clenched white against the tankard he held. "And we must sit helplessly by, wondering who and what will be next!" he ground out. He glanced narrowly at her. "The men mirror the master and de Veasy's lot are foul as they come. You must be careful, Elen. I'd thought your rank protection enough, but after last night I'm not willing to gamble."

He slid his hand into his tunic, coming out with a tiny gleaming dagger. He held it cupped in his hand, shielding it from three soldiers who lounged over their ale several tables away.

"Merciful God, Owain! Are you a fool?" Elen shot a frightened glance over his shoulder. Owain wasn't under strict guard within Gwenlyn, but wherever he went a couple of soldiers lingered nearby. Her own guard had joined the men across the room and was having a breakfast ale. "If you're caught with a weapon, you'll be slain on the spot!" she whispered. "Richard would never grant me your life a second time."

"It's a chance I'm willing to take," Owain responded grimly. Reaching out as if to pass her the bread, he held the dagger close instead. " 'Tis a short blade, scarce the width of my hand," he whispered. "Do you know the places to strike to kill a man with such?"

Elen nodded, taking the weapon and hiding it in the folds of her skirt.

"I pray God you'll not need it," he continued. "But I'd have you carry some protection. I'll not see you used as that girl."

The servant was already returning with the grease. There was little time to talk. "Owain, swear to me you'll do nothing so foolish as this again! I'm too valuable to be harmed . . . at least till after I'm wed," Elen added cynically. "And if my plan works, that time may never come."

Owain's eyebrows rose questioningly.

"There is one power stronger than the king. A power even Edward of England must acknowledge," Elen stated triumphantly. "I will appeal to the Church."

"Take care, Elen," Owain said quickly. "For God's sake take care."

Elen took the proffered cup the servant held, nodding to Owain. It wasn't until she was halfway back to her chamber that she realized her friend hadn't given the promise she sought.

Biting her lip in concentration, Jeanne Basset rubbed a generous portion of soothing unguent into her son's torn back. "Your brother is a brute . . . and jealous of your growing influence with the Baron of Ravensgate! He would shame you any way he could."

She took a deep breath, so angry she could scarcely get the words out coherently. "As God is my witness, I'll see him repaid one hundredfold for this if I have my way!"

Philip winced as his mother's fingers stiffened with anger. "Hush, woman. Leave me be," he remarked irritably. "Some right I'll grant him. I was a fool to get myself into the mess. But I'll not have your interference."

A knock sounded on the door and Philip shifted toward it. Sir Hugh de Veasy stood on the threshold. Philip turned his head, shamed beyond bearing that the powerful man should see his disgrace. "Leave us, Mother," he said stiffly.

De Veasy sauntered into the room. After hesitating uncertainly, Jeanne curtsied and withdrew.

"So, my young friend, I find you a bit the worse for your brother's anger," de Veasy remarked. "In large part, I blame myself. Had I been by last night, he'd never have dared such insolence."

Philip sat up, giving a painful shrug. "He's a bastard. I've known that all my life. He enjoys humiliating me, but he's done so for the last time. I'll slit his cursed throat the next time he lays hands on me!"

"Hmm . . . a commendable plan, but there is one small problem. Your brother's the very devil with a sword."

"Do you think I'm afraid of him?" Philip demanded. "Well, I'm not. With a little more practice I can take him!"

"I'm sure you can. I've seldom seen a man improve in passage of arms of rapidly," de Veasy remarked in a soothing voice. He hesitated, gazing at the boy consideringly. "But there are other ways to lesson an enemy. Ways that would bring no ill to you. After all, Richard is a royal favorite. Do you think Edward would stand by if you killed your brother?"

He smiled. "What would you say to humiliating him

instead, to bringing him down from his place of honor and making sure he advances no further in his unholy quest for power? Unless I miss my guess, he's about to make a bid for a landed and powerful wife—one more to his taste than Alicia de Borgh. But perhaps between us we can stop it."

Philip glanced up, arrested.

"Ah, I see the thought appeals to you even as it does to me. I'm sure if you and I put our heads together, we'll come up with something."

Philip shifted uncomfortably. A fight with Richard would have restored his battered pride, but somehow this scheming seemed unmanly. "I've no wish to involve you, m'lord. I can settle the matter myself."

"Believe me, it's no bother. In very fact, I've long wished to help the impudent jackanapes fall on his face." De Veasy gazed at Philip, the look of amusement fading from his face. "Your brother has weaknesses, like any other, and I've men here to sniff them out. I'm determined he'll not succeed in holding Gwynedd. Are you man enough to strike back, Philip? Will you be willing to assist me when the time comes?"

"Of course, my lord, but—"

"Good. I knew you were a game one—the type of man I would number among my friends." De Veasy smiled again, reaching out to touch Philip's shoulder. "Richard will learn not to underestimate you. That I promise."

Slipping into the chapel, Elen glanced furtively over her shoulder toward the door, then back to the black-robed priest just rising from the altar steps. She crossed herself as she hurried forward, whispering a prayer to the Virgin Mother. "Father," she called softly. "Are you not Father Edmund of Lanwort?"

The man turned in surprise. "Yes."

"I am Elen. Elen of Teifi. I beg a moment's grace on a most critical matter."

"Yes, my child, what is it?"

Elen stared at the stocky figure. The priest clasped pudgy, ringed fingers around the costly golden crucifix in his hand. "Is it true you'll be returning to Lanwort? I've a matter that must be taken before the bishop as soon as possible."

The man surveyed her carefully from inquiring brown eyes. "I am presently confessor to the Lord of Ravensgate, but we will be passing Lanwort on our way south. What is it you wish, daughter?"

Elen shifted uneasily. Could she trust an English priest?

But what choice had she? There was no other way of begging the Church to intervene on her behalf. And after all, he was a man of God. "I've an urgent letter that must be delivered to the Bishop of Lanwort, then on to Archbishop Pecham of Canterbury with the bishop's blessings if possible."

She hesitated, glancing nervously over her shoulder. "It's important none hear of this, for King Edward won't be pleased. I was forced to use a ruse to meet you, Father. I told my guard I would seek you out for confession this evening. It was a lie."

The priest smiled. "But you've just now confessed, have you not? Thus the tale was true."

Elen returned his smile. Perhaps English priests weren't so bad at that. She held out the narrow roll. "It is writ on a scrap. It was all the parchment I could come by," she explained. "Please ask the bishop to give it his consideration. I've heard he has no fear of Edward."

The priest inclined his head. "The Church has no master save God." He glanced at Elen shrewdly. "You said this was a secret request. Who, then, inscribed the letter?"

"None, Father. I write a little. A priest in my household taught me along with my brother." At his frown of displeasure she added quickly. "It was only so that I might assist in keeping household accounts."

The priest took the parchment, slipping it into the folds

of his robe. "I see. So no one knows of this?"

"No one."

"Very well. I will see that the Bishop of Lanwort receives your missive, child. Now go in peace and leave me to my prayers."

Elen dipped into a quick curtsy. "Thank you, Father. I thank you with all my heart!" Turning, she fled back up the aisle, praying earnestly for a speedy answer to her petition.

The priest stood watching as the girl disappeared. After a moment, he untied the carefully bound leather and unwrapped the scroll. His eyes sped along the crowded lines. Carefully rewrapping the letter, he left the chapel.

Moments later, he was knocking at Hugh de Veasy's chamber. The baron's squire swung open the door. "I've come to hear your master's confession," the priest said softly.

Across the room, Hugh de Veasy paused, a goblet of wine arrested halfway to his lips. His dark eyes met those of the priest. "Ah yes, Father, I'd near forgot I asked you to stop by. Leave us, William."

The squire nodded, slipping from the room without a word.

"You've discovered something?"

The priest moved forward, nodding thoughtfully. "Something that should interest you, though I'm not yet certain how it might be used. The girl, Elen, asked me to take this letter to Bishop Vespain. It's a plea to the Archbishop of Canterbury to intervene with King Edward so that she might take the veil."

De Veasy burst into laughter. "A bit naïve, is she not, our sweet bird of the west?" He took the parchment, skimming quickly down the lines.

"And yet it might be useful at that. I mean to have the girl's lands and it will be easiest done if I have her as well. Besides . . ." He grinned. "I've no aversion to taking Richard's pretty mistress from beneath his nose. And I've no doubt she'll be grateful enough to be rescued. He's kept her against her will with a guard to her door. It's my belief he plans to wed her by force now he knows her identity."

De Veasy's dark eyes narrowed thoughtfully. "Yes, I think I see a way." He rose to his feet. "Tell my man, Donald, to have our escort ready to leave tomorrow noon. And find Philip Basset for me. Send him here at once."

"The boy's a hothead. Are you certain you wish to include him in this?"

"Hotheads can be managed, especially young and foolish ones," de Veasy remarked, taking a sip of wine. "Besides, the boy will learn only what I wish him to know. His part will be small, but important."

Rising to his feet, he handed the parchment back to the priest. "Spread the news we ride for Lanwort on the morrow. The bishop and I have much to discuss."

CHAPTER TWENTY-TWO

*R*ichard guided Saladin carefully along the narrow path between rippling fields of Gwenlyn's barley. The crops looked good. By God's grace, Wales had been blessed with a comparatively dry summer just when the seed and young shoots most needed protection from the damp. And if the early frosts held off, the people of Ruthlin would be none the worse for the late planting.

But autumn would be difficult at best. There would be no rest between the busy harvest time and readying the fields for winter crops. Because the Welsh were, by nature, hunters and herdsmen, they didn't take easily to working the fields.

Riding Saladin through Gwenlyn's open gate, Richard continued across the bailey, and then swung to the ground. As he turned to give his reins to a servant, he caught sight of a sweat-stained roan with a dozen mounts being led toward water. His eyes narrowed grimly. He knew that roan gelding. Before God, what was Philip doing here?

He moved slowly up the stairs and into the keep. He had parted from his family with the utmost coolness two weeks earlier. Only his father had grasped his shoulder and kissed his cheek, requesting him to visit Waybridge as soon as possible.

Could that be it? Had something happened to Sir John? His step quickened.

Entering the hall, he noted a small group of dark-robed holy men gathered round a table. To one side of the priests, several soldiers were quenching their thirst from pitchers of ale. Philip rose from a seat nearby and moved hesitantly toward him. "I . . . I wasn't sure of my welcome but came anyway."

Richard sent him a measuring glance. "You are welcome."

Philip dropped his eyes uncertainly. "I don't blame you if I'm not. Just say the word and we'll go."

The boy was so obviously ill at ease, Richard relented. "Remain here as long as you wish. You and your men as well."

Philip raised his eyes. "We may tarry but briefly. I'm escorting these holy men to the Abbey Vale Crucis for Bishop Vespain. But I couldn't pass so near without seeing you." He glanced nervously over his shoulder at his men. "Is there somewhere we might speak in private? Your chamber?" He hesitated. "That is, if you've the time."

Richard frowned. He didn't wish to talk to Philip just now, but his brother obviously had something on his mind. "Of course. Follow me."

When they entered the bedchamber, Richard poured them both wine. "Sit if you will, Philip," he said, gesturing toward a chair. He dropped onto a stool, gazing warily at his half-brother.

"Richard, I . . . I've come to beg your pardon," Philip blurted out at once. "I know I did wrong. You were within your rights to punish me. By the rood, I was a fool!"

Richard studied the boy in surprise. In all his wild imaginings, he'd not expected this. Perhaps Philip wasn't so hopeless as he'd thought. The words of his father echoed in his mind. No doubt, he had been partially to blame for the hostility between them. Perhaps helping the boy was worth a try.

"I . . . I couldn't control de Veasy's men that night," Philip confessed. "I feared they'd not obey me so I went along. It was easiest. I'd no wish to look a fool if they laughed at me, refused my orders. But I should have made an effort. They were my responsibility."

He rose and paced to the window, staring grimly out. "You were put to a great deal of trouble because of my lack of backbone. You've made no secret of the fact you think me naught but a spoilt child. But I swear you'll soon find different!"

"My 'trouble,' as you call it, matters little," Richard remarked. "What you did caused anguish and hardship to a great many people and near destroyed the trust I'd worked months building with the Welsh. But I'd say you've plenty of backbone. You certainly took your punishment like a man. In that moment, if not before, I was proud of you," he added.

Philip glanced back in surprise, his eyes searching Richard's not daring to believe. "But you said I sickened you."

"Your actions and those of the men you were with did." Richard took a slow sip of wine. "You're no spoilt boy now, Philip, but a man full grown. You've yet to learn the ways of command but de Veasy's men would be a hard lot to begin with. I was on my own at an age much younger than you. I had to learn or die. And I learned some bitter lessons most painfully—something I would see you spared."

Philip gripped the window ledge, the old anger spilling out. "You make few mistakes, brother. To our father, you're near perfect. I could never live up to you . . . never!"

"I make a great many mistakes," Richard said. "Some, to my shame, I made with you. I was hard on you when we were boys—when our father wished me to instruct you in use of arms. I'll tell you something now, Philip, something I should have admitted long ago. I envied you then. You had the home I'd been sent from, the love of a mother and father I'd been denied. I've no doubt now, I took out my anger on you. I told myself I scorned you—it eased my hurt to laugh. But it wasn't so. In truth, I was jealous. The problems between us were likely as much my fault as yours."

Philip didn't look at him. "Our father loved you best. He never said so, but I knew he was disgusted by my lack of manly skills. Yet I was afraid . . . afraid I'd not live up to you."

He closed his eyes and took a deep breath. "I longed to go off as you had, to be squire to a fighting man. I used to dream of winning honor and glory and the praise of other men. And the dreams always ended with my besting you on the field."

Richard smiled wryly. "And there was I wishing I might stay home."

"I never knew."

"No, we never talked."

Philip tensed slightly, his eyes narrowing as he stared down into the bailey. When he turned, his face was torn with a look of uncertainty that made Richard study him in surprise.

"Sometimes," Philip began, "sometimes a man makes choices—choices he fears in his heart aren't best. But once made, he's honor bound to see them through. You understand that, I know."

He glanced down uncomfortably. "There is much between us, Richard. I doubt you'll ever forgive me, but I want you to know I regret the trouble I've caused. And I warn you. After our father's death my mother plans to challenge your rights as an elder son, to sue for a partial inheritance for me. I won't interfere with you, though—that I promise."

Richard nodded. "It's nothing I didn't expect."

Philip studied him narrowly. "I'll give you no trouble over Waybridge no matter my mother's plan. Just promise me she'll have a place there despite your anger at me."

Richard nodded. "She'll have a place there as will you

if you wish. I'm little more than a temporary castellan of Gwenlyn and will be off warring for Edward many years yet, God willing." He smiled. "I'll have need of a trustworthy man to keep Waybridge in good heart while I'm away. Between us, we might just make the place pay."

He rose to his feet, moving slowly toward his brother. "We've our differences, Philip, but there's nothing between us that can't be mended. You're welcome at Gwenlyn or any other keep I hold. Can you not stay and sup this evening?"

Philip glanced back down into the bailey. "No . . . my party already awaits me below. It's late, Richard, much too late. I must tell you good-bye."

An errant breeze drifted into the room, ruffling the parchment Elen held. Painstakingly, she copied the last word from a page of Welsh law Richard had requested she transcribe. When finished, the pages would be sent to King Edward along with an explanation of the system of law Gwenlyn used. Though not agreeing with all of Richard's arguments, she had to admit the new codes were fair. And if the king approved, the system would be used throughout Edward's newly created shires in Wales.

A murmur of voices sounded unexpectedly from outside the door along with a curious scuffling noise. Putting the parchment aside, she rose to her feet.

A loud thump came to her along with a short, smothered cry. Her door burst open and three priests lurched in carrying the body of her guard. With a startled gasp, Elen hurried across the floor. "What's happened? Is he ill?"

Father Edmund's well-fed face frowned up at her. "Ill? No child, not ill."

She dropped to her knees beside the man's inert form, noting the large, swelling lump across his forehead. Her eyes went to the staff one of the priests carried. The man grinned.

Father Edmund was already rising from his knees. He dragged a cowled priest's garment from a dusty pack he carried. "Here, child, into these robes and be quick!"

Elen rose, gazing at him blankly. "But I don't understand."

"Bishop Vespain has agreed to take you under his protection," he explained hurriedly. "Archbishop Pecham must put your case to the Holy Father in Rome, but Edward needs money now for mercenaries for the Scots border. Word has it he's already negotiated your marriage settlement. He'll get the thing done before Pecham can move." His eyes held hers. "If you hope to take the veil, we must move now."

The words registered. Elen jerked the robe from his hand, tugging it hastily over her head and smoothing it into place. She gazed at the two priests who were busily engaged in binding and gagging her guard. They looked uncommonly rough for priests—no doubt soldiers in the hire of Bishop Vespain.

She stared down at her unconscious guard. The man had been kind to her and she didn't wish him to suffer for this. "Not so tight," she ordered. "And place him there on the bed. I said, not so tight!"

One of the men glanced up in exasperation, but Father Edmund only frowned, jerking his head in silent agreement. "Listen to me, Elen," he said, turning back to her. "Sir Richard returned unexpectedly, but he's being kept occupied in another part of the castle. We've only a few moments to get you through the hall and out to the waiting horses."

He drew the hood up about her face, frowning at the sight. "Keep your hands folded within your sleeves and your head down as we move through the hall. Whatever you do, don't look up." He frowned again. "You've not the slightest look of any priest I know."

Elen nodded, her heart racing nervously. At this time of

the morning there would be few men in the hall. But could she make it past the servants and the guards at Gwenlyn's gate?

Her thoughts flew to Richard. He would be furious when he learned of this but she didn't want him to worry. She could at least leave a message telling him she was safe.

She moved quickly toward the table with its neat stack of parchment. "I would leave Sir Richard word, else he'll fear for my safety."

The priest caught her arm, his grip far rougher than she had expected. "There's no time, child. We must be away else we'll all be seized." He stared at her narrowly. "We've risked much to help you. I know you'd not wish us to face punishment on your account."

"No, of course not, Father." She bit her lip. "I . . . I suppose I could write from Lanwort."

"Yes, yes, of course. And don't fret. I'll see Sir Richard learns of your safety. Now come, we've not a second to lose."

They slipped out the door, moving quickly along the empty corridor downstairs to the hall. Elen stared obediently at the floor, slowing her step to the solemn, unhurried tread of the priest.

No one spared a glance for the little bunch of dusty priests as they made their way outside to the waiting horses. Elen mounted awkwardly in her robes, keeping her chin tucked down as Father Edmund kept reminding under his breath.

Moments later, Richard and Philip came out of the hall. Elen was surprised to see Philip, and the fact that the boy was involved brought a new worry to mind. Richard would bear the blame for her escape. He was already in disgrace and his failure to hold her would only add more trouble. Naturally Philip would do all in his power to help stir the pot.

She shifted in the saddle, studying Richard anxiously. She hated leaving without even a word, but she couldn't stay, not with the future Edward planned for her. She'd not be sold to some greedy Englishman so the king could finance more wars.

And she could write Richard, she reminded herself. Perhaps he would even come to Lanwort to see her.

Father Edmund caught her reins, swinging her mount's head away from the door. "Come," he hissed, "lest you be noticed. Move toward the gate with the rest of us."

She darted a worried glance back at Richard then obediently rode her horse toward the gate. She would write Edward as well, explain that this was none of Richard's fault. She didn't wish him disgraced on her account—not again.

No shouted challenge stopped them as they passed under the first raised portcullis. She ducked her head lower, holding her breath as they crossed the outer bailey and trotted through the main gates.

Moments later they were cantering along the north road. Once out of sight of Gwenlyn, they lashed their animals into a gallop, putting the keep behind them as quickly as possible.

Leaving the road, the party cut westward through a dense wood of birch and aspen. Branches snatched at Elen's face and robe as she rode through the trees toward the sea. She could smell the freshening ocean breeze, hear the restless surge of sea against land. But why were they hugging the coast?

She followed Father Edmund's awkward, unwieldy figure, clinging to her reins as her mount stumbled and slid down a steep embankment toward water. Armed men sprang from a thicket near the small stretch of rocky beach. At Philip's curt order, they dragged a longboat from beneath a tangle of driftwood and water weed.

Elen reined in sharply, staring at the boat in surprise. "What's this?"

"Did I not tell you? We'll cross first to Ireland to a place of safety for you." Father Edmund pointed over the shallow inlet. A short distance offshore, a small trading ship rode to her anchor. "Though the Church sees only a woman determined to dedicate herself to God, many men would see you as a valuable prize to be seized," he explained. "We must take care to keep you safe until the Holy Father decides your case. Until Bishop Vespain can take you personally into his protection, you'll be fair game to any dishonorable knight who might seize you."

Ireland! Elen stared at him in dismay. "For how long?"

"Only a short while, I assure you."

"The bishop will join us there?"

Father Edmund nodded. "He will join you soon if he is not there already."

"Oh." Elen gazed uncertainly toward the ship. The words of the priest made sense. It was just that this was all happening so quickly. She hadn't had time to think. Still, she had prayed for a speedy answer to her troubles and perhaps this was it. She only wished she could have discussed it with Father Dilwen.

Swinging down from her mount, she watched with misgivings as a soldier came to lead the sweating animal away. The boat was pushed into the water and, after begging her pardon, a brawny seaman lifted her through the shallows and into the boat. The men took their positions at the oars and shoved off. Father Edmund waved to her. "Go with God, my child."

She rose to her knees in surprise. "Aren't you coming?"

"No. I must return to explain all to Sir Richard. You will be safe. These men have orders to see you into the keeping of the bishop."

Elen gripped the side of the boat in a sudden panic. "But you said you were coming," she shouted. "Wait! I've no wish to go without you!"

The seamen leaned into their oars, sending the little boat skimming forward across the water. Father Edmund moved to stand beside Philip, his figure dwindling rapidly with the distance. "The Baron of Ravensgate awaits you on board," he called. "He will see to your safety until Bishop Vespain arrives."

Elen's heart began a wild, frightened beating. Sir Hugh de Veasy—Holy Mary, she'd been a fool! She glanced down at the glittering water but knew she dared not jump. These men would only haul her back in like some struggling fish.

She stared in dismay at the rapidly receding coastline. Dear God in heaven, what had she done? She had flown as foolishly into this trap as a bird into a net. She had put herself hopelessly into the power of an unscrupulous man— the sworn enemy of her people and of Richard as well.

And she had no one she might count on for help. For even if Richard somehow learned what had happened, he had no ships at his command. He would have to send to Edward and it would be weeks, perhaps months, before she might expect rescue.

Father Edmund's words came back to her. She was a valuable prize any dishonorable knight might seize. If the man could wed her, perhaps even get her with child, the marriage would be sanctioned by Holy Church and he would have legal right to her lands. Of course, he would be forced to pay a huge fine to Edward, but that would be no hindrance to Hugh de Veasy. And she had heard Richard say the man wanted control of North Wales.

She closed her eyes, trying desperately to get hold of her rising panic. Think . . . she must think! Was it possible Father Edmund had been part of this plot or was he as foolishly trusting as she had been? And was Bishop Vespain coming to Ireland or had he even heard her request? It didn't really matter. Hugh de Veasy would take care he was too late.

She opened her eyes and gazed narrowly at the ship, her fear distilling to a sharp, crystalline resolve to best the man. Other heiresses had fallen as fair game to similar plots, but de Veasy would find her no easy victim. She hugged her arms close to her chest where the dagger Owain had slipped to her rode comfortingly inside her shift.

At least she had weapons—the tiny dagger and the wits to use it. Small comfort to a woman alone against a man and an army.

All too soon, the little boat reached the waiting ship. Elen rose to her feet, waiting for the men to help her on board. She wouldn't make a fuss now; it would do little good. And if Hugh de Veasy thought her willing it might forestall any use of force—at least for a time.

The baron stepped forward to personally assist her over the side. "Welcome, my lady," he remarked with a bow. "Bishop Vespain has charged me with your safety until he arrives. It's my pleasure to be of assistance."

Elen allowed him to take her hand and lift it to his lips. So he thought to continue this farce a while longer. The idea suited her as well. She forced herself to smile. "You have my gratitude, my lord. I've long hoped for freedom, but it is now my fervent wish to dedicate myself to Holy Church."

"So I've heard." De Veasy returned her smile, his eyes dark, glittering, half closed against the light. "Knowing that to be the case, I had no hesitation in assisting your rescue. Besides, I'd not miss the chance to annoy our mutual friend. Sir Richard Basset grows too large in his own conceit. It's my belief he planned to wed you and put himself above far better born men."

Elen glanced up in surprise. "Wed me?"

"Don't be afraid. I can assure you, he'll get no such chance."

Elen sent the man a thoughtful look. Hugh de Veasy obviously believed she hated Richard. She wasn't sure how to use the fact to her advantage, but perhaps she should follow the baron's lead. "Richard Basset is the sworn enemy of my family," she said slowly. "I would never wed him . . . never! I only hope I'll not be forced to look on him again."

De Veasy took her hand, bending over it once more. "My dear lady, I can promise you won't see him anytime soon at least. We're bound for Ambersly, an estate I hold on the Irish coast. Sir Richard will have no idea where to look for you. And even if he did, he dare not bring armed men there. Edward has expressly forbidden such. Like any well-trained puppy, Richard won't think of going against his master's will."

Elen nodded, de Veasy's words adding to her despair. No, Richard wouldn't go against Edward's orders, not even for her. The tiny hope that he might somehow miraculously appear died a bitter death in her heart.

The rattle of the rising anchor chain signaled the ship was ready for sailing. It dipped forward with a lurch and was at once under way. Elen tried to think of her father, of Rhodri and Enion—what would they do?—but instead she found herself remembering a tall, golden knight smiling down at her in the summer sun.

No matter how dark the hour, she doubted Richard would be afraid. She steadied herself against the roll of the ship, turning her face toward Ireland. Even in his absence, the thought of Richard Basset was comforting.

CHAPTER TWENTY-THREE

*R*ichard held himself stiffly, straining eyes and ears in the ghostly midnight quiet for any hint of his men returning from their expedition. The muted growl of waves against sand came to him along with the eerie call of a night bird winging its way up the Irish coast—but no noise of stealthy footsteps crunching on sand.

He toyed restlessly with his dagger, trying to keep his thoughts on the dangerous business at hand. Despite his efforts, a host of fears rose to plague him. What if he had guessed wrong? What if de Veasy hadn't brought Elen to Ambersly? And what might be happening to her now?

He shifted impatiently from one foot to the other, clenching and unclenching his fists. If de Veasy had hurt her, if he'd touched her...

He drew a deep, steadying breath. If de Veasy had hurt Elen, he would kill the bastard if it was the last thing he did. And Philip, his dear half-brother? Philip would pay for his treachery if Richard lived the night.

He glanced over his shoulder toward the glittering blue-black sea. The royal supply ship he had confiscated at the point of his sword lay well hidden with his soldiers on board. He hadn't dared sail closer for fear they might be seen by de Veasy's men.

The ship from Anglesey had been a stroke of luck for Richard—that and the fact that a keen-eyed Welshman had seen de Veasy's ship and watched the direction it sailed. When Elen's unconscious guard came to with his tale of priests with clubs, it had been easy enough to connect the day's events. Putting two and two together, it had smelled to heaven of one of de Veasy's plots.

And to Richard's surprise, the Welsh had swarmed forward to assist him. Owain had demanded to be taken along and Richard had quickly enlisted his help. No one was better suited to this cat-and-mouse game of midnight raiding than the Welsh. He had taken a score of his own men and a dozen grim Welshmen Owain had handpicked, and they had set out in Edward's small supply ship in hot pursuit.

What bothered Richard most about this affair was Elen's willing participation. Surely those pretend priests couldn't have taken her against her will. What tale could de Veasy have spun to cause her to fly with him into danger? It was difficult to believe she had left like that—without even a word.

A shadow flitted from the thicket and, with no other warning, the Welshmen were back. Startled, Richard muttered an oath beneath his breath. These men were silent as death. Praise God they were with him this night instead of seeking his life. "What did you find?" he whispered.

The stiff body of a bound man was dumped unceremoniously at his feet. "A present for you," Owain said softly. "We reached the keep without mishap and took this man napping at his post. I've little doubt we can make him talk."

Richard knelt in the sand and dragged the gag from the soldier's mouth. "We want information and we've little time to phrase it gently, my man. If you answer truly, you'll live. If not, I promise you'll wish you were dead a thousand times over. Do you understand?"

The man nodded.

"Tell me. Is the Baron of Ravensgate in residence?"

The man hesitated. Richard drew his knife from his belt. "Y-yes. Rode in near sundown."

"Had he a woman with him?"

The man nodded again.

A flood of relief swept Richard that nearly sent him reeling. If Elen hadn't been here, he wouldn't have known where to search. "Do you know where she's kept?"

The man shook his head.

"Think," Richard ordered grimly, pressing his blade against the man's throat.

"Uh, the best apartments be on the third floor, uh . . . the side nearest the sun's rising. The baron lodges there. She'd be near, most like."

Another dozen questions concerning the placement of sentries and the castle's layout, and Richard forced the gag back into the prisoner's mouth. The men dragged him into a thicket. "He's not to be harmed," Richard ordered. "We'll release him on our return."

"What next, my lord?"

Richard turned to Owain in surprise. The stubborn Welshman had never acknowledged him in that respectful manner—and Richard had never demanded it. He grinned in the dark. "I've heard you Welsh climb like flies on a wall. Think you we can make the cliff face on the seaward side of the keep? According to our friend here, it's not guarded."

"A babe could make it," Owain responded scornfully.

"Good. Once at the wall, we'll go over it into the garden and make for that side door the man spoke of. You and your men will wait there. I'll stand a better chance alone than to take this lot clattering about the halls."

"The men will wait, but I'm with you," Owain replied stubbornly. "Elen is my lady and I've sworn to bring her back. Besides, we stand a better chance together."

Richard thought for a moment. The man was probably

right. "Very well. If you've a wish to go, I won't stop you. But no more than we two."

"Aye."

With that, the men scattered soundlessly through the trees toward the coast road. They dashed through the forest shadows paralleling the short track. Richard shifted the heavy rope he carried and glanced up at the night sky. What little moon there was had set long since and the night was near black as the tomb. It was a good night for raiding. If only Elen's safety didn't hang in the balance, he'd be enjoying himself. His comrades were battle-hardened veterans and Owain a wily old fox well seasoned by command.

Richard's eyes narrowed and he glanced across at the tireless Welshman, not liking the thought that had suddenly crossed his mind. No, it was ridiculous. The man he sought was much younger and went by the name of Rhys.

Reaching the cliffs below the ancient stone fortress of Ambersly, the men went grimly to work. Without a word of complaint, they began inching silently up through the jagged scree of rock, heaving themselves along, hand over hand, to the shadowy summit at the the base of the castle wall. Once there, they paused for breath and a few last whispered orders.

After he tossed the scaling rope over the wall, Richard jerked it once to set the hook over the edge. The keep was ancient and poorly fortified. He clambered up easily, noticing the disreputable state of the battlements as he ascended. Christ's body, his men were more like to be hit by crumbling stone than downed by a sharp-eyed guard.

He dropped down from the wall onto all fours and held his breath for any hint of alarm. But there was no sound save the rustle of wind in the trees and the scurrying of some creature in the grass.

He gazed about at the shadowy riot of fruit trees and overgrown hedges. The garden was little more than a wilderness, mute evidence that de Veasy was rarely in residence. So much the better for his purpose tonight.

Owain stepped toward him. "Let's to it."

The two men crept silently along the side of the keep to the door the guard had mentioned. It swung open with a heart-stopping creak. After hesitating a moment they slipped inside. Now came the test.

They reached the narrow spiraling stair which went up from the kitchens past the great hall. The evening meal was long over, but they still risked detection by servants fetching up wine and ale for de Veasy's men.

Richard formed a brief prayer. God grant they weren't discovered in this narrow stairwell. There was scarce room to draw steel, much less make a fight of it. Taking a deep breath, he sprinted upward past the hall, ducking through a doorway into a musty corridor he hoped led to the eastern wing.

Leaning against the moldering wall, he glanced back. Owain was still with him, his breathing no more labored than Richard's own. For all the man's years, Richard recognized a raider of note. It was good to have the Welshman along. "Come," he whispered. "If the man spoke truth, the main stair should be just ahead."

Owain nodded and they slipped noiselessly down the shadowy corridor. Richard began to breathe easier. Perhaps they would make it after all.

Without warning, disaster struck. Two soldiers stepped from a doorway directly into their path. Sword up, Richard leaped to throttle the men, but a shout of alarm rang out.

And suddenly, the entire corridor was filled with fighting men. Richard swung his blade with a fury, cutting and slashing in an attempt to reach the stair. Owain darted forward to guard his back, determinedly holding off the growing hoard of soldiers.

"Well, well... what have we here? I fear I underestimated you, my friend. Welcome to Ambersly."

Sword still swinging, Richard glanced in the direction of

that familiar, mocking voice. Sir Hugh de Veasy stood in the hallway, smiling like a satyr.

"I suggest you put down your weapon and tell your friend to do the same. You might live longer that way."

For a moment Richard stubbornly held on to his sword, but he had no choice and knew it. He couldn't give de Veasy an excuse to kill him—not with Elen depending on him. With a heart full of bitterness and a muttered curse, he dropped his blade to the floor.

Elen paced her narrow room in a growing worry. She had heard distant shouts of alarm and the footsteps of hurrying men. But when she opened the door to look, a guard had gestured her inside. Now she flung herself onto the musty, unused bedding in a fever of impatience.

What was happening? She dared not hope it was Richard, but perhaps Bishop Vespain had arrived after all. She could almost tell herself de Veasy would keep his word and hold her safe for the Church.

Almost but not quite. The memory of those moments between them in the shadowy corridor of Gwenlyn, of his dark eyes studying her this evening had left her little doubt of his plans. Besides, he would do anything to spite Richard.

Quick footsteps sounded in the hallway outside. She had moved the dagger to her sleeve, ready to hand. Now she pressed her arm to her side, the feel of the blade giving her courage. Holy Mary, Mother of God, give her strength and wit.

An impatient knock came against her door. It opened and Hugh de Veasy stepped into the room. His eyes were bright, his face flushed with the excitement of victory. "I see you've not yet retired. Good. We've matters to discuss."

Elen slid to her feet, thankful the bedcovers were mussed from her restlessness. "I was asleep, my lord, but sounds in the corridor frightened me. Is there trouble?"

"Trouble, no . . . only a bit of good sport."

The baron looked so pleased with himself, she almost expected to hear a purr of satisfaction. "Oh? What sport?"

He advanced toward her and she crossed her arms, her hand hovering near her dagger. "You might be amused at that," he remarked. "It seems I underestimated Sir Richard Basset. He followed us here, made it into Ambersly by some ruse and got so far as the main stair." He grinned maliciously. "But he's resting below at present in conditions well suited to his station."

"Richard . . . here?" Elen's eyes widened in a look of horror de Veasy took for fright.

"You've no need to fear. He's quite helpless at the moment."

Elen's throat was so dry she could scarcely swallow. Hugh de Veasy hated Richard and the man had no honor. There was no guessing what he might do. And it was her foolishness that had led Richard into danger. If there was any way she could undo this day's evil, Richard wouldn't suffer for it, she swore. But first she had to find him.

Mustering a scornful look, she gazed up at de Veasy. "Fear? I've no fear of the man. But what a pretty sight—Sir Richard Basset in chains. After months as his prisoner, what I'd not give to see it!"

De Veasy caught her chin, lifting her face toward him in the light. She suffered his touch, forcing herself to gaze back at him evenly. "You may think me vengeful, my lord, but Sir Richard has many sins against me for which to answer. I've sworn to see him repaid."

De Veasy released her. "Yes, I suppose you've earned the right. And it might be amusing at that." He began to smile, a look that sent a shiver through Elen. "Come, I'm sure Sir Richard will enjoy the company."

They moved through the musty castle, down the stair through the first-floor storerooms to the prison below. De Veasy paused outside a barred doorway where two guards stood to attention. Taking a torch from one of the men, de Veasy motioned for the door to be unlocked. "My lord Richard," he called mockingly. "You've guests."

Elen ducked through the low entrance, biting her lip to keep from crying out at the sight. Richard lay bound hand and foot in a matting of filthy straw. And he was obviously the worse for a beating.

The flickering torchlight illuminated another body, and she glanced from Richard in surprise. Owain? What was he doing here?

Merciful God, what should she do? She glanced at the man beside her, calculating the chance of killing him with one swift stroke. But she doubted the tiny blade she held would do the job quickly enough. De Veasy would have time to call the guard.

De Veasy was staring at her expectantly. She had to say something. "What a sight," she murmured, near choking on the words. "My lord de Veasy, it exceeds my expectations."

The baron gave an exultant laugh. "I thought you'd be pleased."

Suddenly the image registered. Rope... Richard was bound with rope! She pressed the dagger close. She had a weapon—a weapon Richard needed desperately.

She glanced at the bound men, giving a contemptuous laugh. "So, Richard Basset, Wolf of Kent. At last I see you brought low. You've much for which to answer. The death of my family, the murder of the man betrothed to me, the countless brutal indignities I've suffered at your hands. I take much pleasure in this sight."

Richard blinked and squinted into the light, unable to believe the voice he heard. After the darkness, the sudden torchlight was blinding. He struggled to a sitting position, ignoring the intense throbbing in his head. Elen? Could that really be Elen saying those things?

His head spun and his battered body ached with a vengeance. Perhaps she had gone willingly with the priests.

The memory of her and de Veasy together in Gwenlyn's hallway danced before his mind's eye.

"You were a fool, such a fool," Elen continued scornfully. "And as easy to dupe as a child. I've longed to see you dead, but before God, this is better! My only regret is that the baron's men were too gentle. I shall pray you soon get what you truly deserve."

She turned to de Veasy. Placing a hand on the hilt of his knife, she smiled up at him. "I've sworn to spill this man's blood. A sacred oath, my lord. May I?"

De Veasy sent her a lazy smile. "No, my dear, we can't kill one of Edward's knights . . . not like this, anyway."

"I've no intention of letting him off so easily. My people know ways a man may die for days."

De Veasy grinned. This was even more entertaining than he had anticipated. "Very well."

Elen drew the knife from his belt. She moved purposefully across the floor, feeling the baron's sharp eyes upon her. Hugh De Veasy was enjoying this but she dared not make a mistake. She had to give him plenty to hold his attention.

Ignoring Owain's frowning gaze, she halted before Richard. "I'd cut your throat with this, but 'twould be too easy," she hissed. "I hope you live long, Richard of Kent. I hope you live long to suffer as I have!"

She placed the point of the knife against his throat, bringing it to his jaw with a steadily increasing pressure. His eyes met hers, fragments of green narrowed with disbelief.

She steeled herself against that look. "This is for Enion," she bit out, drawing the knife lightly across his jaw until the blade dripped red. "I swore an oath to spill your blood. Now I have done so!"

Richard winced as the blade tore bruised flesh, but the hurt was nothing to the confusion whirling through him. It didn't make sense. Her hateful words went on and on, but he closed his eyes, trying not to listen. What was it

Giles had told him about the Welsh and their blood feuds? Holy God, could he have been wrong? Could he possibly have been this wrong?

Elen moved slowly behind him, her knife point pricking his neck, toying with his hair. He remained stubbornly silent, trying to summon the saving energy of hatred, of revenge. But it didn't come.

All at once something fumbled into his bound hands. He felt the sharp edge of cold steel against his palm and his fingers closed around a blade. A dagger—she was slipping him a dagger.

It was an act, this whole thing a ruse to distract de Veasy and slip him a weapon. Sweet Jesus, what a performance! The girl was magnificent.

His eyes shot open, but Elen was already halfway across the floor. She handed de Veasy his knife. "By your leave, my lord, I wish to return upstairs now. I've seen what I came for and the stench here sickens me."

De Veasy nodded. With a word to a guard, he directed the man to escort her above.

Richard listened avidly, every muscle straining for release. He would be out of this cursed cell in short order, and now he knew where to find Elen. She turned at the door and met his eyes. It was all he could do not to laugh.

The door swung shut and de Veasy turned back to Richard. "A bloodthirsty little savage, isn't she—but a lady quite after my heart. I shall have to keep all knives out of her reach once we're wed."

Richard found his voice at last. "Edward won't let you get away with this. He has other plans for the girl."

"Edward will have nothing to say in the matter. I greatly fear my passions are about to get the better of me. By the time my good friend the Bishop of Lanwort arrives, he'll have to make all right by performing a wedding." De Veasy smiled thinly. "Naturally, I'll pay Vespain a fine penance of silver for my sins. By the time I show my face in England, it's my hope the lady will be large with child. And what will your precious Edward do then?"

Richard held his tongue, longing to plunge his knife into de Veasy's throat.

"As you say, nothing." The baron chuckled. "I've friends at court—powerful friends. But take heart, Richard. If the child's a boy, we'll name him in your honor."

Again Richard said nothing. He was already sawing feverishly on the ropes binding his hands.

De Veasy moved toward the door. "I'll leave you now to darkness and solitude. I must see to my bride-to-be." He paused once more, turning back to Richard triumphantly. "Think about it, Basset. I want you to think about it all night."

The door had scarcely closed when Richard tore his hands free of his bonds. Catching up the knife, he hacked viciously at the tight cords binding his ankles. "That whoreson!" he snarled. "If he touches her, I'll kill him!"

"Aye, but slow, lad, slow," Owain growled. "I'd have him gelded and long in the dying."

Richard slid across the filthy straw, fumbling for Owain in the darkness. He found the man's bound hands, and quickly cut through the cords. "She passed you a knife!" the Welshman exclaimed. "By Our Lord Savior, I couldn't make out the mischief she was brewing!"

"Yes, she passed me a knife, but now she hasn't a weapon," Richard responded grimly. "We'd best make haste."

It was an easy matter to trick the guards into the cell. Once inside, Richard and Owain fell on them with a vengeance. Hurriedly, they exchanged their torn and bloodied clothing for de Veasy's livery. Then Richard locked the cell door and they headed up the stairs.

No one called a challenge as the two moved purposefully along the corridors. Richard pulled his cap low to hide his bruised face, but it was all he could do to keep himself to a walk.

They made the eastern stair without mishap. Hurrying along the corridor, they came at last to a guarded doorway. "We've urgent news for the baron," Richard told the soldier. "Is he within?"

The man nodded. "But not to be disturbed." He grinned and raised his eyebrows. "He's got a pretty piece of work this night, for sure!"

Richard shook his head impatiently as Owain moved a half-step nearer. "But this is important. Look here, man—"

Owain threw a muscular arm around the guard's throat, half lifting him with an efficient upward thrust of his forearm. The man slid to the floor without a sound.

Easing the door open a few inches, Richard glanced inside. De Veasy had his back toward the entrance while Elen faced him defiantly, a low table between them. She glanced up, her eyes meeting his for a pregnant moment. Her attention shifted smoothly to de Veasy and she gave no sign she had seen him.

Richard crept through the doorway. Elen raised her voice, covering the slight sound of his footsteps. "You'll never make me agree! Never!" she cried. "And the bishop can't marry a woman with a knife to her back."

"Crude tactics, my dear. I've little use for such," de Veasy remarked. "I've no doubt I'll have your consent before the night is out."

"You wouldn't dare! I'm Edward's—"

She broke off as Richard launched himself across the floor. He struck de Veasy and the two tumbled to the floor, kicking and pummeling each other as they rolled beneath the table.

Richard . . . thank God! She'd not dared to hope he'd come so soon. She gazed frantically about for a weapon to aid him, but the fight was short-lived. Within seconds, de Veasy lay quiet, Richard's knife at his throat.

"Now we'll see who pipes the tune, my fine lord. And I

promise, it'll be no song to your liking," Richard snarled. "Before God, I'll see you die by inches!" He glanced toward Elen, his fury barely controlled. "Has he hurt you?"

She shook her head.

"Tell me true. Has he touched you?"

His expression was frightening. "No! No, Richard, I'm fine."

He nodded, taking a deep breath to get hold of himself. Slowly the black rage eased from his face. "Tear that bed linen into strips to bind this pig. We must be away before anyone's the wiser."

Owain jerked the baron's hands behind his back, trussing them up tightly. De Veasy's eyes narrowed in anger. "You'll never make it. This keep is crawling with my men."

"This keep has a skeleton crew and you know it," Richard corrected, forcing a gag none too gently into the man's mouth. "I'll wager you and Vespain wanted few witnesses to this deed."

He rose to his feet and helped Owain lift their prisoner onto the bed. With a furious grunt, de Veasy began to struggle. Richard pressed the knife to his throat. "What's that, my lord?" he taunted. "I can't quite understand you. Be still, lest I be tempted, like you, to beat a bound man."

Elen watched nervously as Richard tied the baron to the bedframe. How would they get out? Richard and Owain might escape in their guise as de Veasy's soldiers, but she would never leave so easily. The guards at the gate were alert, watchful. Both Richard and Owain might still be brought to grief through her. "Richard, I fear he's right. Oh Richard, I'm so sorry! I never meant to drag you into this."

When Richard turned, without knowing how, Elen was suddenly in his arms. His hard mouth descended on hers and nothing mattered save the feel of him against her, the vibrant life pulsing through them both. He was safe—for now.

Richard tore his mouth from hers, his green eyes alight

with victory . . . and something more. "I owe you, sweet, for a little matter of scaring the wits half out of me. What penance should I exact, do you think?"

"I'm sorry," she whispered again, touching the bloody scratch. "I could think of nothing else to keep him distracted."

Richard kissed her again, long and slow, and her whole heart went into her response. "You were magnificent, sweetheart," he whispered against her lips. "I'd take you on my side to a whole garrison of soldiers!"

Owain cleared his throat. "If you've done now, we should be away," he said gruffly.

Owain! Oh, God, she had forgotten. He glanced at Richard but wouldn't meet her eyes. "I'll see what's about in the hallway," he muttered. He slipped a knife into his belt. "Follow me when you're ready."

Richard brushed a quick kiss against her forehead and set her away. "Have you still the priest's robe, Elen? It will cover your clothing when we reach the darkness outside."

She nodded, hurrying to don the robe while Richard waited. He took her hand, staring at de Veasy. "Come, we'll leave the baron to a peaceful rest." He bowed with a flourish. "By your leave, my lord."

Elen glanced at the man, a shiver of apprehension running through her. Rage was apparent in every rigid line of his body, in the narrow, dark eyes that glittered above his gag. The Baron of Ravensgate would make an implacable enemy. If he caught them now, they'd be better off dead.

Richard eased open the door and glanced out. There was no sign of Owain. Joining hands, they fled silently down the hallway to the shadowy servants' stair. Once inside the narrow turret they raced down, down, down in a dizzying spiral. Another quick passage along a deserted corridor and they were slipping out into the fragrant darkness of the overgrown garden.

The shadowy forms of men materialized. Elen listened as

a few whispered comments were exchanged. Two guards had made the rounds of the wall, but they would give no warning, now or ever. Elen stared at Richard in astonishment. He had brought Welshmen, her people rather than his own soldiers!

Owain heaved a rope up and over the wall. One by one the men clambered up, disappearing silently into the void. Richard turned toward her. "If I lift you onto my shoulders, can you pull yourself up? It's only a short way and there are knots in the rope for handholds."

She tried to see his face in the darkness. She had no idea if she could drag herself up, but she wasn't about to admit it. "Of course. Give me a push."

"Good girl!"

Richard lifted her easily and she reached for the rope. Her fingers slipped and the woven hemp burned through her palm. She caught at a knot, hanging there uncomfortably.

Cautiously bracing her feet against a knot, she began to inch up. It wasn't so difficult—hand over hand, the knots were perfectly spaced. She reached the top of the wall and Owain grasped her wrist, lifting her up beside him.

They knelt in the shadow of the battlements. He placed another rope in her hand, gesturing over the side. "Slow and easy," he whispered. "Don't get in a rush or you'll fall."

She stared uncertainly at his shadowy outline. She needed to explain about Richard. "Owain—"

"Go now," he ordered softly. "Those guards will be discovered anytime."

She hesitated.

He checked the anchoring of the rope, then squeezed her shoulder awkwardly. "Go," he said again.

Elen eased over the side, slipping a little before her hands warmed to the rhythm. She braced her feet against the wall, lowering herself easily into the arms of the men below.

Moments later Richard and Owain had joined them on

the ground. "Owain, wait here with Elen," Richard directed. "I'll take the men with me to silence the guards at the front. We'll have to get past them and use the main road. I'll not risk taking Elen down as we came."

"That way adds a good half hour to the trip," Owain protested. "Besides, the front gate's the only place well guarded. One shout of alarm and the whole garrison'll be after us."

Elen touched Richard's arm. "How did you come?"

"Up these cliffs from the valley, but—"

"Then that's the way we'll return," she interrupted matter-of-factly.

"In the dark? And with that robe flapping about your heels?" Richard growled. "We'll take the main road, and I'll have no argument about it!"

"She can do it. Elen's no fainting Englishwoman," Owain said scornfully. "Many's the time the Lady Gweneth bade me fetch Elen and her brother from the topmost rock of some impossible place."

Richard hesitated.

"We can rope her between us to catch her if she slips. The climb is short and none too difficult for one accustomed to such."

Elen gripped Richard's arm. If Owain thought she could make the climb, she would—or she'd die trying. "It's my life, Richard, my risk. I'll do anything to get away from here."

"Once begun, we'll not be able to turn back. And I'll not be able to carry you," Richard warned.

"You'll not need to carry me!" she snapped indignantly.

Precious seconds ticked by. "Very well," he said low. "We'll chance it."

Quickly, Elen pulled off the priest's robe, tossed it aside and tied up her skirts. Then she stood quietly as Richard looped the rope about her waist. Passing one end to Owain, he tied the other about himself. "Whatever you do, don't cry out," he whispered. He bent to brush his lips against hers, lingering for a moment as if loath to let her go. "Owain and I will have you if you slip. Now go."

Elen glanced down the darkened cliff face into the shadowy void below. For a moment she stood motionless, readying herself for the dangerous descent. Then she grasped the smooth stone and lowered herself over the edge, her slippered foot groping desperately for a toehold. It had been a long time since she and Rhodri had played on the mountainsides. Pray God, she hadn't forgotten the way of it.

She found a small cleft in the rock and levered herself down a few inches. Sweat broke out on her brow and a jagged stone cut her palm. She bit her lip, forcing herself to breathe deeply and evenly. One step at a time. She wouldn't think about how far she had to go or the great emptiness yawning beneath her. One step at a time would get her to the bottom. She couldn't hang back now.

The trip down the cliff was a nightmare she never wanted to think of again. Her fingers cramped painfully from gripping the rock outcroppings and the muscles of her arms and legs trembled with strain. Minutes crawled by. She tore her nails grasping for handholds, scraped elbows and knees in a painful slide against stone. But she didn't cry out. She would not have complained if the torture had lasted for days. After all, it was her foolishness that had brought them there.

After what seemed like hours, they reached the valley floor. Elen's knees near collapsed as she slid to a seat on a ridge of rock, fighting to catch her breath.

Richard bent over her to untie the chafing rope. He squeezed her shoulder encouragingly. "We've still a short way to the ship. Can you make it?"

"Of course. Just give me a moment to rest."

He hesitated. "We dare not tarry longer. The hunt may be up and I'd not wish to be caught on the beach. There's no place to make a fight."

"Oh." Elen was thankful for the darkness. It hid her dismay. She rose to her feet with an effort, her cramped muscles screaming for relief. "I'm ready, then."

They set off at a walk, slowly easing into a jog. Elen sensed the men held back for her, and she fought to keep her limbs moving. But once away from the cramped position of the climb, she was amazed her trembling muscles warmed to their task. Perhaps she would make it after all.

Above the soft sound of a dozen pairs of padding feet, a distant rumble of noise came from behind them. "Horses!" Richard hissed, grabbing her hand and dragging her forward. "The ship's just round this bend. Run for it!"

The sound of galloping hooves pounded closer. Unable to resist the impulse, Elen glanced over her shoulder. A flickering ribbon of torches gleamed through the trees, winding down the hillside in close pursuit. Fear gave wings to her heels and she called on her burning lungs and aching muscles for one last effort.

They dashed around the curve in the road, bounding across the beach toward the sea and freedom. The treacherous sand sucked at her feet, dragging her down to make running impossible. Richard swung her into his arms, carrying her the last few yards across the beach and into the foaming surf. Tossing her into the waiting boat, he shoved it through the shallows, heaving himself aboard as his men pulled at the oars.

Elen collapsed in the boat, praying to every saint she knew to slow de Veasy and his men. There was no sound but the desperate splash of oars against water. Richard knelt tensely in the stern staring toward land.

Seconds later, the mounted men burst onto the beach. Torches glimmered hellishly along the water's edge and a few shouts of frustration followed them through the darkness. Richard edged down beside her, drawing her back against his chest. "We made it!" he said softly, brushing his lips against her hair. "I'm not sure how, but we made it."

CHAPTER TWENTY-FOUR

*T*wo days later, Richard was still asking himself how they had escaped and, more importantly, why in God's name he had allowed the ship's captain to talk him into unloading supplies at Rhuddlan before returning to Gwenlyn Keep. For by some stroke of misfortune, Edward was at Rhuddlan Castle. And if reports were true, the king was in one of his towering rages.

Richard hesitated outside Edward's audience chamber, frowning at the closed door. After nearly two days of waiting, the king had sent a servant to fetch him. It wasn't a good sign. But worst of all, Richard hadn't been allowed to see Elen. She was locked away somewhere and he had only the queen's word she was well.

Taking a deep breath, Richard reached for the door. He had seized a royal ship and taken armed men from English soil in pursuit of a personal quarrel, something Edward had forbidden. And what could he tell his king save the truth?

The king sat at the end of a table, his graying head thrown back, his blue eyes narrow and cold. Richard sank down on one knee, awaiting permission to rise. It didn't come.

"What's this, Richard? I journey unexpectedly to Wales from Worcester and find two of my nobles making war on each other! How *dare* you?"

Richard kept his eyes downcast. It was obvious the king was still fiercely angry.

Edward rose and stalked toward him. "You seize my ship . . . *my ship*! You keep me waiting for supplies I need for my household while you desert your post and junket off to Ireland to pursue a personal feud with de Veasy. Before God, you brave much against my good will, Richard!" Edward paced the floor. "And after I expressly warned you against such behavior! Well, what have you to say for yourself?"

Richard raised his head and glanced up.

"Oh, get up, man, get up!" Edward said impatiently.

Richard rose to his feet. He had seen Edward's rages often enough but had never felt the brunt of them himself until now. "Your ward, Elen of Teifi, was trusted to my keeping," he began slowly. "I sought to fetch her back when Hugh de Veasy took her. The ship I needed was there, so I commanded it on royal business, leaving Sir Giles Eversly to oversee Gwenlyn. To have awaited your permission would have been to give the girl up. I acted as I thought you would wish."

"But you armed Welshmen and took them against an English noble! Were you so sure they wouldn't turn against you?"

Richard met Edward's gaze evenly. "They are good men and were invaluable on the raid. I've no fear of them."

"Humph." Edward moved back around the table and sat down. "Never trust a Welshman farther than you can see him," he muttered testily. "I've done so before to my sorrow."

Richard said nothing.

Edward leaned back in his chair, tapping the fingers of his right hand against the oak tabletop. "So, de Veasy seized my ward. He takes much upon himself," he growled. "Believe me, the man will soon feel my anger. A fat fine to empty his purse will suit me well." His eyes flickered over

Richard's face, missing little. He leaned forward. "How came you by those bruises?"

"They are nothing. A personal matter."

"Ah . . . de Veasy didn't give her up willingly, I see." Edward sighed, his anger ebbing. "Despite your own cursed impudence, Richard, I must confess I'm pleased you succeeded. But the girl be damned—I'll have this matter done! I can't have my barons feuding over the wench. I've near a dozen offers for her, but I'll give her to the first lord who asks with the strength to hold her lands and the coin to garrison the necessary strongholds for England."

Richard stiffened. Though he had expected the words, they were a blow. "I would beg you think further, Your Grace."

Edward's eyebrows rose imperiously. "What?"

Richard hesitated. This was obviously not the time to petition the king, but he had to speak. He couldn't bear to think of Elen wed to some knight Edward might name. "In all our years together, I've asked for naught of you, Your Majesty. Now I do," he began earnestly. "I ask that you think long on the husband you choose for Elen. Give her to someone who would treat her honorably. She is different from our English women. She'll fight any man who misuses her."

Edward studied him shrewdly. "Do you fancy the girl yourself?"

Richard straightened, glancing away. He decided it would be best to admit the truth; Edward would guess anyway. "I've long 'fancied' her, as you say."

Edward brought his fist down on the table. "By God's sword, what foolishness is this?"

"A foolishness I'm loath to confess," Richard replied. "But I've yet to lie to you, Your Grace, and I'll not begin now."

The king gave a harsh laugh. "And did you think to win her for yourself when you took her from de Veasy? Are the de Borgh lands not enough for you, then?"

Richard felt an angry flush creep up his face. "I had no such hope, Your Grace. I know well I have naught to offer for her except my sword—a sword that has been pledged to you these many years already. I sought only to prevent Hugh de Veasy from seizing what was yours . . . and to save her a life of misery."

He glanced at Edward defiantly. "But by all the saints, I'd take her had she not a hide of land as dower. And I'd thank God on my knees if such were the case!"

"Then you'd be a fool. No man can afford to wed without thought to a dower." Edward gazed at Richard keenly. "Take my advice, Richard, this woman can bring you nothing but pain. And one female is much like another anyway. Take de Borgh's daughter. I'll see that it's arranged."

Richard moved to the window, staring out at a depressing expanse of gray Welsh sky. The thought of returning to Gwenlyn without Elen weighed even heavier than he had expected. "I can't," he said softly. "And I know your words are false. Having known Your Queen, Eleanor, can you truly tell me you'd wed another?"

"That's different," Edward snapped.

Richard turned. "I think not."

The king rose to his feet abruptly. "Leave me. I've business to attend and have wasted much time on this matter already. I've determined your action was justified and will pardon your foolishness. But I'll do with the girl as I see fit."

Richard stood his ground. "I'm your man, Your Majesty, and will pledge to none other. Nothing will change that. But for the love you once bore me, will you at least promise not to act in haste where Elen is concerned?"

Edward shook his head. "You're a fool, Richard, a chivalrous fool." His face softened and the hint of a smile touched his mouth. "But you've been a loyal man to me these many years. Now I grant you what you wish. I'll think on this matter and we'll speak of it again."

Richard nodded and moved slowly out the door. It was the best he could hope for, he reminded himself grimly. But somehow Edward's words did nothing to ease the vast emptiness in his heart.

"Pardon, my dear, but may I come in?"

Elen glanced up in surprise. A woman stood on the threshold, but Elen knew by her regal air, her fine clothes, she wasn't just any woman. Eleanor of England stood facing her across the room. Without thinking, Elen dropped into a deep curtsy. Something about the woman commanded it.

Eleanor moved toward her. "Oh rise, my child, rise. There should be none of this between us." She smiled engagingly. "After all, you are a Welsh princess—an older line even than my Castilian blood."

Elen found herself smiling in response. She rose to her feet, unsure what to say. She had been prepared to hate the English king and queen, but this woman's charm was disarming.

Eleanor's beautiful dark eyes moved over her. "Yes, you are as lovely as Richard told me, but—"

"Richard . . . you have seen him? Is he well?" Elen blurted out. At Eleanor's amused nod, Elen turned away self-consciously. "It's just that I've not seen him since we arrived at Rhuddlan," she remarked defensively. "I couldn't help but wonder if . . . if something had happened."

"Richard is well, but yes, something has happened. I fear he is much in disgrace with my husband for rushing to your rescue with a royal ship. He has not been allowed to see you."

Elen glanced up in dismay. There seemed no end to the trouble she had brought upon Richard. "But that isn't fair. Richard rescued me from the Baron of Ravensgate. And he didn't even kill the dog!"

Eleanor's musical laugh tinkled out. "My child, he couldn't murder an English baron! He'd have been in a great deal of trouble had he done that."

"Well, I would have done it and been glad!" Elen said hotly. She thought of those last few moments alone with de Veasy. A quiver of revulsion ran through her as she thought of what would have happened had Richard not arrived. "The Baron of Ravensgate is vile—lower than any crawling thing. He doesn't deserve to live."

Eleanor sobered at once. "Yes, I've never cared for Hugh de Veasy, and I greatly regret your trial. But even such men have their uses."

Elen sent her a bitter smile. "Uses? Yes. To loose them on your enemies. You English have lessoned us well."

Eleanor touched her shoulder. "But I am not English," she said, giving Elen a long look. "Your Richard is a good friend of mine and I'd like to think you could be as well."

"He is not *my* Richard."

Eleanor smiled and changed the subject. "Come, child, it's a gray day but I thought you might take a stroll with me in the fresh air. I've a lovely garden Edward built, with fish ponds and benches where we might continue our talk." She looked Elen up and down. "And when we return, I'll see about getting you fresh clothing. This looks a bit the worse for your adventure."

Elen glanced down at her soiled clothes in embarrassment. Her gown of blue wool was torn in several places and hopelessly stained. She brushed self-consciously at her skirt. "I fear I gave little thought to my gown while I was dangling from the cliffs at Ambersly."

Eleanor's eyes danced with laughter. "Doubtless there were other worries on your mind. You must tell me about it as we walk. Richard was strangely loath to speak." She sent Elen a conspiratorial smile. "Men leave out so many important details, don't you agree?"

Without knowing how, Elen soon found herself telling Eleanor about being tricked from Gwenlyn, about her fear for herself and Richard, then all the details of the daring escape from Ambersly. The queen was a good listener, and

Elen had been so long without a woman to talk with, she found herself confiding hopes and fears she had never thought to voice. "But I shouldn't be telling you all this," she ended in confusion.

"I came here to listen," Eleanor said softly. "But tell me one thing more. Do you truly care for Richard?"

Elen glanced up in alarm. She had obviously revealed too much. "I am Welsh, he is English," she said tartly.

"That matters little. Edward is English and I am from Castile. Do you love him?"

Elen rose from the bench and moved to the edge of the fish pond. The queen's knowing eyes read far too much. "England and Castile are not at war," she remarked, avoiding the question. She swung around determinedly. "It is my intention to seek God's peace and wed myself to Holy Church. I've petitioned the Archbishop, and I'll not change my mind."

Eleanor sat quietly, gazing at her hands. After a moment, she rose to join Elen at the water's edge. "The Church is a great calling but not, I think, for all." Her lips quirked as she fought to suppress a smile. "Somehow, I cannot see you in a nunnery."

A step sounded on the path behind them. Elen turned to find Richard coming along the curving stone walkway toward them. Her heart twisted painfully. Eleanor was right. She would never find peace in a nunnery. She very much doubted she would find peace anywhere.

Richard halted before them, his eyes holding Elen's though his words addressed his queen. "You sent for me, Your Grace?"

"Yes. Now what did I want with you?" Eleanor remarked absently. "I can't seem to remember, but I'm glad you're here. I've a meeting with my seamstress and I fear Elen hasn't finished her walk. Would you act her escort, Richard? You may bring her back when she tires."

Richard shot her a grateful glance. "I'd be pleased to act as your deputy."

"Have a care to the sky," Eleanor called in parting. "Bring her in if it commences to rain."

Elen stared into the pond's shallow, brown water listening to Eleanor's rapidly departing footsteps. "The queen did this on purpose, didn't she?"

"Probably. Eleanor's devious mind near rivals your own."

Elen glanced up. Richard was smiling down at her and the sight flooded her senses with a bittersweet joy. "It's difficult not to like her, you know."

"Yes, Eleanor can charm the feathers from a goose if she puts her mind to it."

She glanced away. "I was worried when you didn't come. The queen says you're in disgrace with the king."

Richard shrugged his shoulders. "He's angry, but the queen tells me the real cause is a petition from the London merchants to lower the wool duty. With trouble brewing on the Scottish border, he needs money for troops. I just happened to get in his way at the wrong time."

"Oh. You won't be banished or recalled from Gwenlyn?"

"No. His rage is shifting to de Veasy now. Edward can set a huge fine on the baron, but he knows there's little he can take from me—one of the comforts of having few worldly possessions." Richard frowned and glanced away. "There should be some compensation, I suppose. Land is wealth and wealth the power to do what you choose. Something I shall never know."

Elen studied Richard's tanned face, surprised at the unaccustomed bitterness of his words. Something weighed on him heavily—something besides Edward's anger. "You have little power because you lack lands, while I am held prisoner due to the extent of mine." She sighed. "Would that we could exchange our positions."

Richard didn't answer. Taking her hand, he tucked it into the crook of his arm. "Come, let's walk a while."

They strolled through Eleanor's pretty labyrinth of pools and hedges, shoulders touching, each caught up in the worry of their thoughts. Upon reaching the end of the pathway, Richard paused. "Elen, there's something you must prepare yourself for." His hands slid to her shoulders and he turned her toward him, his face unusually grave. "I know this foolish notion you have of entering a nunnery, but the King will never allow it. I spoke to him today. He's determined to marry you to someone who can hold your lands for England."

Elen's eyes flashed up at him. "Well, let him try. I'll not do it!"

He gave her a shake. "Listen to me, Elen, and stop this childishness. You're his ward and he doesn't need your consent. He's a king and will do as he pleases. But I've won his promise not to act in haste. He's agreed to speak with me again and I've reason to hope he'll permit me some say in choice of your husband."

Elen stared up at him in bewilderment, the fight going out of her at once. Richard was going to be party to this horrible thing Edward planned to do to her. "You would do that?" she asked softly. "You would truly see me given to some other man?"

Richard's hands bit into her shoulders and his face took on the tormented look of the damned. "I would sell my very life to keep you from hurt, Elen, but there is naught I can do to prevent this! The best I can hope is to have some choice in your husband. There are many who would treat you honorably."

She jerked away from him. "I don't want honor!" She broke off in confusion, fighting back tears. What did she want? Nothing she could ever have. She wanted Enion and her family restored to her alive. She wanted relief from the war in her land and this one in her heart, from the over-whelming guilt and pain of loving a man she should not.

Richard caught her close in his arms. "Elen . . . please, love. Please don't cry."

She closed her eyes against the hurt. "Kiss me, Richard,"

she whispered. "Please don't say any more. Don't ask me to be reasonable—just kiss me."

His mouth covered hers for a searing kiss, brutal in its power but satisfying by its very need. It was a devouring kiss, a kiss that spoke of violent passions too long held in check, of raw emotions too long undeclared. There was nothing of honor or chivalry in that embrace, but its very roughness was reassuring in a way no gentleness would have been.

Elen clung to him, forgetting her fears and guilt in the need that flamed so suddenly, so powerfully between them. She couldn't get enough of him, of the strength of his arms crushing her against him, of the warmth of his hands and mouth. She didn't care that they stood in the castle garden where anyone might see. She wouldn't have minded if a hundred people had stopped to watch. She only knew that she wanted what was happening to go on and on, that she was terrified of the black emptiness that would return when he released her.

She leaned into Richard's body, blindly seeking his mouth, touching her tongue to his, then boldly slipping between his lips with the same movement he used to set her on fire. She heard the uneven rasp of his breathing, felt the taut urging of his body against hers. The knowledge that she could move him to such passion no longer frightened her. It was exhilarating.

With a groan, Richard drew her closer. His head dropped to her bare throat, his lips sending waves of pleasure shivering through her body. His hands ranged down her back, cupping her hips and lifting her tightly against him. She pressed upward, instinctively seeking satisfaction from the empty aching inside, lost to all considerations save the blood that ran hot and fast in her veins and the sound of her own uneven breathing in concert with his.

Richard groaned again. "Elen . . . Elen, before God, we must stop. We must stop or I'll take you now beneath the nearest bush!"

"No, don't stop, Richard. Just hold me."

"Elen, stop tormenting me lest I forget both my honor and yours!" He held her away from him with shaking hands. "We must never do this again. Never! You'll soon belong to someone else and it's hard enough to bear as it is."

Elen kept her eyes tightly closed, struggling to regain control of her spinning world. Richard's kiss was still warm on her lips, the exquisite feel of his mouth still branded on her senses. Suddenly, she knew the pain of wanting—wanting against all reason. Richard was right though; anything more would be madness.

But the thought of some other man holding her, of some rough Englishman touching her intimately made her sick with dread. And it was going to happen. Despite her brave pretense just now, she knew her future was not her own. If she didn't escape Edward, her husband would own her just as he would her castles and lands.

She glanced up. Richard was obviously tormented by that thought as well. The realization gave her new hope. He knew how unhappy she was. Perhaps he would help her escape.

She studied his handsome features. The bruises he had taken for her showed dark against his bronzed skin and his green eyes were narrowed with despair. She wasn't the only one who suffered.

She glanced miserably away. All about them the garden shrubbery bent with an increasing wind, and her heavy skirts billowed and snapped about her ankles. Could she ask such a thing of Richard? He had already suffered pain and humiliation on her account.

A raindrop struck her cheek and the air grew heavy with the smell of the coming storm. She thought of her father, of Owain and Enion—even Rhodri. She had always been able to bend men to her will. And Richard was susceptible now. It was obvious he was torn between duty and desire.

But could she ask this of him? Would he defy his king for her?

The realization came at once. She would never know the answer, for she couldn't cause him the hurt of asking. She reached up and touched his face. "The storm is come," she whispered. "Take me in before we both say things we'll regret."

The next day dawned clear and cool following the storm. The air was filled with the pungent mustiness of the mud flats left by the ebbing tide. Elen stood at her window, trying to convince herself that Richard was wrong, that no true churchman would marry her if she was violently opposed to her groom.

But she took little comfort from her one-sided argument. Bishop Vespain and Father Edmund had both been party to Hugh de Veasy's plot. And if that could happen, Edward of England would have little trouble finding a priest to perform the ceremony—with or without her consent.

Her door swung open and one of the queen's ladies peeked round the panel. "The Queen's Grace sent me to fetch you. You're wanted in the king's audience chamber at once."

Elen's breathing quickened painfully. The king? But she didn't wish to see Edward. She didn't wish to hear his hateful plans for her.

"Come. Quickly, child! The king mustn't be kept waiting."

Elen gave a quick glance to the wimple and veil she had tossed on the bed. Eleanor had gifted her with appropriate clothing—a lovely gown of rich scarlet cloth and an English wimple of finest linen. But she had not been able to bring herself to don the hot, confining headdress. And all at once she was glad. Her bare head would show her contempt for proper English ways. She would wear neither veil nor wimple—let Edward think what he would.

"Very well," Elen responded, moving forward with a show of obedience. She followed the woman along Rhuddlan's twisting corridors but took little stock of their direction. She was about to meet the most dread lord of England, the man she had been taught to hate above all others. And she could admit it to herself, at least. She was afraid.

The woman paused outside the arched doorway of a room where several pages stood in attendance. They stared at Elen, curious, amused. She took a deep breath. Seizing the latch, she flung open the door and strode inside with an air of haughty bravery she was far from feeling.

The king stood at the end of the room, leaning indolently against the fireplace. A small peat fire burned against the damp chill of thick stone walls. He said nothing as she crossed the floor toward him, but his shrewd blue eyes traveled over her, lingering on her face and form in the way of a man who appreciates women.

She sized him up as well. He was tall—taller even than Richard—and his broad chest and powerful arms spoke of the legendary warrior he was. His thick hair had once been golden but was now frosted with silver. She came to a halt before him but refused to bend her knee. "You sent for me," she stated coolly, lifting her chin to gaze up at him.

He shifted away from the wall and moved slowly around her, saying nothing. She stood perfectly still, his silence making her nerves taut. "Now that we have both satisfied our curiosity, may I go?" she snapped.

Edward broke into a laugh. Ignoring her, he shot a glance over her shoulder. "I can better sympathize with your foolishness now I've seen the girl, Richard."

Elen swung around in surprise. Richard sat across the room at a carved oak table. His hair was mussed as if his fingers had ravaged it repeatedly, and he had the look of a man who hadn't slept.

She felt a quick surge of relief. She didn't face Edward alone.

The king glanced down at her, his eyes bright with amusement. "And no, you may not go, Elen of Teifi. As I must be back in England tomorrow next, we'll decide your future today. You have already caused no little trouble. And since I've no desire to have you brewing mischief in my household, I'll not take you with me as no doubt I should."

"I am of age and can decide my own future," Elen remarked in what she hoped was a reasonable voice. "I will pay any fine you name, but it is my decision to take the veil."

"Women do not decide," he responded dampeningly.

"I do."

Richard had moved to stand beside her. He caught her shoulder, giving it a warning squeeze. "Forgive her, Sire. She has been much indulged."

"So I see. Someone spared the rod in her upbringing. Save for Builth, I always thought Lord Aldwyn a wise man. But I wonder at such foolishness."

Elen's voice brimmed with bitterness. "You dare speak my father's name?"

"Elen, hush!" Richard whispered.

Edward gazed at her enigmatically. "Yes, I dare speak of him. He was a man I respected, as were many who fell at Builth. I did not wish them dead, but they chose their paths as I chose mine." He caught a gleaming strand of her hair, tugging it gently between his fingers. His keen blue eyes held hers. "As I will now choose yours," he added softly.

Elen's heart accelerated painfully. Edward's words sent a chill of dread through her. Her defiance was futile. She could do little against any order this man decreed.

Turning away from her, Edward moved back to the fireplace, where he stooped to warm his hands. "As it is, you are too much temptation for my ambitious knights, Elen, and I can't afford personal quarrels among my men. Such petty fights have spilled England's lifeblood too often. You must be married off quickly to someone strong enough to rule your lands and keep your own willfulness in check." He straightened, his face grave. "I must give you to a man I deem ruthless enough to do both."

Elen held her breath while Richard gripped her shoulder painfully.

"After much thought, I believe Sir Richard Basset best suited to the task," Edward continued smoothly. "Though after meeting you, I question if I do him more ill than good."

Elen let out her long-held breath with a gasp. Richard . . . he was giving her to Richard!

Beside her, Richard stood painfully still. Edward was jesting, surely he was jesting. But the king had never been so cruel. "M-my lord?" he stammered.

"You're surprised, Richard? I've determined this the wisest course. I've spoken to your Welshmen. They're a surly lot but seem united in loyalty to you—at least for the moment."

Edward's eyes narrowed and he gazed pointedly at Richard. "Some say you've grown soft, Richard, but they are far from the mark. I say you are shrewd. And I need that. I need someone who can pacify Wales. There's a strong possibility I'll soon be in Scotland and I can't afford rebellion in the west the moment my back is turned—not again. And to that end I also grant you seisin of the demesne of Gwenlyn. You'll do homage to me for the lands in a ceremony this afternoon. Burnell is drafting the papers now."

"B-but Your Grace . . ." Richard protested, still reeling from the shock. "Gwenlyn is a royal keep. I've nothing to offer in return for such a gift!"

"You've given much already. I told you once—in my father's day, you'd have been an earl several times over. I cannot give you lands in England, but Wales is yours for the taking." Edward smiled cynically. "And I've learned men hold their own more readily than they hold for their king. End the rebellion in the north once and for all. Rule quietly and well. Show me my confidence in you is not misplaced."

Richard dropped to one knee, still unable to take in his good fortune. Elen, he would have Elen! And lands beyond his wildest dreams. How like Edward to take him from near penniless soldier to one of the largest landholders in Wales with a marriage and the simple stroke of a pen. "Before God, Your Majesty, I'll not disappoint you!"

Elen stared at Richard, a dozen conflicting emotions tearing through her. Richard . . . she'd never dared hope it might be Richard! But marriage?

Enion's face rose up to haunt her and she saw his bloodied corpse at Richard's feet. Richard Basset—the man responsible for Builth, the man who'd slain Enion, for God's sake! The blood of all her kinsmen would cry out at such a union. And besides, the marriage bed would all too quickly reveal the lie she had spun to protect Owain—the lie she now had such cause to regret.

She backed away a step. "No," she whispered desperately. "No, Richard. I cannot marry you!"

He glanced up in hurt surprise.

"I *cannot*!" she cried again. "I will renounce my lands. You may have them! It's the best I could hope for the people of Teifi. But I must enter the Church. It's the only future possible!"

Richard rose to his feet. "Elen—"

"Enough of this!" Edward snapped. "Enact me no tragedies! You wish for a choice, woman? I'll give you one and one only. You will marry Richard Basset or Hugh de Veasy. He, at least, will know how to deal with such a hellion!"

"Edward, let me speak to her. She doesn't understand."

Edward ignored Richard's words. "You will choose here, and you will choose now, Elen of Teifi. We will dispense with the trothplight and the speaking of banns and I'll see you wed to Richard tomorrow. Or," he added, "I'll take you to London to await de Veasy's coming. The choice is yours."

Elen clenched her fists against her sides, hating Edward, but hating even more her helplessness before him. "That is no choice," she said scornfully.

"Just so," he replied with a cool smile. He turned to Richard. "I forgive this lovely shrew much for the loss she has suffered and because of my love for you, Richard. But take her from my sight before my patience wears thin. And see she keeps a civil tongue in her head when next she comes before me. I might be tempted to teach her the proper respect due her king."

CHAPTER TWENTY-FIVE

The wedding joining Elen of Teifi and Richard Basset, newly created Baron of Gwenlyn, was cold, uncomfortable, and mercifully brief. The hastiness of the affair brought few guests to swell the ranks of the royal household. But to Elen, sitting uncomfortably at the banquet table beside Richard, it seemed that there was a great hoard of Englishmen continually staring at her, laughing and lifting their wine cups in increasingly bawdy toasts.

The rebellion that had driven her yesterday had long since burned out, leaving only the chill, gray ashes of despair. This was her wedding day—a day her mother and father had looked forward to for years. But Enion of Powys was to have been her husband. Enion, the dear friend and companion her husband had slain.

She sent Richard a covert glance. He seemed so . . . so English! Not like the man she knew at all. He sat drinking beside the king in high good humor, discussing the ruling of *her* lands. Richard had scarcely glanced at her all evening. She longed for a word of reassurance or regard, but he had had little to say to her save for questions about Teifi.

A knot of resentment built and tightened in her chest. This man—her husband—was responsible for much of the grief in Wales. She was suddenly ashamed of her brief surge of joy when Edward named Richard, ashamed of the desire she had felt for her enemy. He had wanted her body and he had wanted her lands. Now he had both while the men to whom they rightfully belonged were dead.

She closed her eyes at the thought of the ordeal yet to come, the memory of Richard's passion bringing no answering excitement to fire her blood. In the heat of the moment, she had wanted him, but in the midst of this laughing, leering company of Englishmen she felt more like an animal held to a forced mating than a woman soon to bed with a man she desired.

She lifted her wine goblet and took a steadying drink. Perhaps it was best she had no desire for this coupling. She wouldn't feel her betrayal of her family and Enion so deeply if she took no pleasure in Richard's bed.

Richard's bed . . .

Elen swallowed hard. What would Richard do when he learned she had deceived him about the Fox, that she had continued to lie about Rhys long after he believed her to have told him the truth? He would be disgusted, she knew. But would he wonder why the lie continued, whom she sought to protect? Would he put two and two together and come up with Owain as the Fox?

A hand touched her shoulder and Eleanor bent toward her. "Come, child, it is time."

Time? Elen started violently, spilling a circle of red on the linen tablecloth. She wasn't ready, not for the humiliating ordeal of a disrobing and bedding ceremony before her enemies. But Eleanor was waiting.

She rose stiffly. At once a round of shouting and clapping went up in the hall as the men surged to their feet to mark her passage. When Richard glanced up, the glittering heat of his gaze made her insides tighten with dread.

What did she really know about Richard anyway? She had been comfortable with Enion. She had known and trusted him. But Richard? How did she really feel about him? Love . . . hate . . . perhaps a little of both? Before God, she didn't know.

The women entered a chamber softly lit by beeswax tapers. The bed had been readied and the faint smell of lavender rose from fresh linen sheets. Eleanor took one look at Elen's drawn face and hastened to reassure her. "Richard requested a private ceremony, so there'll be none to make you uncomfortable. Only Father Julian, Edward and myself and the Welshman Richard calls Owain. He will represent your interests and answer you weren't forced to wed a man who's half a man." She chuckled. "Not that there's any question of that, but the forms must be observed."

Elen stood in the center of the room, staring dumbly at the small fire burning sluggishly in the fireplace. At least Richard had asked Owain to speak for her. But could her old friend watch her given to the man they had both hated? It would be an ordeal for them both.

Eleanor rang a silver bell and a maidservant entered, working quickly to help Elen disrobe. The queen took a scarlet bedrobe lined with rich sable fur from the girl. "This is my gift to you," she whispered, slipping it about Elen's naked shoulders. "I know this is far from the manner in which you thought to be wed, but all will be well. You'll see."

Elen shook her head, not daring to speak lest her emotions overwhelm her. She had been fighting tears all evening and they were dangerously close now.

Eleanor stared at her narrowly. "I was told you were no virgin. Come, Elen, you cannot be afraid?"

Elen glanced up. "No. It's just that—" Her throat ached dully with a need to weep that was long overdue. She swallowed hard, trying desperately to gain control. "Richard killed the man I should have married!" she blurted out. "He's slain scores of my people, and—" She choked again, not daring to speak of the Fox. "And now he's my husband. My father would kill me himself were he alive!"

Eleanor dismissed the servant. "The killing is over and done. It happens in a war," she said bluntly. Taking Elen's hand, she gazed pointedly at her. "Listen to me, Elen. Richard is a good man, a man who cares deeply for you. You could easily have gone to Hugh de Veasy or some other warlord just as brutal. That happens to women—especially women of rank like us. Happiness in marriage is a rare gift. I know the joy of it and would see others find it where I can."

"You think he cares for me?" Elen asked bitterly. "He wants me, I know. But I think it's my lands he cares for."

"Land is the most important reason for marriage," Eleanor agreed. "But know this. Richard offered to take you without dower. Edward told me so."

Elen glanced up in amazement. Even serfs must have a pot or tub for dower.

Eleanor squeezed her fingers. "Yes. He's that besotted with you. It's a good beginning, Elen." She bent closer, her voice softening. "Your life will be what you choose to make it—nothing more and nothing less. Differences can be worked out if two people decide it's worth the effort. All may now seem dark and you may be forced to sacrifice things dear to you. But you'll soon find them replaced with things dearer still. And you'll look back, wondering why you were so unhappy at the start."

Her words broke off as the noise of footsteps sounded in the corridor outside. Elen went a shade paler. Edward swept into the room, Father Julian, Richard and the much shorter Owain trailing in his wake.

Eleanor swung around, smiling at the men. "We are ready. And this child is a jewel. Richard, see you treat her well or you'll have me to answer to!"

Richard nodded, not daring more than a quick glance at Elen. The tormenting ache in his loins was bad enough already. To gaze at his bride would make these last few moments of torture unbearable. He struggled to strip off his clothing, strangely clumsy in the simple act of disrobing.

Edward chuckled. "Julian, help the lad. His mind runs too much on the night's work."

Elen kept her eyes carefully averted as Richard was disrobed. In a matter of moments these people would all be staring at her. She scarcely heard the good-natured jests concerning Richard's physical perfection or his obvious readiness to attend to his duty, but when Owain began to speak she glanced up.

His eyes met hers, flinty gray in the flickering light. "I find no physical fault with Richard Basset," he said, his voice unusually harsh. "There be no cause to repudiate this marriage on behalf of Elen of Teifi."

Then the queen was lifting the robe away from Elen's shoulders and she stood naked before the company. A chill draft swept her and she felt Edward's cold eyes perusing her body. She forced herself to focus on the glimmering light of a burning taper, holding her fraying poise together by sheer act of will. *How she hated them . . . how she hated them all!*

Richard caught his breath on a single, indrawn hiss. He had seen Elen naked, but never quite like this. She was tall and willowy but her breasts and hips had become womanly and full in the past few months. Her pale skin gleamed like alabaster in the firelight and her heavy chestnut mane hung to her hips, reflecting a thousand dizzying lights. He swallowed hard, struggling to keep himself in hand as his body reacted intensely to the sight.

Edward finished his leisurely study. "On behalf of Richard Basset, I find no fault in this woman," he remarked. "Father Julian, let the record state there is no reason for either party to repudiate this marriage."

And then it was over. Elen felt the welcome softness of Eleanor's fur robe wrapped about her. The queen kissed her cheek. "Be happy," she whispered, and then she was gone. Owain sent her a last, enigmatic glance, then he, too, filed out after the priest and the towering figure of the king.

The crackling of the fire was loud in the sudden silence. Elen clutched the robe about her, not daring to meet Richard's eyes.

He slipped a robe about his shoulders, then moved across the floor toward her. "You're lovely," he whispered in a strained voice. "More even than I remembered." He halted a few inches away, his eyes devouring her though he lifted no hand to touch her.

Tell him the truth. Tell him now, something warned her.

She met his heated gaze, her eyes shifting uneasily away. No, she wasn't ready to face his anger yet. "C-could we have wine?"

Richard hesitated an instant. "If you wish."

Elen watched him walk to the table. Richard moved with a lithe grace that was beautiful to observe. The queen's words came back to her. He had offered to take her without a dowry. He must care—it wasn't just lands he wanted.

She bit her lip miserably. Be happy, the queen had said. But could she? Could she be happy with the knowledge of a cold December day that stood between them—of a few hours on a bloody field where Richard had done his work, oh, so well? And what would he do if he learned Owain was the Fox?

She drew a deep, shuddering breath, the thought sending her into a panic. Richard was her enemy, for God's sake! He was sworn to hunt Owain down. She couldn't love him, she couldn't!

Richard returned with two silver goblets, holding one out to her. He lifted his in salute. "To our future," he said softly, "and to putting the past behind us."

The past—if only she could. Elen stared wordlessly into her goblet.

Richard waited for several seconds, but Elen didn't speak. He stared at a wavering candle flame, his hope slowly dying. So be it, then, he told himself grimly. He hadn't wanted it like this but if Elen had her way their marriage hadn't a chance.

Without further talk, he lifted her into his arms and carried her to the bed. He loosed the laces of her robe, his fingers trembling slightly against the warm swell of her breast. "We are man and wife now," he whispered, shoving the robe from her shoulders, "and will act accordingly."

The robe slipped to the floor and Elen lay naked before him. God, she was beautiful! He sighed, his patience finally at an end. "I cannot undo what is done, Elen, and I've no power to fight a ghost. Keep Enion between us if you wish, but I'm done with waiting. I'll not have my bed haunted by a dead man."

He brushed her hair aside, his hand trailing slowly along her throat to her breast. He touched her, his body's need warring with the compassion he felt in his heart. "I can do no right in your eyes, Elen, no matter my effort. Forgive me now if I take my pleasure where I can."

He slipped his hands about her waist as he brought his mouth down over hers, hard with a passion he had bridled too long. His arms tightened around her, drawing her hips against the naked heat of his. Lord, she felt good! He'd been a fool to deny himself so long.

Elen remained rigid in his arms. Richard was her husband, she told herself woodenly. He had the right. He had the right to do this to her. And if she admitted the truth, she wanted to love him. But the vision of that bloody field would give her no peace. Could she truly love a man but hate what he had done, hate all he fought for? Could she love Richard, knowing she would fight Edward's armies with her last breath?

Richard's hands, roughened from his hours with sword and lance, slid over her lovingly. She didn't struggle as he pressed her backward onto the bed. His hands caught in her hair, tilting her head back as he sensuously shaped her lips to his, kissing, sucking, stroking her tongue with his in wordless invitation to the passionate kisses they had shared in the garden.

She lay unresponsive in his arms, the thought of Enion a torment. This should have been him. How she wished she had let him love her just once. Perhaps she wouldn't feel such guilt at the pleasure of Richard's touch, at the knowledge that she longed to be his wife in every way.

Richard's fingers cupped her jaw, then slipped downward, fondling her bare breasts, caressing their dusky crests in a way that woke a swift stirring of excitement she fought to ignore. She moved restlessly in his arms, fearing to yield completely, knowing somehow Enion would be gone forever if she did.

Richard drew her closer, his hand moving to stroke her waist, her belly, the velvet skin of her inner thighs. His mouth dipped to her breast, worshiping the creamy mounds his hands had just explored, seizing a budding nipple, alternately sucking and kissing until her desire smoldered and caught fire, a fire no guilt could quench.

She caught his head, holding him away. "Don't," she whispered desperately. "You're tearing me apart. Don't make me love you, Richard. Leave me something of myself!"

Richard hesitated, Elen's words giving him hope. He knew what she was fighting, knew suddenly he could win. "I don't ask for the loyalty you gave your family, the love you gave your betrothed," he said gently. "Only give us a chance, Elen. We're here . . . together now. That other is a past that will never return no matter how you wish it."

He moved over her, sliding his knee between hers, gently forcing her into position. Ignoring his own need, he kissed her, stroked her, calling on all the experience of his years of pleasuring women.

His fingers slid through the soft coil of hair between her thighs, gently exploring the softest, most private part of her. With a tiny moan of pleasure, Elen twisted beneath him, the sound and the movement driving him wild with wanting. His mouth sought hers, his tongue thrusting and withdrawing until hers joined the sensual dance, joined with an eagerness that tore a ragged groan from deep in his throat.

He couldn't hold back much longer—he'd been aching for her all day. His fingers resumed their stroking while he trailed hot kisses over her shoulder, her breast, his tongue moving in slow, building rhythm in time with his hands.

Elen's body tightened with excitement, desire flaming up suddenly, powerfully, inside her.

She caught at Richard's shoulders, arched against his hips, forgetting everything but the aching need inside her. "Richard . . . oh Richard, love me!" she cried out. "Help me forget."

Richard stared down at the incredible beauty of the woman in his bed—the woman who was now his wife. Her hair swept the pillows in a tumultuous cascade of fiery silk, her slanted blue eyes narrowed with passion. God he wanted her, but there was more this time—so much more than with any other woman.

"Elen, before God, I do love you," he whispered. "This isn't a first for either of us, but I'll make you forget the past. I swear it!" He bent and brushed her lips. "We'll begin again. Tonight."

This isn't a first . . .

His soft words registered. Elen's eyes snapped open. Holy Mary, Mother of God, she'd forgotten Rhys—the ridiculous tale of Rhys! She tried to jerk upright but Richard's weight pressed her down. His mouth took hers once more and she felt the taut readiness of his body against her own.

She twisted her head away. "Richard! Richard, wait," she gasped. "I must tell you . . . I'm not—"

Richard's mouth pressed on hers, abruptly silencing her protest. He had no thought now for conversation. Elen's frantic twisting was driving him wild with the need for release. He felt for the soft core of her. She was damp and ready.

Drawing back, he thrust deeply inside her, meeting a resistance that cut through the haze of passion clouding his brain. *Christ, she was a virgin!*

He tried to stop, tried to slow the convulsive thrusting of his body, but it was too late. He had waited too long and now the hot bursting pleasure of release filled his world to the exclusion of all else. He thrust into her, again and again and again, until he finally collapsed, shuddering, against her painfully stiff body.

Beneath him, Elen didn't move. Slowly the spiraling world stilled around him and he registered what had happened. Elen was a virgin, a virgin, for God's sake! But if she hadn't been Rhys ap Iwan's mistress, everything she had told him from the beginning was false.

A surge of anger and hurt washed over him. He loved a woman who was the opposite of all he held honorable, a woman who lied as easily as she drew breath. And he'd just had the incredible stupidity to tell her so. Love? Holy Christ, he was as much a fool as his father had ever been!

He raised his head, staring at her contemptuously. "Is there nothing about you that is not a lie?" he bit out.

Elen struggled to breathe beneath the crush of Richard's weight. He held her pinned beneath him, his eyes glittering dangerously in the light of the burning tapers. Their bodies were still joined, the hurt between her thighs still throbbing. She felt vulnerable and alone and, for the first time with Richard . . . afraid. "Richard, please. You're hurting me," she murmured thickly.

He rolled away from her in disgust.

Elen drew her knees up protectively against her stomach. She twisted to one side, closing her eyes against his scorn.

Richard caught her shoulders, jerking her upright so roughly her head snapped back. "Look at me. How many more lies must I discover? How many more times will you play me for a fool? By the rood, you've made it a cursed habit!"

She stared at him in dismay. She'd expected anger when he learned her deceit, but not this black rage. And it was all the more painful after thinking they had a chance . . . after hearing him say he loved her. The tears she'd fought all evening suddenly filled her eyes. She turned her head away, but he grasped her chin, holding her face toward him.

"Look at me," he bit out. "I want to see your face when you lie to me again!"

"I . . . I tried to tell you, but you wouldn't listen. You wouldn't stop. I wanted to tell you at the last but—"

"Tell me now," Richard interrupted, his voice frigid with mistrust.

Elen sniffed and shoved the hair out of her eyes, struggling for some measure of poise. She didn't want to lie to Richard, she didn't want to deceive him ever again. But what could she say that wouldn't endanger Owain? "There is nothing more I can tell you. I was not Rhys's mistress, but you know that already."

His eyes raked her shrewdly. "Is there a Rhys or is he, too, a lie?"

The question sent a chill through her. There was nothing kind or gentle about Richard now. God help Owain if Richard guessed the truth. She fought to gather her scattered wits. "Of course there's a Rhys. Do you think you fight a ghost?"

Richard's hand rose with his sudden urge to strike her. She didn't flinch.

"Damnation!" Dropping his hand, Richard flung himself from the bed. He stalked across the room, catching up his empty goblet to pour a generous amount of wine. Elen was his wife—how dare she defy him? He could beat her into submission with the full approbation of Church and law.

He tossed off several deep swallows, glaring at her over

the rim of the goblet. She sat where he left her, sitting painfully still in his bed. But her chin was up, her jaw set determinedly. And something in her expression reminded him of that night they'd first met, the way they'd faced each other over drawn steel.

Despite his anger, a hint of admiration stirred. He had a feeling he could beat Elen till doomsday and she would be more defiant than ever. No, he would never force her to change. He would just have to resolve himself to the bitter fact that she couldn't be trusted . . . ever.

"Would you have us still enemies?" he asked shortly. "It is not what I wish."

She tugged the sheet up about her, staring uncomfortably at her hands. "Nor I."

"Then by the mercy of God, cease these tales you tell more readily than breathing!" he stormed. "I'll not have a liar in my household nor in my garrison, and most certainly not in my bed!"

Elen kept herself very still. Honor and truth were everything to Richard. How could she make him understand the divided loyalty she felt, the emotions that were tearing her apart even now? Choices were so simple to him. "I'll lie to you in naught else, Richard. My deceit brings more pain to me than you. I'm torn in a hundred ways you'll never even know."

She hesitated, gathering strength for the words that might close the door between them forever. "But ask me nothing about the Welsh Fox. My loyalty was given to him long before you. I'll not help you trap him nor say aught to help you mark his place. And I warn you—if you force me, in this I will lie."

Richard sighed and put down his wine. At least Elen was being very plain where her loyalties lay. And now that the first surge of rage had ebbed, he felt a glimmer of understanding. If the situation were reversed, he would certainly not betray Edward.

But he wasn't accustomed to such fierce loyalty in one of her sex. Yes, she was different, he reminded himself. That's why he loved her.

He stared thoughtfully at his wife. Obviously the Fox—whoever the bastard was—hadn't been her lover. Nor had her betrothed. His heart lightened considerably at the thought. And she had tried to tell him something at the last. If he'd been more patient, let her have her say, perhaps she would have told him the truth. It wouldn't have stopped his anger, but it would have lessened the shock at least. "I've your word you'll lie in naught else?" he asked warily.

Elen nodded, scarcely daring to hope.

"Swear it."

"I'll speak truth to you in everything, Richard. Everything save what I know of the Fox. I swear it."

"Peace, then," he said, moving back to the bed. "Selective truth," he muttered, easing down beside her. "I never thought it acceptable before."

"You've never wed an enemy before either."

Richard's eyes lifted to hers. Tears glittered behind the heavy sweep of her lashes. As he watched, one slipped from the shadowy fringe, making its way down her cheek. He stroked it away with his thumb. It was rare to see her cry. He hadn't meant to cause it. "Am I an enemy?"

The return of Richard's gentleness near broke Elen's resolve. She took a shaky breath. "No."

To her surprise, a slow smile warmed his face. He pushed the hair back from her face, his hand resting gently against the nape of her neck. "I'm sorry I hurt you just now. I'd no wish for that."

She dropped her eyes. She'd felt more fear than hurt. "It was only a little."

"I could have spared you much had I known you'd not been with a man." He leaned forward and brushed her lips with his. "I regret I didn't listen . . . or that you didn't speak earlier." He grinned. "Learn now—a man in that condition is little given to rational thought."

Richard's smile was enchanting. Here was the man she had ridden with and laughed with and climbed down a cliff in the dark with. Here was the Richard she knew, the man who had become her friend. Gone was the cold, unnatural feeling that had lingered from the stark marriage and bedding ceremony, the sudden fear at his rage.

Taking her courage in hand, Elen stared back at him, their gazes locked in the candlelight. He'd said he loved her, she reminded herself wonderingly. He'd said he loved her and she hadn't returned the words. "Richard, you may not believe me. And I wouldn't blame you now if you didn't." She reached out and touched his face, her heart in her eyes for him to see. "But I do love you. I've tried not to, but I do."

Richard caught her hand, lifting it to press a lingering kiss against her palm. "Of course I believe you. Didn't you swear just now to tell the truth?"

He believed her. After everything she'd done, he was offering the gift of trust. God in heaven, she didn't deserve this man!

Richard's lips traced the veins in her wrist, moving slowly along her bare arm to nuzzle the sensitive skin at the bend of her elbow. "And I swear to give you a hundred reasons to continue to do so," he whispered. "I would have you know more of loveplay than the pain I just gave you. A man can find pleasure even on an unwilling woman. I take no joy in the fact that I gave you nothing in return for mine."

Elen shook her head, her breath quickening as pleasant sensations rippled along her arm. "I wasn't really unwilling. But everything is so . . . so hopelessly tangled. And you seemed strange this evening—so different. I feared I didn't know you."

His lips left her arm, trailing slowly along her shoulder to press against her throat. "Do I seem strange now?"

A delicious quiver of expectation raced through her. "No."

One hand cupped her breast, his other slipping behind her back to ease her down into the pillows. He stretched his muscular length alongside hers, his hands sliding over her, gently molding her against his side.

"Richard . . . are you . . . are you still angry?"

"No."

She took a deep breath, glancing away. "You frightened me."

Richard frowned. "No man likes to be played the fool. Especially by the woman he's just confessed to loving."

"Oh." Elen digested the information. All at once she wondered just how many women Richard had loved—not with his body, but with his heart. Perhaps he said the words easily. Perhaps they meant little to him. She didn't wish to be a fool either. "And does that happen often?"

His lips twitched upward. "What? Being played for a fool?"

"You know what I mean."

He bent over her. His mouth brushed the crest of her breast, making her tremble against him. "No, Elen. It doesn't happen often at all. I'm new to this game of love. Forgive me if I play it poorly for I've never known the emotion . . . never even wanted to know it before. It leaves me feeling unsure and terribly foolish. I'll admit that to you now in the hope you'll forgive my behavior."

Elen closed her eyes tightly. No, she didn't deserve Richard. He'd been attacked, deceived, humiliated and near ruined because of her. And he loved her, trusted her enough to speak honestly of his feelings in a way few men would dare.

She drew his head down to hers. "Oh, Richard, I'm sorry," she whispered, perilously near tears again. "I'm sorry I had to lie. I swear I want to be a good wife to you, but everything is so complicated between us."

His hands continued their sweet torment. "I know, love, I know."

He rolled her onto her back, his mouth sensually teasing and toying with hers, his tongue plunging slowly, deliberately into her mouth, sending delicious waves of wanting spiraling through her body. His hands sought her breasts, gently kneading and stroking, reawakening her desire with an ease that surprised her.

Her arms twined around his neck, then shifted restlessly over his back. She pressed against him, instinctively seeking the pleasure she had come so near to tasting.

Recognizing her growing ardor, Richard lightly stroked her body, his mouth tracing a heated pathway between her breasts to her abdomen and back. He knew what she was seeking. He planned to give it to her . . . and more.

His fingers probed gently through the silky triangle of hair between her thighs, expertly discovering and caressing the places that sent her near mindless with wanting. She arched against him, her hands reaching for him, moving over his body in an uninhibited manner that would have shocked her had she realized what she was about. She called his name, but whatever it was she meant to say was drowned in the rising tide of desire engulfing her.

Richard's breathing quickened and he was surprised to find he was already eager for Elen again. He felt he would never get enough of loving her, of enjoying her exquisite body.

He eased her legs apart, fitting his body against the melting heat of hers. "I won't hurt you this time, Elen," he whispered. "This time it will be good."

Elen strained up against him, instinctively seeking to fill the emptiness inside her. She had no fear of him, no conscious memory of the brief pain of his earlier penetration. She gave herself to him wholly, holding nothing back. The ghosts were gone, the punishing guilt at bay.

Richard's hands continued their tormenting caresses; his mouth seized hers for a kiss of increasing urgency. She felt the probing of his manhood against her and rose up to meet him, crying out with relief as he slid into her, deep and hot.

For a moment Richard didn't move. Then his slow, rhythmic thrusting began and she clutched his shoulders, as an explosive force began gathering inside her and she couldn't think at all. "Richard," she groaned. "Oh Richard . . ."

She gasped for air, for something even more important than air. Then, just when she could stand it no longer, the force within exploded, shattering her being into a thousand separate threads of sensation, fusing and blending into one great cry of pleasure Richard echoed with his own.

CHAPTER TWENTY-SIX

$\mathscr{A}$ distant pounding intruded slowly into Elen's consciousness. Her eyelids fluttered and she snuggled closer to the warm body pressing against hers, a delicious feeling of languorous contentment weighting down her limbs.

"What, Richard, do you lie abed all day? The dawn's far spent—the sun high in the sky!"

The form beside her stiffened and jerked upright. Elen opened her eyes, blinking in surprise as the grinning face of the English king swam into focus. With a gasp of surprise, she caught the sheet to her chest, rising quickly to a sitting position as her mind grappled for order amid the confusion of her thoughts.

Richard brushed the sleep-tousled hair from his eyes, his arm catching Elen to him reassuringly. "By God's ten toes, Edward, don't startle me so!" He grinned. "You had me thinking myself asleep on the field without my sword."

Edward glanced pointedly at the bed. "I'd say 'tis a battlefield more dangerous than most. But you appeared to have a weapon worthy of the fight—at least last night. And by the look of things this morn, the battle was satisfactory. I take it there's no need to send Burnell to Rome for an annulment."

Elen felt her cheeks flame. She was accustomed to bawdy

jesting. If anything, her people were more unrestrained than the English concerning beddings and birthings. But she felt at a distinct disadvantage wrapped in nothing but a sheet before the king. And the bond between her and Richard was still too fragile, too tenuous for the royal wit.

Richard grinned again, pleased with himself, the king, the whole world this morning. "No need at all, Your Grace." He glanced at Elen, his eyes warm. "If I'd my way I would, indeed, lie abed all day. And I doubt you'd find a man in the kingdom to blame me."

"So I thought. It's just as well I came to wake you then. My baggage is loaded and even Eleanor ready to ride. Dress yourself and walk with me below."

Richard slipped out of bed and began fumbling into his clothing. Elen bit her lip, undecided what to do. She wanted to dress and thank the queen for her kindness, but she was uncomfortable in her nakedness with Edward in the bedchamber. "Your Grace," she murmured, forcing herself to speak respectfully. "Do you really leave at once?"

Edward glanced back at her, eyebrows lifting quizzically. "We do."

"I . . . I wished to see the queen. To thank her for everything. She's been most kind."

"Kinder than myself, naturally."

Elen held her tongue, uncertain what to say. But there was no malice in the king's tone, just a high good humor that showed he was pleased with himself this morning. "I will relay your thanks," he said graciously, "and I hope you'll acquit me now of wishing you ill, Madame."

Elen glanced at Richard, the tenderness of the long night between them coming back to her. They had slept and awakened and slept again, loving and talking foolishly together as lovers will. She was amazed she could so readily relinquish her fear and guilt to the friendly darkness and the warm haven of his arms. No, in this marriage, at least, the king had done her no ill. "I do, Your Grace."

Richard was watching anxiously, half fearing what she might say. His expression lightened considerably at her words. He tugged on his boots and moved toward Edward. "I'll be back, Elen. I wish to leave for Gwenlyn today."

Edward strode through the door, Richard hurrying in his wake. "The *Falcon*'s captain holds himself at your command. There's no need to take him at sword point this voyage."

"No, Your Grace," Richard remarked, keeping his face suitably grave.

"Keep an ear toward the doings of Hugh de Veasy. You've made a bitter enemy there. You've told me little enough, but your lady filled the queen's ear with the happenings at Ambersly."

"I can handle de Veasy."

"Yes, you'll have to," Edward remarked. He frowned thoughtfully. "There's little I can do, I fear, save levy a heavy fine. It would be your word against his that he actually meant you ill. Vespain would swear they both sought only to save Lady Elen for the Church, and with her letter as evidence, you'd never prove a thing—especially with the court packed in de Veasy's favor as the bishop could insure.

"But I doubt he'll move against you openly," Edward continued, sending Richard a wicked grin. "From what Lady Elen recounted, he won't wish an account of this recent feuding made public. Christ, I'd give much to have seen him trussed like a pig for roasting in his own keep!"

Richard smiled. "It was a sight well worth a few bruises," he admitted. "But I'll warn Elen to hold her tongue. 'Twould do no good for that tale to get about."

Edward nodded. "I'll have my men watch and listen, but they don't see all. It will be good to observe his behavior toward you at the Shrewsbury Parliament. I'll send word when all is arranged."

Richard glanced up in dismay. Summer was spent, the hard work of harvesting close upon them. He was needed to oversee things at Gwenlyn else the winter would be lean. "When will you call the meeting?"

"Not till Michaelmas or after." Edward's eyes narrowed and his voice took on a harsher note. "We'll have a bit of entertainment after the work of harvest. Dafydd ap Gruffydd will be tried and punished—a traitor to the Welsh when he crawled to me to betray his brother and a traitor to me many times over when he and Llywelyn were reconciled. He'll have a sentence to fit his crimes and I wish all who fought him to see it."

They moved down the stairs into the open bailey. At sight of the king, riders swung onto horses and an expectant ripple of movement went through the waiting crowd.

Richard paused beside Eleanor's white palfrey. "Good morning to you, Your Grace."

"And is it a good morning?" she inquired, a quizzical tilt to her eyebrows.

"It is indeed. I've much to thank you for, I've no doubt."

She smiled at him in response. "Me? Why, I've done nothing at all."

Richard grinned. "I've a notion this stew was one of your making. It bears all the marks."

Her eyes twinkled mischievously as she held out her hand. Richard carried it to his lips. "Don't be hesitant to speak your mind openly next time," she whispered, bending toward him. "I near had you in the wrong pot."

Richard squeezed her fingers and stepped away from her horse. "Godspeed, Your Grace."

Edward motioned to a waiting groomsman. Taking the reins of his fretting stallion, he swung into the saddle. For a moment, he sat staring at Richard as if searching for words. "Love matches can be dangerous, Richard. A woman who holds a man's heart in her hand may rule him in a thousand little ways. Take care, lest you be so ruled." He glanced at the window fronting the chamber Richard and Elen had shared. "I've a hunch that woman would castrate a lesser man."

"You've seen only the worst in her, Your Majesty, the part I saw in the beginning. Elen has another side. I've seen it and rest content in my choice."

"So Eleanor says," Edward responded doubtfully. "Just remember the girl has other loyalties. The Welsh oft turn on each other to rend and tear, but when it comes to fighting an outsider these northerners usually back their own. Don't force her to a choice, for you might not like her choosing."

Richard nodded, last night's argument still fresh in his mind.

Edward gazed at him searchingly. "Have a care, Richard. I wish you joy in possessing the wench, but I pray I've done you no disservice with this match. A man may love too well."

"You've done me no disservice," Richard responded, smiling. "You've made me the happiest man in Christendom."

Edward leaned down and caught his shoulder in a rare public display of affection. "I've no need to tell you Eleanor and I will miss your presence at court. We'll see you at Shrewsbury, though, and visit at Gwenlyn ere long. Go with God now, Richard, and trust not these Welsh overmuch."

Evening was fast approaching, twilight silver blurring the contrasts of rugged mountain and placid sea. A gentle breeze rocked the *Falcon* as the ship dropped anchor at Ruthlin. Elen clutched Richard's cloak about her, watching her husband ready his men for the landing.

Owain moved to stand beside her. It was the first moment of privacy they had shared since her wedding. "Rest you content in your choice? The Englishman who slew Enion? By Our Lord Savior, your memory is short enough!"

Elen glanced up in surprise. The attack hurt the more because its bitterness was unexpected. She thought Owain might understand her predicament. "Choice? What choice had I? Edward offered me Richard or Hugh de Veasy. That is no choice!"

"That kiss at Ambersly bespoke your choice," Owain muttered. "And you appear pleased enough at the arrangement. You stare at the man as a doting hen does her only chick. It seems the English conquer with more than the sword," he added dryly.

A flush of shame warmed Elen's face. She'd been foolishly open in her newfound happiness. It had obviously disgusted Owain.

She gazed at the cliffs above the village. Gwenlyn's towering curtain walls frowned down at them, a bitter reminder of England's might. "I've not forgotten Enion, nor any of the rest," she said softly. "I see English castles of stone on lands held by Welsh families for hundreds of years. I see English pennons unfurled over lands no Englishman should tread. I see Welshmen reduced to cowering in the shadows hoping for crumbs to keep their families from starvation. I know my husband helped bring this about, and it eats at my soul, Owain, like a sickness that has no cure. But Richard is not like the others. He has treated us honestly." She glanced back at him. "Can you say different?"

Owain shook his head. "He's a warrior I respect, a leader I could serve were he not the Wolf of Kent. And for now, he's best for Wales. But he'll not rest till his duty be done." His eyes narrowed and he stared blindly at the far horizon. "Richard of Gwenlyn will be the one to end all hope for us—for Dylan and the rest who fight on. And he'll take the Welsh Fox, Elen. Don't ask how I know, but I do."

Elen caught his arm, turning him toward her. "No! I won't let him."

"Don't think to rule him, Elen, for you won't," he warned. "He cares for you and that is my comfort. Even as it tore my heart to give him what belonged to Enion, I knew 'twas best for you. But not even you will turn him from his duty."

"Owain, you'd not..." Elen faltered, frightened by a thought that chilled her heart, "You'd not seek his life?"

"No, Elen. Not even to save my own."

Richard shouted: "Owain! Fetch your men here to me."

Owain glanced up at Richard's order. "Think on my words, Elen, and decide who you are—Elen of Teifi or Elen, Lady Basset? You cannot be both."

"Would you tear me in two?" she whispered.

"No, I would save you that." The hard gray of his eyes softened for a moment. "Decide your loyalties now and you'll be the better for it."

He moved away and Elen stared across the darkening waters where rose-hued clouds rode a sea of slate. His words echoed in her mind. Decide your loyalties now.

But she already had.

"Come, sweet, are you ready?"

She glanced up into Richard's smiling face, her whole being quickening at the sight of him. She couldn't guard against Richard, even if she wanted to. He had accepted her last night with the partial loyalty that was all she could give. And if the truth be told, she longed to give him more ... not less.

Richard smiled again, his emerald eyes darkening to smoky jade in the failing light. "Continue to look at me like that, love, and I'm apt to forget the host of people waiting to welcome us and spend the night right here."

Richard and Owain. She loved them both—refused to give up either. Owain was wrong, she told herself fiercely. She would make it so!

She placed a hand against Richard's chest, leaning slightly toward him. "But there's no privacy here," she murmured. "I'd much prefer our chamber in Gwenlyn."

Richard's eyes narrowed with a smoldering sensuality that made her whole body tighten in expectation. "Your wish is my command," he whispered, sweeping her up in his arms. He kissed her, his lips lingering on hers for several seconds before he forced himself to break away. "Take care with my lady, Geoffry," he admonished, easing her over the ship's side into the arms of a brawny trooper. "If she's wetted, I'll have your head."

The grinning soldier nodded. "Never ye fear, m'lord. She'll be safe as a babe."

That night there was much feasting and drinking in Gwenlyn's great hall. Richard sent Elen a long look as she left the room, and she knew he would follow as soon as he could excuse himself from the host of well-wishers.

She entered the bedchamber she and Richard would share. A maidservant had already moved her things into a large coffer chest Richard had provided. The girl helped her out of her clothing and Elen wrapped herself in the luxurious bedrobe Eleanor had given her.

Dismissing the servant, Elen walked to the window and stared out. Beyond Gwenlyn's walls the mountain peaks of Gwynedd glimmered iridescently in the moonlight.

Somewhere out there Dylan and the others still fought for a Wales ruled by Welshmen. And it was a dream she still held, despite her marriage to Richard—a dream she refused to relinquish, even for him.

She folded her arms on the window ledge, leaning her chin upon smooth stone. In the distance, the surf beat rhythmically against the cliffs below Gwenlyn. It was a lonely sound.

Strangely enough, it was her mother she longed for this night. How good to have another woman to talk to—someone who would understand her longing to please Richard, her need to be herself. But her mother lay in a shallow grave on a mountainside, a grave marked by nothing save a simple cairn of stone.

And her father? Had the men died unshriven at Builth? Visions of the carnage there had haunted her for months. She knew coins were scarce; Richard had little actual money. But somehow she must find enough to buy masses for those she loved.

Behind her the chamber door opened, then closed, and Richard's light footsteps sounded on the floor. His arms slid around her and she closed her eyes as he drew her back against his chest.

His hands slipped between the edges of her robe, encircling the warm flesh of her waist. He nuzzled her ear, then bent to press a kiss against her throat. "It was a damnably long meal," he breathed, "and knowing you were here waiting didn't make this last half hour any easier."

Caressing her, his hands slid slowly along her ribs to feel the fullness of her breasts. Despite Elen's pensive mood, the sharp contrast of silken fur and the gentle roughness of his hands sent a shivering pleasure radiating through her.

She leaned against him, shifting her head, allowing him better access to the sensitive area at the base of her throat. "You have only to touch me and I care not what lies between us."

Richard stiffened. "Are we back to that?"

She shook her head. "I'm sorry, Richard. I didn't mean to bring it up. It's just that—"

"What?"

"Forget my words. 'Tis nothing."

"What is it, Elen? What troubles you?"

"The bodies . . . what happened to the bodies—my father, brother . . . ?"

He knew at once what she meant. "The savagery wasn't so bad after Builth as no doubt you heard. Edward gave permission for Christian burial. Llywelyn's body and that of your father and brother, and others of rank like Enion who could be identified, were taken to Abbey Cwym Heir. Edward paid for masses." He turned her gently toward him. "I was there, Elen. It's a peaceful place, a beautiful valley. I'll take you there if you wish."

Elen nodded, closing her eyes and leaning into the arms Richard held out to her. His embrace was comforting, his arms warm with the promise of a friend who shared her grief. "And I want to go home, Richard," she whispered desperately, "home to Teifi."

"Yes, Elen, we'll go. But I must make sure all is stable here first. We'll go in the spring." He waited a moment. "What else disturbs you, love?"

She shook her head.

"Come," he coaxed. "Tell me. Remember you swore to speak truth."

"My mother," she whispered, burying her head against his chest. "It's my fault she's dead. I've blamed you all these months, but it was my fault, only mine. She wished to flee England for France, but I wouldn't go. I should have realized she was ailing—she was never strong. But I was so caught up in the fighting, so caught up in planning the next ambush. . . ."

She closed her eyes against the pain of her confession, clutching convulsively at the soft wool of Richard's tunic. "She begged for a priest at the end, but we didn't have one. S-she died unshriven, Richard." A shudder ran through her at the memory of that grim burial. "There was scarce time to dig a proper grave. We scraped a hole in the hillside and covered it with stone. It was such a lonely place, Richard. I . . . I can't stand to think of her there!"

Richard held her comfortingly, stroking her hair as he would a small child. "The times were hard. Many died last winter on both sides. But have you thought of this, Elen? If she were ailing, the Lady Gweneth would never have survived a voyage to France. It's cold and wet and there are storms that make a man's blood freeze in his veins. Sea travel in winter is only for the hearty. You know that."

He lifted her chin toward him. "As it is, she died in her own country. Come spring, we'll take her remains to the Abbey so she might rest beside your father." He brushed a kiss across her forehead. "And we'll buy a hundred masses for her soul if you wish it, sweetheart."

Elen took a deep breath. "I wish it above all things."

Richard drew her away from the window. "Come to bed now, love," he whispered. "I would have us both forget our worries for a time."

Richard's embrace was warm, the strokes of his hand comforting. But Elen soon sought more than comfort. They made love leisurely then, with a tenderness that had been missing in the fiery passion of the night before.

Long after Elen lay sleeping in his arms, Richard stared into the darkness. So Elen had helped to plan the raids against his men. The words had slipped out with her agonized confession and he doubted she was even aware of what she'd said.

He closed his eyes, almost wishing he hadn't heard. The idea of a woman involved in such a task was so farfetched he would have dismissed it had the woman been anyone but Elen. He had no doubt his wife was entirely capable of such a feat. But would a Welsh fighting man actually listen to a woman's counsel in matters of war?

Only if he had known her since she was a babe, Richard told himself grimly. Only if he had been trained since then to think of her as his mistress.

Elen shifted in her sleep, pressing more closely against him. He tightened his arms around her, hating the seed of suspicion planted at Ambersly, the idea that had taken firm root in his thoughts last night: that there was no Rhys ap Iwan after all.

CHAPTER TWENTY-SEVEN

𝒯he busy days of August slid into the hectic ones of September. The hard work of harvest was upon the land, and every day, Richard rode out with his bailiff to oversee the day's activities.

While he was gone, Elen looked to the management of the castle and the efficient husbanding of the scant remaining stores. She had much to learn regarding the running of an important English keep and the many manors and granges that supported it, but many of her mother's long-forgotten instructions came back to her. Though she had always believed women's work vastly inferior to the exciting adventures in which the men of her family were involved, she was grateful now for the knowledge her mother had passed on.

And in her softened mood, Elen saw her role differently. She had no desire for the tumult of war or the planning of raids. Richard depended on her to see to his household, and his satisfaction when he returned to his peaceful, well-managed keep was ample reward.

Her heart had even been lightened concerning Owain's danger. After his help in her rescue, Owain had been granted a pardon. Richard had appointed him village reeve and the Welshman now lived in Ruthlin, representing the people in all dealings with the lord. Surely he'd not have been given such position if Richard had the slightest suspicion of Owain's identity.

In such a setting, Elen flowered into womanhood with all the trusting abandon of any seventeen-year-old bride who knows herself well loved. She learned the names of Richard's men and servants, seeing to their needs as if they had been her own. She even grew to enjoy the pleasant conversation with his knights after meals.

When she and Richard retired to their chamber was when the day truly began for Elen. Richard had opened the door for her to an undreamed world of pleasure and she sought to return the favor. Having once been shown the way, she was an uninhibited lover seeking to please the man she loved in a hundred little ways.

Michaelmas came and went and with it Edward's call to the Shrewsbury Parliament. During Richard's absence, Elen busied herself and the servants with a vengeance. The old, soiled rushes were swept out and every floor in Gwenlyn scrubbed and laid with a carpet of fresh rushes sprinkled with herbs. The bedchambers were aired and cleaned and even the foul-smelling garderobes emptied and washed down.

Now, entering the bedchamber she shared with Richard, Elen's whole body quickened with longing as she thought of his return. The days and nights had seemed endless since his departure, the great, curtained bed empty and cold without him at her side. She knew she was being foolish, that there would be weeks and months when he would be away far longer than this. Still, she attended Father Dilwen's mass every morning, and prayed thrice daily for Richard's quick and safe return.

And she had learned a surprising fact about herself. She was jealous—terribly so. She knew few men were faithful, even told herself it didn't matter if Richard took some woman when she was not around. It was only a physical thing—Richard had told her he loved no other. But the truth was it mattered. It mattered a great deal.

Sudden shouts rang out in the bailey. Elen hurried to the window and glanced down. Men were moving about excitedly, but with no alarm in their motions. They couldn't be under attack—it must be Richard!

She whirled toward the sheet of polished metal hanging above her coffer which she used as a mirror. Jerking the leather thong from her fat braid, she tied her hair instead with a blue ribbon Richard had brought her. There was time for nothing more. By the time she had tucked a few wisps of hair behind her ears, the sound of steel-shod hooves rang on the lowered drawbridge.

Smoothing her skirt into place, Elen hastened to the hall, calling orders for food and drink as she hurried outside. Giles was already there, welcoming Richard and his men as they dismounted.

Elen shot a glance over the group. The men were muddy and travel-stained, their mounts showing evidence of hard riding. She sent a brief prayer heavenward. Whatever the trouble, she was thankful they had returned safe.

Richard's eye caught hers over Giles's shoulder. After a few brief commands, he hurried up the stairs.

They met halfway and he caught her to him, his mouth seizing hers for a fierce kiss. "Next time I take you with me, sweet," he mumbled, kissing her again. "I'll not spend another two weeks like these last!"

So he had missed her. Elen wound her arms around his neck, not caring for the stares and good-natured grins of Richard's men. The steel of his hauberk dug into her flesh but she ignored it, enjoying another long kiss of welcome.

Richard was the first to draw away. "I've ruined your gown," he muttered, staring down at the mud staining her clothing. "And before God, I must smell like a goat. How can you stand so near?"

Elen linked her arm through his, drawing him with her

toward the hall. He smelled of nothing besides horses, sweat and healthy man. "I happen to like goats," she remarked, smiling, "and the gown can be cleaned. But what of you?" She glanced back at the lathered horses, her worry rekindling. "Was there trouble?"

"Trouble? No. But I'd an unholy urge to reach Gwenlyn this day. I'd no wish for another night on the road."

The look in his eyes sent a delicious shiver of anticipation down her spine. She glanced quickly away lest he sense her eagerness. "Come inside. There's naught but bread and cheese and some smoked fish to hold your hunger till supper, but there's ale aplenty to quench your thirst. And I'll have a bath readied for you upstairs."

"But I thought you liked goats," Richard murmured as they entered the hall.

"I do, but they belong outside." She gave him a push toward a maidservant who held out a bowl of water for handwashing. "See to your master, Agnes, while I make sure food is readied."

Elen stayed below only long enough to see the servants passing food and drink among Richard's men. When she was sure all were being cared for, she hurried upstairs to check that her husband's bath was being prepared.

Richard followed a short time later, still chewing on a large hunk of bread he had brought from the hall. "I see someone's been busy during our absence," he remarked. "I doubt Gwenlyn has ever been so clean or well run."

Elen warmed to his praise. "With winter coming on the men will be much indoors. I thought it best to take care of the matter now." She smiled at him across the room. "Besides, it helped pass the time."

Richard put down the bread and began to unbuckle his sword belt. He'd obviously bade Simon remain below. Elen sent the servants from the room, then crossed to help her husband disrobe. "Did you see that dog, de Veasy?" she inquired, lifting off Richard's heavy steel hauberk. "I pray every day he will die of a bloody flux!"

Richard chuckled. "I saw the man, but we kept a polite silence. I think he fears my wit if he provokes me. He'd appear a bit foolish were it known two lone men entered his keep, bound him fast, and stole his treasure." His hands lifted to her face and he held her head gently between his palms. "And what a treasure you are," he whispered, lowering his mouth to hers.

Elen leaned into his embrace, the tender kiss rapidly deepening into passion. How could a simple kiss so rock her world? "I missed you," she admitted when he lifted his head at last. "Each day seemed twice its length."

"And I missed you, sweet, though I'll confess the long, dull nights were more my enemy than the days."

Elen's heart was racing painfully. Had he eased his desire with someone else? She stepped away from him, turning to lay out towels beside the steaming tub. "Oh? I heard you were a favorite among the queen's ladies," she remarked, trying to speak as if in jest. "Were they so unattentive to your needs?"

Richard bent and stripped off his chausses, moving deliberately to climb into the tub. So Elen was jealous. He scarcely dared believe it. "They were attentive enough," he remarked blandly, "but none can hold a candle to a certain chestnut-haired hellion I know. I fear my stay in Wales has given me a taste for a woman who can near burn up the sheets in my bed."

Elen blushed and bent to gather Richard's scattered clothing. She wasn't sure his words were a compliment. He was telling her she was different from the English women he knew, but he hadn't said he hadn't bedded with them. She felt a flicker of doubt. Perhaps it wasn't good to be so obvious in her desire for him.

Schooling her face to show no emotion, she moved toward the door. "I'll just give your things to the servants and—"

Richard caught her wrist as she passed, drawing her back

to the tub. "You'll do no such thing," he said softly. "I didn't ride my horse near into the ground to have naught but a moment of your time, Madame. And as for your question—there's been no other woman for me since Beaufort. Now are you satisfied?"

No other woman since Beaufort; he had waited for her a long time. Elen's confidence returned and she smiled bewitchingly. "Yes, my lord. But I hope to be even more satisfied ere long."

Richard leaned back, his lips framing a sensual smile. "Then I suggest you remove your gown—unless you wish to have it washed on your back. I want you with me . . . now."

"Richard . . ." Elen tried to draw back, but he held her wrist firmly. She began to laugh, but when he rose up from the water and made as if to lift her into the tub, she drew back with a gasp. "No, no, wait!" she choked out. "Give me a moment."

"A moment only. Then you're coming in, clothing or no."

She moved away from him, quickly slipping out of her gown, but leaving her shift in place. She hastened to the mirror and unfastened her braid, letting her hair become a thick, shining mass down her back. Stepping out of her shift, she turned back to the sheet of polished metal to secure her hair atop her head with a set of ivory combs Richard had given her.

Each movement was slow, deliberate. She knew Richard was watching, felt the heat of his gaze warming her like the sun. She put down the brush and moved toward him. "Is this what you had in mind, my lord?"

"Witch . . . come here and I'll show you what I had in mind."

She halted beside the tub, staring down into Richard's narrowed eyes. His mouth was set, the pulse beating visibly in his tanned throat. Wordlessly, he rose and lifted her over the tub's edge, returning to his seat on the bathing stool as he settled her in his lap.

Elen wound her arms around his neck, closing her eyes and lifting her head for the kiss she was sure would come. But to her surprise, Richard didn't kiss her at once. Squeezing water across her shoulders, he drew the cloth across her body, encircling her breasts in long, lazy movements that near stopped her breath.

His hands dropped lower, drawing the cloth slowly across her belly then down to wash her legs, the sensitive place beneath her thighs. His mouth sought the taut peak of her breast, tugging at it until she was gasping.

Such inflamed play was new to Elen and all the more rousing for its unexpectedness. The silken warmth of the water enfolded her, Richard's lips enticing, demanding, hot against her skin. Her hands slid over his chest and she sighed his name, shifting against him as a rising tide of wanting built between them.

Richard eased her from his lap, deftly moving her against the side of the tub. He pressed against her, his mouth urgently seeking hers, their bodies all but joining. "You've burned up my bed, love, now you set my bath aflame as well," Richard whispered against her mouth. "How am I to think about duty, work, anything save making love to you?"

His eyes were dark with passion. Elen gazed back at him, her whole being afire with his touch. "Stop talking and love me," she whispered. "Love me, Richard, before I come apart."

Richard swept her up in his arms, climbed out of the bath, and strode to the bed. Dropping her in the center he dragged the combs from her hair, tumbling it about them in a fiery sea of silk.

Elen caught him to her, tangling her legs with his, wanting him with a desperation that was almost frightening. Their mouths joined, separated, joined again. And then he entered her—the release immediate, uncontrolled, shattering.

Some time later, Elen awoke. The last burnished gold of evening filled the room; she could tell it was growing late. She eased cautiously out of Richard's arms, but he slept the sleep of exhaustion and didn't stir as she left the bed.

She gazed about the room in amusement. Clothes were scattered everywhere and as much water was out of the tub as in. The servants would have a good gossip over this, she thought with a grin.

Gathering up the clothing, she put it aside to be washed, and quickly restored the room to as much order as possible. She hesitated beside the bed, staring down at Richard, trying to decide whether sleep or food was his most pressing need.

Richard slept on, unmoving. Her face softened. Dear God, how she loved him—more than she had ever dreamed possible! She had never known this shattering ecstacy she felt at Richard's touch, this deep need to be with him despite all reason to the contrary. True, she had loved Enion, but she had come to realize it was in much the same way she loved her brother Rhodri. She still missed her family, still missed Enion's easy laugh and teasing ways, but the men were dead and she and Richard alive. And life went on. As Eleanor had said, the war and killing were done, the past best forgotten. The Wolf of Kent was no more.

Slipping out of the room, Elen closed the door softly behind her. She would fetch up supper on a tray and, when Richard awoke, he would have whatever he needed without having to stir from his bed.

She entered the hall, ignoring the knowing glances a few of the men cast her way. She made her way along the side of the room, seeking Agnes to gather what she needed from the kitchens. But within moments, all thought of food was forgotten.

"I'll tell you, friend, the Welsh dog weren't so high and mighty when our Edward's horses dragged him to the gallows through the streets of Shrewsbury!"

"Before God, I wish I'd been there!"

"Aye, they cut him down while he was breathin'. Had his entrails torn out and burnt before his eyes, he did! His screams were something like." A round of cheers went up and, for a moment, the speaker's deep, bass voice was drowned.

Elen swung around, staring at the men in horror. A handful of soldiers who had remained at Gwenlyn were crowded eagerly around the end of the trestle table where one man was holding forth. "Aye, York got a quarter, Chester a quarter, and Northampton a quarter, though we left afore 'twas decided where the last bit of him would go." The man took a gulp of ale. "Naturally the traitor's head'll grace a pike on London Tower."

Elen felt her gorge rising. They were speaking of a man . . . a Welshman. She moved slowly toward the high table where several of Richard's knights still sat. Unbelievably, their talk ran on much the same lines. Everywhere men were gleefully discussing the execution of Llywelyn's brother, Dafydd ap Gruffudd.

Her heart hammered against her ribs, her pulses throbbing painfully in her head. Richard had been there—Richard had been at Shrewsbury. She moved woodenly toward Giles, seeking someone to tell her this tale wasn't so, that Richard hadn't been part of it.

Sir William of Hereford was loudly explaining things to a man on his left. ". . . and Edward called the council to vote. Every knight voted death. I tell you, men'll think twice before raising a hand against our king!"

"And did Richard vote, William? Did your lord urge death for my kinsman?"

Elen's cold, brittle voice silenced the group immediately. Sir William swung around, the look of dismay on his face almost ludicrous. "Lady Elen. I . . . we didn't see you, m'lady."

"Did he vote?" she snapped, her fists clenched at her sides. "Tell me!"

Giles took one look at her ashen face and rose from the table. "Elen, come with me," he said gently. "I'll explain—"

"Did . . . he . . . vote?"

"Yes. But the council voted only on Dafydd's guilt or innocence, Elen," Giles said quickly. "Not the execution of the sentence."

His words barely registered. Richard had sent her kinsman to a horrible death, then ridden back here and taken her to bed as calmly as you please. And she had been foolishly eager for it. She hadn't even minded that every inhabitant of Gwenlyn knew what they were doing.

"I want the hall cleared, Giles," she said coldly. "I want every English bastard out of here now!"

The men gazed at her in dismay. "Now!" she snarled. "Do you hear me?"

The men glanced at each other sheepishly, then began rising from the table. Giles leaned down to Simon. "Fetch Richard here," he said tersely. "Hurry!"

Elen's order rippled slowly through the room, sending an uneasy wave of quiet sweeping the hall. Men began to rise and edge uncomfortably toward the door.

Finally Elen stood alone beside Giles. "Elen," he tried again, "you know—"

"Get out!"

Giles gave her a long look. "Very well."

Elen watched Giles leave the room, hating him in that instant, hating all the English in Wales, her husband included. She gazed at the lofty grandeur of the empty hall, thinking of Dafydd's massive Castel Y Bere, Llywelyn's beautiful palace at Aber, her own home at Teifi . . . all now in English hands.

Drawing her dagger from her girdle, she moved purposefully toward the canopied seat of the lord. She climbed onto the table, slashing down the scarlet cloth, ripping Edward's golden lions from the frame. Throwing them to the floor, she ground them viciously underfoot.

Hot tears began to flow unchecked. The English, the greedy, grasping English! They took what they wanted, her husband included. And they didn't care what pain they inflicted in the process. No, she corrected herself, from what she'd heard just now, they reveled in it!

She stared at the scarlet and gold ruin at her feet as if only now realizing what she'd done. The dagger slipped from her hand and she turned away, moving blindly toward the chapel.

It was there Richard found her, huddled miserably on the steps below the altar. He hesitated a moment as if uncertain how to approach her. "Elen . . ."

"Don't speak to me!"

He began walking slowly up the aisle. "I didn't like it any more than you."

"No?" She glanced up at him, her eyes swollen, her face streaked with tears. "But you spoke for it. Giles said so."

Richard sighed. "I agreed Dafydd was a traitor—the punishment for that is death. But before God, I'd no idea what the manner of it would be." He glanced away. "It's a new method of execution some devil dreamed up. They call it drawing and quartering."

Elen's hands clenched against her skirt. Her breathing was short and shallow. "Why . . . why didn't you tell me?"

"I was going to."

"When? After you'd had your pleasure again?" She stared up at him bitterly. "Did you fear I'd not be so eager knowing another kinsman's blood stained your hands?"

Richard had the grace to look embarrassed. "I should have told you," he admitted. "But I'd not seen you in over two weeks. I knew you'd be angry. I didn't want our reunion beginning like that." He eased to a seat beside her. "I meant to tell you afterward, only I . . . I fell asleep."

He reached to take her hand.

She jerked away. "Don't touch me now, Richard. I can't stand it!"

His hand fell back to his side. "Elen, I was wrong not to tell you. I'd not have had you find out this way. But you know as well as I Dafydd was a traitor—to both your people and mine. He deserved to die, though I'd not see any man go like that."

"I didn't care for Dafydd—no one who loved Llywelyn could. But this will inflame all of Wales. Even Welshmen who despised Dafydd for his treachery will be outraged by this. He'll be a martyr," she added slowly.

"I know."

"There's no hope for us, is there?"

He gazed at her in surprise. "Of course there is. This changes nothing between us."

"You don't understand, do you, Richard? You really don't."

"Understand what?"

"Who I am."

He frowned. "You're my wife, Elen. You're Lady Basset of Gwenlyn."

She stared at him, hearing the haunting echo of Owain's words. "Yes, but I am also Elen of Teifi. And I've yet to learn to reconcile the two."

"Richard . . ."

They both glanced up. Simon stood in the doorway, his face pale beneath its tan. "What is it?" Richard asked sharply.

The boy moved toward them, visibly shaken. "A rider . . . a rider from Beaufort. The Welsh burned the place to the ground. Every last man, woman, and child slaughtered—even the servants." He swallowed. "And Sir Thomas was butchered like an ox for roasting, the parts of his body wrapped in . . ."—he hesitated—"in the pelt of a red fox."

Richard sat unmoving. "God save us," he murmured after a long moment. He swung to his feet, his face emotionless. "Send Henry to Ruthlin. See if the Welshman called Owain can be found."

Owain, he wanted Owain. Elen scrambled to her feet, Dafydd's hideous fate forgotten. "W-what will you do?" she asked unsteadily.

"Do?" he repeated. "Why, I must take the Welsh Fox, Elen. Do you doubt it?"

She stared at Richard, the strength draining from her limbs. *He knew. Before God, he knew!*

She grasped his arm. "Richard, don't go! Please. Let this be. Rest a day at least."

"Wait? After this?" He turned back to Simon, his answer in the curt orders he clipped out. "Have the men prepare to ride. Send to the stables to see if horses can be found fresh enough to carry us. Spread the word we travel light and fast. Go now."

"Richard, please . . ."

He glanced sharply at her. "Don't ask it, Elen."

"I'll never forgive you if you hurt him, Richard," she cried out. "Never!"

His eyes softened, his hand moving slowly over her face as if to memorize her features. "I've no choice," he said softly. With one last searching look, he began walking up the aisle.

"Richard . . ."

He glanced back.

Elen stared at him, her heart breaking. "Have a care, Richard," she whispered. "Have a care to yourself."

CHAPTER TWENTY-EIGHT

*W*ales was aflame with autumn. The high, wild hillsides ran golden with bracken, red and yellow with leaves of oak and ash and beech. Elen rode out often, seeking escape from her worry in the freedom of the hills, in the sweet sigh of wind in the spruce and the vast sweep of countryside spread out below her.

She drew rein on a hilltop overlooking the pass into the mountains. Sometimes she sat there for hours watching for any sign of Richard. He had been gone over a fortnight, and she worried that his men might return without him . . . or that he might return with so much blood on his hands she could never forgive him.

Her worst nightmare hadn't been realized. During the raid on Beaufort, Owain had been working diligently at his post in Ruthlin. But it was obvious Richard had suspected him, that he had even had the Welshman watched.

Elen could scarcely conceal her fear, but Owain had merely shrugged his shoulders. What would be would be, and he was interested more in who had claimed his notoriety. Both he and Elen suspected Dylan was the man.

The plaintive cry of a curlew sounded from the heather-covered slopes below, its mournful call sinking Elen's spirits even lower. What would she do when Richard returned?

Despite their differences, she loved him. She had never doubted that. But given their conflicting worlds, would that be enough?

Suddenly her mare's ears pricked forward. A puff of dust rose near the road's farthest bend. Elen squinted against the light. She could just make out a flash of red—Richard's banner. Touching her reins to Ceiri's shoulder, she sent the mare careening down the rocky hillside, easing into a smooth canter along the grassy verge of the roadway.

Richard must have seen her. Reining Saladin out of the column of men and horses, he waited for her to one side of the road.

She drew her mount to a halt, her heart hammering painfully. What had happened these last weeks? She was almost afraid to learn. But at least Richard was safe. There was no hint of injury in the straight, proud way he sat his horse. She searched his face. It was cold and impassive, his green eyes as wary as hers. "I'm glad I see you well," she murmured stiffly.

"And I you, Elen."

She sent a questioning glance down the column of men filing past. "Were you . . . successful?"

"Yes."

Her eyes flew to his. They were shuttered, remote, giving nothing away. "You took the Fox?"

"You tell me."

Elen nudged her mount forward, passing the English soldiers quickly in her effort to see the prisoners trudging behind Richard's men. Dylan walked at the head of the group, heavily bound and guarded. Her eyes widened in recognition, her stomach churning sickly at sight of this once-proud man brought low.

"You know him, I see," Richard remarked, watching her intently. "Some say he's the Welsh Fox."

Elen didn't respond. She stared at the men moving past, a dull ache growing to fill every part of her. Just as she and

Owain had suspected—Dylan led the Welsh rebellion. Or at least he had.

"Come," Richard said heavily when she made no effort to speak. He caught her reins, swinging both mounts around. "We've wounded to see to . . . yours and mine."

Some time later, Elen finished stitching up the last of Richard's men. The Welsh had been caught by surprise as they lay in camp and the fighting had been vicious. Simon had taken an ugly gash in his shoulder and even Henry Bloet had been wounded in the struggle to overcome Dylan and his men.

But Richard's soldiers were being carefully restrained in Elen's presence. They had learned their lesson. None were discussing the fight or boasting of the number of Welsh they'd dispatched. And if she hadn't felt so much like weeping, she was sure she would have laughed at their courteous restraint.

With a heavy heart, she put away her bone needles and salves. She'd had but a moment to speak to Dylan, a moment to tell him she would do what she could. She wondered now what that might be. She dreaded facing Richard with this between them, but she knew they must reach some compromise. She couldn't let Dylan be put to death. He had long been a friend and he and Gruffydd had risked their lives for her.

Quickly instructing her maids on the proper use of Saracen's root to dress one man's fractured arm, Elen gave another maid a quantity of sicklewort in the event Simon's wound began bleeding again. She checked Richard's squire one last time before going in search of her husband.

Simon caught her hand as she rose to leave. He motioned the maid away. "See to Richard," he said softly. "He's a wound in his right thigh but wanted none to know."

Elen glanced around. Richard was nowhere in sight.

"He's already gone above."

Her eyes widened in alarm. "Is it bad?"

"Not now. But it wants tending."

She gave Simon's fingers a quick squeeze. "My thanks."

When she reached their chamber Richard was stretched out on the bed. She eased quietly inside and shut the door.

He rose on one elbow. "I'm awake."

She moved toward the bed, anxiously searching his face for any sign of fever. Her father had been just such a fool. He had never wanted notice taken of his hurts.

Richard smiled wryly and sat up. "I see Simon's mentioned the cut I took. 'Tis nothing to look so fearful about."

"Why didn't you tell me? I'd have seen to you at once." She frowned. "Even small wounds can poison and kill. You know that."

Richard had removed his surcoat and hauberk. He bent now to unwind his crossgarters. "And would you care so greatly?"

Elen dropped to her knees, quickly performing the task for him. The question hurt. "You know that I would."

"Elen . . ."

She glanced up.

He caught her shoulders, lifting her into his arms. She held him tightly. "Oh Richard," she whispered, "how can you ask such a thing?"

He rained gentle kisses on her face and throat. "I'm sorry, love, but I had to. I saw the look on your face when you watched the prisoners this afternoon. First Dafydd, now this. I greatly feared I'd gone beyond what you could bear."

"I don't know what I can bear, Richard. I pray I don't find out."

"I love you."

She stared up at him. "Richard, could you not—"

His lips moved over hers, gently silencing the request before she could put it to words. "Don't ask, Elen," he finally murmured. "Please don't ask."

He drew her down into his arms, shifting until he had her beneath him. She would think about Dylan later, Elen

promised herself. She would think of some way to save him
. . . later.

She threaded her fingers through Richard's thick hair,
giving herself up to the sweet pain of loving him. For now
there was only Richard.

"I can't let this go on, Elen. I've no choice."

Elen stared into Owain's grim face. Sweet Mary, how she
had come to hate those words! "Of course you have a
choice," she snapped. "It's ridiculous for you to admit being
the Welsh Fox. They'll only kill you both!"

Owain dragged a hand through his graying hair. "Yes,
but I can't let Dylan face the death they've planned for
me. Edward wants the Fox alive. You know what that
means, Elen." He glanced up, his eyes meeting hers. "What
they did to Dafydd will be child's play in comparison."

Elen caught his hand across the width of the table,
searching for any argument that might sway him. "Think
what you're saying. With both you and Dylan dead there'll
be none left to lead us. The resistance will be finished,
Owain. You and Dylan are the end of all our hopes."

"The resistance is finished," he remarked wearily. "There
are too many English and they've horses and armor, weapons of finest steel and castles of stone. We can't fight that,
Elen."

"Yes we can! We just need time."

He shook his head. "Wales has run out of time."

A servant moved purposefully toward them. "The lord
will see you now," he said, pausing at the table. Owain
drained the last of his ale as the man moved away. "I must
speak to Richard on this matter of the village butchering
day. We've not enough salt for the meats." He rose to his
feet with a sigh. "Holy Christ, butchering day, indeed!"

"Owain, listen to me," Elen said desperately. "Swear to
me you'll do nothing foolish yet. I . . . I'll speak to Richard
again about Dylan. I'll make him listen!"

"Elen, Richard is a soldier. He'll not listen to you in this."

She glanced up at him. "You would."

He smiled and raised his hand, moving his fingers slowly over her cheek in a rough caress. "Aye, but I'm an old fool, snared by your wiles when you were naught but a babe seeking the world on all fours." His eyes suddenly misted. "Don't cry for me, little one. I've had a good life."

Elen's throat closed up and she fought back tears, tears that seemed to come so easily these days. She caught his hand, holding it against her cheek. "Give me another day. Swear to me you'll not speak to him of this for at least one more day!"

Owain began to shake his head.

"Swear it!" she snapped, the ache in her throat making her voice unexpectedly harsh. "I order it so!"

Owain smiled in spite of himself. "Very well, my lady. I'll wait another day. Now release me," he remarked, gently disengaging his hand. "Your lord has made time to discuss the needs of Ruthlin."

Elen watched him move away across the hall, her vision blurred. She had begged and pleaded with Richard in every way imaginable. They had argued, been reconciled, and argued again. And he had forbidden her to bring up the subject of the Welsh Fox. She had no idea what she could do, but she would have to think of something.

Elen struggled with the problem all morning, finally coming up with a plan so simple it might work. But the scheme was a hateful one, the idea of putting it into practice nearly breaking her resolve. It would take Richard a long time to forgive her . . . if ever he could.

She would speak to him again, she told herself resolutely. She would make him listen. He had to.

When the master of Gwenlyn finished his afternoon conference with the bailiff, Elen was waiting for him in the corridor. "Richard, may I speak with you?"

He took one look at her face. "Not if it concerns your friend below," he remarked, still walking.

Elen matched her stride to his. "Tell me something. What does Edward plan for the Fox?"

"I don't know."

"Does he call the man traitor?"

Richard frowned. "You know that he does."

"And did you not say this hellish drawing and quartering is now meant for traitors?"

Richard kept walking. "Yes."

His voice was stern, unyielding, offering little hope. "You can't mean to go through with this," she said desperately.

"I must."

Elen stopped abruptly. "You would do this? You would have a man I care for sent to such a death? You would do this knowing how I feel?"

Richard swung around. His face was set, his eyes bleak but determined. "I've no choice, Elen. We've been over this a hundred times. I've no wish to see this happen. I'd kill the man straight and clean were it up to me—a damn sight easier death than what your Rhys gave de Waurin! Now peace . . . I'll discuss it no further."

Elen stared at him. No, she didn't suppose Richard had any choice. But neither had she. "Richard." She hesitated as he glanced up in irritation. "I love you," she said softly.

That night at supper, Elen was unusually quiet. The light meal she had eaten shifted uneasily in her stomach as she gazed at Richard's men, trying to decide which to use in her plan. The most logical to ask was Simon, but the boy would never forgive her for forcing him to betray Richard. And during these months since her marriage she'd come to look on him like a brother. It wouldn't work to pretend she might do him harm, he would know she was bluffing at the outset.

Her eye fell on Henry Bloet. Yes, Henry might do. He

trusted her, but she suspected he stood a bit in awe of her as well. Yes, Henry would be the one.

She rose from the table, moving quietly to fetch the salves and herbs she used in healing. She made the rounds of the hall, seeing to the individuals in her care, unhurriedly checking wounds, speaking a word or two of encouragement to each man. Belatedly, she had come to realize that men were alike whether Welsh or English. It was difficult to hate a man when you dressed his wounds, asked after his wife, spoke of his children. It would be painful to hear any of these men had been lost in battle.

Finally she came to Henry. His arm was healing. "Have you a few moments to spare me, Henry?" she inquired, giving his bandage a tug to ease the bind. "There are prisoners below whose wounds need checking as well. I'd not bother you but Richard insisted I take a dependable man when going below." She gazed at him with a show of concern. "If you don't feel equal to it, just tell me. I'll ask someone else."

Henry bristled. "A'course I'm equal to it. Happy ta take ye below, m'lady."

Elen dropped her eyes. How she hated this. Henry would be furious and Richard might never forgive her. She swallowed hard, willing herself not to think of Richard's rage. Of course he would forgive her . . . eventually. But she would never forgive herself if she lost both Owain and Dylan, knowing she might have prevented their deaths.

They trudged down the stairs into the dreary dungeon block. Elen nodded to the guard on duty at the landing. The man's name was Roger. He had a wife and two small sons back home in Sussex. She didn't want them orphaned. "I'll be down here an hour or more," she said, turning to Henry. "With you here, Roger might as well go above for his meal."

The soldier glanced hopefully at Henry.

"Go on, lad. But see you're back and no dawdling."

Elen glanced away uncomfortably. It was easier than she'd dared hope. The men trusted her and she was about to make fools of them. And Richard would look the greatest fool of all.

Her hands began to tremble as she hurriedly checked the wounded Welshmen. She tried to speak lightly to them as she worked. She dared not let this visit appear any different than the others she had made. "One more," she said to Henry at last. "The man Richard calls the Welsh Fox needs his bandage changed as well."

Henry frowned. "Lady, I dare not."

Elen gazed straight into his eyes with the lie. "Richard has given permission. Send above to ask if you don't trust my word."

Henry shifted uncertainly. Of course, she couldn't let him actually ask. " Come into the cell with us if you don't trust me, Henry. I've no secrets to tell him. I'll promise to speak only English if you wish."

Henry gave a relieved sigh. "I'd breathe a sight easier if ye would, m'lady. Not that I don't trust ye," he added respectfully.

His words were a lash. Dear, loyal, unsuspecting Henry . . . merciful Father, don't let him force her hand!

Henry unlocked Dylan's cell and they moved together into the tiny room. A faint gray light filtered in through the iron grate in the ceiling. Elen's eyes met the Welshman's and she sent him a warning look. Placing her bag of salves on the floor, she moved forward to stoop beside him.

Dylan snapped out a question in Welsh, but she shook her head, touching her lips and pointing back to Henry. She motioned to his arm, as if trying to convey the fact that she was here only to see to his bandage.

Dylan watched her narrowly. She peeled the bandage back, sending him another sidelong look. Rising to her feet, she crossed the floor to her bag of medicines, her heart pounding so heavily she wondered the men didn't hear.

She opened the bag, slipping out the knife she'd placed there earlier. The narrow length of steel gleamed wickedly in the light. She swallowed hard and glanced back at Henry. He was watching Dylan suspiciously, his back toward her.

She caught up the knife and moved behind him, steadying herself for the task at hand. She no longer had the stomach for killing, especially not Henry. Dear God, she prayed, don't let him be foolishly brave.

And then she moved. Seizing Henry's square chin in one hand, she pressed the knife tight to his throat with the other. "Drop the sword," she ordered coldly.

Henry growled an oath. He lurched forward, but Elen moved with him, trying desperately to keep the knife from severing the veins in his throat. She felt the slick warmth of blood coat her palm, but it wasn't the spurting gush she had feared.

"You fool! Another hairsbreadth and you'd be breathing your last," she threatened him. "Don't force me, Henry. I've no wish to see you dead. Now drop the blade!"

He snarled out some English words she'd never learned. Something highly uncomplimentary, she'd wager. "You're stronger than I, Henry, but that matters little." She shifted the blade against his throat to give him the idea. "Drop your sword."

For several tense seconds the man didn't move. His muscles were coiled, ready for action. Elen's heart was in her throat, her stomach churning. Then the sword fell to the floor with a muffled clatter.

She drew a deep, shaky breath. "Good. Now kneel here in the straw. For the love of God, do as I say! Richard needs you."

"Ye betray us like this and speak his name in the same breath. God's truth, ye Welsh are a treacherous lot and yer worst of them all!" he snarled.

She tried to ignore the words, tried to ignore the sick feeling intensifying in her gut. "I'm sorry to do this, Henry, but there's no other way. Now kneel. And don't try anything. Please, don't try anything."

He eased slowly to the floor and Elen knelt with him. She released his chin, holding the knife even more snugly against his throat. If he moved now, there'd be no way she could stay the blade. Drawing another knife from her girdle, she fumbled for Dylan's bonds, never taking her eyes from Henry.

"I knew you'd do it, Elen!" Dylan cried exultantly. "I knew you'd do something."

He strained toward her, working the rope against his wrists as she fumbled blindly with her left hand. Suddenly his bonds gave way. He grabbed the knife, and she heard him hack at the bindings about his feet.

He was up in a flash, an ugly laugh ringing out. A sharp blow sent Henry sprawling in the straw. Dylan swung the knife toward him.

"Don't! Don't touch him!"

Dylan glanced up in surprise.

"Bind and gag him, but I'll not see him hurt," Elen ordered.

Henry spat contemptuously at her feet. "Welsh slut!"

Dylan directed a vicious kick to Henry's stomach and the Englishman doubled up with a groan. "Hold your tongue!" Dylan snarled in a voice laced through with hatred.

"Dylan, no!" Elen's hands were shaking. The look on Henry's face spoke volumes, and all at once she wondered if the rest of Richard's men would feel so strongly. A loyal wife didn't protect her husband's enemies, and loyalty was near a religion to these English.

Perhaps this was a worse crime than even she had anticipated—but there was no turning back now. "No, Dylan," she repeated in a shaky voice. "I'd have no harm come to this man."

Dylan's dark eyes narrowed thoughtfully and he lowered the knife. "As you wish, Elen. But I fear you grow soft."

Using the rope that had bound him, Dylan hastily tied the Englishman's hands and feet, lashing them together, so the man couldn't rise. He ripped a piece of cloth from his tunic, making it into an effective gag.

Elen pointed toward her bag. "I've clothing bearing Richard's badge there in the bottom. The guard at the stair is at supper so your way is clear to the corridor above. Make your way out the postern door. Most everyone is in the hall, so this is your best chance."

"I know the way. I've been here before," Dylan remarked. "Only I left without Gruffydd."

Elen sighed, the name and the memory causing an old familiar ache. "Yes, I remember." But she had a new pain, a new question. "Dylan . . ." She hesitated, not certain how to ask. "Did you truly put all at Beaufort to the sword?"

"I did. And I plan a like fate for all the English in Wales," he responded bitterly.

She stared at him in horror. Until this moment, she hadn't believed the tale. "But there were children there, Dylan, mothers and babes! I didn't believe it when they told me."

"They didn't spare my Enid," he said harshly. "Of all people, I shouldn't need to remind you, Elen."

Elen shook her head, the thought of the massacre at Beaufort sending a chill sweeping through her. "Enid died in childbed, Dylan. She wasn't murdered in cold blood!"

His face was hard, contorted with hatred. "She'd not have died if not for them. And they've murdered women and children before—scores of times. Don't weep for them, Elen. They're but getting their own justice back again."

Elen shook her head. "No, Dylan. What you did was wrong. War is bad enough, but this—"

Dylan moved toward her. He caught her shoulders, his dark eyes holding hers with a fanatical intensity. "I've no time to argue, but know this, Elen. Wales isn't finished yet. There's new hope breathed into our cause, new hope and new blood." He grinned unexpectedly. "'Tis the devil's own jest, as the English will learn to their sorrow."

She stared at him questioningly. "What?"

He brushed a kiss against her forehead. "I must go. God keep you, Elen. Lord Aldwyn would be proud of you this night!"

He turned, but Elen caught his arm. She stared pointedly at the knife. "One thing I ask, Dylan. Take no life as you leave here unless it means your own."

His eyes narrowed and he sent her a long look. "Very well," he said at last. "For you, Elen."

She moved with him through the doorway, watching as he disappeared down the shadowy corridor. After several minutes, she stepped back inside. Henry lay at her feet, a seething heap of impotent rage. She dropped to a seat beside him, taking a cloth and reaching to clean the ugly cut at his throat.

He jerked away from her hand, but she caught his head, forcing him to lie still. "I'm going to see to this, Henry, so you might as well stop struggling," she informed him. "I know you hate me, but that's no reason to lose your life for want of care."

He glowered at her over the gag but stopped straining against her hand. She cleansed the cut, then gently dressed and bound it. He might, indeed, have been a hairsbreadth from death.

After her work was done, she sat quietly, trying to keep her mind from the bitter scene to come. Richard would be in a rage, but he would be hurt too. He had trusted her and she had betrayed him—again. Suddenly, she was afraid that this last treachery was worse than all the rest combined.

She glanced back at Henry. He was staring at her as if she were the lowest creature he could imagine. And if Henry was reacting this violently, what in God's name would Richard do? Her stomach knotted uneasily and she felt she truly might be ill. But she had done what she had to. Dylan was away and Owain needn't confess to being the Fox. And she had only her own hurt and Richard's to endure.

Henry was still glowering at her. "I'm sorry, Henry. It was wrong to use your trust in such a way," she said, softly. "You may never forgive me. I know that. But this man has long been dear to me. I couldn't let him face the death Edward planned."

Henry glared at her, unblinking.

She tried again. "Would you let Richard face such a death without moving heaven and earth and risking your own soul to save him?"

Henry's expression didn't change.

Elen sighed and gave up, sitting quietly until she judged Dylan had had sufficient time to escape. Then she removed the gag. Henry began cursing immediately.

She freed his hands and he tore his ankles loose, leaping to his feet in a burning rage. "Good Christ, do ye know what ye've done, woman?" he bellowed.

"Yes, Henry, yes I do. I know far better than you."

He moved toward the door to raise an alarm.

"As you love Richard, let me be the one to tell him this," she said, stopping him. "I owe him that, at least."

He swung back toward her. "I'll grant ye that, all right. And God have mercy on ye both."

CHAPTER TWENTY-NINE

*R*ichard stared at Elen incredulously. "You what?"

"I released him. I released the Welsh Fox. He's gone," she added when Richard made no response.

A host of conflicting emotions swept his face. Disbelief ... rage ... hurt ... then back to disbelief. He glanced from her to Henry and back again.

"It's true, m'lord," the wounded Henry muttered, "though I feel a fool admittin' it. I've men scouring the place now on the lookout fer the devil." He stared uneasily at the floor, unwilling to gaze on the emotions ravaging his master's face. "Strip me of my post, sir, I deserve it."

Richard didn't speak. He looked, in that moment, as if speech were truly beyond him. Elen watched anxiously, her heart aching at the hurt she had caused. The pain of her betrayal was etched on Richard's face, the look more daunting even than that she'd seen in the dungeon of Ambersly. "I ... I'm sorry, Richard, but I'd no choice. I couldn't let him be put to death. Not like that."

Richard's throat worked convulsively, but no sound came forth. The silence was unendurable, worse than any harsh words could have been.

Elen held her breath, preparing for an explosion of rage. She wanted it to come, prayed for it to come. Anything would be better than this look of stunned hurt.

But the explosion didn't come. "I'll want . . . an explanation of this, Henry," Richard finally got out. He took a deep breath, struggling for command of himself. "But it's I who should be stripped of my post. I should have foreseen this. Edward warned me. But I was too blind, too damned blind!"

He broke off abruptly and turned away, as if he couldn't stand the sight of his wife any longer. "See Lady Basset to her chamber, Henry. She's not to leave it for any reason." He moved toward the door without another glance in Elen's direction. "I'll be in my audience chamber. Bring me word if there's any sign of the man, but I've no wish to be disturbed for aught else. See to it, Henry."

This icy restraint was terrifying, far more frightening than the rage she had expected. Elen took a step toward him. "Richard . . . we must talk."

He didn't even look up. "Talk? I've nothing to say to you, Madame. Our talking has all been done." He walked away and Elen sprang after him. She couldn't let him go. Not like this!

Henry stepped into her path, a solid wall of simmering English indignation. "I'll see ye upstairs, Lady Elen. And I hope ye'll give me no trouble."

Elen stopped short. She took a deep breath and closed her eyes, willing herself to think rationally. Richard was furious now, but they would talk this out later and he would understand. She'd make him understand, she promised herself. "No, I'll give you no trouble, Henry," she responded with a strained smile. "I've done that already, I fear."

She moved ahead of him to the bedchamber she and Richard shared. She heard the door slam behind her, the sound of guards being posted in the corridor outside. The action shook her. Surely Richard didn't believe she would try to leave!

An hour crawled by, and then another. The candles

burned low and Elen slumped tiredly in a chair, waiting for Richard. Never had she felt so utterly and hopelessly alone. She had been forced to hurt the one man she longed to please above all others, to hurt him in a way he would find difficult to forgive. Richard's honor and honesty were such he would never have dreamed his wife would betray him, that she would scorn the trust he had so readily given. But had there been any other way?

She must have dozed, for the candles had guttered out and a faint gray light filtered into the room. Elen glanced around in confusion. It was day—but it couldn't be. Richard hadn't come.

She rose to her feet more frightened now than she had been during the night. She had never dreamed he would stay away. Knowing Richard's temper, she had expected a terrible argument, had even planned what would be best to say. But he hadn't come.

The sound of horses and the jingle of harness drew her to the window. She stared down. The men of Gwenlyn were making ready to ride and Richard was moving about among them. She watched as he took his reins from a groom and vaulted into the saddle.

He was going to leave without even speaking to her. He was angrier than she had realized. She leaned over the window ledge, longing to call out to him. But she didn't dare.

Holy God, let him look up! Let him at least look up.

But Richard wheeled his stallion, crossing the bailey without a glance in her direction.

Elen swung away from the window, leaning her heated cheek against the cool stone of the wall. Her throat closed up and a sick feeling swept her more intensely than it had last night. She'd gone too far this time. Richard couldn't forgive her.

Her mouth began to tremble and she pressed her hands against it, remembering the look on Richard's face as he had left her last night, the unrelenting set of his shoulders as he had ridden out just now. What if he never forgave her, or worse yet—what if he never came back?

Tears squeezed from behind her tightly closed lids. She would make it up to him, she swore. She would make it all up to him—if ever she got the chance.

The men of Gwenlyn didn't return for three days, and then they returned empty-handed. Dylan was still free.

Elen waited impatiently for Richard to come to her, but her hope died in tiny, painful pieces as the minutes dragged into hours, the hours into a day. She strained her ears for any sound of movement outside, but the only footsteps that halted were those of her maid, Felice. Not even Giles was willing to befriend her now.

Simon dealt the death blow to her hopes. He appeared at her door near sunset, and with a curt nod, set about packing Richard's things.

Elen sank onto a stool, watching helplessly. "Is he . . . leaving Gwenlyn?"

Simon shrugged. "I've no knowledge, Madame. He only bade me fetch his things."

"Oh, Simon . . . what am I to do?" she choked out.

He whirled on her angrily. "It appears you've already done it! You've betrayed him . . . shamed him before his men. And Holy God, I hate to think the damage done if Edward hears of this before we get the bastard back!"

"I . . . I didn't mean for it to be like this," she whispered, struggling for control. "But a man's life was in the balance, Simon. A man very dear to me."

His lip curled contemptuously. "Yes. Dearer than Richard."

Simon obviously thought the worst. She wondered if the rest of the men thought it as well—if they believed Dylan her lover. She cursed herself for the thousandth time for that foolish tale of Rhys. If only she could tell them it was Owain, all for Owain.

She shook her head vehemently. "No, he is not dearer than Richard. No one is that, Simon. But the man you call the Fox has been a friend all my years. He's protected and guarded me, risked his life for mine on countless occasions. Would you have me turn my back on a friend like that, Simon? Will you try to make me believe you could do so . . . or that Richard would?"

Simon didn't speak, but his movements became slower, much less indignant. The idea of loyalty he could understand, but it was Richard who owned his allegiance and all of his boy's heart.

"Tell me," she said softly. "How is he?"

For several seconds Simon didn't speak, then he put down the tunic he held and turned around. "Not good. He doesn't talk much . . . refuses to discuss you at all." He stared at her accusingly. "You've hurt him, lady."

"I know that, Simon. I would to heaven there was a way to lessen the damage. But he won't see me. He won't even let me explain." She studied him hopefully. "Would you ask him to come? Tell him I've asked for him?"

Simon frowned. "No. He doesn't wish it."

Elen clasped her fingers together desperately. How could she ever make Richard understand if she couldn't even talk to him? "I've written a letter. A letter explaining things as well as I could. Would you at least see that he gets it."

Simon thought for a moment and finally nodded.

She rose from the stool, quickly fetching the sheets of parchment. She had agonized for hours over the words, hoping to make Richard understand her actions without endangering Owain. But her guards wouldn't even speak to her much less take the letter.

She watched as Simon slipped it into the stack of Richard's clothing. She felt better now than she had in days. The boy was obviously still angry, but he would see Richard got the letter. Richard would read it and understand. And he'd forgive her. She wouldn't even think about what would happen if he didn't.

But an hour later Simon was back. He held out the parchment, its heavy seal unbroken.

Elen's tenuous control snapped. She reached blindly for the unopened letter, tears slipping unheeded down her face. She didn't care if Simon saw them. She didn't care for anything now.

"I . . . I'm sorry," Simon stammered. "He didn't wish to read it."

"Did he send any message for me?"

"No. No message."

"M'lord. The Welshman is still waiting."

Richard scowled at the wary servant. "I told you bid him wait!"

"I did, m'lord. But that was midday and it's now past supper. I . . . I thought mayhap ye'd forgotten."

Richard rose and paced the floor. He didn't want to see Owain. He didn't want to see any of these damned Welsh. They were totally mad, beyond redemption and utterly incomprehensible. And he wished the whole lot of them to the devil, his wife included. Especially his wife. "Tell him I've no time to—"

"You had better take time."

Richard glanced up in surprise. Owain stood just inside the doorway, his square, soldier's face set in grim lines. Mad . . . they were totally mad. "You dare enter here unbidden?" Richard bit out, his temper raw, easily fraying.

The servingman wisely withdrew.

Owain stepped away from the doorway, unmoved by Richard's ire. "Yes. My lady's welfare is at stake."

"Your lady is damned lucky to be alive!"

Owain stared back at him, unblinking.

Richard took a deep breath, struggling to restrain his anger, the anger that sprang from a hurt still too fresh to probe. "Your lady is fine," he remarked more calmly. "You know well enough I'd not hurt her."

"That's not the talk in the village. Word is she's ill."

"Well, she's not," Richard snapped. "She's kept in perfect luxury with anything she desires."

"Have you seen her?"

Richard turned away. "No."

"Then I'll see her myself. I'd not have her suffer for what she can't help."

Richard swung back, his words deliberately insulting. "For being a treacherous, lying jade? No, I don't suppose she can help that. She's Welsh!"

Owain didn't rise to the bait, but his eyes flickered warningly. "For being a woman loyal to those she loves."

To those she loves . . .

The words couldn't have been better calculated to wound. They cut through Richard like a blade. That, of course, was the root of his problem. Elen didn't love him, at least not as she did this Welshman named Dylan. And he had loved her—blindly, foolishly, so much he'd never dreamed she would betray him even with all the warnings he'd had, so much he could finally understand his father's neglect. A man in love saw only what he wanted to see. "She's fine," he repeated sourly. "Now be gone."

Owain stood his ground. "The people of Ruthlin'll not stand for her abuse. I tell you that in all honesty."

Richard's voice sharpened. "Do you threaten me?"

"No. I only tell you true."

"Christ's blood!" Richard stalked to the door, shouting for the servants. In a matter of moments, Elen's trembling maid stood before him. "How is your lady?" he bit out.

"W-what mean you, my lord?"

"How is she? Does she sit? Does she walk? Does she eat?" he snapped impatiently. "How does she fare?"

"S-she's not well, I fear," the girl quavered. "She eats naught but a bit of bread and cheese. And when I coaxed her to try more, s-she grew sorely ill."

Richard's green eyes narrowed. "A trick."

The girl stared up at him, gathering her courage with difficulty. "I think not, m'lord."

After a few more questions, Richard sent the girl away. "Very well, I'll see her," he remarked, the words hard-won. "I still think it a trick. God knows she's got enough of them to—"

He broke off. He would never forgive himself if Elen were ill, but he hadn't planned to see her just yet—not until he'd hardened himself to send her away to another of his manors. He couldn't afford a wife he couldn't trust, at least not until he convinced himself she no longer ruled his heart. "I'll send word how she fares," he said slowly. "If she's truly ill, I'll fetch you."

Owain nodded and turned toward the door. "That's all I ask."

Richard gazed at him thoughtfully, struck by the Welshman's fierce loyalty to Elen. Few of his own men were willing to face him in this mood, but Owain hadn't hesitated. And in a race renowned for their many creative ways of skirting the truth, the Welshman offered an unsparing honesty Richard had come to value. He only wished his wife had the trait as well. "You dare much for her sake, don't you, Owain?"

"I do. She's my lady."

"And she'd dare much for you?"

Owain glanced back, his face unaccountably bleak. "Yes . . . to my sorrow."

Richard frowned. He had half convinced himself this man was the Welsh Fox, at least until that raid on Beaufort had taken place. Now he wasn't sure what he believed. He gave a fleeting thought to simply asking Owain outright, but he was afraid the Welshman might answer. And then he would have to act.

"I'll catch him, you know," Richard muttered. "I'll catch the Fox."

Owain's clear gray eyes met his unwaveringly. "I know that, my lord."

"Henry heard the man's true name, and we know now what he looks like. This Dylan will make another mistake, and I'll be waiting when he does."

"Dylan's a fool," Owain said low. "He can't understand the fight is over."

"And do you? Do you believe it's over?"

A long look passed between the men. "It was buried at Builth," Owain replied heavily. "It's been over a long time now, my lord. A very long time."

For nearly an hour after Owain left, Richard remained in the room, steeling himself for the painful effort of seeing his wife. Elen had tricked him, lied to him, deceived him from the first moment they'd met. His foolishness over the girl no doubt had him a laughingstock at Edward's court. Given her treachery, it should be easy enough to cut her out of his life. He hated that in a woman... hated it in anyone.

But to Richard's dismay, instead of brooding on his wife's deceit, he found himself remembering the way Elen's smile lit any room she entered, the way she reached for him in the night and the sleepy, contented way she curled against him after their lovemaking. She claimed she loved him, but it was a strange love that put loyalty to another man ahead of loyalty to her husband.

How much was a lie? he wondered darkly. How much of their marriage was nothing but one of her clever acts?

He put down his wine cup and rose resolutely to his feet. Better to get this over with quickly and try to get some rest. His first hurried foray after the Fox had been unsuccessful, and he had been forced to turn back for lack of supplies. But he was taking his men out again at first light. This time they were provisioned for a month. He planned to search every mountain, every valley, every miserable hillside. He would take the bastard if he had to dig him out of the earth!

Ignoring the two stone-faced guards outside Elen's chamber, Richard swung open the door and went in. He wouldn't give Elen the courtesy of a warning. He wouldn't give her fertile mind time to dream up some new plot.

But the sight that met Richard's eyes halted him on the threshold. Elen was gowned in the scarlet bedrobe Eleanor had given her, a brush in one hand as she stroked her unbound hair. He had watched her this way on so many nights, so many times as a prelude to their lovemaking. A sharp pain twisted through him and his body ached with the memories. Christ, how much of it was a lie?

Elen glanced up. The brush fell to the floor with a clatter as her startled eyes met his. He leaned against the door facing, his voice as cold as he could make it. "I hear you are ill, Madame. You look perfectly well to me."

Elen rose slowly to her feet. She had hoped and prayed for this moment, but now that it was here, her mind swam in a dozen dizzying directions and she couldn't begin to think what she wanted to say. "You heard wrong. I am well."

Richard's gaze shifted over her. They both lied. Elen didn't look well, she didn't look well at all. Her face was far paler than it was wont to be, her great blue eyes heavily underscored by dark shadows of sleeplessness. They gazed back at him now with a desperate hope that somehow angered him. Sweet Jesus, did she think he had come crawling back so easily after what she'd done?

"We ride at first light to take your friend Dylan. I thought you'd wish to know."

Her eyes still held his, searching for any sign of weakening. If she wondered how he knew the man's name, she didn't give it away. "I expected it," she said only.

He glanced about the room. Her supper tray sat untouched on a chest. "You've not eaten. Do you think to win sympathy by starving yourself?"

"I eat enough. You've no need to concern yourself."

Damnation! Why didn't she say or do something he could

scorn? Why didn't she weep or rage at him; he was prepared for that. But this cool self-possession took him by surprise. She didn't appear contrite. She wore her treachery as she wore every other emotion—with a fierce pride he knew he would never break, that he had never really wanted to break. God in heaven, what they might have shared if only she'd loved him enough!

He swallowed hard and swung on his heel to leave. The warm, candlelit room sparked too many painful memories. He was far too weak to be here, to have Elen sharing his roof. If he gave in to her now, she might rule him completely. "Ready yourself to leave Gwenlyn," he said coldly. "Giles will escort you to my manor at Belleterre. You'll remain there until I decide what to do with you."

His words were like a blow. Richard was sending her away. There would be no chance for a reconciliation, no chance to start anew. Not until this moment had she truly realized the extent of what she might lose.

She stared at his stiff back, suddenly recalling the black, unreasoning hatred in Dylan's glittering gaze, the ugly smile when he had mentioned the massacre at Beaufort. Merciful God, what if Richard fell to the man? She would have helped to cause it!

"Richard . . ." She felt the threatening heat of tears, the ache in her throat that presaged a storm of weeping. "Have a care tomorrow," she managed. "He . . . he favors river crossings for ambush."

Richard's head snapped up. "Christ, woman, make up your mind! Whose side are you on?"

"Both . . . and that is my misery!"

Richard turned, all pretense forgotten, his bitterness a palpable thing that hung in the air between them. "Why, Elen? Why did you do it? Why waste what we might have had?"

"Because lives hung in the balance."

Her reply was honest, unrehearsed. Lives. Not life. One

part of his mind registered the word, but the rest was intent only on his own hurt. "Edward warned me not to force you to a choice, Elen. I should have heeded him. But I was so sure of you, so damnably sure you cared enough—"

He broke off and turned away, reaching blindly for the door.

"But it wasn't a choice!" Elen cried out. "I saved a man from death, a death I can't bear to think on. I didn't choose him over you. Your life wasn't at stake!"

Richard glanced back. "If it came to that, to his life or mine, which would you choose?"

"Don't ask. It's the one thing I fear above all others."

He stepped toward her. "I'm asking it, Elen. Which would you choose?"

"There is no choice, Richard. I'd give my life for yours if it came to that—mine and any other were it necessary. I spare no effort, no risk for those I love." Elen's mouth twisted wryly. "You should know that by now."

Richard said nothing. He was staring at her as a man betrayed too often, a man who dares allow himself no luxury of belief.

But he was listening, she realized. He made no move to walk away. "You knew my loyalties when you married me, Richard. I made them no secret," she continued. "I told you at the outset this marriage wouldn't work, begged only to be allowed to enter the Church. But your Edward wouldn't have it."

Her eyes were luminous, filled with unshed tears. "Well, we almost made it work, you and I. We almost built something beautiful from the hate of two worlds. But if you insist on blind loyalty, insist I sit idly by while friends who've risked their lives for mine are murdered for the profane sport of a stupid, vengeful king—"

She broke off, taking a deep breath. "Then what we've built is a mockery and your love not worth the having."

Richard shifted uncomfortably. For the first time he felt

unsure of his ground, slightly shaken in his unquestioning belief that he was the one who had been wronged. "You're my wife, Elen. My loyalties become yours, my enemies your enemies," he said stiffly. "That is the way of things."

"Who decided that, Richard? Who decreed it must be the woman who gives up all? Where is it writ in holy law that the wife is the only one who must compromise?" She stared at him bitterly. "I've lost everything to you, compromised all for your love. And now I've forfeited that as well for saving the life of a friend. Sweet Jesu, where is the justice in that, Richard?"

Justice. Elen had found little justice in the past year— he couldn't argue that. She had lost home, family, friends— even been forced into marriage with the man largely responsible for her grief. She had warned him where her loyalties lay the night of their wedding. Why punish her because he had failed to remember she wouldn't act like any obedient English wife.

"Perhaps you're right," he murmured. "You've been forced to make your share of compromises." He stared at her narrowly, aching to touch her, aching to take her in his arms . . . knowing it would solve nothing. "But how can we go on like this? How much more can we take?"

Elen shook her head, unable to speak around the lump in her throat.

"You're wrong about one thing, though," he added softly. "You've not yet forfeited my love."

Elen caught a deep, shaky breath, struggling against the wild urge to explain about Owain, Dylan, everything if it would only put things right between them. "Don't, Richard . . . don't say that unless you mean it."

He touched her cheek. "I love you, Elen. I love you, but I can't trust you." His eyes searched hers. "But how long can love dwell where trust does not? I only wish I knew."

"I . . . I don't know, Richard, but I understand," she

choked out. "I'll ask nothing of you. You don't have to trust me, ever. Only have a care tomorrow."

His arms went around her. "Oh, Elen," he whispered, gathering her against him. *"Oh, Elen..."*

She buried her face against his chest, clutching the material of his tunic so tightly her fingers ached with the strain. His lips found hers, the kiss warm, but tentative. His arms tightened around her, drawing her against his hard length. "I want you, Elen," he said softly. "I want you now... tonight. But I'd have you know at the outset this doesn't change the questions, doesn't change the doubts. Tell me to go now, if you'd rather."

"I want whatever part of you, whatever part of your life you'll let me share," she replied. "I love you, Richard. If this is all we have, then so be it."

Wordlessly, he drew her toward the bed, sending her robe to the floor along with his weapons and clothing. They made love then with a fierce urgency, a wild desperation to blot out the pain between them, to put things right if only for a moment in the night. And much later, after the passion was spent but the peace of sleep hadn't come, they lay in each other's arms, neither daring to speak of the future or question the other's thoughts.

Finally, Richard broke the long silence. "You know, it's haunted me for weeks," he remarked thoughtfully.

Elen waited, but he didn't continue. "What, Richard?"

"I thought I recognized your friend, but I've finally remembered where I saw him before. Your Dylan is the man who held William hostage that night of our raid." He paused, his words deceptively soft. "He's not the Welsh Fox, is he, Elen?"

She froze in his arms. She wasn't on guard and Richard knew it.

"Never mind," he said gently. "I didn't really expect you to answer that."

She wanted to speak, wanted desperately to deny the

words, but no lie would benefit her now. She had given Richard the answer he sought and it was obvious he knew it as well.

His arms tightened about her. "Sleep," he whispered, drawing her back against him. "It will be dawn soon enough and I must ride."

CHAPTER THIRTY

$\mathcal{T}$he rattling sound of a rising wind filtered into the bed-chamber, nearly covering the stealthy tread of footsteps across the rush-strewn floor. Elen opened her eyes, watching as Felice tiptoed across the room checking the fastenings of the heavy window shutters. "I'm awake," Elen said softly.

The girl turned about with a smile. "I hope I didn't wake ye," she remarked. "'Tis grown colder outside and I only sought to be sure ye stayed snug."

Elen smiled back. "I'm warm enough. I just hope the men were prepared. . . ." Her voice trailed off, her smile fading. Richard had taken his leave of her at dawn. He had kissed her tenderly enough and told her he loved her. But neither had dared mention the Welsh Fox or the problems confronting them.

"The men'll be warm enough. They'd blankets aplenty," Felice remarked briskly. She sent her mistress a sidelong glance, unable to contain her excitement any longer. "Oh m'lady, the guards outside your door be gone! Lord Richard sent 'em away."

Elen sat up, amazement sweeping all else from her mind. "You're certain? No one's there?"

"The likes a them'd be hard to miss," Felice replied with a grin.

Elen leaned back against her pillow. So she was no longer confined to her chamber. She knew Richard didn't fully trust her, but at least he wouldn't keep her confined. She breathed a sigh of relief. But what did it mean? Had he forgiven her? Did the night between them mean more than he would admit?

"I'll fetch ye some breakfast. Mayhap ye'll eat better this fine morn," Felice remarked with a smile.

Elen glanced up, her stomach twisting uneasily at the words. "I'm not really hungry. A bite of bread will be plenty."

The girl paused beside the bed. "Ye must eat," she said softly. "If not fer yerself, than fer the wee one ye carry."

Elen's eyes widened in surprise. Was it so obvious? "I . . . I'm not certain yet," she faltered. "It might only be some passing illness."

Felice gazed at her skeptically. "Yes, an illness that'll pass in some six or seven months, I'll be bound. Does Lord Richard know?"

"No. And I'll not have him learn of it yet," Elen replied, her voice sharpening. She didn't want Richard keeping her with him simply because of her pregnancy. And if there were no child, if this queasiness were due to an illness, she'd not have him suspecting she had lied to regain favor. "I'll not have him or anyone else know of this until I'm certain there's a babe. Do you understand, Felice?"

The girl nodded and Elen realized her maid probably understood all too well. But Felice was right; she needed to eat. For nearly a month she had hoped she might be pregnant, but this past week, she'd scarcely cared.

Now she smiled to herself. A child . . . Richard's child. Her spirits began to lift. "Bring me bread and cheese and a bit of watered wine. Oh . . . and a handful of dried apples," she said softly. "I can recall my nurse, Tangwen, telling me that sometimes helped."

While Elen breakfasted with a heartiness she hadn't felt

in days, the maid chattered on about the happenings within Gwenlyn. Henry Bloet had been left in charge of the castle while Giles had ridden out with Richard. And much to his dismay, Simon had been left behind. The rub of his shield had reopened his shoulder wound, and Richard had left him to Elen's care.

Elen dressed and braided her hair, winding it into the tight knot she usually wore. With nothing more to be done, she moved resolutely toward the door. She had to go downstairs sometime. She might as well face Henry at once.

When she reached the hall, Richard's captain stood talking with a group of soldiers. A sudden hush swept the room. Elen's step faltered but she lifted her chin, moving directly toward Henry. She kept her eyes on his face, not daring to glance at the others. "I would speak with you, Henry," she said. "Now, if you don't mind."

"Certainly, my lady."

His eyes were watchful, alert, his voice cool but shaded with the proper deference. He stepped aside, pouring wine and placing it before her as she seated herself at the table.

She didn't really want wine, but she took a sip anyway. "It's foolish to pretend nothing has happened, Henry. We all know that it did. I don't expect your forgiveness or your respect, but I would have your honesty." She glanced up. "What is my status here?"

He met her gaze evenly. "Yer the lady of Gwenlyn and Richard left orders to that effect. Any man or woman acts otherwise and I'm ta see to it."

Elen took a deep breath and closed her eyes. Not only had Richard given her her freedom, but he had restored her to full honor as mistress of Gwenlyn. For a moment she didn't think she could bear it.

"Yer ta have the same status as before," Henry continued, "only not to go outside the gates . . . not without Simon or myself."

"I understand." She forced a smile. "I suppose I'd best

talk with the steward, then, and check what supplies we have left. Someone should see to the chaos Richard no doubt left."

Henry nodded. "An I'd take it kindly if ye'd see to my arm . . ."—the briefest of smiles touched his face—"and my neck."

"I'd like to do that for you, Henry," she said softly. "I'd like that very much."

The next morning Elen awoke refreshed and hungry after the first really good sleep she had had in over a week. Though she was obviously still in disgrace, Henry seemed inclined to forgive her and Richard's men had treated her with respect. Even the servants had leaped to do her slightest bidding.

She lay snugly in the great down bed, listening to the howling autumn wind outside and the rain that slanted against the wooden shutters in occasional tumultuous gusts. She thought of Richard lying cold and uncomfortable in some damp tent, of Dylan alone and on the run, not daring to remain long in any one place.

The memory of that last conversation with Richard returned. He doubted Dylan was the Fox, but that didn't mean he could prove Owain was. And she would take precious care Owain gave him no further cause for suspicion. If only Dylan remained free, if only Richard would call off this cursed hunt, she told herself desperately. They could work through this problem. They had worked through difficulties before . . . if only Richard didn't decide to send her away on his return.

She rested her fingers lightly against her abdomen, wondering if a tiny babe were nestled beneath them. The thought was comforting. She hummed the lilting tune to a lullaby she could remember Tangwen singing. She missed her old nurse, but the inquiries Owain had cautiously put about had met with little success. The woman had been seen in various camps but none knew her whereabouts now and Elen had long feared the worst.

Rising gingerly to her feet, Elen called for Felice. She dressed hurriedly in the chill room, thankful her nausea had subsided. After a hearty breakfast her maid carried up, Elen sent for Simon. His shoulder hadn't looked bad yesterday, but she did plan to check it again this morning.

But before the boy could appear, Father Dilwen burst into her chamber. With a frown at Felice, he flung back his dripping mantle. "I must speak with you, Elen. Alone."

Elen glanced at him in surprise. The priest was damp and disheveled, his gaunt face chiseled in lines more than usually grave. "Very well." She nodded toward the door and Felice obediently left, closing it softly behind her.

"Your lord husband and his men are riding into a trap," he began bluntly. "Dylan has gathered every rebel and malcontent in Wales for one last effort. And they receive support from a most unexpected source . . . England."

Elen stared at him in bewilderment. "What?"

"Money for arms and men has been flowing across the border for weeks. A force of Gascon mercenaries has been quietly assembled. Dylan pays them and they'll fight any foe he names."

Elen felt as if the floor were breaking away from under her. "But that's impossible!" she exclaimed. "Dylan has no money."

"England," Father Dilwen repeated softly. "The money comes from England."

"De Veasy!" Elen spat the word with such venom, the priest was momentarily silenced. "I would to heaven I'd killed that hellspawn at Ambersly!" She glanced at Father Dilwen. "We must warn Richard. Have you knowledge when this trap will be sprung?"

"Tomorrow . . . or as soon as they reach the pass the English call Devil's Foot."

"Tomorrow?" she echoed bleakly. "We'll never reach

them in time. Richard will have two full days' march on us!"

"I know."

"Merciful God!" Elen took a deep breath, fighting the suffocating panic that threatened to engulf her. Richard would walk into an ambush in that mountain pass, only there would be more than Welsh longbows awaiting him and his men. When the English scattered for cover as they had finally learned to do in waging Welsh warfare, the armor-clad mercenaries would sweep in to finish them off.

She closed her eyes, clenching her fists so tightly her nails dug into her palms. If Dylan planned well, the men would never even have time to re-form their ranks. They would be easy targets, could be picked off one by one. They had to be warned!

She glanced at the window, listening to the howling wind outside. There was a trail, a little-known track over the mountains a man need be half mountain goat to tread. It took a direct route east while the trail Richard traveled with troops and supply carts meandered along a river course through several mountain valleys.

But would that path across the heights of Eryri be passable in this weather? And could she even be sure she could find the way again? She had followed it only once, once when she and her father had been Llywelyn's guests at his hunting lodge near the coast. Word had come that the Lady Gweneth was taken ill, and Lord Aldwyn had spared neither man nor horse nor even his own daughter to reach his wife's side.

"There is a way we might reach them in time," she began. "There's a trail I know . . . perhaps someone at Ruthlin will know it as well. Fetch Owain and—"

She broke off as Simon thrust his head through the doorway. "You said you'd remove this foul-smelling poultice this morning," he said, extending his arm with a grin. "Well, I'm here."

The grin faded abruptly as he took in Elen's ashen face, the grave countenance of the priest. "What's wrong?"

"It's Richard. He's riding into an ambush tomorrow, and we've little time to give warning. It's not just the Welsh, but a host of hired mercenaries as well." Elen's eyes narrowed coldly. "Hugh de Veasy's work, I've no doubt! This is what Dylan meant when he spoke of the devil's own jest. God, if only I'd made him explain!"

"How do you know this?"

She glanced at the priest. "Father Dilwen learned of it."

Simon was eyeing the man suspiciously.

"It matters not how I learned of it, lad," the priest remarked coolly. "What matters is getting a warning to your lord. Lady Elen knows a way we might reach him in time, but we must leave now if we're to have any hope. Can you fetch us horses?"

Simon shook his head. "Not so fast. I'm not sure I believe this tale. Not even Hugh de Veasy would join forces with Welsh rebels against an Englishman! And the Lady Elen can't go anywhere. Richard left orders she's not to stir past the gates without Henry or myself." He hesitated, his expression hardening. "And I think perhaps we'll keep you below until Richard returns, Father. You'll have some explaining to do then, I'll be bound."

"Oh Simon, don't be daft!" Elen exclaimed impatiently. "We're wasting time. Your history and ours is riddled with English who sided with Welsh and Welsh with English against common enemies. You know de Veasy, you know what he's capable of doing. And Dylan hinted as much to me before he escaped." She caught his shoulder. "Richard's life is at stake, Simon! We can't just stand here arguing."

"I can't trust you, not either of you!" Simon burst out. "I'll ride to warn Richard, but the two of you remain here!"

"You don't know the way," Father Dilwen reminded him, "nor do any of your men. Elen is the only one who might be able to reach Richard in time." He hesitated, then said softly, "You're a fool if you believe any thinking Welshman wants Edward's favorite slain by Welsh treachery. Holy God, the bloodbath would drown all Gwynedd! Your English king would leave not a man alive were Richard Basset slain in such a manner."

"Simon, listen to me," Elen said earnestly. "We must warn Richard or he, Giles, William... all the men of Gwenlyn will die in that wretched ambush. They'll be facing not only the Welsh, but the best soldiers the Baron of Ravensgate can buy. Mercenaries, Simon, hardened mercenaries who care not a damn who they fight for so long as they're paid!"

Simon was obviously torn. He wanted to believe her. She could almost see him calculating the chance she might be right, weighing it against the commands Richard had given him. "Simon, I once heard Richard tell you a man must sometimes disobey orders. Well, this is one of those times. If you don't trust me, if you don't help me now, Richard may die. Henry will never believe me, would never let me go. But you can easily fetch provisions and horses. We can be gone before Henry even suspects."

Simon drew a deep breath. She could read the decision in his eyes. He would help her because he dare not do otherwise. "Very well, lady. I'll help. But if this is another of your tricks...."

His words trailed off, but the threat in his hard blue gaze was clear. Simon was no longer a boy but a man, Elen told herself wryly. And he'd need to be for what they might face.

A short time later Simon and Elen were riding through the gates of Gwenlyn. But once outside the castle's protective walls, they entered a world grown harsh with winter. Heavy storm clouds boiled across the heavens, darkening the morning and obscuring all but the lower slopes of the mountains in layers of swirling mist. An icy wind bent nearby trees, scattering dead leaves before it like a flock of sodden birds, whipping the manes and tails of the horses and snatching at cloaks and hoods as if to deny the riders what meager comfort the wraps provided.

Elen gasped as the first force of the wind slapped her face. She dragged her cloak closer, thankful for the woolen tunic and chausses she had borrowed from Simon. She hunched her shoulders against the cold as they rode along the verge of the rain-swept sea, past the village of Ruthlin and into the forest beyond.

Simon was obviously ill at ease. He stared wordlessly ahead, fidgeting nervously with his reins. And when three men broke from the cover of the dripping trees—Owain, Father Dilwen, and Heffeydd Sele—the boy swung around, his sword half out of its scabbard.

"It's all right, Simon," Elen put in quickly. "They're with us." She exchanged a few terse sentences with the men in Welsh, then turned back to explain, "Heffeydd Sele has traveled the first half of our route before. There are others in Ruthlin who know it much better, but Father Dilwen feared to trust them with our plan."

Simon glanced uneasily at the three silent Welshmen, his hand still hovering near his sword.

"You're free to turn back if you wish," she remarked. "This ride will be a hard one."

He shoved his sword back into its scabbard. "I've already let you out of Gwenlyn," he muttered. "Richard would have my head if I left you now. Ride on."

Elen smiled grimly and nudged her horse into a brisk trot. "We must make time while we can," she called back over her shoulder. "We'll soon reach places where even walking will be an effort."

As the morning wore on the trail became steeper and far more treacherous. They were forced to dismount and walk almost as much as they rode, dragging their reluctant mounts up some rocky incline or edging along the narrow rock shelves that hung suspended halfway betwixt man and God. And for the first time Simon could see why the Welsh so often traveled on foot. In this type of country, a horse was a deuced nuisance.

The air grew colder. Icy rain still fell intermittently but now occasional sleet stung their faces, rattling against the few gaunt trees they passed and glancing off the rain-darkened slate of the mountainside.

Elen fretted openly each time the rugged terrain slowed their passage, but she knew they dared not travel faster. The track was slick with wet, occasionally icy; the horses were nervous, their riders ill at ease. It would do Richard little good if they slipped and went crashing down the mountainside.

They paused to eat with nothing for shelter save the dark arc of sky overhead. They had only their own weariness and hunger to gauge the passing time, for with the sun obscured, it was impossible to judge. But for a certainty, the night would come early.

And Elen had a new fear to drive her. The dull aching that had begun in her back hours ago had now spread to her groin. It was possible this ride to warn Richard might cost her her child. But she couldn't stop to rest—she didn't dare.

Gradually they began moving lower. Woods of spruce, ash, and oak again darkened the landscape, and Simon pointed to a distant glimpse of silver curling through the valley below. "Look, there's the river. Richard should be camped somewhere nearby."

Elen glanced anxiously at the darkening sky. "We'd better hurry or it will be too dark to travel. There'll be no moon tonight and we dare not risk lighting a torch for fear of Dylan's scouts."

The party hurried on through the twilight world beneath the dripping trees. Elen felt so miserable it was all she could do to sit upright. The pain swept over her in waves, each grown worse than the last. She fought to block out the hurt, praying earnestly to the Holy Virgin for the life of her child . . . for the life of its father.

The wood continued to darken, and Owain finally dismounted to lead Elen's mount and lessen the possibility of her falling. Just as she began to doubt they could stumble on much farther, a shouted challenge echoed out of the brush. "Who goes there? Stop now, or we'll cut ye in two."

The words were English, a blessed sound. "Lady Basset of Gwenlyn," she called back. "We've urgent news for Lord Richard."

Two men tumbled from the shelter of the bushes, staring at her as if she had sprung up by witchcraft. But after a hurried conference with Simon, they waved the party on. Richard's camp was only a few hundred yards ahead. They would make it after all.

Their entrance into the English camp was as spectacular as even Simon could have hoped. Men began gathering from all sides of the camp as the riders pushed through the ranks toward a tent sporting the rampaging boars of Richard's banner.

Elen held herself erect with the last of her strength. The pain in her side was continuous now, the pounding in her head making thinking nigh impossible. One of the men would have to explain, she told herself. She had finally reached her limit. She had done all she could.

Richard threw up the flap of his tent and stepped out. His blazing eyes cut from his wife to his squire. "You'd best have a damned good explanation for this, Simon! Before God, I'll see you whipped from Gwenlyn to London and back again if you don't!"

"Richard . . . no." Was that her voice sounding so strained? "We've come to warn you. Y-you ride into a trap tomorrow." Elen wavered in the saddle and Richard leaped forward to catch her. "Hugh de Veasy's men," she murmured as he eased her to the ground. "They fight with Dylan now."

The campfires spun and pitched, the faces of Richard, Giles, Owain, swimming in and out of focus as they bent anxiously over her. Someone was calling out orders. It sounded like Richard but the voice was coming from a great distance. A wave of unnatural heat swept Elen's shivering body and she closed her eyes with a groan, certain she was about to disgrace herself by becoming violently ill.

"Stand back, my lords. The child needs air to breathe."

Tangwen's voice? She was dreaming, she must be!

Gentle, competent hands slid over her. "Bring blankets. She's wet through and chilled to the bone."

Richard's voice was frantic with worry. "What is it, woman? Is she ill?"

"Ill? No." The woman's dry laugh cackled out. "I'll wager 'tis only the baby grown weary of the ride."

"*What?*"

Elen opened her eyes, reaching feebly for her nurse's hand. "Tangwen . . . no."

The twisted old woman was staring at Gwenlyn's lord with a look of amusement. "Are you so green you know not when you've caught a woman with your babe, my fine lord? God save us if you're to rule Gwynedd!"

CHAPTER THIRTY-ONE

"*H*ow do you feel?"

Elen glanced up from her comfortable pallet of warm blankets. Richard knelt beside her on the floor of his tent, his eyes searching hers anxiously. She gave a tentative stretch, glancing around for Tangwen. The Welshwoman had remained with her most of the night, coaxing Elen to drink some foul-tasting posset she had brewed and constantly changing the hot stones she kept against Elen's aching back. But the woman was gone; Elen and Richard were alone. "Much better after my sleep," she said softly. "The pain is eased and I've had no bleeding. Tangwen thinks the child is safe."

It was obviously still dark outside but the flickering light of a single candle told Elen her husband was booted and dressed for riding, his hauberk and surcoat in place. She sat up with a frown. "What is it? Surely we don't ride yet."

He shook his head. "Less than an hour till first light. But you're not riding anywhere for a while." He took her hand, lifting it to his lips to press a kiss against her fingers. He studied her over their clasped hands. "Why didn't you tell me of the child? Could you possibly think I'd not be pleased?"

Elen hesitated. "I wasn't sure at first. Then, when it

began to seem more likely, I . . . we . . . we weren't getting along."

She broke off, drawing her hand from his, unable to meet his eyes for fear of what she might read there. But if this marriage were to survive they needed to be honest about their intentions. She needed to tell him how she felt. "I know you were angry with me, Richard. God knows you had reason. But there was cause in what I did as well. I'm sorry you were hurt—I never meant that—but I'm not sorry for what I did! You should know, I'd do it again if I had to. I'm not like to be an obedient wife, Richard, so send me away if you feel you must. I'll not spend my life thinking this child the only reason you keep me with you!"

Richard didn't seem disturbed in the least by her torrent of words. His voice was soft, his eyes holding hers evenly. "We haven't had an easy time of it, Elen, but you must never think that. There are a hundred good reasons I keep you with me—not the least of which is the fact that I need you as I need the air I breathe."

His eyes were tender. "By English standards, what you did was wrong. But I understand. Perhaps I even sympathize with your situation. Because of my loyalties I can't approve, but I honor your loyalties just the same."

A faint smile replaced his worried expression. "And I'm beginning to see what being loved by a woman like you can mean. You meant what you said about sparing no man—Henry and Simon are proof of that. And someday, my lovely hellion, I'll tell you exactly what I shall do to you if ever you put yourself or any of my unborn children in this kind of danger again!"

Elen stared up at him, afraid to believe his words, afraid to hope Richard could forgive her as easily and uncondi- tionally as this.

He leaned forward, brushing her lips with his. "Kiss me, love. I dare not linger. I've an important meeting with some anxious rebels up ahead."

"What?" She gazed at him incredulously. "You can't mean you're riding on?"

"Yes. Hugh de Veasy wants an ambush—an ambush he shall have."

"Richard..." She clutched his shoulders frantically. "But it's a trap! They'll have the advantage of you in numbers, position—"

"But we'll have surprise," he interrupted. "Thanks to you and your Welshmen."

Elen began to protest but he silenced her with a long kiss. "Someday I'll let you argue strategy with me, Elen," he said at last. "I'm sure it would prove interesting. But for now, I must go. We need to march into the pass just after sunrise."

Elen clung to him, saying nothing. It would do no good to protest; Richard's mind was made up. And in her heart she understood his reasoning. If he didn't fight now, he risked stumbling into some other trap Dylan and de Veasy would lay—some trap he might not know about. Richard had weighed the risks, calculated the chances, and decided to face what he knew. But dear God, what if he never came back? What if Richard rode out like the men of her own family had done, and what if he never came back?

"All will be well," he said, sensing her thoughts. "With any luck, I'll be back with you by midday."

She swallowed hard, struggling to keep the tremor from her voice. "What will you do?"

"Divide my army," he replied, understanding her need to see his plan in her own mind. "I'll move in leading the first half as unsuspecting as the rebels could wish. Giles will hold back with the rest of the men in the wood. We'll break for cover at the first sign of ambush, making the rebels believe their plan is working." His voice hardened. "But when de Veasy's Gascon troops march in to finish us off, they'll get a little surprise. Giles will sweep down with my reserve to take the heat of the fighting, giving us time to rally. And I'll be much amazed if we don't spark a full-scale rout."

Elen's fingers tightened against his shoulders. War was no stranger to her; she knew what he left unsaid. "Not so easy as you make it sound, I fear."

He smiled. "Well, perhaps not so easy as that. But I've fought both with and against mercenaries, Elen. They're good troops when the battle is even, but they're loath to give up their lives for a shilling a day. They'll never hold if we once begin pushing them back. And the mood my men are in, no foreign troops can hope to hold them. They're so outraged by de Veasy's treachery, they'd charge Lucifer himself if I asked it!"

Elen nodded. The English had often used Gascon troops in Wales. It was the kind of talk she'd heard all her life. "A good plan," she forced herself to say. "Only . . ." It was growing harder to keep her voice steady. "Only you have to stay alive till Giles relieves you."

"I will, Elen. I will." Richard held her tightly. "And no worrying. Spend these next hours planning for our child. I'll want a name both your people and mine can pronounce."

He kissed her again, hard and possessive, then eased her back into the blankets. Rising to his feet, he stared at her thoughtfully. "You've not spoken of Dylan, so I take it you've made your choice. It would be foolish to tell you I'd try to spare him—you know I won't. But I promise you this. If we meet in battle and God favors me, I'll not take him alive to be made sport of by my people. That much I will grant you."

Elen nodded. It was all that he could offer and more than she had dared hope. "Just take care, Richard. Dylan's so twisted with hate, he's scarce human."

"I'll take care, Elen." He sent her a long look. "And I'll be back."

Ducking under the tent flap, Richard hurried across the

wet grass toward his horse. The blackness outside had shaded to pearl-gray. It was light enough to march.

He took his reins from Simon. "See to my lady," he directed. "And whatever you do, don't let her talk you into bringing her to the pass." He flashed the boy a grin. "I'd not put it past her to end up in the middle of this fight."

Simon nodded glumly, furious Richard had ordered him to stay behind once more. Richard swung into the saddle, edging his mount away from the campfires toward the trampled clearing where his men were already gathering. From the shadows beneath a large, gaunt beech, a flash of movement caught his eye. Owain was watching the English soldiers, his face heavy with the knowledge of what was to come.

Richard drew rein. "I've not yet thanked you for helping to save my life," he remarked softly.

The Welshman only shrugged.

"I'm well aware you could have left camp anytime you wished, that you could be riding to warn Dylan even now." Richard hesitated a moment, gazing at the man searchingly. "Might I ask why you're not?"

"I'll take no sides in this battle," Owain responded. He nodded his head in the direction of the pass. "My heart is with them. I know why they fight and I feel the same, yet I've the wit to realize the dream is over. Dylan no longer thinks on what is best for Wales. He cares only for a personal feud. Were you to fall there'd be a hundred more to take your place." He looked at Richard. "And none the man you are."

The reluctant praise was pleasing. "Better the devil you know, eh?"

Owain smiled. "Yes . . . and there's a little matter of the lady we both admire. Elen's vengeance would put Edward's to shame if she thought I'd lifted steel against you."

Richard glanced back at the tent. He was sure of his strategy, confident of his own abilities. But ofttimes in battle, fate took a hand. "Owain... in the event things don't go as planned, I count on you to get Simon and Elen away safely. Take them back to Gwenlyn. Henry could hold the place against de Veasy's men indefinitely."

He glanced at the lightening sky, the shadowy mountains of Eryri taking shape with the dawn. An unexpected feeling swept him—this fierce, proud land was home. "I'd like my child born in Wales," he added softly. "Tell Elen that for me if the need should arise."

Owain was staring at him strangely. "I'll see to it."

Saladin jerked at the bit, impatient to be gone. Richard held the stallion a moment more, his eyes meeting those of the Welshman. Elen and Owain, inseparable it seemed. And she *had* said lives that night... not life.

He held up a gauntleted hand in tribute. "We were well matched you and I, Owain. Very well matched, indeed."

From the shadowy concealment of the forest, Richard stared down the misty river valley, his soldier's eye noting every ridge of stone, every patch of trees that could hide enemy bowmen. The river curled through the wood below, a murky, fog-shrouded ghost twisting through the trees.

Dylan had chosen well. Richard cursed the route that would take him in such proximity to the water. He had no desire to find himself trapped with his back to the river— not with the amount of steel he wore.

The sun had just lifted above the mountain peaks to the east, sending warm, golden light to bathe the western rim of the valley. The eastern side, the track they must travel, was still cloaked in shadow. He had timed it perfectly. His men would make poor targets for Welsh bowmen moving through the deep shadows darkening the valley floor, but the Welsh would be forced to begin the attack or risk allowing them through the pass.

He breathed deeply of the cold, crisp air, watching his breath rise in a warm cloud about him. Dylan's scouts would have reported their movements at dawn. The Welsh should be in position by now.

He wondered who was leading de Veasy's mercenaries. Not the great lord himself, Richard knew for a certainty, nor even anyone who could be traced back to him. The Baron of Ravensgate was far too wily to be caught with a charge of treason. He was probably at court now, passing the time as innocently as possible while he waited for word of Richard's death.

He turned back to his men, suddenly eager for the waiting to be over. "Move out," he ordered, swinging into the saddle. "Let's get this done and go home."

The men moved unhurriedly out of the cold, wet woodlands, marching down the rocky hillside into the valley below. Faces were grim, nerves stretched to the breaking point as they waited for the attack to begin. Richard thought of Elen, of his child on the way. Never had he ridden into battle with so much to lose.

He was actually relieved when the first whine of arrows cut the air. His mind emptied of all save the will to survive as he swung from his mount, tossing his reins to one of the squires. "Into the trees with the horses, lad!" he shouted, ducking behind a rock.

He glanced out from his dubious sanctuary, noting with satisfaction that his knights were following his example. The ground was too rocky and uneven here to even think of remaining mounted. Yes, Dylan had planned well.

Feathered shafts flew about them, thick and fast, and an arrow thudded into a gnarled tree, inches from Richard's shoulder. He jerked behind the rock with an oath. Christ, he didn't dare lift his head so intense was the fire!

But Richard's own archers had taken up position behind a small ridge. A barrage of arrows was returned up the hillside, slowing, if not stopping, the murderous Welsh fire.

A sudden blood-curdling yell rent the air, and the Welsh swarmed down the mountainside, screaming and yelling, a hoard of vengeful demons sprung up from hell. Richard took a deep breath and steadied himself. The sight was one to make an Englishman's blood run cold, and he was thankful his men were well seasoned.

He waited until the last possible moment, then swung out to meet the enemy, his men surging out from behind rocks and trees to do the same. The fighting was furious, hand to hand, but the most difficult time was still to come, the time when de Veasy's armor-clad mercenaries moved in.

He parried the furious thrust of a Welshman's sword, swinging his blade inside and under his enemy's guard with the ease of long practice. With a cry the man went down. These men wore no armor, carried shields made of wood and hide. They excelled in lightning ambushes, but were no match in pitched battle with trained knights.

Richard's own divided force was outnumbered and the Welsh were attacking with a single-minded fury. He could feel the hate in the air like a tangible thing, could sense the zeal that drove them to fling themselves against armored knights and trained men-at-arms. Give him an enemy who fought for pay any day over one who fought for a cause!

Gradually Richard and his men began giving ground before the onslaught. He realized what was happening and redoubled his efforts, shouting at William, his other knights, apprising them of the danger. Merciful Father, why didn't the Gascons move? If Giles brought in the reserve too soon, they would lose the advantage of surprise. But Richard's men were rapidly tiring. They couldn't hold much longer.

He parried another thrust and swung out with his blade, holding off three Welshmen attempting to encircle him. His sword was bloodied to its hilt, his surcoat and armor liberally splattered with red. He had no doubt these men knew him; each wanted to be the one to take the Wolf.

He darted a quick glance over his shoulder, measuring

his distance from the river. There was still room to maneuver. If they could hold their ground, his men would be in no danger.

Then he saw it—a flash of sunlight glinting against mail. De Veasy's Gascon troops marched out of the trees, precision perfect, swords and shields held before them as they advanced to finish off the beleaguered English.

Richard shouted a warning, knowing the next few minutes of the battle would be most critical, the time when he and his men would be set upon from all sides by a hopelessly superior force. But just as the Gascons made ready to engage, confusion seemed to sweep their ranks. Men were veering off toward the river, others surging forward in an uneven line against Richard's desperately struggling men.

Richard lunged forward into the chaos, fighting his way to the forefront. What fool was giving the Gascons their orders, he wondered. He didn't know, but he thanked God for him!

He pushed on, so hard-pressed he no longer even tried to strike quick and clean. He swung at whatever part of his enemy's anatomy was exposed. He slashed at hands, heads, bellies, even kicked a Welshman viciously in the groin, taking him out of the way as he raised his shield to fend off the well-aimed blow of one of the Gascons. There were no rules of chivalry here; it was kill or be killed in whatever manner possible.

And all at once, Richard realized the cause of the heaven-sent confusion in the enemy ranks. Philip . . . his fool of a brother, Philip, was shouting out conflicting orders. For one incredulous moment Richard couldn't believe his eyes. Then his lip curled contemptuously. The Almighty was indeed merciful. He was cursed with a brother hell-bent on seeing him dead, but at least the boy was plagued with the worst battle instincts Richard had yet seen!

Richard pushed blindly away in the opposite direction, knowing Philip would be little menace to any of his men, more than a little loath to meet his brother over steel. But his push carried him too far. He was now dangerously near the muddy, reed-choked banks of the river, with little room to fight and four wiry Gascons closing in for the kill.

He backed away from the men, eyeing them warily. There was no offer of mercy if he threw down his arms, no request for ransom as was usual when a great lord was taken. These men were obviously working together, bent on killing. And Richard had a sudden inkling he knew why. De Veasy must have offered a substantial reward for the man or men who took his life.

He feinted toward the right then swung back to his left, darting a few paces away to put the thick, protective trunk of an oak at his back. It was the best he could do, and he glanced desperately over the seething, chaotic field, searching for someone to come to his aid. But the few men who might reach him in time were locked in their own desperate struggles.

Then he heard it—the echo of his war cry wavering over the field as Giles came surging down the valley leading the attack. But Richard knew the men would never reach him, would never even realize he was in danger until it was too late.

He stared grimly at the circling soldiers, wondering how long he could hold them at bay. One darted in and Richard swung at him with such force he felt the shattering ache all the way to his shoulder. The man howled with pain and staggered away, blood welling from his chest. The stroke had been a lucky one, severing mail and cleaving living flesh.

The remaining men hesitated, none wanting to be next, but Richard had no time to congratulate himself on reducing the odds. Philip suddenly materialized out of the melee, an unholy grin on his grimy, bloodstained face.

The sweat was trickling into Richard's eyes, his breath coming in deep labored gulps as he recognized the bitter irony of his situation. Philip had dreamed of besting him on the field. His half-brother would never be man enough to take him down alone, but he'd damn sure enjoy being in on the kill!

Philip raised his sword in salute. "To the Wolf," he said mockingly. "I never hoped to see you treed. You'll forgive me if I mention you appear more cat than wolf at the moment."

Richard's fury was cold, deliberate, born of outrage. It burned through him, sending new strength coursing along his limbs. "Then come and get me, little brother," he challenged. "Mayhap you can take a cat. God knows you've not the courage to take a man!"

Philip held his sword in one hand, drawing his dagger with the other. He leaned toward one of his companions, making a jibe at Richard's expense. Then coolly and efficiently, he sheathed his blade in the man's throat.

For just a moment, Richard stood, amazement rooting him to the earth. Then blessedly, his instinct for survival took over. He lunged forward against one of the soldiers, fighting with all the desperate strength of a man unexpectedly reprieved from death. He hadn't any idea what Philip was about, but he wasn't waiting to find out. Men who pondered battlefield deliverance seldom lived to enjoy it.

He hacked his way forward, glancing back at his half-brother from the corner of his eye. Philip was fighting the other Gascon, more than holding his own.

"Ware, Richard . . . behind you!"

Philip swung his sword in a half-point and Richard twisted in time to meet two onrushing soldiers. But so intent were the men on racing away from the battle, they paid him little mind. The rout had begun.

CHAPTER THIRTY-TWO

$\mathcal{T}$he autumn wind sighed brokenly through the pass, drying the sweat still soaking Richard's body and making him shiver unexpectedly. He sat on a grassy hillock, rubbing his aching right arm. In the aftermath of the furious fighting, the abused limb was already growing stiff. Farther down the valley, his men were still checking the field, searching for comrades, dead or wounded, searching for any sign of the elusive Welsh Fox.

He gazed up at the sun, surprised it had moved but a short distance in its journey across the heavens. The life-and-death struggle enacted in this valley had taken scarcely an hour. It never ceased to amaze him that so many men could die, that the course of history could be changed in such a short space of time.

The wind picked up and he drew his cloak about his shoulders, as he watched the activities below with an odd feeling of detachment. Three men broke away from a milling group of prisoners and made their way uphill toward him: Giles, and William, his half-brother, Philip, walking between.

They came to a halt. "We found him," Will stated gruffly. "Down by the river, just as you said. And unhurt, more's the pity!"

Giles said nothing. His sharp eyes traveled from Richard to Philip and back again.

Richard gestured for the men to be seated. "I owe you my life, Philip, but before rendering effusive thanks, I'd best discover just what the hell you were doing here in the first place."

"I don't want your thanks," Philip said sharply. He dropped to his knees, then shifted to sit cross-legged in the dead grass. "Consider it payment of a debt owed. And as to what I'm doing here, you'd not believe it anyway."

"Try me."

Philip shot William an angry glance. "I know what you think. I realize what this looks like, but it's not that way at all. We all know this ambush is Sir Hugh de Veasy's doing. But I left his service weeks ago."

Richard's voice was cold. "So why are you here?"

Philip plucked at a twig, breaking it into pieces. For a moment silence reigned among the men, and the cries of the wounded, the shouting of Richard's soldiers could be heard clearly from below. "Sir Hugh never wanted my friendship as he claimed," Philip admitted, each word measured, won with a price. "He used me to get to you. I see that now, should have recognized it long ago."

His eyes met Richard's evenly. "For a long time, I've regretted the Judas role I played for him last summer. Christ's blood, I regretted it even as I did it! I wanted to pay you back for what you'd done to me, but I never knew Sir Hugh actually planned to have you killed. I'd not have been a part of that for any reason."

"And yet when I was last at Waybridge you told me you'd see me dead." Richard's eyes narrowed, his expression hardening. "I remember it distinctly."

"Y-you didn't really believe that," Philip stammered. "Christ Jesus, Richard, that was schoolboy stuff! I was furious and that was the worst I could think to say."

"In light of the present circumstances, I must consider it at least," Richard remarked dryly.

"Believe me as black as you wish, but don't think I'm fool enough to commit treason for something so petty as a beating!" Philip exclaimed. "Lord, if you think I'd join the Welsh——" He broke off and took a deep breath. "I guess you might at that."

"Just tell me what you're doing here, Philip. I'll decide what to believe later."

"I left de Veasy, left him some weeks ago," Philip began. "I wanted to put things right but didn't dare come to you. But I'd no wish to return to Waybridge and face our father either. So I moved north through Marcher country, hoping to sell my sword to one of the border lords if I could find one who'd have me.

"I'd reached Chester when I ran into a man I recognized, Lile de Ponsant, a Gascon, a mercenary captain I'd once seen at Ravensgate Castle. I struck up a conversation with the man, thinking to find out who was taking on soldiers. But he put me off, swore he didn't even know Hugh de Veasy when I mentioned where I'd learned his name."

Philip frowned darkly. "By that time I was suspicious. I followed Ponsant, saw him join up with a small group of soldiers once he passed over the Welsh border. And the further we got into Wales, the more men began to gather. They came under cover of night in small groups, four or five at most. I didn't know what was in the wind, but from the way Ponsant acted I figured de Veasy must be behind it."

He glanced up. "And I knew it didn't bode well for you, Richard. Believe what you will, but I swear on the surety of my soul, I only followed those men with the intention of warning you. I thought to make amends for the harm I'd done before—that maybe you'd not think so ill of me if I were able to help you somehow."

He shrugged. "But you stumbled into us this morning and you know the rest."

William snorted derisively, unable to contain himself.

"That's why you were out there in the thick of it just now, fighting with the bastards! I notice you didn't step forward to help until the scale tipped decidedly in our favor."

"Peace, Will," Richard said softly. "If you noticed, the lad was shouting out the most ridiculous commands I've ever heard in my lifetime."

Philip grinned unexpectedly. "Ponsant went down early. When I charged by giving orders, some of the foot soldiers were eager enough to follow a mounted knight, especially one ordering them away from the thick of the fighting." He glanced at Richard, his voice bitter with self-mockery. "Not being blessed with your military genius, brother, it was all I could think to do in the press of the moment."

"Holy Jesus, Mary, and Saint Joseph!" William exploded. "You're not going to believe this outlandish tale."

Richard hadn't taken his eyes from his brother's face. "Think, Will," he murmured. "Hugh de Veasy is many things, but he's no fool. Do you really believe he'd send a man so easily identified with himself on a mission of treason?" His gaze shifted to his friend. "After what we all witnessed at Shrewsbury?"

William's bearded face turned thoughtful.

"No," Richard continued. "He'd move heaven and earth to keep Philip from this place, to keep from being implicated in such a way. It's the one thing I know beyond all doubting."

He rose to his feet, extending his hand to Philip. The boy took it hesitantly and Richard swung him to his feet. "And since I can think of no other reasonable cause for the lad to be here, I find I must, in truth, believe this outlandish tale."

His eyes were cool, still wary, but he held Philip's hand a moment longer than necessary. "If I must question brotherly love from long habit, I do believe self-interest—the Baron of Ravensgate's self-interest. Welcome to Wales, Philip. You've service with me if you wish."

• • •

Elen glanced up anxiously as Heffeydd Sele broke from the cover of the forest. "They come," he announced in Welsh.

She rose to her feet, reaching to clutch Owain's arm. Her heart was beating painfully. "Richard . . . ?"

"At the head of his men. He took no hurt I could make out."

"God be praised!"

Elen leaned weakly against Owain, staring up at the sky through burning, tear-blurred eyes. Of a sudden the vault above seemed bluer than ever she'd seen it, the winter sunshine more brilliant, more warm. Joy flooded through her like a draught of new wine, making her knees feel strangely shaky, her head light as thistledown.

But Owain's terse words were sobering. "Any sign of Dylan?"

Heffeydd shook his head and the men exchanged looks. The Welsh leader hadn't been taken prisoner. He was either dead or still free in the wood.

Elen turned away. Richard was alive. He was coming back to her. She had thought that her only concern, but the fact that Richard had prevailed meant her people had lost. How long could she stand being torn in two like this? Richard had told her she had made her choice, and she had. But she didn't have to like what it meant.

She glanced back at the two Welshmen, seeing the same grim thoughts writ deep on their faces. Along with Father Dilwen, they were responsible for what had taken place in that pass. And the knowledge didn't sit easy on any of them.

Moments later one of the English sentries rushed into camp shouting of Richard's coming, and a state of near hysterical rejoicing swept the men who'd been left. Simon raced straight for Elen, catching her up in his arms and swinging her around in a dizzying circle. "He did it!" the boy shouted exultantly. "Was there ever such a knight!"

Richard rode into view, and Elen found herself swept along with Simon and the rest of Richard's men. Her mind registered the significance of the blood staining her husband's chausses, the clean surcoat he had undoubtedly donned to hide the worst of the damning evidence. But all at once the killing didn't matter, nothing mattered when weighed against the precious gift of his life.

Richard drew to a halt beside her, leaning down to lift her onto the saddle before him. "I'm back as I promised," he said softly. "And as near midday as I could make it."

His eyes held hers, the intensity of his gaze telling her something of the hell of the last few hours, of the question he feared to ask. She flung both arms about his neck. "I don't care," she whispered in answer. "Whatever happened, I don't care."

Richard's arms closed about her, nearly crushing the breath from her lungs. "I didn't find him," he murmured, and she knew he was speaking of Dylan. "In all that blood-soaked pass we never came together." His mouth sought hers, the fierce kiss exorcising all suspicion, all anger, all hurt from the past.

Elen clung to Richard as Saladin sidled and fretted in the midst of the noisy clamor. So Dylan lived still. She refused to think of the consequences, was only thankful she need not mourn his loss.

Giles and Philip rode past, and Elen choked off a surprised oath.

"Easy, sweet," Richard murmured, following the direction of his wife's furious glare. "I do owe Philip my life. We've made our peace, and I hope you will do so as well."

"Your life?" Elen echoed, her resentment of Philip paling beside her renewed fear for Richard. "You're not hurt are you, Richard? This blood's not your own?"

He shook his head. "It's a strange story and I'll tell you all once we've a moment to ourselves. But I fear the next hour belongs to my men."

Some time later, Richard finished the hasty meal Tangwen had prepared for him and Elen. He sat on a stool in his tent watching as his wife played a game with the dark-haired child the wrinkled old Welshwoman had dragged into camp with her.

The woman had walked boldly into camp two nights earlier, asking for food and shelter in the Lady Elen's name. She was brought immediately before Richard, and he realized she was the old servant his wife had been seeking. He had not yet asked Elen the babe's identity, sensing she would tell him in her own time.

Simon was hard at work caring for Richard's weapons and mail. The blood and dirt had to be removed, each metal piece carefully cleaned and dried lest the gleaming steel rust and become useless. "Simon."

The boy glanced up.

"See if Father Dilwen can be spared from tending the wounded. I would speak with him."

Simon rose with alacrity and was off on his quest for the priest.

Moments later, the gaunt, black-robed figure ducked into the tent. Richard waved his squire away. "You can guess why I've sent for you, Father," he began. "I would know how you learned of this ambush."

"And that is something I cannot tell you," Father Dilwen replied calmly. "It is sufficient you were warned."

The priest's cool insolence rankled. Richard fought to control his anger. He did, in truth, owe his life to this man.

"I'm sorry, Father, but that isn't enough." Richard fingered the hilt of his dagger, noting the priest now wore a like weapon openly at his waist. "It's my belief you are or were in league with the rebels. What have you to say?"

Father Dilwen didn't hesitate. "I was."

Richard leaned back, his eyes narrowing coldly. He hadn't expected this open admission, had only made the accusation in hopes of surprising some fleeting look of guilt or indignation into that austere face. "So you were in on that plot to slay me in Gwenlyn's hall. Yet when I questioned you then, you swore on holy relics you knew naught of the plot. A priest who damns himself eternally?"

His voice trailed off. He was struggling with the realization that no matter Father Dilwen's crime, he couldn't reconcile executing a man who had just saved his life. Doubtless the priest recognized that fact as well.

"I knew naught of that plot," Father Dilwen replied. "By the time that took place, I'd come to believe you were like to be Gwynedd's salvation rather than the scourge we'd all believed. I tried to sway the others, agreed to get Gruffydd and Dylan into the keep only so they might see for themselves that Elen was well treated, that you dealt honestly with our people. I foolishly believed them when they agreed to my terms."

"Did you know then my wife's identity?"

"I did."

At the gasp from the back of the tent, Richard's eyes cut to Elen. This was obviously news to her as well. He wasn't the only one stumbling about in the dark.

"I'm sorry, Elen. I regret not being able to tell you," the priest said softly. "I knew and loved your lord father. I came to Gwenlyn for the express purpose of helping to free you any way I could. Yet the longer I stayed, the stronger became my belief it was better for you and for Wales that you remained where you were." A wry smile lightened his dark countenance. "Our Lord Savior does work in ways too deep for men to fathom. Besides . . . I always knew I could get you out if the need arose."

"Just how many rebels do I harbor in my household?" Richard snapped. "How many met set to do your bidding instead of my own?"

"None. Let us just say that you harbor men of conscience, men who seek what is best for Wales amid the wreckage of Llywelyn's dream."

Richard frowned. "You speak eloquently, Father, but I'm afraid that won't do for me. What if their conscience and my orders diverge? I must know I have their loyalty."

"We Welsh are different," the priest said slowly. "We are not bred to blind loyalty like you English. We do not follow any lord because of his title or birth. Treat us fairly and you will be treated fairly in return. And loyalty? That comes with love, the kind of love the people of Teifi had for Lord Aldwyn, that all Gwynedd had for Llywelyn, the kind that makes men willing to die . . . for a man or a dream."

He sent Richard a sharp, appraising look. "You will not see that kind of loyalty for an Englishman in our lifetime, my lord, but you will see trust and respect. You've reaped their fruits already. They are the very reason you will watch the sun set this day."

He gestured to the child tumbling about Elen's knees. "And perhaps in her lifetime such loyalty between a Welshman and an Englishmen will be possible. That is for the future and your children and children's children to decide."

Elen sat young Enid on a pillow, giving Dylan's curious daughter Richard's empty scabbard to explore. Elen had listened to the priest in silence, fearing Richard might resent any interference from her. Now she moved to her husband's side, placing a hand on his shoulder. Her people were different. Why was that so difficult for Englishmen to understand? "I fear he's right, Richard," she said slowly. "The people of Gwenlyn have come to believe you mean what you say, that your word can be trusted. Don't destroy that trust by seeking out for punishment men who once sought to best you." She squeezed his shoulder. "People change— loyalties can as well. We've both learned that."

Richard raked a hand through his hair distractedly. "Enemies who are allies, countrymen who are adversaries, priests who are rebel spies—Holy God, I suppose this is Wales!" He jerked to his feet in exasperation, picking up a flagon of wine to pour a generous measure into his cup. "You force me to a difficult decision, Father."

"As you have forced me on several occasions, my son."

Richard took a long drink. "Let it be known, then, that the rebels who lay down their arms and swear to live peaceably will be pardoned." He scowled down at the wine. "Even those who participated in the bloodbath this day. I suppose you've ways to do that," he added, directing a hard look at the priest.

Father Dilwen returned the look. "Yes. I've ways."

Richard nodded curtly. "Then do so."

The priest took his leave and Elen moved to stand beside her husband. Taking the earthenware cup from his hand, she drank deep, then handed it back. "Let's go home," she said softly. "Let's go home to Gwenlyn."

CHAPTER THIRTY-THREE

$\mathcal{W}$eeks passed and the anniversary of Builth came and went. Richard ordered a day of mourning on that occasion and Father Dilwen performed a mass in honor of the dead of both sides. Yet the people of Gwenlyn's demesne seemed eager to put the memory of war behind them. They had had enough of sorrow, enough of bitterness and hate. There was an almost frenzied need to put their thoughts and energies into plans for the approaching Yuletide season, and Richard, sensing the sentiment, planned for a far more elaborate Christmas than he could well afford.

Guests had been invited, both English knights and Welsh of good standing in Gwynedd. People thronged in and out of Gwenlyn's open gates and the castle kitchens labored night and day to keep up with the increasing hoard of hungry mouths gathering to be fed. Players, minstrels and jugglers strolled about within the walls, plying their craft and taking their wages in whatever manner they could—a coin now and again, or a free meal and a warm corner of the stable in which to sleep.

The great hall was adorned with sweet-smelling evergreen boughs, and mistletoe was placed strategically in window alcoves and doorways throughout the castle. Even the weather conspired to bedazzle the eye, for a fine, powdery snow had fallen, blanketing the countryside with a carpet of glistening white, spangling rooftops and naked trees with nature's shimmering, ice-encrusted ornamentation.

Elen watched as a group of laughing, struggling men dragged in the immense Yule log. It would be lit tonight, Christmas Eve, and would smolder in the great fireplace throughout the twelve days of holiday merrymaking.

Her gaze wandered slowly over the mix of people gathered in the hall. In one corner three Welshmen strummed harps, singing a lively ballad in their rich mellifluous voices while even the English listened, occasionally joining in for a verse. She felt a swift, sharp pang of regret, a deep longing that her mother and father, her brother and Enion could be here to enjoy the season.

But such thoughts were fruitless. The old life was being replaced with the new, even as the queen had predicted. Though death and heartbreak had been no stranger the year past, Elen was yet aware she had much for which to be thankful. Dylan had not been heard from since that disastrous battle weeks before and peace now reigned in Gwynedd—a peace most hoped would be permanent. Richard had made no effort to seek out the Welsh Fox or his followers, and though she knew her husband suspected Owain, the Welshman continued in his duties as reeve, working alongside Richard's trusted bailiff and even the master of Gwenlyn himself. Even Tangwen had found her, at last.

Richard had written his sovereign concerning Hugh de Veasy's treasonous machinations, and though there was no evidence sufficient to charge the powerful Baron of Ravensgate, enough suspicions and ill will were engendered that he had removed to his derelict Irish estates until the scandal blew over and Edward's wrath cooled.

And Elen's most personal cause of joy—her child—continued to grow. Her hand slipped to her thickening waist in a reassuring gesture that had now become habit. She had not lost her babe in that breakneck ride to warn Richard.

She had yet to feel its movement, but Tangwen assured her that all was proceeding as it should.

"Madame . . . what say you to a walk with your lord husband? The din here is enough to wake the dead."

Elen swung around in surprise. So intent were her thoughts she hadn't even heard the sound of approaching footsteps. She smiled at Richard, her welcome taking in Philip and Giles who flanked him on each side. "Certainly, my lord." She nodded at Philip. "Would you gentlemen care to accompany us?"

"No they would not," Richard put in firmly. "They've other business to see to, I'm sure."

Philip grinned, comfortable now with both Richard and Elen. "My thanks for the invitation, but my brother's subtle hint hasn't escaped me. Giles and I will play the hosts if you two wish to slip out for a breath of air."

The idea of a moment alone with Richard in all this press of people did sound wonderful. Elen caught her cloak from a peg on the wall, tucking her hand in her husband's arm as they ducked down a back hallway, and slipped out into the garden.

The air was crisp and still, the sky opaque, gray-white like the milky surface of a frozen mountain lake. They walked along in companionable silence, the soft snow crunching underfoot. But the sight of so much pristine white was too much temptation for Elen. She skimmed a handful of snow from a yew hedge as they passed, gazing innocently ahead as she squeezed it into a ball.

"Don't even think it," Richard warned softly.

But it was too late. Elen had already spun sideways, dropping back for refuge behind the hedge as the missile left her hand, splattering against the russet wool of Richard's cloak in a clump of wet snow.

Richard was quick to avenge the attack. Grabbing up handful after handful of the white stuff, he fired a dozen snowballs in such quick succession, Elen had little time to marshal a defense. He followed up his lightning assault by breaching her yew fortress, catching her hands and forcing them to her sides as he dragged her into his arms. "Quarter?" he queried with a grin. "Cry quarter and perhaps I'll have mercy."

Elen's lungs ached from the cold as she struggled to breathe despite her laughter and Richard's tight hold. "Never! I'll never ask quarter. I'll beat you yet!"

Richard stared down at his laughing, struggling wife. Elen's rich chestnut hair was dusted with snow. Sparkling crystals gleamed on the thick fringe of her eyelashes and powdered the front of her cloak where his missiles had scored hits. The cold and her exertion had brought the color into her cheeks and she looked so lovely, he promptly forgot their skirmish and bent to cover her chilled lips with his own.

The kiss was long and slow and deep, and when it ended another began. Elen's resistance crumbled, and she slid her arms inside Richard's cloak, holding him against her, relishing the contrast of cold air outside and warmth building within. "Quarter," she whispered breathlessly. "You don't fight fair, Richard."

"I'll accept your surrender, but only upon my terms." Richard's eyes went very green and his mouth curled upward in a devastating smile. "Meet me in our chamber in twenty minutes. I'm damned tired of having no time alone with you."

"But Richard, our guests! We can't just disappear. It wouldn't—"

"You've surrendered, Madame. You don't cite conditions," he interrupted. "Upstairs . . . twenty minutes." His eyes twinkled brilliantly. "If you wish to save life and limb."

"Very well, my lord. Since I've no other choice, I accept your terms." Elen lowered her gaze demurely. "Twenty minutes." She drew away from him and began retracing her steps up the path. But the fight wasn't done. In a lightning move she bent, swept up a handful of snow, and let fly a snowball that caught Richard squarely in the chest.

He sprinted forward to catch her, but she was already racing away, her triumphant laughter floating back to him as she reached the safety of a group of milling carolers at the edge of the bailey.

"Damned Welsh," Richard murmured with a grin. He swept her a low bow, granting her the honors of the exchange. Life with Elen might occasionally be exasperating, but it would certainly never be dull.

Elen was still flushed and breathless and thinking of Richard's kiss when she entered their bedchamber a short time later. She had sent Felice up earlier to ready the room while she hurriedly checked preparations for the evening feasting.

She glanced around. It was obvious her maid had come and gone. The shuttered room was alight with two burning tapers, while a small fire blazed brightly in the hearth. The bed curtains were drawn back and a plate of the sweet Yule wafers Richard loved sat on a table alongside a flagon of wine and two wine cups.

She moved forward, unpinning her snow-damp hair and reaching for her brush to untangle its length. Richard should be along in a few minutes; that is, if he didn't get caught up with some of their guests.

She began to smile, then to laugh, the sound spilling into the chilly stillness of the bedchamber. She and Richard were acting like two heedless youngsters so hot for each other they couldn't even wait for the coming of night— and she an old married woman with a babe on the way!

"Share your mirth, Elen. I see little cause for joy this Yule season."

Elen spun around, gasping at sight of the unexpected figure. "Dylan! For the love of God, what are you doing here?"

"Some unfinished business. A matter of a promise to Enid," he said softly.

Elen moved toward him, intent on one thought. Richard would be along any minute and she had to get the Welshman hidden. "Dylan, you can't stay here. It's not safe!" She bit her lip anxiously. "There's a place down the hall— just a cupboard really, but you can hide for a time till I think where best to keep you." She caught his arm. "Come, we must hurry before you're seen."

His hand closed about her wrist. "I think not, Elen." He glanced about the cozy chamber. "It looks as though you expect only one. I think we should await your lord's coming together."

His dark gaze settled on her with a look of such hatred it took her breath. Dylan was here to kill Richard. It wasn't finished yet!

She tried to swallow, but couldn't, tried to draw her hand away but his grip only tightened. She could scream, but the noise wouldn't carry far through thick stone walls. And no one was in this part of the castle anyway.

"Dylan, you can't possibly mean what I think you do," she began, struggling to find her wits. "You'll never leave here if you take Richard's life. Don't waste yourself for this. You're a leader men will rally to—the last hope for us, the last hope for Wales!"

"You'd sound a bit more convincing if you and that cursed priest hadn't sent over a hundred countrymen to a needless death," the Welshman said coldly.

Elen caught her breath. So Dylan had learned of her warning to Richard.

He read her face easily. "Oh yes, I know of that. I know of far more than you'd like." His dark gaze slid over her contemptuously. "I know you fawn over Richard Basset like some whore does a rich merchant. That you share his bed and carry his child." His voice trembled with anger. "You, Elen of Teifi—Lord Aldwyn's daughter! Thank God he died never knowing this day!"

Elen fought to keep her composure. "My father loved

Wales. He never favored senseless killing—you know that. If he were alive today, he'd have made his peace with Richard. He'd have done what was necessary to protect his people and win concessions from Edward . . . just as I have done."

She took a step nearer, her cool blue gaze on a level with his. "And you speak of my betrayal, but what of yours? At least Richard is a good man, he gives us justice as no other Englishman has before. He cares about Wales, about us. But that bargain you struck with the Baron of Ravensgate was conceived in hell, Dylan. You can't lie with the devil and not expect to be burned. You must know he wants Richard dead so that he can rule Gwynedd. And God help all Welshmen if that day comes to pass!"

Dylan shrugged off her words. "Englishmen are all alike so far as I am concerned. Let them kill each other. There'll be that many the less for us to fight."

"They're not alike," Elen said hotly. "Talk to the people of Ruthlin, the people anywhere in Gwenlyn's demesne. They prosper, both Welsh and English. They'll tell you Richard Basset is a fair lord to all."

"The time for talking is done, Elen. I've sworn an oath to kill the Wolf. I owe him that for Enid." Dylan's voice dropped, his eyes went very hard. "Despite your betrayal, I've no wish to harm you. But I will if you force me."

"Dylan, listen to me!" Elen cried out. "Enid wouldn't want this, you know she wouldn't. And your daughter is here. Richard knows who she is but he hasn't used her to hurt you. Dylan, you can still live! You can go far away, make a life with your child. Richard isn't even looking for you!"

But Dylan wasn't listening. "Lie down on the floor," he ordered. "Facedown."

"Dylan—"

She broke off as he drew his knife, shoving her to her knees. He was right. The time for talking was done. She steadied herself against the floor with her free arm, then twisted suddenly, throwing all her weight against his legs to knock him off balance.

But he must have expected something of the sort. He was braced for her attack and it scarcely shook him. He forced her against the floor, his knife at her throat. "One false move, Elen, and I'll end your life . . . yours and that brat you carry."

She stared up into his hard face, remembering all the times they'd shared, the good and bad. "I can't believe you'd kill me, Dylan," she whispered. "I just can't."

His gaze shifted away. "Believe it. I've already slain one woman this day. Margaret, that half-breed bitch who betrayed our camp to Richard last spring."

He grinned as Elen jerked toward him in surprise. "So you didn't know." He dragged her hands behind her, roughly binding her wrists and ankles. "Well, she's been repaid for her treachery. She sold us out to Richard then resold him to me for a bit of Hugh de Veasy's silver. But I'll not be needing her information any longer. I'll soon be done with Gwenlyn and back in the hills where I belong."

Elen stared narrowly at her old friend, but could find little trace of the man she had once known. This stranger just might kill her. She didn't know, but she had to take the chance. Perhaps someone would hear.

Twisting her body away, she began to scream, biting down hard on Dylan's hand as he covered her mouth to silence her. But he quickly ended the struggle, forcing a gag into her mouth that abruptly smothered all sound.

For a moment, he squatted on his heels, regarding her intently. Then he swung to his feet and moved to the door, opening it a few inches to peer into the corridor. He must have been reassured, for he returned to her at once. "Now we wait," he remarked, drawing his sword.

Richard hurried along the corridor, impatient with the delay two English guests had cost him. He had listened politely as they expounded on the Welsh problem, then made good his escape at the first opportunity.

He grinned and shook his head, wondering at the men's expressions if he had simply told them the truth, that he was on his way to bed his wife and couldn't tarry to discuss such nonsense. Actually, having seen Elen, they'd probably understand. Pregnancy hadn't dimmed her allure, had only heightened her beauty.

He opened the door and moved through the outer chamber. "Elen," he called softly. "Elen, I'm—"

He broke off, his breath catching at sight of a man bending over Elen—a man holding a sword. Then his own steel was out and he was hurtling toward the crouching figure.

"Not a step closer if you wish her to live!"

Richard stumbled to a halt. Dylan! He swallowed hard, struggling to get command of himself.

"Drop your sword," the Welshman hissed. "Drop it!" he repeated sharply as Richard still hesitated. "Don't think I'd spare her because she once saved my life. I know 'twas she warned you of our ambush. I've no mercy for traitors!"

Richard's fingers clenched against his sword hilt, his rage almost choking him. Could the Welshman be bluffing?

Dylan's sword shifted against Elen's throat. "Your English lover puts little value on your life. A pity, Elen."

"Wait!" Richard pitched his sword to the floor. It was a chance he dare not take.

"That's better. Now kick it there . . . under the bed."

Richard did as he was told. Fear and fury settled into a cold, tight knot in the pit of his stomach. Elen lay very still, and for one agonized moment, he feared the Welshman had already made good his threat. Then he caught sight of the rapid rise and fall of her chest and he steadied himself. "Your quarrel is with me," he said curtly. "Let her go."

Dylan smiled. "In good time. But first there's a little matter of making you pay for your crimes." He gave a bitter laugh. "The Welsh Fox outwits the English Wolf in his own den. I want a moment to savor the victory, a moment to watch you sweat."

Richard studied the Welshman warily. The man's rage blazed in his eyes, simmering beneath the surface, barely controlled. But a man who hated so deeply was seldom wise, seldom patient. "I thought you more cunning than the rest," he began scornfully, "but it pleases me to find you no different than any other Welsh fool. Do you really think to escape here once you've done with me?"

Dylan grinned. "I do." He prodded Elen with his foot. "Your wife and unborn child will insure my safe passage. None will touch me so long as I hold Elen."

Richard forced himself to laugh. "The joke is on you if you think my men will worry for the safety of another Welsh slut, more or less. Christ Jesus, we've killed enough in the last year. I'd certainly not have made this one my wife had she not brought a generous piece of Wales as dower. Your women mean little to us and I've brats to spare scattered throughout Gwynedd."

"Hold your tongue," Dylan bit out furiously. He took a step toward Richard. "Hold your tongue or I'll pleasure myself by cutting it out!"

"Can you now? I doubt you've the stomach for it," Richard goaded. "You'd not the backbone to meet me on the field. I doubt you can best me even at this."

Dylan moved closer, his face white with fury. "I'm going to enjoy this," he snarled, raising his sword. "I'm going to—"

The noise of crashing furniture and splintering pottery filled the room. Dylan swung about instinctively and Richard dove for his enemy.

Elen rolled away from the table she had kicked over, cutting her arm and staining her gown in the wreckage of broken cups and crumbling, wine-soaked wafers. She stared breathlessly at the struggling men. Richard's attack had knocked the sword from Dylan's hand and the two now fought furiously for a dagger.

Help . . . she had to get help!

Rocking herself up on one elbow she braced her shoulder against the wall, then pushed herself to her feet. She swayed there a moment, her eyes never leaving the fight. The men's ragged breathing filled the chamber, punctuated by grunts and snarls as knees and elbows connected viciously with soft, unprotected flesh.

She glanced at the door. She had to get round them to reach it. She hobbled toward the bed and rolled across it, easing herself to the floor on the other side.

A strangled cry rang from one of the two men, sending a shiver of dread down her spine. She pulled herself up to look at them.

"Richard?"

The combatants lay in a tangled heap. Neither moved. Panic swept her. "Richard?" Her voice rose, hysteria threatened. *"Richard!"*

"Hush, Elen. It's all right." The words were English, blessed English.

Another groan sounded and Richard finally moved. He shoved away from Dylan, clasping the bloodied dagger as he struggled to catch his breath. He rose to his feet, crossing the floor and cutting her free. "It's all right, love," he murmured, taking her in his arms, clinging to her as if he needed the reassurance as much as she.

"Oh, Richard, I was so afraid. So afraid he'd killed you!"

"Elen . . ."

She stiffened. The sound was half word, half gasp.

"Elen . . . please."

Richard released her and they gazed back at the crumpled figure on the rush-strewn floor.

Elen began to tremble, a host of conflicting emotions flooding through her: regret, pain, relief—but anger most of all. *Why, Dylan? Why did you do it?*

"Go on," Richard said, understanding her far better than she did herself. He gave her a gentle push. "Make your peace if you can."

She moved hesitantly away from Richard, sinking to the floor beside the dying Welshman. Blood welled from the ragged wound in his chest. His eyes were closed, his complexion rapidly graying.

"Dylan." She touched his cheek. His eyes fluttered open.

"Elen." He stared up at her. "I . . . I'd not have hurt you. I want you to know that."

She took his hand, cradling it against her chest. "I think I knew that, Dylan," she said softly. "I feared for Richard, not myself."

His throat worked convulsively as he tried to speak. She leaned closer to hear. "Enid," he whispered. "Tell my daughter . . . about me. The good things."

Elen's throat closed up. Her eyes burned with unshed tears. There were good things—but Dylan was a young man—there could have been so much more. "Yes. Yes, I will."

"Tell her . . ."

Elen was vaguely aware of the sound of hurrying footsteps, of a babble of voices filling the room. Giles, Simon, Will— Richard's men had been summoned.

Dylan's dark eyes were glazing rapidly. Each breath was a struggle. She squeezed his fingers encouragingly. "Tell her what, Dylan?"

"How much . . . how much I loved her mother."

Grief cut through her then, wiping out all that remained of her own fear and anger. How had it ever come down to this? How could love beget such hate? "I'll tell her, Dylan," she whispered around the ache in her throat. "I swear it."

His fingers contracted briefly against hers. A harsh sigh escaped his lips and she breathed a prayer as his soul slipped the confinement of his body.

Releasing his limp hand, she rose to her feet, stumbling blindly into a solid, familiar form. Owain. Richard had summoned Owain, the one person who would understand. "Why, Owain? Why did he do it?" she choked out. "I thought he was gone . . . to France like we planned."

"He'd hated too long. 'Twas his reason for living," Owain said softly. "But Dylan was a good man before the bitterness sickened him. Remember that, Elen."

She nodded miserably, watching as two men bent to spread a blanket over the Welshman's body before they carried him out.

"Leave us . . . everyone," Richard demanded.

Elen turned to discover her husband watching her, a troubled frown on his handsome face. He gestured toward his men. "Giles, tell our guests what has happened but keep them below. And order the men to keep their gloating to themselves. I'll have no baiting of our Welsh guests."

Giles nodded and the men filed slowly from the room. Owain squeezed Elen's hand and turned to follow. "Not you," Richard said softly. "I would speak with you two."

He waited until the last man had departed and the chamber door was closed. "The Welsh Fox is dead," he began, "the rebellion ended. I'll send word to Edward as soon as the weather breaks."

Owain met his eyes evenly. "My lord, why not end this game between us, why not—"

"Peace!" Richard snapped. "Dylan confessed ere he died. Knowing the penalty for treason, only a fool or a madman would admit to being the Fox." He was studying the floor intently. His frown deepened into a scowl. "Now I wish to hear no more of this. In so far as I am concerned the Welsh Fox is dead."

Elen drew one deep, shuddering breath. Richard knew. He knew the truth, but for once in his life he was turning a blind eye to duty. "Richard, you will probably never know," she said softly, "how very much I do love you."

His eyes lifted to hers, his grave expression softening. "Owain, take my wife from here. I will join you as soon as I've had someone restore the room."

• • •

The last rays of the sun had broken through the thinning layer of clouds by the time Richard went in search of Elen. One of the guards had reported seeing her on the battlements. But that had been near an hour ago.

Richard climbed the steep stone stairs in growing concern. Elen must be hurting more than he had guessed. God grant him the words to ease her pain. There was enough between them already for a lifetime.

Stepping out into the glow of a wintry sunset, he searched the shadows along the wall. He saw her at once. A cold wind, blowing in from the sea, stirred the powdery snow from the ramparts, swirling it over her dark cloak and unbound hair.

He moved toward her. "You'll catch your death up here in the cold."

Elen didn't answer, didn't even turn around. She was watching a half-dozen eagles circling and diving for fish in the darkening waters beneath Gwenlyn's gray stone walls.

"Do you wish to speak of it?" he asked softly.

"No."

Richard took a deep breath. "Not with anyone, or just not with me?"

She swung around at that, her eyes searching his. "You can't possibly think I'd have it any other way, Richard. I've been up here thanking God, the Holy Virgin, and all the saints for your life. And yet . . ."

Her voice grew suddenly shaky. "And yet a part of me is sad, Richard, so sad. As if it died too. I can't explain. The old ways are gone. Everything has changed. I . . . I don't even know who I am, what I want anymore."

"We've both changed," he said thoughtfully. "For the better, I think. Compromise takes a strength, a wisdom, simple winning doesn't require."

A long silence stretched between them. The shrill cry of an eagle echoed overhead, and Richard watched the birds wheel gracefully over the castle, the fierce creatures lending him sudden inspiration. "Eagles don't survive in captivity," he said softly. "They've not the ability to adapt that their cousin the falcon has. They can't be trained to do the bidding of a keeper."

He studied his wife. "Dylan couldn't compromise. He'd never have reconciled himself to living with English rule. He'd have forced his own end sooner or later. If not this time with us, it would have been another."

"But why us, Richard? Why did he force us to do it?" Elen glanced up. "I feel as if I put that blade in him myself. Someday I'll have to tell young Enid we took her father's life."

"A far kinder fate than the other he faced," Richard said stiffly. "Don't punish yourself, Elen. Dylan chose his own end."

Elen turned and leaned against the battlements, gazing at the snow-covered mountains lifting beyond Gwenlyn. "Eryri," she whispered, "haunt of eagles." Her eyes filled with tears. "It's really the end for us this time, Richard... a twilight of eagles. There will be no more Llywelyns, no more Dylans to lead us. There will never by another Welsh prince of Wales."

Richard remained silent for several long moments. He had no words to comfort her, for she faced the truth at last. He slid both arms around her, drawing her into the warmth beneath his cloak. "The ending of these bloody wars between England and Wales has to be a blessing, Elen. So many have suffered and died so pointlessly over these few square miles of ground. And the end of one things may be the beginning of something better."

"But it will be so... so difficult," she said, stumbling a little with her effort for control. "We Welsh don't take easily to change."

"Yes, but it will come, Elen. In time it will come. And I'll be here to help."

Richard forced her to look up at him. "Things of value

are seldom easily achieved. Just look at us. We've been to hell and back again, Elen. Perhaps it took that to learn the value of what we have."

Elen stared at her husband, knowing she'd never really realized how much she loved him until this moment, realizing all at once she was free, blessedly free to give him all of her loyalty and all of her heart. "Do you remember asking me if I could forgive you Enion's death?" she whispered.

"Yes."

"Well, ask me again, Richard."

His eyes held hers, his gaze never wavering. "Can you forgive me, Elen, for Enion, for Dylan . . . for all the grief I've brought you?"

Her arms went around him, a smile lighting her tear-streaked face like sunshine after a storm. "The grief came first, but joy followed after. I could forgive you anything on this earth or beyond, Richard. As you said . . . sometimes endings are beginnings."

Sweeping from the wild Scottish Highlands to tapestried castle halls, from court revelries to battlefields, from the unstoppable desire for power to the unquenchable hungers of the heart—they struggled passionately toward a triumphant destiny.

HEARTSTORM

ELIZABETH STUART

"A vibrant tapestry of highland castles and lochs, of passionate love and conflicting loyalties."
—**Elizabeth Kary, author of *Love, Honor and Betray***